NEBULA AWARDS SHOWCASE 61

NEBULA AWARDS SHOWCASE 61

The Year's Best Science Fiction and Fantasy

EDITED BY

STEPHEN KOTOWYCH

Nebula Awards Showcase 61: The Year's Best Science Fiction and Fantasy

Cover design by M.L. Clark
Interior layout designed by Laurie McGregor / Page Turn
Typesetting by M.L. Clark

San Lorenzo, California, United States

ISBN 978-1-958243-10-7 (print)
ISBN 978-1-958243-11-4 (ebook)

2025 NEBULA AWARDS®

Presented at the Crowne Plaza Hotel in Chicago, Illinois, and online on Saturday, June 6, 2026

Toastmaster: Tananarive Due

Novel

★ **Winner:** ***The Buffalo Hunter Hunter*** **by Stephen Graham Jones,** published by *Saga/Titan UK*

When We Were Real **by Daryl Gregory,** published by *Saga*

Katabasis **by R. F. Kuang,** published by *Harper Voyager US; Harper Voyager UK*

Death of the Author **by Nnedi Okorafor,** published by *William Morrow*

The Incandescent **by Emily Tesh,** published by *Tor Books*

Sour Cherry **by Natalia Theodoridou,** published by *Tin House*

Wearing the Lion **by John Wiswell,** published by *Penguin Random House*

Novella

★ **Winner:** ***The River Has Roots*** **by Amal El-Mohtar,** published by *Macmillan Publishers*

Disgraced Return of the Kap's Needle **by Renan Bernardo,** published by *Dark Matter Magazine*

The Death of Mountains **by Jordan Kurella,** published by *Lethe Press*

Automatic Noodle **by Annalee Newitz,** published by *Macmillan Publishers*

But Not Too Bold **by Hache Pueyo,** published by *Macmillan Publishers*

"Descent" by Wole Talabi, published by *Clarkesworld Magazine*

Novelette

★ **Winner: "Uncertain Sons" by Thomas Ha**, published in *Uncertain Sons and Other Stories* (Undertow Publications)

"Our Echoes Drifting Through the Marsh" by Marie Croke, published by *Beneath Ceaseless Skies*

"We Begin Where Infinity Ends" by Somto Ihezue, published by *Clarkesworld Magazine*

"The Name Ziya" by Wen-Yi Lee, published by *Reactor*

"Never Eaten Vegetables" by H. H. Pak, published by *Clarkesworld*

"The Life and Times of Alavira the Great as Written by Titos Pavlou and Reviewed by Two Lifelong Friends" by Eugenia Triantafyllou, published by *Uncanny Magazine*

Short Story

★ **Winner:** "Laser Eyes Ain't Everything" by Effie Seiberg, published by *Diabolical Plots*

"Through the Machine" by P.A. Cornell, published by *Lightspeed Magazine*

"Six People to Revise You" by J.R. Dawson, published by *Uncanny Magazine*

"In My Country" by Thomas Ha, published by *Clarkesworld Magazine*

"The Tawlish Island Songbook of the Dead" by E. M. Linden, published by *PodCastl*

"Because I Held His Name Like a Key" by Aimee Ogden, published by *Strange Horizons*

Ray Bradbury Nebula Award for Outstanding Dramatic Presentation

★ **Winner:** *Murderbot*: Season One, written by Chris Weitz & Paul Weitz (Apple TV+)

Sinners, written by Ryan Coogler (Warner Bros Pictures)

Severance: "Chikahi Bardo", written by Dan Erickson & Mark Friedman (Apple TV+)

Pluribus: Season One, written by Vince Gilligan (Apple TV+)

Superman, written by James Gunn (Apple TV+)

KPop Demon Hunters, written by Danya Jimenez, Maggie Kang, Hannah McMechan, Chris Appelhans (Netflix)

Andre Norton Nebula Award for Middle Grade and Young Adult Fiction

★ **Winner:** *Into the Wild Magic* by Michelle Knudsen, published by *Candlewick*

The Tower by David Anaxagoras, published by *Recorded Books*

Gemini Rising by Jonathan P. Brazee, published by *Semper Fi Press*

Wishing Well, Wishing Well **by Jubilee Cho**, published by *Atthis Arts*

Sunrise on the Reaping **by Suzanne Collins**, published by *Scholastic*

Goblin Girl **by K.A. Mielke**, self-published

Game Writing

★ **Winner:** *Clair Obscur: Expedition 33* **by Guillaume Broche and Jennifer Svedberg-Yen,** published by *Kepler Interactive*

Spire, Surge, and Sea **by Stewart C Baker,** published by *Choice of Games*

Hollow Knight: Silksong **by Ari Gibson and William Pellen,** published by *Team Cherry*

Dispatch **by Ashley Jeffalone, Chad Rhiness, Chris Rebbert, Mavanna Berrin, Pierre Shorette, and Suzee Matson**, published by *AdHoc Studio*

Hades II **by Greg Kasavin,** published by *Supergiant Games*

Blue Prince **by Tonda Ros**, published by *Raw Fury*

Comic

★ **Winner:** *Mary Shelley's School for Monsters: The Killing Stone* **by Jessica Maison**, published by *Wicked Tree*

Second Shift **by Kit Anderson,** published by *Avery Hill*

Carmilla: The Eternal **by Amy Chu**, published by *Berger*

Helen of Wyndhorn **by Tom King,** published by *Dark Horse*

Fishflies **by Jeff Lemire**, published by *Image*

Strange Bedfellows **by Ariel Slamet Ries**, published by *HarperAlley*

The Flip Side **by Jason Walz**, published by *Rocky Pond*

The Stoneshore Register **by G. Willow Wilson**, published by *Berger*

Poem

★ **Winner: "The World to Come" by Jennifer Hudak,** published by *Strange Horizons*

"Though You Always Are" by Linda D. Addison and Jamal Hodge, published in *Everything Endless* (Raw Dog Screaming Press)

"They Said Robots Are" by Casey Aimer, published by *Penumbric Magazine*

"The Mourning Robot" by Angela Liu, published by *Uncanny Magazine*

"To Be the Change" by Nico Martinez Nocito, published by *Strange Horizons*

"Care for Lightning" by Mari Ness, published by *Uncanny Magazine*

Other Awards

Damon Knight Grand Master Award
N. K. Jemisin

Kate Wilhelm Solstice Award
David Langford

Kevin O'Donnell, Jr. Service to SFWA Award
Gay Haldeman

Infinity Award
Roger Zelazny

TABLE OF CONTENTS

INTRODUCTION

INTRODUCTION

As we celebrate the best works of science fiction and fantasy from 2025 in *Nebula Awards Showcase 61*, it is remarkable to me how unremarked upon the quarter-century mark of the 21st Century was.

We commemorate the 25th anniversary of the most trivial things—TV shows like *Friends* and *Survivor*, the debut albums of the Spice Girls and *NSYNC, movies like *Coyote Ugly* or *Legally Blonde*, and even fad toys like Tamagotchi and cultural ephemera like Pokémon have all been fêted for their 25th in recent years.

Yet our silver anniversary with the future came and went, and we, as a culture, just ignored it. No wistful remembrances, no collective stock-taking. Total silence.

Maybe it's because, after all the buildup, once we actually got there, we discovered that the future kinda sucked.

No orbital colonies. No meals in pill form. No flying cars.

Turns out that the future was (to invert what historian Arnold J. Toynbee once said about the past) *just one damned thing after another.*

It was not the future we were promised. We were promised a better tomorrow. A final frontier. We were promised fully automated luxury gay space communism!

(Though, I'm not too bent out of shape about the flying cars, to be honest. Have you seen how people drive? Do you want to watch them fly? Me neither.)

I'm being silly here in imagining a future straight out of *The Jetsons* or *Star Trek*, obviously, but I'm hardly alone in feeling that the future turned out to be underwhelming. Psychologically, when the cosmic odometer turned over from 1999 to 2000, wasn't the future supposed to feel *different* from the past?

What we got instead was a lot like the past, but with better interfaces. No definitive rupture, but rather continuity with the same fragile human vanity, cruelty, and institutional failures, only now delivered faster, scaled globally, and rendered in high definition on screens we can't stop checking.

Was that most science fictional year of 2001 a new start or a best-before date?

I am guilty of giving the future too much credit. And I suspect I'm not alone.

In hindsight, we probably should have been more skeptical of the 21st Century. The warning signs were there.

Consider how the 2000s began: millennial anxiety and the Y2K bug, the bursting of the dotcom bubble, a botched American presidential election, and then 9/11, which shattered the world's post–Cold War idyll and put an end to the "end of history."

Since then, experiencing the first quarter of the 21st Century in real-time has felt less like a futuristic era and more like a series of stress positions. The phrase "unprecedented times" has lost all meaning, as historic shocks arrive with farcical frequency: twenty years of war in the Middle East, a global financial crisis, austerity, Brexit, a global pandemic and *another* global financial crisis, war in Europe, an energy crisis, trade wars, *another* war in the Middle East and then *another* one, *another* energy crisis, growing right-wing authoritarianism around the globe, the steady background hum of compounding ecological and climate degradation, *and a partridge in a pear tree...*

Just one damned thing after another.

And perhaps most offensive to fiction writers is how *utterly preposterous* this future is, narratively. We have arrived less in *2001: A Space Odyssey* and more in *Idiocracy*.

I have lost count of the number of times in recent years when, seeing the latest outrage in the news, I have thought, "There is no way an editor would ever accept this story if I submitted it!"

Politicians and billionaires so cartoonishly evil that Bond villains would tell them to tone it down a bit? Media barons buying online platforms and TV networks to hollow them out as propaganda machines? Billionaires funding private space programs while civilization's basic mechanisms are starved for resources? Paramilitary goon squads unleashed on American cities? Threats to invade Greenland? *GREENLAND!?!?*

Please rewrite and resubmit. No one will believe this as-is.

Yet this is the *actual future* a quarter of the way through the 21st Century. Truth is stranger than fiction, as the saying goes, because fiction is obliged to make sense.

It is worth noting that neither the fantasy nor science fiction genres escaped the growing pessimism of the early 21st Century unscathed. At a time when real-world institutions felt like they were failing us, even our imagined worlds began to lose hope.

The rise of grimdark fantasy—so prominent in the late 2000s and 2010s—tracked almost perfectly the disillusionment following the global financial crisis and the Great Recession. Science fiction cycled through trends of dystopia, zombie apocalypse, and retrofuturism, looking back to a time when we still believed in the future. Nostalgia, as Richard Greenberg once observed, is just a longing for a time we know we can survive.

Please don't misunderstand: this isn't a slight against grimdark or post-apocalypses. The trends in genre over the last 25 years have all yielded wonderful works. Rather, it's an observation that the farther we got into living "the future" the harder it seemed to become to imagine "the future" anymore. Or at least a future we would want or hope for.

Maybe that's because, as William Gibson has assured us, the future is already here, but it's just not evenly distributed. I'm not sure that's correct, though. That idea assumes there is one coherent "future."

What we're experiencing are *fragments* of many imagined futures all at once. Utopia and dystopia butt up against each other. Sleek *Star Trek*-inspired design and late-capitalist cyberpunk decay grapple for aesthetic dominance. It's like viewing things through a kaleidoscope, with each turn revealing a different configuration as the shards of our futures reorient themselves into our Now.

Turn the kaleidoscope and you've got slick touchscreens and pocket supercomputers. Turn it again and you get digital platforms controlled by tech-bro oligarchs. Another turn, we've sequenced the human genome. Another turn, democratic decay. Turn for billions fewer people living in extreme poverty than at any point in human history. Turn again for staggering wealth inequality. Turn for climate catastrophe. Turn and humans return to the moon.

And yet, this is *precisely* why speculative fiction remains indispensable.

Because in a moment when reality feels unreal, feels incoherent, when we are grappling with a fragmentary Now, speculative fiction still insists on asking: "What comes after this?" Speculative fiction demands we confront and reimagine what comes next, challenging us to assert agency over what the future could and should be.

What matters to us? What kind of world is this becoming? More than that, speculative fiction can ask not just what future we expect, or what future we fear, but what kind of future do we actually *want*?

To hold in mind a vision of a future you would choose (rather than one you would merely endure) is a radical act of resistance in the face of a world seemingly bent on driving us to despair. Such a vision is how we clarify what we value. How we identify what we're willing to fight for and defend. What we might still build.

To plan, to wonder, to *speculate*—that, increasingly, feels like something worth preserving, and speculative fiction is a unique vehicle for doing just that.

Because, at its best, speculative fiction isn't really about the future at all.

Like most good fiction, it is about the human condition: about who we are under pressure, and how we might react when circumstances change. The high technology, the distant planets, the magic, the dragons—these are not the subject so much as the lens. Because speculative fiction is about the Now, about us as people of the present.

Science fiction takes contemporary concerns—political, social, technological—and wraps them in the guise of the wondrous or numinous or alien not to escape them, but to let us step back from the present, from our own assumptions and blind spots, and ask, at a safe distance: what kind of a world are we building, and is it one we want?

Fantasy, while often less concerned with the future *per se*, is no less interested in the realities of the human condition. Power, duty, loyalty, corruption, sacrifice—exploring such concepts is the raw material of fantasy. If science fiction asks what kind of world we are building, fantasy asks what kind of people we are within it and who we might yet become.

The future, despite everything, isn't a destination, and it's not something that happens to us. It is something we assemble, piece by piece, out of the Now.

So, as we look through the kaleidoscope, the question is not whether things will change (they will) but *how* they will be arranged when all is said and done.

Speculative fiction gives us a way to turn the lens experimentally, to see not just what is, but what might be, and to imagine the final pattern we want.

In the stories that follow in *Nebula Awards Showcase 61*, and in the longer works on the Nebula finalists list, you'll find fiction that speculates about all this and more.

Stories that center on the redefinition of identity and the fragmentation of the self, the burden of generational legacies and the tension between preserving memory and moving toward the future. Stories examining the encroachment of the artificial and its displacement of the human. There are meditations on the power of storytelling and memory, and on the nature of power and the struggle for agency against systematic control.

So, let's turn the kaleidoscope a quarter turn and another and *another* and see how our futures might sort out.

Welcoming New Categories to the Nebula Awards

And speaking of the changes the future brings...

The Science Fiction & Fantasy Writers Association (SFWA) is pleased to welcome two new categories to the Nebulas this year: Poem and Comic.

The Best Poem category is open to a science fiction or fantasy poem of any length, and the Best Comic category is open to a science fiction or fantasy story of any length told using sequential art. These mark the ninth and tenth new categories added to the Nebula Awards since their inception in 1966 and are among the nine active categories of awards presented this year.

So, with those welcomes made, all that remains is to welcome you to *Nebula Awards Showcase 61*.

Stephen Kotowych
Kitchener, ON
April 2026

SHORT STORIES

LASER EYES AIN'T EVERYTHING

Effie Seiberg

The Super-Abled 501 Local Union building wasn't ADA compliant.

I sat in my wheelchair next to the three steps that led to their front door, and groaned. My brand new laser eyes didn't exactly fix my mobility problems.

Two weeks ago, I'd been zapped by a falling piece of alien spaceship debris and developed laser eyes. Ten days ago, I'd lost my job at the City Planner's office because of budget cuts. I wasn't even mad though, because I could never push my projects through and you know who gets stuff done without anyone getting in their way? The super-abled. As soon as I got home I filled in my union application.

Yesterday I'd gotten notice that I could join after I demonstrated my new laser eyes in person. And now here I was. Stuck.

A rubbery guy walked out the front door, legs stretching and compressing like a slinky.

"Excuse me!" I said, brandishing my paperwork. "Is there another way into the building?"

Stretchy-legs looked me up and down. "You sure you're in the right place?"

I sighed and took off my sunglasses, then lasered the small patch of grass next to the sidewalk. "Yeah. So. Is there another way in?"

He shook his head.

"Socooo could you get someone to come out? Nobody's answering the phones."

"Right. Sure. Hey, why are you in a wheelchair if you're super-abled?"

I took a deep breath and reminded myself that ignorance wasn't malice. "Laser eyes ain't everything. Can you go grab someone?"

Eventually a harried intern came and explained that testing had to be done inside where specialized equipment made sure nobody was cheating, but if I wanted we could get one of their super-strong members to carry me and my chair in.

Normally I'd never submit to such indignity. But, figuring I could get this sorted more effectively as a member than a non-member, I said OK.

A large woman who looked like she was made of striped sedimentary rocks clomped over and gathered me up, wheelchair and all, like I was just a bag of groceries. Humiliating, dehumanizing, and not exactly the best first impression in a professional context. Once she put me back down I hoped that everyone, myself included, would forget that ever happened.

Inside, in a room full of lenses and sensors, I lasered things. I turned paper into ashes, melted concrete into a glowing blob, and then, because nobody was saying anything, with great care I lasered the wobbly words 'is this enough' in char marks on the wall.

My application was approved.

I'd been trying to get traffic circles built since I'd started at the City Planner's office. As an assistant I hadn't had much sway over anything.

Each time there was a different reason. Sometimes there was no budget. Sometimes it wasn't what the voters wanted, though, had anyone actually asked the voters? Of course not. Sometimes there was no time to spend on this and really I should be focusing on the important things like fixing the coffee machine.

But the super-abled? They could do anything they wanted. They had no bosses to tell them no, and what were you gonna do, try to stop a super-abled person from doing, well, anything?

Over the next week I went through the list of superheroes in the union roster and started contacting them, one by one. I introduced myself and gave my little spiel about how traffic circles save lives compared to regular intersections, and how this little change could make a big difference, and weren't we super-abled all in the business of saving lives...?

The responses weren't encouraging.

ExpandiRay wouldn't lend me his raygun to grow an intersection wider so that I could carve it into a circle after, because insurance wouldn't cover it.

AscendAnt said she was too busy with an autograph signing to get ants to dismantle bits of pavement and carry them to a new orientation.

NiteFlite wouldn't lift and move sections of street without consulting with the union PR rep, who wrote that redoing city infrastructure wasn't "on brand" for the union and maybe I should just find a nice supervillain to fight instead.

The Smash sent me back an email that looked like she'd mashed her fists all over the keyboard and called it a day.

But most of them didn't respond at all.

They still hadn't built a ramp, and meetings were in-person, so I joined the union meeting by video. The HR rep made a big deal about making a "special exception" for me since I "didn't really need this accommodation" because "someone could always carry me in like before." I managed to keep my smile plastered on my face.

The union leader, a woman named "Big Dig" with hands like gopher claws, went through the agenda. Most of it was assigning press stuff. But eventually we got to the one real thing on the agenda—the union wanted to defeat Doctor Croc, a green scaly menace who'd been razing buildings, most recently a conference center.

I knew that place well. Its front doors were too narrow for my chair, and the one time I'd gone to a conference I'd had to get in near the dumpsters in the back. Which had meant waiting by the dumpsters for an hour, until I too smelled like garbage, until someone brought up the service elevator. Which meant my boss was so grossed out he'd sent me home to shower.

Destroying a conference center wasn't great, but if you absolutely had to, I'd choose this one.

When it was time, I introduced myself and said "Sorry I'm not there in person to meet everyone. I'll be glad to join you once there's a ramp!"

Crickets.

"So I was wondering when there was a chance to suggest new business? Traffic circles save lives over intersections, and I was thinking that if someone like PhazeMatter could turn an intersection's pavement into a liquid and then we reroute it and solidify it back, we could make a big difference to the city without a lot of effort... I have a research paper on traffic circles... if anyone's interested..."

I trailed off. Nobody was listening.

The union leader ahemmed and said "Everyone, there's snacks outside, mingle and enjoy! RazorBeam, can you stay on a minute?"

She waited until everyone else filed out of the room. "I wanted to touch base. The 501 really cares about accessibility. But with dues the way they are, we can't afford to put in a ramp right now."

"But the ADA says—"

"This building is old enough to be grandfathered in. Besides, if we built a ramp for you, we'd have to make adjustments for everybody. Backless chairs for Lizzardbeth so her tail would fit better, upgrade the bathroom plumbing for RockGal, you get the idea. The budget would explode! There's even a rule in the union handbook, from about seven years ago, that says we don't do accommodations when it's for just one member."

Temporary ramps were pretty cheap, but I tried switching tactics. Maybe I could still get something else done. "Can we talk about traffic circles then?"

"Unfortunately it's not on our list of priorities for the year, so maybe some other time. And we'd rather you not bug all the other union members about it. But hopefully you can join us in person for the next meeting! You're missing out on the networking," she chirped, and hung up.

I breathed deeply. Then lasered a hole in my living room wall.

Throughout the next week, I waited for my union-issued superwatch to vibrate and call me into action. On Friday it finally did, telling me to come to HQ.

Yet again, I hit the problem of the stairs, but it turned out not to matter. They wanted me for an outdoor photo shoot as the newest member of the team, together with an interview with a local journalist.

During the interview, the PR rep held giant cue cards with what I was supposed to say to the journalist. The whole exercise seemed pretty meaningless.

But then the journalist asked, "And RazorBeam, how do you feel about Doctor Croc getting away yesterday, after he smashed up the craft supplies store on Main Street?"

The PR rep's eyes widened. Probably the journalist hadn't vetted this question with them. And I was taken aback too—I'd had no idea that there was a new Doctor Croc incident.

"Uhhhh... I'm sure we'll get him next time?"

"What's really important here," jumped in the PR rep, "is that we have a wonderful new member of the team. Our diversity makes us stronger, and that lets us better serve the people of this city. Thank you for your time!"

After the journalist was hurried out, I asked the rep what had happened.

"Oh it's just a craft store, don't worry about it."

"Why wasn't I called to help? I was free, and maybe if I was there he wouldn't have gotten away."

"Oh well." They looked me up and down. "We want to save your abilities for the projects that use them best. I'm sure the next time you'll be called. See you then!"

As they sauntered away, I lasered a patch of grass into a charred black splotch in frustration.

But why a craft supplies store? What would a supervillain have against pipe cleaners and construction paper and rolls of fabric? A convention center was the center of big meetups and commerce, it was a big deal to a city to get that destroyed. But a little craft shop?

I wasn't a fan of that store, not that I needed a lot of craft supplies. But I'd gone once to get poster board and thick markers to make a sign for a rally, and the aisles of supplies were crammed so close together that I couldn't really maneuver in there.

Still, a craft store made no sense.

Two weeks later, at the next union meeting (still via video), I came prepared with a proposal.

If I could get help blocking traffic, I could sort of make traffic circles happen myself. I'd spent the last few weeks experimenting with asphalt and found that after I melted it I could sort of push it around with a shovel. It wasn't the most efficient, but it could work.

I never got to talk. There'd been another Doctor Croc attack that nobody had invited me to, and it was at a perfectly wheelchair-accessible gym. This time they put up some photos from the gym fight. (They'd brought the journalist! But not me!)

I'd been to that gym. It was a crappy old place where the windows didn't properly close and all the fluorescent lights flickered and there was a greasy sheen of something on all surfaces, so not that many people went to it anyway and I doubt many people were sad it was destroyed. What was Doctor Croc's goal here, anyway?

Nobody was trying to figure out what the pattern was, though. And it seemed like nobody could stop the guy. ExpandiRay was in the hospital with a shattered femur from some barbells Doctor Croc had thrown at him during the fight. And RockGal had some new epoxy-filled cracks on her face.

I didn't even try to bring up traffic circles.

The attacks kept coming, and I kept not getting an invitation to come help.

I did experiments in my own backyard on how far I could accurately laser things, and sent the results to Big Dig. It didn't change anything, even though I was pretty sure I had the most reach out of any of the super-abled who had distance or projectile abilities. (I got an angry letter from my landlord who saw the charred remains of my experiments and I had to buy a fire extinguisher, so I guess one change. But that was it.)

If I couldn't help fight, perhaps I could help predict. I went to the library and read all I could about Doctor Croc, and found nothing that made sense. There was no obvious vendetta I could find, nothing about past grudges, or feuds, or specific needs for revenge. As a twentysomething he'd had an airboat accident in a swamp and had been bitten by a mutated crocodile. The toxic waste plant that had oozed its sludge into the swamp to affect the crocodiles had long since been dealt with. There'd been lawsuits, cleanup efforts, the works, and it hadn't been in business in years. It looked like the site was now an ecology museum with exhibits about the dangers of pollution in wetlands.

So I needed a new theory. I made one of those conspiracy boards at home, with the printed out pictures and thumbtacks and pieces of string connecting pieces of information. He'd destroyed the conference center, craft supplies store, and gym, and previously had demolished an ancient movie theater that showed old movies on a rattling old projector, and a little hardware store crammed full of tools and paints all the way to the ceiling, with really high checkout counters that displayed even more goods beneath them. After weeks of trying to put together the puzzle pieces, I still had nothing.

Chez Louisette was the one fancy restaurant in town. And it was having a grand re-opening on Wednesday. It was no crappy gym or dusty craft store, but it was an opportunity with a lot of press so maybe, just maybe, Doctor Croc would be there? Maybe?

So on Wednesday morning I sent a note to Big Dig about my theory, then went to stake the place out.

Not only was I right, but Doctor Croc had beat me there. As soon as I got near I heard a big crash. And another. And then two green scaly fists burst through its wall, raining down bits of brick.

Nobody else was here, but this was my chance! Maybe if I could take him down alone, the union would take me seriously, and we could get something done.

I lasered a giant hole in the wall, which then tottered and fell forward, revealing a very angry crocodile man. He was about eight feet tall, mostly a torso on stubby green legs, and his arms were muscular, massive, and gearing up for another punch.

"Hey!" I said. "Doctor Croc! Put your hands in the air!" I remembered protocol, and pushed the button on my new superwatch for the union to send backup to my location.

He looked me up and down. "You?" he said. "YOU. Of all people. Are trying to stop ME."

I suppressed a scream. Why were people so difficult everywhere! "Disabled people can be super-abled too, you know. Now I can laser you dead from here in less time than it'd take you to throw a chunk of wall at me, so I suggest you put your hands up."

"You don't get it. Do you know what this restaurant's been doing?"

"Uh, being snooty?"

"They won't reveal their ingredients, which is dangerous for people with allergies and Celiacs and whatnot." He looked smug, as though this magically explained everything.

"I mean, that's awful, but that's no reason to destroy the whole building. Or any of the other places you've been smashing up. Now, you're under arrest, by the order of the Super-Abled 501 Local Union! Hands up!"

He scoffed, but slowly raised his hands and stepped out towards me. Behind him were the twisted stainless steel remains of what had been a kitchen. "Still a believer, huh? Tell me, did the 501 ever add any outdoor handrails?"

"What does that have to do with anything? No..."

"I was a member seven years ago. Asked for some accommodations so my kid could join on Take Your Child to Work Day. They never added any. Each time it was 'there's no budget' or 'that decision was made by the previous leadership' and nothing. Ever. Changed. Eventually they had a vote that said that any changes to the union of any kind, which benefit only one person, were out. Specifically to shut me up. Even though accessibility accommodations help loads of people, and they wouldn't even know how many people weren't applying in the first place because the building was inaccessible."

Sounded familiar. And enraging. "It's crappy," I said, "but still no reason to destroy everything."

"Oh yeah?" he asked, moving closer. "Have they built you a ramp yet?"

"Um. No..."

"Didn't think so. They just can't be bothered."

"OK so they suck, fine, but why destroy all these other buildings?"

Doctor Croc continued, "Nobody can be bothered to make accommodations. The ADA's only enforced when people bring lawsuits. I'm in a giant Facebook group of parents with disabled kids and basically nobody has the time and money to sue, ever. And even then most lawsuits fail. But when I destroy an inaccessible building, the insurance covers it, and when they rebuild, it's no longer so old that it gets an accessibility exemption. Plus, it's safe since everyone gets evacuated. No people get harmed, and we get the accessibility we need. There was nobody here this morning when I started smashing."

"That can't be right," I said, as his hands started floating downwards. "Hey, hands stay up! Look, I used to work for the city. There are plenty of avenues to ask for accommodations. And besides, what was so inaccessible about that gym? Or the other places?"

He put his hands up again. "That gym had flickering lights, which can trigger migraines, seizures, or meltdowns. The movie theater never bothered to add closed captioning devices. The hardware store had high checkout counters and never let its cashiers sit even when one of them broke a leg."

"OK, that makes no sense. Why not just destroy the gym's lights? Or the hardware store's checkout counters? There's no reason they couldn't rebuild with the same exact problems. Plus I doubt anyone even knows that this is why stuff's getting destroyed. You're not exactly getting headlines that say 'Doctor Croc Destroys Another Inaccessible Building'."

"Huh," he said, lowering his hands briefly then thinking better of it and shoving them up again. "Yeah that's a good point. Probably should've just smashed up those counters, and probably should've left a note or something. Hey you're good at this! You should join me!"

"I'm not going to start smashing up buildings! I'm one of the good guys."

"Oh yeah? Those good guys that can't even get you a ramp? Those things cost what, like $200 at Home Depot?"

He had a point. With the union taking a percentage of all sponsorships and deals, and members working with giant brands like Nike, they could absolutely find space in their budget for a measly $200. They could get a single backless stool for Lizzardbeth for cheap. They just weren't bothering to take those two minutes to think of solutions to help. Even I hadn't thought of the problems with flickering lights and old movie equipment.

Most of all, *nothing was getting done.* The local 501 was so busy with its public image it wasn't doing jack. Here I was, talking to their archenemy for a good five minutes, and nobody else was showing up.

"This is ridiculous," I muttered.

"It is ridiculous! We'd make great partners, you and me, actually make some changes around here. What would you do about the movie theater?"

"Huh? I don't know, I guess I'd laser 'GET CAPTIONING DEVICES OR ELSE' on their walls. Or send a note to local insurance companies that says that their clients are at risk of expensive damages if they don't shore up accessibility, and they have two weeks to fix things." I shook my head. "But that's irrelevant!"

"See? Those are great ideas. You're full of them. So join me, whaddaya think? No more smashing up buildings when you've got a better plan, I promise." He gave me a crocodiley grin, showing all his teeth. "My garage is fully accessible and is a great place to meet. And I make a mean dairy-free hot chocolate."

Something inside me snapped. It had been years since someone thought about accessibility for me without me having to even ask. And maybe this way I could actually get something done, especially if Doctor Croc was willing to let me focus him. Get him laser-focused, if you will. And with a bit of time I could probably come up with some better plans that were less destructive and more effective.

"Hell," I said. "Only if we make some traffic circles too."

"Oh I read those things save a lot of lives! Great idea, let's do that next. You in?"

"Why not," I said, and grinned back.

And just for some much-needed catharsis, I lasered an already-wrecked piece of kitchen behind him. The metal melted into a ramp-like shape.

Effie Seiberg is a fantasy and science fiction writer living in the San Francisco Bay Area. Her stories include a Nebula and Hugo Award finalist, a finalist in the AnLab Awards, and a finalist for the Subjective Chaos Kind Of Award. Her recent work can be found in *Diabolical Plots*, *Lightspeed*, *Fantasy Magazine*, and *PodCastle*, amongst others.

THROUGH THE MACHINE

P.A. Cornell

"Steve, over here! Turn to your right. Can we get a smile?"

He falls back on his training easily enough, turns to the cameras, gives them his famous crooked smile, tilts his head just so as the flashes go off so they can capture the smoulder that highlights his cheekbones. The one he's practiced countless times with his manager, Ethel.

The red carpet extends before him, and up ahead he sees the actress he's been paired with in this film. His co-star and onscreen love interest but in reality, a total stranger. He only knows her name because the photographers keep shouting it, asking her to turn so they can capture her svelte profile. She tilts her head obligingly, long blonde hair falling seductively over one eye, teasing the lenses and through them the millions of fans who'll one day see these images. She's a pro, like him. She's clearly had the same kind of training he's had. She's been through the machine.

It's a phrase he heard years ago from a late night talk show host. It refers to the way Hollywood turns you into a product. You start out this average person, just trying to make it as an actor, then as your success grows, more and more people come into your life to turn you into something else. A movie star. A fairytale ideal of celebrity perfection. He'd told himself that would never be him. He was in it for the art, not the fame and fortune. But here he is.

"Steve! Daphne! Can we get some shots of the two of you together?"

The blonde up ahead reaches a hand toward him as if beckoning a good friend, though this is the first time they've met. She smiles at him in a way that almost looks genuine. He returns his best leading man grin, flashing the expensive set of pearly white teeth his manager arranged for in the earliest days of their partnership. He puts an arm around Daphne. They both pose, turn, look at each other and smile over and over. Then both look serious, then smile once more. Then she leans in for a peck on the cheek as instructed by the shouting crowd, just before they're both ushered off to find their places inside, where the film will be screened.

Once they're away from the cameras, he extends his hand to Daphne.

"Hi. Steve Randall."

"Nice to meet you," she laughs. "Daphne Everheart."

"You seen any of it yet?"

"Not even the trailer," she admits. "Did they send you the screenplay?"

He shakes his head.

Someone in her entourage grabs her by the arm. She gives him a small wave as they lead her off. He wonders if he'll even see her again after this premiere. Maybe. If the film does well opening weekend, there could be a sequel. They could find themselves at another premiere for a movie they appear in together, but that neither of them has acted in.

Steve lets his own people show him past curtains and cocktails to a theater with plush red seating. He takes his place staring up at the screen, trying to conjure up some of the excitement he once felt as a kid about to watch his favorite actors. But the excitement feels more akin to anxiety as the opening credits appear. He sees his own name—or the one his manager gave him, anyway. That's when *he* appears.

Seeing himself like this is unsettling, to say the least. He turns to the people seated around him and they're all looking up at this face that resembles him but isn't him. Do they not see it? Do they not feel that uncanny valley sickness in the pit of their stomachs that weighs his down as the thing on screen billed as Steve Randall starts to speak? It's his voice, but he's never said these words. Never read the script they came from. Who wrote this, anyway? He wonders. Or rather, *what* wrote this?

The film's runtime is ninety-five minutes. It's a romantic comedy, but the word 'comedy' is generous. Steve doesn't so much as crack a smile. He watches this AI-generated doppelganger and his equally digitized scene partner as they traverse the uneven landscape of the disjointed plot—flimsy even for this genre. They flash smile after smile, kiss with ever-deepening passion—if you can call it that, and ultimately, after a series of contrived misunderstandings, they get their Hollywood ending. All set to an AI-generated score bereft of any feeling that might conjure atmosphere or elicit an emotional response from the viewer.

As the lights come up and people start to clap, Steve glances down the row of seats at his co-star. Daphne, seeming to sense his stare, glances back. She looks as though she's about to be sick but gives him a brave smile—a trained smile—and starts to clap along with everyone else. He does the same. This is his job now, after all.

The scan was taken a couple of years ago, during pre-production on a movie in which he played an astronaut. They had to scan him for proper fit of the spacesuit they were having made, as well as for some of the more intricate effects. The voice they came by even more easily. From all the ADR he'd done, voicework on some animated stuff, and of course countless interviews already accessible online. He hadn't given the scan much thought, at the time. It had made sense for the work they were doing. He'd never imagined it would lead to this.

There's an afterparty and people keep coming up and congratulating him on the movie. He says what he's been trained to say, graciously thanking them for their praise, taking pictures with people for magazines and entertainment shows. Evidence that he is in fact still a real person that exists in the world, even though it's not him on screen. Not in this movie and not in a handful of others, several of which he hasn't even seen. If Hollywood could turn you into a product before, this is on another level.

His career has become, almost exclusively, one of public appearances. His L.A. agent has him booked for a store opening tomorrow, and some time in the spring a series of meet-and-greets at conventions. The sorts of gigs that used to be thought of as 'has-been' work, but Steve, by all accounts, is still a bona fide movie star. He was *People Magazine*'s 'Sexiest Man Alive' just last year. Fans still somehow manage to find out what hotel he's staying at in any given city all over the world, just so they can catch a glimpse of him walking in and out. How has it come to this?

At the end of the night someone pushes him into a shiny black town car and the spectacle of this farce fades away in the car's rear lights. He exhales, trying to get the image of the *thing* on screen out of his head. It's not so bad, he tells himself. SAG made sure he'd get paid for the use of his image. It's not as much as he might've liked, maybe, but it's decent, and they use it often enough that the cheques enable him to maintain his standard of living. The public appearances add to that. He can't really complain.

But the sick feeling in his stomach remains.

When he's back in New York, he calls his manager.

"It was fucking weird, Ethel." He tells her. "Seeing myself in a film I wasn't actually in. No chemistry between me and my co-star because, well...neither of us was actually there to do any acting. This isn't what I signed up for."

"Sweet boy," she says, using her years' old term of endearment for him, though he hasn't been a boy in quite some time. "I know. But this is how it works with the studio films these days. Be glad your image is still worth something."

Steve sighs deeply. "I know. It's just...I worked so hard to get here. We both did. The work mattered to me. I miss challenging myself, figuring out who my character is and how to best convey that through my performance. I miss being able to disappear into all those people and live their lives for a time."

"Of course, of course," says Ethel. "That's one of the reasons I took you on as a client. Even at sixteen, you had such passion. You loved the art of it. But what's the alternative, Stefan?"

She only ever uses his original name when she's serious. He knows her hands are as tied as his. It's this or give up the business altogether.

Over drinks with a friend the next night, he airs his frustrations, his tongue loosened by more than a few shots with beer chasers.

"I'm bored," he tells Frank, who doubled for him in an action film franchise that now continues without need of either of them. "I miss acting. It's like all they left me with are the worst parts of fame. The parts where I still can't walk down the street in peace without some paparazzo shoving a lens in my face, and where I can still get cancelled online for any stupid shit I might say without thinking. But the good parts, they've all been taken over by some digital version of me that frankly gives me the creeps."

"I hear ya, Steve," Frank says, raising his beer. "It's not just you though, brother. At least you still have a marketable presence. Companies still send you free clothes and shit so you can be spotted using it."

"Sure," he tells Frank, "but all that amounts to is that I'm now pretty much just this human billboard. I'm not even an actor anymore."

"You're breaking my heart, man. But think about guys like me. We were getting your crumbs even in the good times. If you think things have gotten rough for you, imagine what's left for us. I haven't been called for a stunt gig in months. And that last one ended up cancelled last minute when they decided it was cheaper to use AI. I've got a family to support, and all three kids are gonna need braces. Not to mention the first wife who's on my back if I'm even half a second late with her alimony. What I wouldn't give for my ugly mug to be in demand."

Steve knows he's right and feels bad for whining. Things could be so much worse. Whatever jobs he's lost to AI, there are countless more jobs lost by less famous actors, crew, and other support personnel like PA's and craft services. He can't begin to imagine how they're all making ends meet these days. Many of the ones he's still close with, like Frank, work multiple jobs, even outside the industry, just to cover what their once stable careers did.

"Drinks are on me tonight, by the way," he tells Frank.

"You'll get no argument here, pal."

Later, in the privacy of his loft, Steve allows himself the luxury of self-pity. He can't help thinking of the kid he once was. The chubby little dork with the accent. Too shy to talk to girls. Pushed around by the guys he so wanted to be. Acting freed him from all that. It had allowed this kid who didn't feel comfortable in his own skin to become someone else. In time, it had given him confidence, and as he continued to hone his craft, it had brought him the attention he'd craved and opportunities he'd never imagined.

It hasn't always been easy. There'd been plenty of lean years before his big breakout role turned him into a household name. Years during which covering rent had been a struggle, and meals had often consisted of half-eaten scraps left by patrons of the restaurants in which he'd waited tables. But he'd loved acting enough to stick with it, and he'd thought it worth all the sacrifices.

He gave up his very name for this profession. He lost the accent and the baby fat. He's spent a sizeable portion of his income on fixing his teeth, and on five-hundred-dollar haircuts sometimes paired with a treatment to achieve that perfect shade of chestnut brown or a shave that still left enough stubble to keep him looking 'manly' in a marketable way. He's gotten regular tans to conceal his naturally pale complexion—a condition the L.A. agent refers to as his 'vampire' look. He's hired a stylist, a personal trainer, and a dietitian to help him maintain what the grueling workouts have chiselled him into. He's had more hours of media training than he's had acting classes. Hell, at times he's even dated women he's been *told* to date. All of it to create this perfect image of Hollywood glamour intended to seduce audiences into filling theater seats.

He's been put through the machine—and willingly let it happen—just so he can go on doing what he loves.

He hadn't realized this image wasn't him. It was just a product. Something that could be sold, and then re-sold again and again, with little if any say from him as to how it might be used.

Feeling down about his situation, Steve turns to Instagram. He doesn't follow any fan accounts but now and then, when he's alone, he looks up the hashtag that bears his name. The fans have a way of making him feel better about himself. Their comments on his pictures—especially the shirtless ones—always make his day. Their support for the charities he's championed over the years warms his heart. Sure, there are always trolls, but those are in the minority and easy enough to block.

He scrolls through his feed and finds the *People* photoshoot. His feelings about the shoot are a mix of pride and embarrassment. Pride that the chubby kid with the Polish accent showed his high school bullies up, but a little shame at the fact that he still cares so much about what they might think. Still, a few of the pictures from the shoot are really good. He recalls how the photographer's great sense of humor put him at ease, and how welcoming the magazine staff were.

Continuing to scroll, he comes across a picture of himself he never took. This isn't one of those amazing fan art images he's seen over the years made by outstandingly talented artists that managed to capture not just his appearance, but his essence. This is some kind of Frankenimage, clearly AI-generated. His hair is a honey blonde he's never sported, not even on screen. The cheekbones are oddly exaggerated and too narrow, giving him an almost gaunt appearance. In the picture he holds an infant, staring down at it like a proud father. It hurts him to see it. He's always wanted a family, but this hasn't happened for him in real life.

Steve scrolls some more and comes across another AI image. In this one he's dressed in a patent leather getup; cut to reveal tattoos he doesn't have. A red blindfold covers his eyes. His arms are cuffed behind his back. His expression is one of ecstasy. Behind him stands another known actor who holds the handle of a whip against his chest as he leans in to lick the side of Steve's face. The actor is a good friend. They've worked together a few times but never as onscreen lovers. Fans have imagined their characters as a couple for years, which seemed harmless enough, but seeing this is something else. Against his better judgment, he reads the comments.

"I ship them."

"Gorgeous art. Love this."

"Yes, please."

And so on.

"I wanna see them getting down in a movie together," someone's written.

There's a response to this last comment from someone who's handle indicates they work for a major studio. "Don't worry. You won't have to wait much longer for that. And let's just say this one's not going to be the family-friendly fare you're used to seeing these guys in."

Steve isn't homophobic. He's played gay characters more than once and has been fine with kissing or even simulating sex with other male actors. But there's something about being paired with a close friend in this way without so much as a heads up, that seems like a violation. It's one thing to work with another actor that you've built trust with and talk through a scene to make sure you're both comfortable depicting something intimate that everyone can be proud of in the end. It's quite another thing when your image is used to quell strangers' salacious appetites, in a way you didn't consent to.

Steve feels sick. He takes screenshots of both the AI image and the comment about the movie and texts them to his friend. He follows that up with the message:

Did you know about this?

The reply comes almost immediately.

Fuck. Are you kidding me?

Wish I was.

Damn man. I love you, but not like that. At least not without the kind of money we used to get for our movies.

Steve smiles in spite of himself. At least his friends can still have a sense of humor about these things.

I feel like we need to push back on this, he tells his friend.

Yeah, I get it man, but we signed the contract. I know we didn't have much choice, but the law doesn't care. We agreed to this. Pretty sure it's too late to stop them.

The fans don't even seem to care it's not really us, Steve types.

Why would they? his friend replies. *They don't even really need us anymore. We just get in the way of their fantasies.*

Steve doesn't respond to that. He deletes his Instagram account.

He shudders to think of what they're doing with his image on TikTok. Or worse, on the dark web.

"This sucks, Ethel." Steve puts the phone on speaker and sets it down on the kitchen counter to pour a bowl of cereal. "I'm going stir-crazy here. I need something to challenge my creativity again."

"Well, I heard about one thing, but I'm not sure it's really for you, so I hadn't mentioned it," she says.

"What? Tell me?" He opens the fridge and reaches for the almond milk then thinks, *screw it*, and grabs the whole milk he bought yesterday instead.

"There's this Broadway musical. I know one of the producers, but you'd have to audition."

"That's exactly what I need right now," he tells her, over mouthfuls of Frosted Flakes. "It'll be good for me to go back to my theater roots. It's been too long since I've performed in front of an audience."

He pushes the thought that it's a musical to the back of his mind. He's never been known for his singing, but he can work with a voice coach or something. At this point he'll do anything to perform again.

"It's been a long time since you've had to audition, let alone for live theater," Ethel says.

"Just tell me where and when. I've got this."

When he gets the lead in the musical, Steve's thrilled, but also mildly surprised. He'd felt good about the audition, but he'd heard some of the other actors sing and they were clearly better than he is. He figures they must've seen something in him—an intangible quality that suits the part. Why overthink it?

His illusions come crashing down early on in rehearsals. During a break, he talks with one of the stagehands. An older guy named Bill. Steve vents a bit about how he can't really act in the film industry anymore.

"Thank god for Broadway. The last refuge for actors like me."

"Yeah. For actors like *you*," Bill agrees.

Steve isn't sure what he means by that and says so.

"Look, you seem like a decent enough guy," Bill says, "so don't take this the wrong way, but you're here because you're a name. They need something to put on the billboards that'll draw a crowd, is all. It ain't about talent no more."

Steve is taken aback, and his expression must show it.

"Don't get me wrong," Bill continues. "You're good. Up there on the big screen, you were a real standout. But this is a whole different animal. All I'm saying is there's actors more cut out for the stage than you that can't get hired anymore because the guys who used to work the screen are taking their roles."

Steve's about to respond when Bill points to a group of actors sitting together talking.

"See the guy in the collared shirt?" Bill says. "That's Wayne Garnet."

Steve knows Wayne from rehearsals. Nice guy. He has a small part but gives it his all.

"Wayne's a Tony-winner. Used to be *his* name on the marquee. Now even he has to settle for bit parts since AI started taking chunks out of the film industry."

Later Steve Googles Wayne Garnet and finds he's actually won *two* Tonys. He's also known for his singing voice, which he loaned to several animated films before they started digitally recreating it.

Steve feels sick. He approaches Wayne during the next rehearsal and offers to bow out to make room for him. Wayne is gracious and tells him not to.

"There's no point, Steve. They'd just get another big name movie star to replace you. My days as the lead are done. I'm just happy I still get to be on stage at all. At least for now."

"What do you mean?" Steve asks.

"AI's coming for all of us," Wayne says. "It's not just the film industry. This crap is spreading like a virus throughout the arts. There's already talk of a new play, AI-written, of course, where instead of live actors they're projecting digital performers onto the stage. It's strictly off-Broadway for now, but give it time."

Steve is appalled. Doesn't know what to say.

Wayne continues. "I'll take whatever I can get these days. You know what they say, 'There are no small parts.' I just hope that when the roles run out, someone will want to scan *me* to use in a projection so I can at least cash a cheque now and then."

At home one night, after the play's run has ended, Steve settles in to watch TV. He scans his options, stumbling upon one of his early roles. A serious drama in which he played a depressed teen, struggling with his parents' divorce and his older brother's untimely death.

Even all these years later, the dialogue comes back as he watches one of the more emotional scenes.

"It's not like I don't want to talk about Tommy," he mouths along with his younger self. "I do. It's just that..." Young Steve can't finish because he's started to cry.

Present day Steve remembers shooting the scene—his first time crying on cue. He remembers harnessing all those emotions and tapping into all the pain he'd ever felt, and all of it somehow pouring out of him in that moment. He remembers the director taking him aside later and saying, "You nailed it, kid." He smiles thinking of this now, but then he's sad again, missing the sense of accomplishment of pulling off a scene like this. The exhilaration of seeing an audience respond to it later.

He watches the remainder of the movie while eating peanut butter by the spoonful right out of the jar. Halfway through he crumbles in an entire Kit-kat bar like he used to do when he was a kid. By the time the credits roll, the jar is empty.

Steve's personal trainer leaves frequent voicemail messages asking when he's coming back to the gym. He knows he should, but it's tough to get motivated for a workout when he feels like all anyone's going to see is his AI clone. Still, it's in his contract to try to resemble the digital version of himself as much as possible. He knows his skin could use a bit more color these days too, and his hair's starting to show some gray he hadn't even realized he had. He makes a mental note to focus more on his appearance.

All that can wait until after he returns from the convention though. He's surprised to find he's actually looking forward to connecting with his fans again and maybe seeing some of the ones that have become familiar faces over time.

The energy at the con is intense, and Steve feels electrified, like he did during his stint on Broadway. One by one he greets his fans as warmly as he possibly can. He makes time to speak with them in the few minutes he has while they take pictures with him. He gives them not his practiced smile, but his real one, and makes sure to thank each one for their continued support.

Things get a little weird during the signing. Much of it is what he's used to, with fans handing him old headshots or pictures from his older films to sign, and in some cases art they've made themselves. But he's also handed quite a few more AI-generated images than he's used to. He feels like a fraud signing them. Like he's putting his autograph on someone else's headshot. Still, he tries to be gracious and humble with the fans. They've been there for him through his rise to fame. It's the least he can do.

By the time it's all over and he's on his way back to the hotel, Steve's feeling good about the event. So good, in fact, that he revives his Instagram account to see what fans have been posting. He smiles at the pictures they took with him earlier in the day. Many of the fans are dressed like his characters. Some of the props and signs they've brought are so creative, they bring a smile to his face. But soon he notices that not all the comments under the pictures are kind.

"Is it just me or is Steve rockin' the dad bod these days?" someone asks.

"Yeah. I hate to say it, but I was a bit disappointed that he didn't look as hot as he does in *Burning Brand II*," replies the account holder. "He's looking older too. I mean, don't get me wrong, he was nice and all, I just wish the picture was better."

"Just fix it so he looks hot," someone else suggests.

"Yeah, I probably will."

Steve doesn't even know what *Burning Brand II* is. Another of his films he hasn't seen—or acted in—he assumes.

He closes the app and wonders why he even bothers. If the fans don't care what's real and what isn't, why is he even doing this?

He goes for a run the next morning. It's been a while, but he soon finds his rhythm. It's early in the day and the streets are quiet. He likes this time of day. It's peaceful. Gives him a chance to clear his head.

When he stops for a rest, he notices a small theater. A sign over the door proclaims that the theater shows only movies made by and starring living human beings. The acronym 'AI' is painted in one of the windows with a red slash cut diagonally through it. But what really gets Steve's attention is the man changing the posters. He replaces one with another that features a pensive-looking Daphne Everheart. His former co-star, if you can call her that, looks younger in this poster. He's never seen her act before and he's curious. He decides to return later in the day when the theater opens.

The film's called *Grace*. In it, Daphne plays a young woman trying to convince her wealthy parents to take her seriously as an inventor. The story's moving, as Daphne's character struggles against societal expectations to achieve her dreams. Steve likes the score too, and decides he'll stay to read through the credits to see who composed it. He also enjoys the style the director has brought to the project. But what he likes most is Daphne's performance. She's good. It kills him to think that someone who was clearly a rising star, is now relegated to appearing only as a digital ghost of herself in half-baked movies that would've been an embarrassment at another time.

How many other talented actors have been forced out of the industry altogether? And what of everyone else whose jobs have been made irrelevant?

Steve feels the tears well up, in part because of the movie, but also because of his thoughts. He blinks them away and looks around to see if other people are equally moved. That's when he notices that nearly every seat in the theater has someone in it. He watches their expressions as they react to Daphne's performance. He sees the story affect them, and by the end he understands that there are still people for whom this art still has meaning.

After the movie lets out, he calls Ethel.

"I'm thinking of doing something a bit different," he tells her. "I want to start a production company. Make movies the old way. I have a whole list of people I can call who'd jump at the chance to collaborate on something real again."

"That sounds wonderful, sweet boy. It's nice to hear some excitement in your voice again."

"I was calling to ask you something," he tells her. "You wouldn't happen to know how to get in touch with Daphne Everheart, would you? I don't have a project yet, but I'd like to gauge her level of interest. I'm sure we'll find something for her. The world deserves to see how good she actually is at this.

P.A. Cornell is a Chilean-Canadian speculative fiction writer. A two-time finalist for the Nebula Award, her stories have been published in over seventy magazines and anthologies, including *Lightspeed*, *Apex*, and eight "Best of" anthologies. In addition to becoming the first Chilean Nebula finalist in 2024, Cornell has been a finalist for the Aurora and World Fantasy Awards, and in 2022 won Canada's Short Works Prize. When not writing, she can be found assembling intricate LEGO builds or drinking ridiculous quantities of tea. Sometimes both. For more on the author and her work, visit her website pacornell.com.

SIX PEOPLE TO REVISE YOU

J.R. Dawson

A parent or guardian
Someone who has known you since childhood
A mentor or teacher
An employer or coworker
A spouse, partner, or close intimate friend
Someone who does not consider themself a loved one

RED

The form is one page long. No back. Just a front. It should be longer. There are six copies of the form, all different colors. Like I'm working my way through the rainbow to the end where I'll finally find peace.

Red. A parent or guardian. I meet my mother for lunch at the little bistro down the street.

She's an anxious person, and it is hard for her to find her way in this part of the city. She wanted to meet at the McDonald's near her house. But I wanted to stay in my neighborhood, and this place has outdoor seating.

It's summer. It's nice. While the rest of the world burns, it seems like Minneapolis holds onto normal temperatures and we're still living up here in a bubble. Some flooding. The last two epidemics, yeah. But no fires, no heat days. Just a cool 85 degrees.

Mom sits down, her lips already pursed. She crosses her legs. She looks around at all the people, like they're going to laugh at her. She hates going outside. I need to make this count for her.

We order food quick. I make sure she knows I'm paying. She asks if it's okay if she gets a pop. I say yes. She asks why I'm wearing my mask around her. "Do you think I'm infected or something?"

"No," I say. "We're just being really careful."

Before she asks anything else, I take out the red form. One sheet. Five questions after the initial information fill-in-the-blank. Rachel Wendy Coleson. 59. F. Mother. Etc.

"So you're doing it," she says, eyeing the paper as I put the other colors away back into the folder with the logo of the hospital on the front. REVISION LABS, TWIN CITIES.

"I am," I say.

"Well, I think it's smart," she says. "Therapy hasn't been working, and how many years have you been doing that? This seems cheaper, even with your copay."

I swallow. "They want you to answer this form, and I brought a pen..."

"So," she says, taking the paper form over the wire metal table and giving me a wry smile. "I can just write, 'I want her to give me a million dollars' and that's okay?" She says it like a joke. But there's something behind her words that sticks out like needles hidden in carpet. I should have asked my father. I should have parents who don't smile like that.

But this isn't a revision for her. It's a revision for me.

"Sure," I offer a very uncomfortable laugh.

She takes out her reading glasses, puts them on her face, looks down her nose, and scans the form. "Well, this feels like a trap," she says. "You're not gonna like anything I put on here."

"Like what?" My mind is already whirring. There's never knowing the depths of how much Mom's truths are going to hurt.

"Like...can they...change anything?" she says.

I nod. Because I need to know the truth. "There's a place at the bottom, after you answer the questions about the current draft as they call it...what is now... who I am now...where you can write your top three, from most important to least important."

"Just things I would change about you?"

"Things that would make life easier for me," I say.

She taps the pen to her chin. And then writes, a little too fast, three things.

She passes it back. She sets back in her chair. Bracing for me to read it. I know every muscle in her face, every twitch in her body, I've been translating them like runes for survival since I was a child. I know she wrote something that will curdle my blood.

The doctor said it would be best if I don't read anyone's answers until the end.

My therapist said that it might shed some light if I do.

I had already agreed, within myself, that I would read them before the end, but not in front of the person.

And I would not tell Sadie about any of this until it was already finalized and I absolutely had to get her to write in her own answers on the blue-colored copy.

But the way my mom is looking at me.

I have to look.

1. *Liza's life would be much easier if she was happy with her given gender. That's my biggest wish.*
2. *Liza would be a wonderful mother, if she actually wanted to be.*
3. *We couldn't afford to fix her teeth.*

None of these come as a surprise. But the fact they're written on this sheet...I remind myself the doctor said if there was a real reason for concern, my therapist could sign off and get a request negated. I know my therapist will have my back on number one. But...

"You shouldn't be surprised," she says.

"I'm not," I say.

And that night, I will probably think of a thousand things to say beyond that. But right now, I'm just dead inside.

At least she wouldn't have me give up Sadie.

ORANGE

Ryan has known me since I was in the third grade. He has a shit memory and we haven't spoken for a few years. But we always seem to come back to each other whenever we have a moment and come up for air from our busy lives.

I've mailed him the orange sheet. He texts me to let me know it should be arriving today, back at my house, all stamped and sealed and ready.

Sadie won't see that Ryan has written me, because Sadie doesn't get the mail. I do. Sadie is at work on her computer inside the house when I check the box and there it is. In this day and age with postal workers being shady, I don't know why Revisions wants us to use the fucking snail mail but here we are. Just some junk and an overstuffed envelope.

I rip it open.

> *I just have one thing. Liza is super standoffish. If they could just trust people more, I think they'd be happier.*

And there's something that twists in my stomach.

A memory, of Ryan punching a wall and leaving homecoming. The two of us hanging out at the park dome, him saying my clothes were too baggy. The time he got drunk and called me, saying it was my fault I was alone because I never gave the good guys a chance.

I put the orange copy with the red copy.

YELLOW AND GREEN

I can hit two in one.

I work at the high school where I graduated.

After work, when the students have finally straggled out of the music room, I meet up with the band teacher next door (Mr. Carson, or Tony), and then Mrs. Rhodes joins us from the English department upstairs. Because Tony is band and I am choir/vocal, we have a connection that comes from being in the spring musical trenches together year after year. We don't go out for coffee. He doesn't know my real pronouns. He hasn't seen my house. But I know he's been cheating on his wife with the guidance counselor and loves watching the sun come up over the parking lot at 6 a.m. In the same vein, he knows that when the kids are gone and I think no one is listening, I'll improv on the piano to get my feelings out. He knows that I miss my grandma every day. He knows that sometimes when the kids cuss me out, I go into our shared office and cry. It's an intimacy between teachers on the front lines.

Mrs. Rhodes told me to call her Rhonda years ago, when I started working here. But Rhonda Rhodes will never be a peer for me; she'll only be my senior English teacher with the horn-rimmed glasses of undiscernible age. Like a mythical demigod that Odysseus comes across on his travails. Above humanity, beyond comprehension. As an adult, I was horrified when I was sitting in the faculty lounge one day and she came in holding her pantyhose in one hand and her shoes in another (Don't ask, she'd shot off, before dodging into the bathroom). Other than that one incident, I was still Liza to her. She was still Mrs. Rhodes.

This is all to say, if there are coworkers and teachers I trust with knowing I'm going to Revisions, these are the two I can trust not only to not judge or ask prying questions, but answer truthfully. They know me, sides of me no one else did. I admire them. They know what it means to be a teacher.

So we sit down in the practice room behind Tony's and my classrooms, make the keyboard a makeshift table, and each take a bench or a small stool to circle up and fill out the worksheets.

"Seventy-two?" Tony snorts as he peers over at Mrs. Rhodes's yellow copy. "You're not seventy-two."

"I am," she said stiffly, the same horn-rimmed glasses bobbing on the edge of her wide nose. Tony shakes his head.

"I'll be long retired by the time I'm seventy-two," he says, going back to his green sheet.

"Now, Miss Coleson," Mrs. Rhodes says. We still haven't decided on what to call me. She used to call me Liza. Just Liza. But now my role here at school is Miss Coleson. Or Miss C. Maybe she calls me this out of respect, like she knows I don't see myself as an equal. Welcome to Mt. Olympus, Miss Coleson. Miss. Coleson. Miss. "I'm sorry I don't understand this, what is this?"

"You can't tell me you haven't seen Revisions ads everywhere," Tony says, scribbling while he talks.

"I just don't understand why they need to know what we think," Mrs. Rhodes said.

"Capitalism, probably," Tony says. Still scribbling.

"Well, I chose you because you know me," I say, honestly. "You had me as a student, so...just maybe write down the things that you think would help me focus?"

"You were an exceptional student," she says.

Tony scribbles. A part of me wants him to say I'm an exceptional teacher, too. But he doesn't. There is a worm inside me that eats away at a hole, making it bigger and bigger.

"Okay, well, was I a happy kid?" I say.

"As happy as any teenager is," she says. "You're such a pretty girl, I don't understand why you're going through this."

"It's not plastic surgery," Tony sniffs.

"So I don't write down anything physical?" she says.

"You can if you want," I say.

"Oh really?" Tony laughs. A joke. It's a joke. I force a laugh, too.

"Well, I suppose it would make your life easier if your hair wasn't so curly," she says. She pats her own curly hair, short and tight to her head. "I know it can be a bear in the morning, and sometimes...well, to be honest, you look tired sometimes. That could make things easier?"

"I guess," I say. "It's up to you."

"So what do I write?" she asks.

"Uhm...I can't really tell you?"

"Just something such as...straight hair?"

"Sure," I shrug.

"I feel like a fairy godmother!" Mrs. Rhodes giggles, writing down in cursive, *straight hair*. "Giving you a gift!"

Tony slams his pencil down and flips his green sheet around, in the same manner as a fourth grader who just wrote "farts" a lot. But after they both leave, their totes over their shoulders and them both fishing for car keys while the practice room door shuts behind them...I look to see what he wrote.

1. *Liza could do with a little more confidence.*
2. *Liza should play the piano more often.*
3. *Better posture will help with singing and confidence.*

Could be worse. But something about it still churned inside me. Oh really, Tony had laughed. Better posture will help with singing and confidence. Oh really. Oh really.

I was being sensitive. Literally nothing written was bad.

I put the yellow and green sheets back in the folder.

BLUE

I'm not ready to tell Sadie.

I was going to tell her when she came down for breakfast, but now that she's two feet away from me, pouring cereal from the bag to the bowl, I can't say anything. The sheet is in my hand. I could slip it across the table when she sits down.

She sits down.

I fold the paper up and put it in my pocket.

"What do you have going on today?" she asks me, digging into her Cheerio knockoffs.

I shrug. "Typical Saturday."

We go our separate ways, Sadie weeding the garden and me locking myself up in my home office. I click into the video chat room, to see that my therapist's other client is already there. We don't know each other, but I know his name is Noah and he's gone through the revision.

I click on my video, and he does, too. We reveal ourselves to one another. Me, a mess in my messy office. Him, his hair perfectly parted and his Saturday lounge clothes nicer than what I usually wear to a funeral. His eyes are bright. His skin is clear. He's had eight to ten hours of sleep. Somehow, even with the world on fire outside our windows, he is internally a tranquil pond full of dancing swans. Our therapist thought we'd get along because we're both originally from St. Paul and we play piano. Two things that can bring any strangers together.

He smiles. "Hey, there, Liza." He says it like we've been good friends since college.

I offer a smile. "Hey, uh...Noah."

He tells me about the procedure, how they knock you out, you wake up, a couple of days to "come back online" he jokes, and then you're home. "It does take about forty-eight hours for the brain fog to lift," he explains. "It doesn't hurt. It's barely disorienting. It's like when you wake up in the morning and have to remind yourself where you are."

Or who you are.

"Do you miss anything about before the revision?" I say.

He thinks about it for a second, honestly, and then with a small crack in his smile he says, "I don't listen to as much music as I did, I suppose. I used to bang on everything, shove it through my car speakers, tinker around on my keyboard... it was very annoying and overstimulating for those around me. So it isn't so much that I miss it, it's that it's something I remember enjoying and now I don't enjoy it. That doesn't make much sense. I guess I *would* say I miss my snaggle tooth. It was just something very ugly but also you know, it was me. But I suppose this is also me. Everyone changes through life, even if they don't have a revision."

PURPLE

The last time I saw Caroline, we were twenty-three and I was moving out.

There's something poisonous about knowing someone so well, having your heart the closest to theirs, so close you could touch souls...and then they are strangers. The tone they always took with the cashier at your favorite restaurant is now softer and kinder than the one they reserve for you.

Once, Caroline and I stayed up late in our dorm room sophomore year, throwing popcorn and drinking Baileys, watching old Kevin Smith movies.

Now, Caroline sits with a straight back at the bistro where I met my mother. She would like this place. Maybe that's why I picked it a few days before, because I was picking it for her. Because maybe, I could show I'd changed enough to be worthy of her voice.

It had taken some messaging to get her to meet me.

I knew she was in the Twin Cities area. We both had gone to college here. We both had never moved. And yet, I hadn't seen her in fifteen years.

When I'd moved out of our senior apartment, she just gave a wave and a goodbye and that was that. I don't even remember the last glimpse I got of her. We were supposed to go on a road trip later that summer. We didn't.

It wasn't supposed to be goodbye.

Sadie wouldn't care I was here. Caroline had never been with me. We had been sisters. And yet, I hadn't told Sadie where I was going.

Because there was no reason to see Caroline. Unless I wanted to unearth fifteen years of pain.

"Hey," I offer. My voice is too loud.

Caroline, slim and sleek and wearing just the right clothes...a cooler version of who I wished I was...she just looked over her phone to me and forced herself a pithy, "Hello." Her eyebrow raised and her eyes lowered back to the phone as she said it. Like it took everything in her to shove the word out.

Sometimes, there aren't big blowouts between people. Sometimes, people just grow in two different directions until there's nothing left to see of the other.

"Thank you for meeting me," I say. I take a seat. Scoot it in too loud. Put the folder and my purse on the table. Maybe in another life, in another dimension, we meet here every week and I could ask to see pictures of her kids...or I could at least know if she had kids...that used to be our trajectory. And maybe we would be talking about the weather or the next soccer game or something other than...this.

"So Revisions, you said?" she offers.

A part of me is glad she didn't sink her teeth into a bitter, "it's been a long time." We know it has been a long time.

"Yeah," I say. "I uh...the last page, it's..." She sighs, puts her phone down on the wire table, and leans back with her arms and legs both crossed. I lose my train of thought. She does not want to be here.

I do.

I want to see her. To know her. I wish I had been a worthy human to have her friendship forever.

That's why Purple had to be her.

She can tell me how to be fixed.

"So the last witness I need," I say, "is someone who doesn't consider themself a friend. Someone who...well...is the opposite of a friend, no offense, I don't mean to—"

"No, no you're right," she says.

The way people move when they say heartless things. She looks down her nose as the table, like she is speaking to me but I have hair made of snakes.

I'm right.

Fifteen years ago, this person stopped taking my calls. Fifteen years ago, I started wondering why. My stomach sinks.

"Well, I guess then you're the perfect one to do this," I say. I pull out the purple sheet from the folder and pass it to her across the wire table, although it feels like I'm crossing a boundary by putting any limb closer to her radius. Who am I to hand her something? Maybe she won't take it.

She takes it.

What did I do, Caroline? I want to ask. Why do you hate me?

She takes out a pen that she has in her purse. She scribbles out the information. She starts it too fast, and then ends it too slowly. A waitress comes in halfway through her writing and interrupts. She just looks up at the waitress with that smile she reserves for people she wants to like but doesn't know.

"Oh, I'll take a jasmine tea to go, please," she says. "Thank you so much."

To go.

"I uh..." stumbling, I say, "Same."

She flicks her eyes at me, and then scribbles something else.

Finally, she sets it down on the table a little too hard. She puts a saltshaker on top so it won't fly away. She says, "Well. Good seeing you and good luck."

She stands.

"Wait, that's it?" I hear myself say.

She stops, like I have gone off script. "Yes." I have never heard an "s" sound so sharp.

"Okay," I say. "Can you...it's...been fifteen years."

She rolls her eyes. "I knew this was gonna be a whole thing. Lizzie, there are people dying in the streets. The world is on fire. No one has time for your...all this." She waves her hand.

Lizzie. No one has called me that since college, and it burns in my stomach like a warm fire. Back when I believed I could be someone beautiful.

"Goodbye, Lizzie," she says. "Good luck on your procedure, and may you heal fast."

She's gone.

The purple sheet is still there.

I look to it.

> *L is self-centered.*
>
> *L is too sensitive.*
>
> *L is a hypocrite.*
>
> *But again, I haven't known L for years. The fact she's getting this done at all makes me believe she is still warring with herself. She needs to buck up and stop leaning on others. She needs to let things go. She needs to understand the rest of us don't think about her.*

BLUE

It has been a month.

The folder sits on my side of the closet, between some old U-Haul boxes that smell like even older laundry.

Sadie hasn't found it. Maybe a part of me wanted her to.

I can't lock in my surgery day until I have all the paperwork filled out.

I finally hit her up as we're sitting in the attic's library, and she's reading and I'm fucking around on the computer. It's built in me like a festering electric storm. I've waited too long to say it, and with every time I've put it off, the harder it's gotten to open my mouth.

Finally, I say, "So you've heard of Revisions?"

"The thing all the billionaires are pushing in ad space? Yeah," she says. She doesn't put her book down.

"They say they can make you happy."

"A lot of people say that," she says. "If it was that easy, they wouldn't need to flood my feed with it."

"But what if it can?" I say. "Deirdre had it done, at the beginning of last summer. She looks great. She says she feels great."

"Deirdre?" Sadie says.

"She teaches English at the school."

"Oh," Sadie says. "Okay. Huh. Well, good for her."

I pause. "Sadie," I say, "Deirdre doesn't go to therapy anymore. She's gotten Teacher of the Year. She gave me the name of her doctor...she says our insurance covers it and I checked and...I would really love to give it a chance."

Sadie puts her book down. She looks to me. Not in surprise. But with those big eyes like she wishes she could pick me up and hold me. "I know you do," she says. "They've been sitting in the closet for a month."

"So you did see them."

"I didn't go poking through them, no," Sadie says. "The logo is on the outside of the folder."

"Well if you'd read them, you'd see how much work needs to be done."

Sadie nods. "I looked up who needs to fill out what in order to give the doctors pinpoints to change. I'm guessing you asked your mom. Caroline. Probably Ryan. And you're about to ask me."

"Yes," I say. Just yes, to it all.

Sadie nods. She quietly stands up from her overstuffed chair, forgetting her book. In her soft way, she crosses the carpeted floor to her desk. She opens a drawer and takes out a manila envelope.

She hands it to me, her socks tip-toeing across the room like a ballerina. "Here," she says. "I'll fill out your blue sheet. But only if you read these."

"What is this?" I say. "I told you I checked our insurance—"

"They're from our friends," she says. "A couple of your students. Your brother and your uncle and your aunt. My mom and dad. Charles next door and your graduate student cohort. People who know you, and love you." She holds out her hand. "Where's the sheet?"

"You're...not gonna stop me?"

"It's your choice," she says. "No one else's. It's what *you* want changed. Not Caroline. Not your mom. Not even me."

We trade paperwork.

I open up the envelope, undoing the little string on top. Winding it off the pin.

It is a thick stack of all different colors of paper. Mauve and pink and aqua and deep purple and even some blank white computer paper.

Liz is a really wonderful singer.

They have been a wonderful auncle to our children. They always know how to turn anything into a game. One time they turned our table into a time machine after dinner. The kids still play the time machine table game, even after all these years.

They are exceptionally good at remembering birthdays, even without Facebook notifications.

They are always one to cry with a friend, no matter how late it is.

Video games make them smile. And their smile is contagious.

I remember when they were little and I took them to the zoo and they memorized all of the names of the animals in one afternoon.

They are brave and courageous to be themself. My daughter is worried about being gay, and seeing Liz and Sadie together has really been a life-saver.

They care about their community.

They are honest.

They don't kill spiders.

They play really beautiful music.

They always know how to find the best parking spot.

They mask, even when no one else does. I'm immunocompromised, so I notice.

They still love stuffed animals.

They bought us baby formula when we couldn't afford it. And when the third lockdown happened, they bought us a little inflatable playground for the backyard.

They drove me to get flowers for my grandma's funeral when my car broke down.

They made sure I got to work.

Liz laughs.

Liz knows what it means to be themself.

Liz is kind.

Liz is kind.

They are kind.

Liz is kind.

Then Sadie's handwriting on the last paper. A bright robin's egg blue.

Liz, you are the sun. Please don't try to tame that wild light. Let it glow. See who follows it to their shores.

MANILA

I was going to turn in the papers today.

Instead, I drive north. I pack my mask, my hand sani, all the things we need now to go through the world, and I cut through the chaos to find a small untouched piece of shore near the river.

I sit there, with this folder full to the brim, sitting on my lap.

There was supposed to be peace. But it isn't here, and the thought of having straight hair or happiness in another pronoun that isn't mine...even if I make the whole world happy, the world will still be on fire.

I pull out the manila envelope. I fish a pen out of my purse. I write my own list on the back.

A person who genuinely cares.
Someone who loves theme parks and musicals.
A queer, complicated mess who is still alive.
A wife, a teacher, an auncle.
Someone who considers themself worthy.
A human who wants to love themself.

It's six lines long. It is the only thing in this entire Revisions folder that is written in my handwriting. So it is the only thing I take with me when I stand up, walk past the trash can, clean up after myself, and find my car again.

I follow the setting sun back home.

J.R. Dawson (she/they) is the Golden Crown award-winning author of The First Bright Thing. They have had shorter works in places such as *F&SF*, *Lightspeed*, *Reactor*, and *Uncanny*. Dawson currently lives on Dakota land in Minnesota with her loving wife. She teaches at Drexel University's MFA program for creative writing and fills her free time with keeping her three chaotic dogs out of trouble. Her latest book, *The Lighthouse at the Edge of the World*, is a sapphic Orpheus retelling.

IN MY COUNTRY

Thomas Ha

My country may seem strange to you.

There are times when it seems strange to me. I wake and work. I work then rest. And in between I say things, and I don't say things. Because, as you'll learn, in my country, what you say is important. But what you don't say is perhaps just as, if not more, important.

Like all neighborhoods, mine has a blue house.

If you live here, yours too will have a house nearby that is blue. A man sits in the blue house, and he listens to the wind. And when he smiles at you, you smile at him. When he greets you, you, of course, will always greet him. When you come home and find him in your living room, you offer him tea. When you find him sitting in your bedroom, in the dark, you close your eyes and go to sleep, until he decides to leave. You listen, you wait, until he eventually leaves.

I once had a son and a daughter who asked about these things.

Like all neighborhoods with a blue house, there is, of course, a school. My son and daughter went to the school, before things quieted down. The schools are still around, but they are all much quieter now. Before the curricula were liberated, my son and daughter would ask me about the school. Where are the other children who were there before? Why are the teachers going to the far fields? Are we going to the far fields too?

I would point to the blue house, raise a finger to my lips, and smile.

One day, over dinner, my son asked: Who is the king?

What?

I did not mishear. My son asked, again, the same question. Who is the king? We read a story about a man who ruled another world, and it called him a king.

We're a very special place, we have no king, I explained.

The man in the blue house, and the other men in the blue houses, they seem like kings.

I don't think that's true, I said. Why do they seem like kings?

Because a king is someone who does what they wish. And the men in blue houses do what they do, no matter what. We greet them and let them into our homes, no matter what.

Oh. Well, the men in blue houses only do what they do because of the local officials. And (anticipating his next question, I said) they only do what they do because of the district officials, provincial officials, and national officials. No single one of them has sole authority. Not any one person can do what they want to do. And so, you see, not one is a king.

What about the First Citizen?

Yes. I hesitated. In a way, the First Citizen might seem like a king. Here I waited again, looked at my son and daughter and listened to the wind. Behind the picture frames, and down the long hall in the full-body mirror, I detected the slight film of a static charge. I could see the eyes and the ears of men in blue houses within our walls. The First Citizen is something, I said, but he is no king.

There is no king.

Listen to what I say. Listen to what I *don't* say.

My children nodded, and we did not speak about it for a time.

In your country, you might be afraid to talk about your king. In our country, we don't have to be afraid because there is no king. In fact, people are welcome to criticize the First Citizen, who some mistake for a king. Many people take part in criticizing the First Citizen. They say he is ugly and stinks of shit. They say he cannot speak or understand or direct matters of importance.

Between the day-work ending bell and the night-work starting bell, we watch many men and women discuss the country and its officials on our televisions. They are free to say good things and bad things. So long as they pick one or the other. The important thing is to be sure to pick one or the other and talk to fill the time. When you fill the time with talk, there is little time for unproductive contemplation and other small ruins.

After a while, and lots of talk, my children grew.

My son became a writer at our university. There are many fine things about becoming a writer at a university like ours. My daughter was still in the neighborhood school, but she thought she might be a scientist or a teacher, she would have to see.

One day, over Sunday supper, my children said the usual prayers for their mother (who was no longer with us, like many mothers who were no longer with us after the closure of the state hospitals). But the children were unusually quiet, even for Sunday supper quiet. So I asked why both of them seemed so quiet.

Someone, a boy they knew from the neighborhood, a childhood friend, went to the far fields after a conversation with a man in the blue house.

Oh. Well, that is not the worst outcome, to go to the far fields after a conversation. People are sent there for a time to work in place of incarceration and other antiquated barbarities. But my son and daughter seemed not to agree. It was like they had seen and discussed things I had not seen or discussed with them. This was the first time I suspected they knew things I did not know.

It's always the other thing, they said to me in reply.

What?

It's always the other thing, when they say it's the fields. Fields aren't fields. Not when they say it that way.

What are they then?

My children listened to the wind, looked at the pictures, the mirror, and did not answer me. Their fingers flitted one way and the other with hand signals, back and forth to each other, something secret and silent communicated. I waited patiently and ate. I offered something of comfort:

At least the boy didn't die, I said reassuringly. It's incredibly rare, but sometimes these conversations take a turn, especially for those with certain sensitivities. I remember it happened to someone once, when I was young, someone with certain sensitivities died.

Death isn't death, either. Not when they say it like that. This time, my son and daughter laughed, almost ruefully. When the men in the blue houses say someone has died, especially when they insist upon it, it means something else entirely, my children said.

My daughter used hand signals again. She pantomimed a small man, using her forefinger and middle finger as two legs. She showed him running off, running away, escaping. Then she held up her hands and stretched out her fingers, like claws.

You mean they got away and joined—

My son coughed.

Listen to what we say, he intoned. Listen to what we *don't* say.

The children looked on, smugly, smiling, and I felt they were teasing me. They were, just a little. And that was fine by me. I had a laugh too. We finished the meal and retired to our rooms.

My son wrote.

He wrote and wrote and wrote. He wrote stories about many things, and I liked his stories. Many people liked his stories. They were strange and outlandish stories about strange and outlandish things. Other planets and other places. I think many of us liked reading about other planets and other places.

Then one day, he wrote a story that did not feel so outlandish. It was about a sickness. It was about a sickness that made chickens turn black and limp in their cages. It turned their feathers into flecks of dried skin and their eyes into weeping sores. When people ate the chickens, they would feel unwell, shut themselves in their homes, and never emerge.

Someone who worked with the chickens on the farm tried to warn his village, and other villages, against eating them. But someone with a long rope, someone called the Rope Man, paid the worker a visit before he could get very far or tell any of the others about the chickens. The story did not end. The story did not end, but it stopped abruptly, when the Rope Man paid the worker a visit.

It occurred to me that my son's friend—the one who had been sent to the far fields—had worked in health inspection, but I did not say anything at the time.

The story would be trouble, I already understood, even then.

We have all kinds of art in this country. Triumphant art. Depressing art. Silly art. Pornographic art (subject to procreative code). You can do anything and everything, and some will support it or rail against it and talk about it in turn. There is only one kind of art you cannot make here. There is only one rule about what you cannot make here.

There can be no ambiguity to the art. It must be clear.

Everyone from the First Citizen down to each person in each neighborhood knew that stories had to be clear. Anything said had to be one thing or the other thing. Pick one thing or the other thing. So long as it was not an in-between thing. The in-between things were where problems lay.

My son knew, too, that he had flouted the law of clarity.

His stories grew increasingly odd.

One was about a machine operator. The operator worked a machine that directed bridges to raise and lower. But the machine stopped working properly. Something about the machine was beginning to break down, but the operator pretended it was not breaking down. Sometimes the bridge did not raise when it should, and boats crashed below. Sometimes the bridge went up when it shouldn't have, and cars crashed above. Many times, no one was around or saw the machine fail, and nothing happened at all.

The machine operator did not tell anyone else in the city about the error. Everyone assumed it was caused by something other than the machines. Boat captains were blamed. Drivers were blamed. The operator assumed he would, too, be blamed and lose his job, or worse. Instead, the Rope Man appeared at his door and delivered a letter promoting him. The operator became the boss of all of the machine operators, each one with their own machines. And he soon learned, all of the other machines were equally flawed and never operated with any consistency either.

I don't know if I like that story, I told my son.

That's okay, he said. Liking or disliking it is not important. So that's okay.

Can you write nicer stories? Nicer worlds?

I write things I can imagine, he said. I can't create things I could never possibly imagine.

Months later, my son wrote another piece, a similar sort of piece, about a banker who lived a life of indescribable luck. Every day the banker received adoration, gifts, and support. But about forty miles away from the banker, people would die. An invisible circle with a radius about forty miles, no more than forty miles, no less than forty miles, from the banker, was where many people would die. It was a force of nature, this invisible circle around the banker, where people died. The banker never knew he was the cause of their deaths. He thought the people he met simply disappeared from his life, and he never gave it much thought.

He continued comfortably, until his children grew up and left home. But the moment they left his sight and crossed that invisible circle, they died like all the others. He assumed his children just wanted nothing to do with him, when they disappeared and never came back. And he simply went on, never knowing why his children, and many others, never came back. There was no Rope Man in this story. But I read it again and again, looking for some sign that the Rope Man was around.

Do you know what the story is about? I asked my daughter.

I don't think they're supposed to be about things, she said. The stories are the stories. What did it make you feel?

I am not sure what it made me feel.

Maybe think about that then, she said.

And I did. Whether I wanted to or not, that is what I did. The story made me feel unfocused and unsettled. I felt a connection to the lucky banker, though I couldn't say why. I started thinking of my wife, and her death in the state hospitals after the birth of my daughter, though I couldn't say why.

There was no reason for the association. The story said nothing of state hospitals or births. But I thought of her again. I thought of how she disappeared from my sight. I thought of how many people disappeared from my sight, and I had no way of knowing if they were coming back either.

I started seeing longer shadows. People talking. I worried that they were talking about my son, or about us.

A man with a crooked nose walked through our neighborhood. The crooked nose was bent at the bridge, indicating it had been broken several ways, long ago. His eyes were unreadable and unmoving, like he only had interest in capturing the images in front of him but not studying them in depth. And I recognized him, from idle neighborhood talk, as our man in the blue house. It was a rare thing, to see the man in a blue house outside on the street rather than inside a house. Why was the man in the blue house outside rather than inside the blue house? And why was he looking my way? Why was he looking at me?

He nodded.

I nodded back.

He smiled.

I smiled back.

It was not long after I saw the man in the blue house and smiled, that my son finally wrote the story about the deviant.

The deviant story was particularly popular at the time of publication.

The deviant was a character who became excited whenever people told him he did something incorrectly. There was nothing more he enjoyed than doing things incorrectly, so that people would tell him he had done things incorrectly. His greatest fear, more than death, was fading away from existence. His thoughts were so twisted, that he believed his degradation was a strange form of immortality, because it made him so prominent in people's minds and memories.

The deviant employed several men to effectuate his perversions. They sounded similar to the Rope Man from the other stories, these men. And they would gather people up for the deviant, like fodder, to tell the deviant he had done things incorrectly and satisfy his needs. The story ended with the deviant reaching orgasm in front of a giant crowd of hateful people, brought just to scream at him. Or perhaps he wasn't orgasming, perhaps he was ascending to another level of existence, like his mind was no longer limited to his physical form, because he had achieved such an extreme level of incorrect bliss, of immortality, like he had always dreamed. The text made it very difficult to tell what happened, to be frank.

This one made me the most uncomfortable. It made me uncomfortable because of what was said, but also because of what was not said. The deviant bore a striking resemblance to the First Citizen. Little things about the character, mannerisms, the color of his hair, the way he spoke, reminded me of the First Citizen.

Is this a satire? Of the First Citizen?

My son would not answer the question.

Satire was, of course, permissible, encouraged. But my son would not say whether or not the work was satire. I found it frustrating and concerning. And I grew more concerned when the stories became more widely read.

I worked at the train station near our country's border, much as I do now. Greeting foreigners and visitors, like you, I would direct them to the information booth or the local processing hall, much as I do now. And I would see commuters, travelers, exchanging newspapers and tracts. I could see the magazines that carried my son's stories, more and more of them, floating around.

A co-worker told me he'd read my son's stories and found them intriguing.

Why? I asked. Why do you find his stories intriguing?

I don't know, my co-worker admitted. I'm afraid I just do.

You're afraid you just do, I repeated.

Yes, he said, and that was all. I'm afraid I just do.

After the usual prayers for their mother and before our Sunday supper, I told my son, I'd like to know the point. Of these stories. I'd like to know the point. He and my daughter looked at one another and did not speak for a time.

There is no point, he answered. Not in the way you mean, at least.

But in some way. You may not think I understand much, and I may not understand much. But I see that it's there. I am worried about how people will think and how they will interpret these things because of what's there.

Well, my son replied, I cannot control how people will think or interpret these things. My job is to be attuned to the way we are living. And, if you are attuned, sometimes what you create seems a certain way to others. I cannot control how it is interpreted or how it seems to others.

You could write it differently. You could write it more clearly.

If it's not clear, maybe the way we are living is not clear.

What does that mean?

You know what that means.

My son and daughter silently flitted their hands in signals to one another. Rapidly, they went back and forth while I ate, annoyed. The wind was quiet, and no one was listening. But I was still annoyed. My son knew he was going a way that would make people unhappy, make me unhappy, but he was still going.

Is this really what a writer is? I asked.

I don't know about other writers. I only know about me, he said. And even then, I am not sure I always know about that.

My son's work continued, and as it continued, it attracted the attention of certain elements. You can probably guess which elements those were. In our country, they refer to themselves as the Fallow. In your country, they may go by another name. The Fallow is a reference to a famous revolutionary poem about drained farmlands. A reference to soil, rocks, bugs, dreaming wearily of recovery, in this revolutionary poem. The goals of the Fallow, as I understood them, were to overthrow the First Citizen and his men, and replace them with some other kind of governance.

I did not see the Fallow come to our home (they never appear to people like me), but my son said he saw them, that they came specifically for him. They overrode signals in the mirrors and glass one night. He said he was in his bedroom, and one of the Fallow appeared within the glass, a strange face, blurred behind my son's reflection within that glass.

We read your story about the deviant, they apparently told him. My son said the voice sounded empty, synthetic. The face was partially flesh and partially something embedded in that flesh. The hands of the speaker were stiff and metallic, replaced with augmented prostheses. Claw-like, the telltale sign of the Fallow. They divested themselves of certain parts to gain others, or so the rumors said.

The ending of the deviant story. Did the deviant die? Some among us believe the ending implies that the deviant may have orgasmed and then died.

My son, both frightened and perhaps set in his ways of writing, did not answer.

This story, your story, has been flagged by several Bureaus. As we speak, memos are being written to analyze associated risks. Many analysts are interpreting this as veiled political criticism. But its ambiguity makes it more dangerous than typical criticism.

I cannot control if others believe it is dangerous, my son replied.

The problem with ambiguity is that it demands interpretation. The demand for interpretation welcomes a different magnitude of contemplation and unanticipated dispute. Already, the Bureaus are seeing influence in other writings. And reductions in worker productivity in regions exposed to these writings, more so than happens with permissible criticism. They will inevitably determine that these stories go beyond permissible criticism.

If that is what they decide, that is what they decide, my son said.

Do you hate the First Citizen? Do you wish for his death? Is this story about how you wish for his death?

My son did not answer.

If you tell us, we can help you. We can help you, if you tell us. There are dedicated functions, established places, for alternative views and dissidence. But before we can help, we must be sure of the precise intent. We may require a demonstration of that intent.

My son continued to give no answer.

Words matter. Do you not agree?

Words matter, my son repeated. It was a phrase often uttered by the Fallow and their sympathizers. It was meant to distinguish their cause from the obtuse First Citizen, his officials, and their enforcers in the Bureaus, for whom words carried little weight. I want to agree, my son answered. But I'm not sure I would always agree. Experiences matter. Actions matter. But words are only signifiers, means, for both. They are not an end in themselves. I don't write words because of the words.

Why then?

Again, my son did not provide them with an answer. After several more questions with unproductive results, the Fallow faded away from behind the glass, and my son found himself alone in his bedroom, again.

I asked him, later, if he did not answer those questions because he was afraid it was some kind of ruse. Or perhaps because he did not hate the First Citizen. Or perhaps because the men in blue houses were somehow listening in to the signal.

No, my son replied. Those were not my reasons. Declarations to the Fallow, affirmative or negative, would be contrary to the stories. I am happy to make declarations elsewhere, to state my views, to pick one thing or the other thing, in other ways, separate and apart from the stories. But admitting one meaning, one purpose, within those stories, precludes other possibilities within those stories.

And that was precisely the trouble within those stories, I realized.

The possibilities.

It was because of the possibilities that the ideas stuck like tiny fishbones in the throat, not easily eaten and forgotten.

I would hand out pamphlets to visitors at the train station who were thinking of immigrating. I would point to posters of the First Citizen as I explained our naturalization policies, and in the back of my mind, I would still be thinking about that deviant. Against my will, a link had been made somewhere in my brain that I could not unlink. I kept thinking about the First Citizen, surrounded by men and women yelling at him, and his orgasming, or ascension, or death. And the powerful, stern, paternal image of the First Citizen was replaced by a perverted shadow.

Each time I halted my car at a bridge crossing, or drove by a bank, or ate chicken, I would think about the stories. There was an unexpressed dread, a potential energy that was more ominous because it refused the catharsis of full articulation.

One night, I woke to low voices in the house.

I crept to the door and peered, unsure if I had even fully woken, out at two shapes sitting in chairs in the living room. I could not see clearly, but I knew one shape to be my son. I would know that shape, even if I could not perceive any other detail, to be my son.

The other shape, however, was not my daughter. It was a strange man. In the puzzlework of light and darkness in the room, I could make out the angles of a crooked nose broken in several places. It was the man in the blue house, inside of our house, I realized.

And the man in the blue house, now inside of our house—he held something. It looked long, and it dangled there, like a cord. I recognized it as a Bureau restraint, though I'd never seen one this close. A hempen material designed to be worn like a noose around the neck, as well as the wrists and ankles from several shorter branching cords. Something about the patented hempen material was painful and prevented a captor from straining. They also could generate a small shock to the nervous system if necessary. From behind the door, where I stood, it looked much like rope to me.

My son said something, like he was answering a question.

I have my theories, he said.

What are your theories? The man in the blue house in our house asked.

I suspect clarity is a comfort to you. It's finite and enclosed. You can argue with it, disavow it, disprove it, undermine it. It is also short-lived. An opinion, once stated, is accepted or rejected and disappears into the void. Do you agree?

I do agree.

There is also inherent power in asymmetric ambiguity. You are allowed to have multiple meanings, to keep things veiled. Citizens do not have that right. Their minds have to be open to inspection. And you have learned that most people are actually quite eager for inspection when they think of it as presentation. Do you agree with that as well?

I do agree.

Something you fear, then, is the art which obscures, for two reasons. The first is because of you. You cannot see how it moves, who it moves through, why, and how deeply. The second is because of us. Because when we do not understand something, we question, we grasp, and we connect. Even if the connection makes no technical sense, we create the connections. With each other, with ideas, with something else. We empathize. We engage. We become unpredictable and unknowable. That is mystery, faith, compassion, whatever number of words you want to give to the compulsion you cannot circumscribe. Things you'd prefer we forget.

The man in the blue house in our house sat perfectly still.

And it felt as though I were not watching my son and a stranger, but representatives of something else, as though they were speaking for others I could not see. Something old before our time, or so advanced that I would not live to comprehend it. They were themselves, but they were something else. I said I knew the shape of my son, but that was incorrect. I knew the shape of the boy I had given life and raised and talked to at the dinner table, but not the whole of him. I felt as though I were the child, not the parent, back there, eavesdropping on matters beyond my simplified world.

My son looked in my direction, and I pulled back from the doorway.

We should continue this conversation elsewhere, I heard my son say. I will go with you. Let's leave this house be and take the conversation elsewhere.

I listened, waited, for the two men to leave, and I did not sleep for the rest of the night.

The next day, I received a letter of congratulations.

My son was being honored for his writing and taken to further his education in the far fields. There, he would be given an opportunity to write other stories, wonderful stories, that would no doubt be improved by his time in the far fields. He was promised to return from the far fields upon his request, but no one ever requested a return from the far fields as far as we knew.

My daughter read the letter and screamed. She slapped me across the face twice. She went to her room and did not come out to see me. She was unspeakably angry and blamed me for something. I did not understand, and I also understood perfectly.

I sat quietly with the letter. I felt tears I didn't know I was still capable of crying. I went to my son's room and sat on his bed. I sat with the letter, I thought of my son, and I sat in his room and on that bed.

I tried to imagine him working in the far fields, the way we had been told. I tried to dream of it, too, when exhaustion inevitably came to take me away from my repetitive thoughts. But I couldn't see it, or him, in the far fields, not even inside my head, where I wanted to see him most.

In the weeks after, I read and reread his stories. I was not so much looking for things in the stories. I just wanted to hear his voice. And something about the detached way I read the stories this time made me appreciate them more. There was a wryness I did not pick up the first time when I was trying to place the words within my rigid understanding. A certain sense that this was a game, a game that did not suit a rigid understanding.

One evening, I found the dusty pages of an unfinished piece in my son's desk. It was called, "In My Country." It seemed like it was written when he was very young. I suspect he did not finish it, because he felt it was immature and too direct for his liking. It was not as layered or careful as the stories he wrote later. It was about a little family in a little house in a little neighborhood. A father told his children, very confidently, that they could be at ease, because even though kings were something to be feared, there was no king in their country. One of his children questioned that belief. I had difficulty reading the story, and I was grateful when it stopped. Then I reread the story and found myself wishing that it had not stopped.

Stories were released by the Bureaus in the next few months, released under my son's name in state-edited magazines. Supposedly written from the far fields, these were stories of perfect clarity, fables, digestible moral quandaries, easily untangled. Stories that were not in my son's voice but were in my son's name in these magazines.

These stories were not as popular, and I understood, now, why that would be.

Not long after was when my daughter said she was leaving the house.

She left, but before she left, she told me she forgave me.

I said I did not do anything that needed forgiveness.

There was something wrong with her hands, when she told me she was leaving and that she forgave me. She was hiding them in her coat pockets. And her voice was different too. There was a certainty to her posture and tenor that made her almost unrecognizable.

No. I forgive you for everything you did not do, she said. We all do different things, but we all do something. The one thing we cannot afford to do is nothing.

Oh, was all I could bring myself to reply.

Days later, I was woken by a strange tide of lights and sirens, in a time long after the night-work starting bell had last rung, when there should have been little light or sound. I emerged from my son's room, out into the street, where others in the neighborhood had gathered in the darkness, in their bathrobes. Emergency vehicles were caravaned around the blue house.

They tried to hide the grotesquery behind plastic sheets, but we could see from the curbside, a body. It had been strung up by a hempen cord and tied in an unusual position, like a tangled marionette with broken limbs. Between the flesh and the cord I recognized a crooked nose, red and purple, and empty eyes, staring from the blue eaves.

An investigator took me aside with a firm grip and a sober expression.

At the time of the incident, the man in the blue house had been in conversation.

In conversation?

With your daughter.

With my daughter?

I am so sorry to inform you that she was killed in the attack too. We cannot announce this yet, but the Fallow were involved. It was very unfortunate, and she was caught in the crossfire. I'm sorry to tell you, but she is dead. Your daughter is dead. It will be some time before we can release the cremated remains. Ongoing investigation. You understand.

Dead?

My mind reeled emptily, then settled in our home, at the table, over Sunday supper. To conversation about things, what they meant and what they didn't mean. I listened to what the investigator said and what he didn't say.

Dead?

The investigator looked perplexed. Yes?

Dead?

Yes.

Dead? I smiled.

Yes.

Dead. I laughed.

He recommended that I go home and told me I would be contacted when the cremated remains were ready. He apologized again. I told him I would have no need for the remains. I had no need for any of those remains. I left the scene, the neighbors watching, whispering, while I laughed and went home and sat in the darkness again.

People know me here as the man with one child who is alive and one child who is dead. They are right, in a certain way, and in a certain way, they are not.

The train station where I work is quieter than before. Like the whole country, all quieter than everything before. They are having a harder time filling it, though they do not say it. Just like the schools, hospitals, factories, offices, everything is quieter. And with those changes, the First Citizen and his Bureaus have shifted their stricter immigration positions, relaxed certain policies to stimulate an influx of labor. It was not that way yesterday and may not be that way tomorrow. But for today, for now, they demand the influx of labor.

So, I explain the way of things, in the country, in accord with certain procedures. But sometimes, I wander a little with what I say and don't say. There are fewer men in blue houses to listen to the wind, to listen to me wander with what I say and don't say. I like to share passages from my son's work. I'd like to share this one, from his unfinished story, if you don't mind.

My father says there is no king. What I believe he really means, whether he knows it or not, is that there are many kings. Neighborhood kings, city kings, money kings, legal kings, machine kings, political kings. There is no singular king, yes, and no one king by that title, but there are many who think they bear the mantle nonetheless. They surround us. Suffocate us. They step on our backs. They coordinate without even knowing they coordinate to coerce and control.

But now I think my father was correct in a different way. Unintentionally, maybe. But secretly, accidentally correct. There is no king.

There is no one, or many, who can rule for long. They can divide and categorize and simplify to make the rest of us forget a greater thing. Make themselves forget that they, too, are part of that greater thing. But they are not above or below or beside or apart for long.

They know there is no king.

I know there is no king.

There is no king.

I think about this passage often. I repeat this one to new arrivals, like yourself, most often. I am not clever like my son or brave like my daughter. But still, I think about their stories and talk at the dinner table, and I find myself repeating this passage most often.

I spend the days watching the train windows, the series of glass panels, pulling in, pulling away from the platform, and sometimes, I see a static charge, and with it a blurred, almost unrecognizable face, partly flesh, partly something else, looking back from behind each reflection that passes me by. The blurred face behind the reflection does not look at me directly when I smile. She is not ready to look at me, I think. But that is fine. I am just glad she is still there watching and passing me by.

Just like I'm glad when I sleep, and I can almost see another face in an unbroken darkness, obscured. A shape of someone I know and do not completely know at the same time. A voice that is his voice and my voice, blended together, so that I can't tell who is speaking anymore, whether it is him or it is me. And in that other place, I share my thoughts without fear. Everything that I say. Everything that I don't say. I share it all.

Thomas Ha is a writer of speculative short fiction whose work has been nominated for the Nebula, Ignyte, Hugo, Locus, and Shirley Jackson Awards, among others. You can find his work in *Clarkesworld*, *Lightspeed Magazine*, *Beneath Ceaseless Skies*, and *Weird Horror Magazine*, and other publications. His work has also appeared in *The Best American Science Fiction & Fantasy* and *The Year's Best Dark Fantasy & Horror*. Thomas grew up in Honolulu and, after a decade plus of living in the northeast, now resides in Los Angeles with his family.

THE TAWLISH ISLAND SONGBOOK OF THE DEAD

E.M. Linden

The living have been leaving Tawlish for centuries; this evacuation is only the latest and last. There are good reasons for it: the freshwater spring gone brackish; the water, always encroaching; the colicky, relentless wind. No schools for the children. No doctor. We should have seen it coming, but sometimes we forget what the living need.

We cannot cross salt, so we watch from shore. Our loved ones and descendants wade into the sea. The men strain to hold the boats steady against the waves. Everyone's weighed down by possessions, a village crammed into sacks and lifeboats. Spoons, spindles, fish-hooks, balls of yarn. A clothes-peg doll in a twist of old apron. Seabirds' eggs wrapped in blankets: habits ingrained by generations of scarcity. They've even dug up their potatoes.

Katie Zell's mother is already on the boat. The songbook is tucked inside her jacket.

Thirty-seven people. Only some of them look back.

They leave cold firepits and fulmar bones, middens, empty crofts with the thatch already collapsing. Sheep they've blessed and turned loose to fend for themselves.

And us. The dead of Tawlish.

Katie Zell's father has been dead longer than she's been alive. Before he drowned, he'd hoped to sing her lullabies: the ones he sang to her older brothers, the ones his grandparents sang to him. Now, in farewell, he rests his hand briefly on her curls. Most of the living are oblivious to the dead, but the Zells are a noticing kind of family.

Katie raises her hand to his; perhaps she mistakes the cold brush of it for sea-spray. It's enough. He smiles. That's all there is time for: Katie's uncle lifts her from the shore, over the churn of the sea, and seats her next to her cousin on the boat.

Old Maureen Stornaway is furious, sees evacuation as defeat. She clenches a knuckle of island rock in her pocket. Tiny luminosities watch her from shore: the ghosts of three of her children. She strains her eyes and peers back through the sea-mist. Maybe something shines there. After decades of loss, of wishing them still with her, this is the first and last time that she almost makes them out.

The rector, smug, takes nothing. He doesn't need to. He has a house on the mainland, and — as far as he's concerned — he's saved thirty-seven souls.

A Tawlish tradition: the living and dead send each other gifts. The living give tobacco and carved pipes, posies of sea-vetch, griddle-cake. Packets of seeds for Lizzie Knell. Wooden rattles and teething rings. Handkerchiefs embroidered with our names. They slip our gifts into the flames so that they'll cross over to our side. Burnt offerings. The wind chases the sparks out of the sky. The gifts arrive smelling of smoke.

Our gifts are less generous. All we can send are dreams.

Tonight, all together, we dream safe passage for the living. Grudgingly, because they're abandoning us; jealously, because we want them here: their songs and laughter reminding us who we are, their bones buried beside ours in the thin Tawlish soil. We dream them returning.

We dream them bringing our songbook home.

The songbook holds all the magic of Tawlish. Spell-songs that nudge the wind and sing fish into nets, that knit bones and heal coughs and call the drowned ashore for burial. The rector feared our spell-songs, but they made life here possible.

We wish the living had left the songbook behind. Burned it as a farewell gift, perhaps. There's no magic on the mainland, after all; the spells work nowhere but Tawlish. Perhaps we're being childish — what use to the dead are spells for fishing and healing? — but we want it back.

We miss the songs.

Somewhere on the mainland where only our dreams can reach, Katie Zell, her mother, and her two older brothers are making the best of a narrow, cramped house, far away from even the horizon line of the sea. We don't know any of this. More things we don't know: The air smells wrong to Katie. She misses the sound of gulls. But she loves the flowers in the town's gardens, bright beneath the coal-dust in the air; daffodils instead of potatoes and turnips.

Katie's mother gives thanks for jobs and schools and electric lights. A working stove. Unchapped hands. The neighbour gives her seeds.

"You see?" Katie's mother stands in their small kitchen, shakes the packet at her three uprooted children. "We can grow here."

None of them mention their dreams.

Katie's mother insists they go to church, and Katie scowls at their rector and swings her legs. She doesn't fully understand what's happened to her life, but she knows it's somehow his fault.

We don't see it, but Katie's mother wraps the songbook in the shawl that Katie and her brothers were baptised in, and tucks it away in her drawer. She props a blurred photo of Katie's father on the mantelpiece.

"Who is that man?" Katie asks.

Her mother doesn't answer. Tears gather in her eyes, and Katie thinks of sea-spray.

Maureen Stornaway struggles to hold what's left of her family close to her. In her life she's wrestled loss and grief and hardship, but never distance. She has no experience of loving someone far away. One by one those of her children that survived to adulthood move away for partners, bigger cities, better-paying jobs. They do not need her, she announces, and they should never have dragged her from Tawlish in the first place. She won't visit. She's still saying this when the first of her grandchildren is born, and she boards the overnight bus with her bags full of knitting.

Always in her mind, the three she buried on the island. The glimmer of small ghosts.

As for them, they cannot imagine what their mother is doing, have no idea that they still haunt her at all. They've no reference points for anything beyond Tawlish. They know they were once precious; all of them remember being held. And they achieved things, important things, while they were alive. One of them touched the sea. One took his first steps. One lasted only hours but she heard and approved of a lullaby. But now, despite all this significance, they think themselves forgotten. We don't know how to comfort them.

Years ago, the rector burnt a violin. He intended to destroy it, but instead it came to us. We, the dead, squabbled over it. Tore that little violin out of each other's hands, wrenched it back and forth, cried over it. It was agonising: we knew it contained music, but without the songbook, we could not remember how to play.

Music, we remember, leapt like fire and waves. Music was one of the few bright things on Tawlish.

The rector, though. He was always a mainlander at heart. If we think of him at all, we roll our eyes and laugh. We have his measure. Our dreams are wasted on him.

In the graveyard of Tawlish's only church, Lizzy Knell hovers, polishes her headstone. In life, they said she had a green thumb. She was the only person on

Tawlish who grew flowers. She gave them to her neighbours for their weddings and adorned the church with them in spring. She cannot tend the flowers that grow over her grave, but she kneels close and pushes her hands among them anyway. Can almost feel the tickle of sea-lavender. The churchyard is a lovely spot: high but sheltered, overlooking the smaller harbour. Maybe she thinks of the rector more than most.

We, the dead, clutch our shreds together, try to distinguish ourselves from the morning mist that breathes all over the island, hold tight to the gorse and use the rocks as anchors when the gales get up. There's a formlessness without the living here. We erode; the land slips into the sea. We miss the cradle of our bones.

It's cold, without the living. It's very quiet.

Katie's father worries no one's watching over her. We can't comfort him either.

Visitors still come to Tawlish occasionally: bird-watchers, historians, scientists. But they don't notice us, and none of them bring what we need.

There always used to be singing. All through the generations the living sang, to the dead and to each other. Strands and skeins of song between our ancestors and our descendants. Sometimes lyrics changed, notes were dropped, new songs written and others forgotten, but the songs always told us who we were. Wove us together and held us in shape. There was always music. Over the rocks and harbour, mingling with the peat-smoke, hanging under our eaves. Between us and the painfully clear stars.

But the threads have gone slack. Silent. The living are letting us go.

We wait and dream, but they don't return.

At first we think: our descendants are fortunate. They've safely crossed the strait. They're living long lives.

But still nobody comes. It dawns on us slowly. Our families will never return to Tawlish. Not even to rest.

Even so, we send our dreams of good fortune and protection across the strait. We keep calling them home.

Maureen Stornaway and Katie Zell take the train to the seaside. Brightly painted changing sheds and matchstick boats. Wavelets. A pier lined with striped booths: fortune-tellers and sticks of rock. Nothing that could withstand a Tawlish storm.

By now Katie Zell hardly remembers Tawlish. "This is nothing like home," she says, and pretends it isn't a question.

Sometimes, Katie worries that she has no claim on the island. It is inarguably home for her mother and brothers. The moods of the sea are in their voices: lilt and rage and laughter. But Katie's accent is imbued with coal-dust. She coaxes sunflowers from the narrow strip of yard their landlord calls a garden, but she never learns how to tie the knots for wind and fortune.

If we were there, we'd teach her. If we knew her worries, we'd send her dreams of welcome. *This is always your home*, we'd say. Katie would smile, and we'd remember the living need us too. It would be another kind of gift.

At the seaside, Maureen nods. "Nothing like Tawlish." Privately, though, she welcomes the weak sunlight, the pale golden sand, the ice-cream van's jingle. The seaside colours disappoint Katie, but Maureen is grateful for little disappointments. She needs distance. If this place were too like Tawlish, she'd be sunk.

Bad enough when a toddler trips in the sand. The mother picks the boy up and comforts him. Maureen's arms unconsciously mirror the mother's, shaping themselves around the remembered heft of her own one-year-old son. She left him on Tawlish with his smaller sisters.

She turns her face away. Too late: she's spinning through thirty, forty, fifty years of memories. The pain is new and bright as a white-hot coin. No. Not that. A coin is small and can be handled. Grief is the sun itself. Everyone talks about it as if it rises and falls, as if it has seasons. The truth is, she'll orbit it her whole life, and she'll never be able to look at it without flinching.

"Are you all right?" Katie asks her. Katie's a good girl, but how can you explain things to the young? Maureen Stornoway clenches her knuckle of island rock. The daylight could split her wide open.

Katie's father would be so proud if he could see her now. He doesn't know it, none of us do, but Katie is the first Zell to go to university. Her mother is thrilled enough for the two of them. Katie studies anthropology and travels the mainland, collecting Tawlish stories from the other evacuees. She listens to everyone: her mother, Maureen, even the rector.

At first none of the others see the point, but they take it in good part. Katie's one of them, after all. And once they start reminiscing most of them can't stop: the weather on Tawlish, the food, the beauty of the skies, the singing, the hunger, the gnawing cold, the way the damp crept into their lungs, the gleaming fish. Katie crams her notebook with stories and memories. She hears about the gifts for the dead, and who was buried where, and who had grudges and who died too young. She hears about her mother's songbook. The Tawlish islanders tell her about her father and their own loved ones and insist that one day — any day now, maybe next summer—they really will go back to tend the graves.

Finlay Price gives her tea as thick as porridge and an old guitar of wood the colour of honey. "Your father sang," he says. "He could coax a tune from anything. Your mother played the fiddle. Thought maybe you'd like to try."

Katie doesn't know it, but she has her father's knack for music. Her mother's ear. Her own singing voice. On weekends she bar tends in a pub and plays for ceilidhs at the community hall. Saves up for a violin.

Katie's father never hears how easily music comes to his only daughter. If he knew what he was missing, his greatest regret would no longer be drowning. It would be that he never heard Katie play. She spins joy and tears from her listeners like yarn from wool. She has them up and dancing. She plays all the old ones. *Fishermen's Jig. Wedding in May. The Weaver's Loom*, that's her favourite; it's one they danced in the ramshackle hall on Tawlish. Feet stamping. Dancers criss-crossing the floor.

But her father never knows any of that. He never hears her play.

Our songs were twisty, tidal, sea-breeze things. Swells and surges, seabird squalls, glimpses of cloudless sky. We remember the dancing. Hands thumped on tables, feet on swollen floorboards. Pipes, fiddles, and goatskin bodhráns. The calling of the women and the men.

Even now, Tawlish is not silent. Gannets shriek against the wind and waves. But we cannot help it: we only hear what's missing.

None of us know that we're still remembered. How could we? The living don't dream to us the way we dream to them. It's not just that we miss them. We're losing ourselves without them, our shapes and our names. We've no reason to carry on.

The island scares us now: we scare each other. We're thinner. Perhaps it's good they've left, we tell each other; we're too hungry to be near them. We can't trust ourselves.

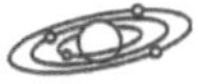

Sometimes the rector worries about the state of his soul. There is a woman back on Tawlish buried in consecrated ground. Lizzie Knell.

Lizzie chose her own end. Because of that, she should be buried outside the walls on the sinner's walk, a rocky strip of land already falling away into the harbour, too badly eroded for mourners to visit. But the rector insisted she be buried in the churchyard. He knew it wasn't right, but he was also human. He couldn't bear to think of her family grieving more than necessary, having no grave to visit. Didn't want them to feel shame over this bright, sad woman who grew flowers even on Tawlish, who whistled to her sheep and made her neighbours laugh.

In his prayers, he offered to carry the weight of her sin himself. He hides it from his congregation, can't admit it even in his prayers, but after Lizzie Knell he finds he no longer truly believes in sin.

He's not perfect. The islanders didn't even like him that much. But he's satisfied with how he's spent his life. Thirty-seven souls. Thirty-six, shepherded safely in small boats to the mainland. And Lizzie Knell, with flowers on her grave.

The latest Stornaway baby is named Lily. They wanted to call her Maureen for her grandmother, but old Maureen refused.

"Old-fashioned name," she says. "Never liked it myself."

Baby and mother are doing well. But only because of certain interventions, procedures that had never been available on Tawlish. Maureen dandles Lily, supports her head with years of practice, and lets the conversation wash over her. It's only women talking, so the details are bloody and true. *Monitor,* she hears, *induction, falling heartbeat.* She doesn't understand all of the medical terminology. *Emergency caesarean. Blue. Resuscitation. Thriving.* Understands enough. This baby stuttered back to life because they're here. Mainland doctors and midwives, medicine and equipment.

The baby spits up a little on her shoulder, and Maureen forgives the mainland with her whole heart.

"Songs," we remind each other. We, the dead. We're almost gone now. "Music. It was like..." We trail off. We can't remember who of us is which anymore, who belongs to whom. We've lost the names. Faces. Families.

We wish we could have seen them grow. We'd have danced in secret at their weddings, hovered next to them when they wept, welcomed the babies, kept watch at cribs and wakes. Instead, this rupture.

Another of us tries. "It was," one says, "like a sound. A long sound."

"It was words," another says. "Or sometimes not."

"It was wood," one says. "Like that violin."

We have to admit it. We've forgotten our songs. We've forgotten.

We don't know that Katie's life is music. She plays at Maureen Stornaway's wake. She marries and has children; her children have children. She sings them lullabies. Passes the little scraps she remembers of Tawlish on to them.

We don't see Katie inherit her mother's songbook. *Our* songbook. We would have been jealous, but also pleased to see the care she takes with it. She unwraps the little book and thumbs through its salt-splashed pages. She tries to make out the blurred notations of the songs.

One by one we slip into sleep. All we have now are our dreams.

One day two young men arrive in a small rowboat. One navigates the deadly currents as if by memory. We surface from our dreaming to pay closer attention. We shake ourselves a little. Scent the air.

When he climbs ashore, his feet already know the rocks.

We drift closer; all we are now is hunger. Almost all. But names start coming back to us, distinct from dreams and hunger. We'd forgotten other things existed. As we wake fully we find our voices. We whisper among ourselves: *He is Finlay Price's grandson. No, he's Zennor Canne's youngest child.*

We know one thing: He's been listening to the dreams we send.

The other man sketches seabirds and purloins feathers. We ignore him. We only care about our young man.

A Stornaway, we mutter. *Look at his blue eyes.*

They build a campfire. Fire on Tawlish, after all these years. Another gift. We lean closer, we clustering dead, marvelling at its warmth.

We speak close by his ear. *A Quarn: see the red of his hair.*

He jumps, rubs his arms, stares wide-eyed around him.

"What's wrong?" his friend asks.

"Nothing." He shakes his head. "Just thought I heard someone."

Heard! We are delighted. *He's a Zell*, says Katie's father, proudly.

"Come on, get this over with," the friend says.

We shush each other, our hunger forgotten. Our young man pulls a sheaf of paper from his rucksack and unrolls it.

"The Tawlish Island Songbook," he says.

Our songbook. A hum of excitement goes through all the dead. It charges the air, glitters like sunlight on the waves, sends flurries of seabirds skywards. Our young man looks around in wonder. He shakes his head. "Odd weather."

"Seems a waste." The friend, who hasn't noticed, frowns. "Your grandma really said to burn it?"

"She has copies; the original's barely legible now. But yeah, Nanna Katie insisted."

He sits by the fire. The three tiny Stornaways curl close to him: one on his boot, one on his shoulder, one tucked in the crook of his arm. Maybe he thinks it's sea-spray; most likely he doesn't notice them at all. But he moves gently, as if he's taking care not to disturb something he knows is nearby.

He thumbs through the songbook. We crowd close to see. There are the songs we once knew. And at the back, a new sheaf of pages, trimmed to fit and stitched into the cover. New songs.

They're for us and about us. There's one about Katie's father. One about Finlay Price's sheep. One for the tiny Stornaways, a lovely threnody set to violin and flute. Even one about Lizzie Knell and the rector. These songs aren't magic the way the old ones are; they don't bring favourable tides or sing fish into nets.

They're something else. They're proof.

We didn't know, but the living never forgot us. They carried us with them over the salt of the sea.

The threads have never gone slack. They criss-cross the strait, our weft, their warp: love and loss, life and death, past and present. We've always been dancing with the living.

Katie's grandchild places the songbook in the flames. It rises with the smoke.

A gift.

The songs are there. The spells. Snatches and strains. Some are warped by time, others missing, others new. But we recognise Tawlish, the old magic woven from wind and seawater. The music. New songs and old. We're dead; our people will never return. But one after the other, we sing.

E.M. Linden (she/her) is a writer from Aotearoa New Zealand whose work has appeared in 20+ publications including *Strange Horizons*, *PodCastle*, and *The Deadlands*, as well as on the Locus Recommended Reading List. She likes coffee, owls, and the sea.

BECAUSE I HELD HIS NAME LIKE A KEY

Aimee Ogden

When I met the young Mr. Turing, I had not yet ascended as Autumn's King. Nowadays it has become fashionable for the sons and daughters of the lesser fey gentry to improve their position in the shifting hierarchy of the Courts by virtue of intrigue, scandal, and the naked blade; but in those times, it was the custom to advance one's position through the collection of human bagatelles. Poets, polymaths, politicians—all manner of mortal myrmidons who flourished, in turn, during their time under the butterfly-bright attention of this Court or that one.

A changeling, of course, affords the best expectation of loyalty, but I have never had the patience for cultivating a companion from scratch; nor have I ever seen reason to abandon the comforts of the Courts to scrounge through cradles low and high. Instead, I opened doors. Anyone worth having would come to me. To ride searching and screaming over the worlds—that is the purview of the Wild Hunt, and my taste for flesh has never been of a kind with theirs.

On what was for me a quiet morning, he jogged into my Fellforest parlor through a door I'd tossed—in a fit of pique or boredom—at a musty potato cave in Dorsetshire. A few mortals had wandered through it before, as well they might; but never yet one wearing sodden-wet running shorts and trainers. (Indeed, the most recent visitor to use that door had done so some hundred years before running shorts had come into fashion.) He turned from me at once to survey the door through which he'd come. On the other side, rain pattered down through bud-tipped branches. Yes, he said, I thought as much; and he nodded with satisfaction in a hypothesis duly supported.

Visitors have most commonly responded with awe, or fear, or simple confusion, when they first arrive, through my intervention, in Elfhame; there are those, too, who step across my threshold a-shiver, with simple hope or elaborate greed, that they will find among the Lords of Faerie such things as they have been denied in their own world. To be met instead with this supple curiosity presented me the rare gift of novelty, and I could only laugh, for I knew that such a creature would be the envy of all the Courts.

At the sound, his shadow moved first—realizing for the first time, perhaps, that it was not bound to him in the same ways, not in the sunless light of

Elfhame—and it strained toward mine where it lay on the carpet of dry leaves at my feet. Alan himself turned to me and offered a rueful smile and his apologies for entering uninvited, and without any sort of decent greeting besides. Still a youth, then, tripping around the rim of manhood and waiting to tumble into his majority. When he spoke, steam billowed from his mouth, to match what rose from his rain-dampened shoulders: good afternoon, sir, or—He paused there, taking account of the wan light that streamed down through the woven branches of the parlor roof, before he continued: or perhaps I ought to say good morning.

I passed the correspondence with which I had been occupied to a waiting raven and stood, so that my shadow slid across my visitor's. He seemed entirely unconcerned by his sudden arrival, and I said as much; to which he replied that there was little enough utility in being disturbed by the unconventional method of transport. I'm here now, in any case, he said, and he smiled again, and asked me how my door worked.

While our shadows cavorted, playing a coy hide-and-seek in the patches of darkness beneath the branches, I showed him the runes I had drawn upon the trees that formed the doorframe: those markings which guided the path he'd traveled and other like-minded routes from his realm to mine; those which bound world to world and held them fast against one another. He scratched his head and said that he'd hoped for a stronger basis in the natural laws with which he was familiar, though he confessed that he wasn't much of a physicist. And he craned his neck for a better look into the Fellforest and asked me if I might show him around.

That carried us into the disappointment of familiar terrain: lacking true power of their own, mortals grasped instinctively at any they saw. Even now, as Autumn King, I watch my human petitioners stare up into my face, seeking nothing deeper than some glimmer of their own reflection. I had already indulged him in one curiosity, and I reminded him, velvet politesse draped over the blade of meaning, that nothing in Elfhame was freely given—even if you did not know the cost, it would come to be reckoned in its course.

He protested then, with a hint of abashment, that he had not brought his billfold nor anything worth trading on his long jogging route, and at that I laughed again, and suggested that we might exchange something beyond mere material goods.

Time can be a gift, he said, one not always fully appreciated when it is given. And his eyes went to the wooden chessboard that rested in its place of honor atop a polished stump, its rows of rooks and redcaps, queens and courtiers.

Time, yes, a passable euphemism. But to ensure my intent did not slip past him, I allowed my shadow enough rein to rise from the rough earth—my visitor had not learned the game of control over his own, not in his realm where a man's shadow bends unthinkingly to his every whim, and his followed mine into the air. As speech is not in the nature of a shadow, these silhouettes told each other of their desires without words, and in doing so, they also told Mr. Turing of mine. We slipped out of our clothing and our shadows alike, so that we and they might couple privately and like unto like.

I found him eager but not desperate, attentive but not self-effacing, and not long after we had finished, with the lacework of sweat and semen drying on our skin, he stood up again and dusted away the bits of leaf and soil that clung to him, and he said he'd had a fine time but that he ought to finish his jog before it got much later.

Though this son of man towered over me, I did not trouble myself to rise. He still had no shadow to drape over me, with his and mine alike still elsewhere at their play. Cool air or English shame drove him quickly to dress himself, but, unbothered by either of those, I propped myself up on one elbow to watch him. Did he not, I wondered aloud, wish a proper introduction to my Court? Here, he would find pursuits that would put his time to better and more interesting use than trotting to and fro. Here, he would be understood and appreciated in a way he never would be there. Here, things were sweet and simple.

He brushed the leaf-litter out of his hair and told me that as he himself was neither sweet nor simple, he thought he would rather not stay. But he hesitated, and I knew then that I had adequately baited the hook after all. He would return in time—and what matters time, to the timeless?

If you like, I said carelessly. I warned him that he would not be able to use the same door twice, but told him, too, that there were others that would make themselves known to a watchful eye.

He nodded gravely, and said he hoped we would meet again, and as he turned to go, he said to me one more thing: My name is Alan, by the by. Alan Turing.

A true name freely given, without a thought as to how I might use or abuse it. I offered him something in turn, a figment of a name to call me by—the north wind's passing fart, a grasshopper's cough, and he smiled, and thanked me for it, and when he trotted off back into Dorset, rain quickly darkened the dry patches on his shirt.

He did return, as good as his word and better, without me ever having to yank on the chain of that true-given name. By his reckoning, some three years had passed, while I had seen the rise and fall of three would-be fey dynasties all in the course of a single evening's ball. When we allowed ourselves the opportunity for closer examination, his body had changed in innumerable little ways, which was a profound curiosity to me; and mine had changed not in the least, which he found an impossible riddle.

He did not much appreciate my explanation that I was as old as my world itself, and also born anew with each falling leaf and encroaching early frost. A human mind is an incomplete thing, and I knew there was no way to express my nature to him in a sense that he could have understood, and yet he continued to desire all along that I try, and I cannot say that my explications were enhanced for his wishing me to speak with his fingers in my mouth. Among his faculties he did not count a capacity to let things rest in their native duality—he demanded a single phenomenon with unifying explanatory power.

Later, while our shadows played a well-matched game of chess, Alan sketched out a shape in the dirt between the roots of a yellow-leafed beech tree—a fortuitous choice, for the beech grove was young enough not to take offense at this forwardness, and this specimen in particular was too shy to interrupt Alan with questions about his thought experiment. There must be some means, he said to me, by which matter is processed—transformed—as it is moved from a realm with one set of physical laws to a domain with another set entirely. Imagine, then, a circle that exists on a flat plane, a plane of only two dimensions (and he indicated the shape in question where he had scratched it on the ground).

Easily enough done, I said, and having done so, I suggested that we move on to pursuits of a more challenging nature, be it intellectual or physical.

But he urged me to possess myself of a moment's patience, and he placed a round acorn-cap atop the circle. Imagine again, he said, that the circle passes through a portal, or indeed a doorway, of some sort, into a world of three dimensions. And there, our circle finds that the shape it possesses in two dimensions represents a mere cross-section of the whole, and that only now, senses transformed, can it perceive itself in its entirety.

I laughed, and moved the acorn cap out of its circle. A circle altered by its passage into a greater world, I suggested, might well perceive new qualia outside its ken. But perception and ascension were two different things.

He looked at me then, out of the corner of one dark eye, and he got up to retrieve his things—not to depart, he said, but to offer a small gift: a handsome watch on a chain. Truly the gift he gave was the gift of labor, for he taught me how to wind it and asked me to do so regularly, and showed me a twinned timepiece that he kept in the pocket of his own waistcoat. When next he came, he said, he would compare the time that had passed between the two devices, and so develop his understanding of how our worlds aligned. He said, even a simple circle can grow into a third dimension, once he knows it is there.

I laughed and told him that talking in quite literal circles had grown tiresome, and offered him apple wine and roasted hazelnuts, and he ate of what I brought forth, and spoke with both his mouth and mind full and overflowing: of hypotheses and raw-cut first principles. Of experiments. Of proof—proof of natural law, he said, but what he truly meant to prove lay deeper than data.

And by then he had freely given his name, and freely eaten my food. Even when a flat shape perceives an added dimension, it may not always understand what it has been shown. When I next return, he had said, and I knew it for a certainty.

He spent three days in the mortal realm, searching all the while over a long holiday weekend for another door, before he strolled back into my parlor. Nearly all that while had I been drowning in the rot-and-honey oubliette of the Dawnsun Court (for my *faintest* of associations with the youngest principality, before his failed coup). Before I knew I would be captured, I had entrusted the watch to the care of the wisest pine marten in my parlor. Before she died, she had taught her daughter how to wind the wretched thing, and her daughter taught her own son in turn; and because they were good and loyal subjects all, the watch had known a fastidious custody across their generations.

And yet Alan was not best pleased when he re-examined it, for in his absence each of the numerals had become a small blinking eye, twelve in total, and when he went to wind it he found that the gears had turned into a maze of interlocked, white-enameled teeth (which still turned, and the hands on my watch's newly vigilant face kept pace with the hands on his).

In sympathy—for he had exclaimed with great dismay over the predicament I had suffered—I offered to alter the watch in accordance with his wishes. What would he prefer it to say? How might I bring it more neatly in line with his expectations?

But he gave the watch back to me, keeping back, this time, the insistence on its care and feeding. I still believe the premise is sound, he said, and he put his mouth to mine as if searching for what honey might linger.

On that occasion he did stay long enough to accompany me to the Seaward Court, where he made exactly the impression that I had desired upon my fellows. The attention of a Tide is an enduring thing, waxing and waning but always present. All manner of watery fey came and went while Alan explicated his mortal mathematics. A fundamentally flawed system, as he described it, what he called the Entscheidungsproblem: incomplete, inconsistent, fumbling attempts to grope for a truth that was at its roots unknowable.

A cold-water Current with limpid blue eyes draped herself over Alan's shoulders. A pitiful thing, she said solicitously, that there existed no power nor principality in the mortal realm who might address such inadequacies.

But, Alan protested, what was not *complete* did not inherently equate to what was not *interesting*. The greater significance of his findings lay, he went on, as the Current receded and was directly replaced by a Tropical Breeze, in the notion of a Universal Computing Machine. Another of his thought experiments, which he explained at length; a thought experiment that argued against its own very existence. And yet, Alan averred, a computing machine of less than universal capacity could, and would, still be achieved. Whatever computational capers a mortal might be capable of, this machine could reproduce, and yield an identical output. Such a computation machine would be governed by written rules to impose upon it the structure of mathematical law, to recapitulate the human capacity to memorize formulae and figures—differing chiefly, Alan noted, in its inability to deviate voluntarily from the structure imposed by those internal instructions. A computational golem, with a set of algorithms carved into its soul.

I wondered aloud whether that was any difference at all, for it seemed to me that a mortal mind found itself ruled in all things by the labyrinthine law engraved upon it by habit, by social custom, by biological demand. Any difference lay only in scale.

But what of free will? asked Alan, and he frowned at the eddy of laughter that spun around him.

Come now, I said gently, you are too old to believe in such a children's tale as that. In your day-to-day life you must pretend yourself free to choose—to feel oneself an automaton should be intolerable—but in such exalted discussion as this, it is time to fold away your delusions until you need them again. You are more like your machine-computer than you are like to any of your present company.

Am I, he repeated.

Though he did not say this as if to argue the opposite, he spoke with a distance I did not appreciate, not while I still hoped to burnish my reputation with the careful application of his intellect. In my impatience, I said: It is very well to make a machine that behaves like a man. If you could contrive one that thinks like the fey, now, that would be something else entirely. And a deep-sea Current trilled a laugh, and a sea-devil asked on what sort of fuel this fey-machine would run, and as the wheels of conversation settled onto these new tracks, Alan excused himself and retrieved his shadow from beside the dessert arrangement.

It would be some time by both of our reckonings before he returned, and my circumstances and his were both much altered. The turn of his years had carried his world into war, while mine had elevated me into a position of power. When Alan first stepped into the Goldbower, he was much taken aback, and protested that he had never known I was the son of some great lord. I was no such thing, and before he could ask more than I wanted to tell, I said simply that a position had opened and that I had availed myself of it quickly.

Our shadows slunk off hand in hand—for their bond was possessed of a simplicity lacking in our own—while I showed Alan the rest of my new estate's grounds. The Firstfrost Garden, the Hall of the Dying Sun, the acres of vineyards that tumbled down sloping hills and arbors whose leaves melted into every warm and welcoming color that light has ever touched. He said I had done well for myself, and I told him I could do well for him, too. He could be my royal mathematician, or an Architect Prince of the realm I had won. He could build for me a tower of flowers and calculus.

Perhaps he could, he allowed, but he had work already, of a sort that engaged him, and people dearly relying on its completion. And he refused to be convinced, and refused to be more than politely impressed by the Goldbower, and refused my advances when I pressed myself against him in the Crimson Gallery. Was there not somewhere more private, he protested, and gestured at the servants who hurried through, who watched us intently through a flimsy veil of indifference. He was not that kind of man.

But you could be, I said, this once, for me, and amid a flood of endearments and sweet words, he was, yes, just as I asked of him, he was. Yet he did not linger long before he made his excuses and dressed, saying moreover that with the war and his work, he was not sure whether or not he would be back again any time soon—or indeed at all. The bombings, you know, he said. Might get caught out by the Blitz any day now, or any night rather.

I freely confess that I did not like to hear that, and I offered him again titles, riches, attention, all of which he brushed aside. None of it would last; his mortal body would grow old, and—he said, with a rueful gesture at his face, not as smooth as it once had been, his belly, not as flat—youth's blossoms had already faded.

And so what? Both my world and his would use him up in their course, but only one would love him first for who, for what, he was.

He stood with that in silence, listing as if against an unseen wind. Finally he said that an argument could be made in favor of open earnest cruelty over the shabby facade that had stood between him and every fey creature he had met in his time among my kind.

The temptation to wield his name rose within me, but I did not enjoy his company because of his tractability, and I knew—had traveled before upon—the compliant ruts that I would wear into him, should I rely too heavily on what I had been given. Instead I lay a last offer before him: If he stayed, I would grant him the power to invent a new arithmetic that would obey every command he set before it, as pliant as a pussycat. Not this nightmare of illogic that he must deal with in the mortal realm.

He smiled, and allowed that there were days where he would have enjoyed that. Do you know, he said, I sometimes imagine that a fey lord got his hands on mathematics before human beings had fully got their minds around it. And he clasped my hand, as if I were an old classmate or a coworker at Bletchley Park, playing his goodbyes in a key of formality to which he had never before tuned himself. He walked through the door and out of the Goldbower. Not for good, not forever, though it seemed so at the time. And because I held his name like a key, and because he had eaten of what I had offered, he left a part of himself behind, and did not notice what he lacked.

I nodded to his shadow where it shuddered on the carpet, unable to follow its master, and bade it make itself welcome.

In later days, mortals would whisper that it was fey magic that broke the machine's stubborn code. They would say, too, that it was Alan's time in Elfhame which bent his desire toward the attentions of other men: breathing our strange air, aping our strange customs. Human beings tell stories to understand what falls beyond their ken: wild-eyed mutterers squatted around a primeval campfire, reassuring one another that the raging thunder is the voice of the gods, that the sun soars and sets on the backs of winged horses. That these things are lies does not matter to them, so long as their fears are, for a moment, assuaged. But Alan remained as infuriatingly unmoved by his visits to my world as any man has ever managed to be. Nor did he ever carry his work with him. When he came, he came for an escape—albeit only ever a temporary one—and so he never offered an explanation of his code-machines to me, and I did not ask for one.

What he longed to explain was how things could be one way for me, and another for him. And what I asked was that he stay. And we were both ever disappointed.

Perhaps in the mortal world, hewing to mortal custom, our next meeting would be painted with the same formality: stiff brushstrokes of small talk, reminiscences, the steam rising over a cup of tea. Perhaps there, distasteful news could be received without taking on a life of its own. Certainly human beings have found innumerable ways to convince themselves to live with the intolerable—else they should have run themselves into madness long ago, and from madness into extinction. The wind-up toy, tracing its aimless circles, was not made to look back and understand the trajectory of its journey.

But he came, as he always had, to my realm, and his news trailed after him like a shadow should have done: a fiancée, a wedding date. If he had tried to hand me an invitation like some kind of unearned prize, I could not have held back my wrath. Bad enough that he told me, and then sat with the telling as if he thought I might be glad for him. Was he here, then, to post the banns, I wondered? Did he hope to dress his darling bride in fey-made lace, to make her the envy of mortal women?

Only then did he make note of my ire, and he dared to look put out about it. I had hoped—he began to say, but I did not let him finish, for I knew what he had hoped, and told him so: a human wife for daily wear, a lord of Elfhame for holidays and special occasions. I had killed men and fey alike for lesser insults.

He protested at that—she was his best friend, he would build a plain and mortal existence atop that trustworthy foundation, he had not come to ask anything of me. But he had come, had he not, and the act seemed to me in itself a kind of petition. He had not asked, but I would give, and I gave him his true name and all the obligation it bore. Whether he knew or not that he was compelled, he could not help but follow the tug of the lead. And in the end, if he was in any way truly distressed, it was not to such a degree that he failed to enjoy the fullness of his pleasure.

I kept him for only three days. Three days of dancing, of a whirlwind tour through all the Courts that called me friend or ally, of every kind of congress.

He ate what he was offered and slept beside me in the highest tower room of the Goldbower while a dozen Winds capered and sported outside our windows. On the fourth morning, I told him he might as well go back and see to his fiancée. He knew then where he belonged, I said, and I let go the lead.

When he felt his liberty return to him, he cocked his head, a hound listening for its master's call—or for the thunder. He took my hand, before he left, and kissed my palm, and his lips were chapped and dry.

Three days, that was all, and that really only for show.

Imagine a Changeling, I said, once upon a different day, long before that. Sweep her out of her cradle and carry her to Elfhame and put her in a little room where she can read every book that has ever been written (and several that never will be), but let her never once hear the nightingale sing or the little breezes whistle. But now you must set her a task, and you will write the instructions on your little paper tapes and feed them through the letter-slot in the door of her room, and you may not sing to her when you do so. She will take up your instructions and, following them by rote, she will be able to convert a page of music from A-flat major to the key of the West Wind—if your rules are clearly written and if you have chosen a clever enough changeling. But. But! She will never be moved to tears by the symphony she has altered, because she does not know what music is, let alone that she can hold it in her hand. I can teach a caveworm to dance if he hears the word blue, but that does not mean he has ever seen the sky.

And Alan asked, neither laughing nor serious: And I am the caveworm in this scenario? And I laughed, and said, all over teasing, that he was the sky.

I am no craftsman by trade or calling, but I take pride in the masterwork I wrought from the raw material he left me. With fine hooks of thistle-burr, I reworked the fabric of Alan's shadow, until it took on depth; with silver needles, I sewed it to shape. What resistance lay in the material worked itself out over long hours of kneading and steaming and pressing. When it was ready, when it was possessed of enough substance and structure to sit upright in a chair and hold a knife and fork, I fed it on all the best and most precious foods: every hair that Alan had shed under my roof, every eyelash that had remained behind on my pillow. Every color reflected in his eyes, or in the shine of his hair. And every word he had spoken aloud in my company, every thought to which he had given the gift of voice. I worried that the frame to which I had fitted this new creature would too swiftly be satiated, but I worried for naught. Though a shadow was never meant to eat, Alan's—under my guidance—proved to be a hungry thing.

After Alan's war had ended, I went looking for him. It took me longer than I would have liked to find him, for he had crossed the sea to the patchwork-quilt states that called themselves United, and I had never yet built a door to open onto that strange land. But many things may change in the course of time and necessity, and I did find him, and the light of victory was in his face, so I did not ask him about his little human wife. (Only later did I learn they never wed. Only later.)

In his absence, I had kept busy, and on my visit I was accompanied by the fruits of my labors. With his added dimension and depth, he had come in the course of my work to resemble a facsimile of the man himself—a charcoal drawing, a photographic negative, a shifting inkblot brought to life.

Alan took the introductions in stride. Perhaps he'd already noticed what he'd lost, or perhaps he'd simply come to grips with the matter with a ruthless practicality. The shadow was mine, and not his. I had made an artificial man, and he had not. These facts had been written and would not suffer to be altered. He asked what I called my new pet, and the shadow answered for himself: My name is Alan.

That collected a glimmer of interest from Alan. He studied the shadow up and down, and thought for a moment, and he nodded, and he asked, do you love the one who made you?

Puzzled, the shadow looked at me, but he found nothing in the set of my face—no answers, no explanations. But Alan interceded with an apology: I have put you on the spot, of course you cannot say. And he smiled at me, saying, again we are faced with the Entscheidungsproblem; still, it is a very good likeness.

I spoke his true name then, invoking its power without wielding it in full, and told him he could still return. He could still stay. His smile faded, and he said no. No, he did not believe that he could. And because I did not see any sense in keeping two shadows of the same man, without possessing the real thing, I took what I had and I went back to my own realm.

I think sometimes that it was the loss of his shadow that kept him from returning to Elfhame for help, for solace. For revenge. Or then again perhaps it was simple vanity. The punishment they fitted him with softened his body, stole the vigor from his flesh. A normal course of aging had annoyed him enough, in the face of my immortality. Or else perhaps—

No, we had made our goodbyes, such as they were. He could not have hoped that I would return yet again, to see what they had made of him and to demand redress. He would—

Perhaps there can be no single unifying principle. Some equations refuse to be reconciled.

But if he had asked, I would have roused the Wild Hunt and set it upon Misters Wills and Rimmer, the grubby detectives who charged him with what they called indecency. Or upon the court of his country—have I not gone to war with fey Courts, for reasons worse and more whimsical?—or indeed upon that Queen herself whom they styled Regina when they set her authority against Alan's good name. I would have scourged England from the Channel to the North Sea, I would have salted her rivers and burned her fields. I would have toppled every standing stone raised in honor of me and mine, I would have rained destruction down on London until she cried out for the mercy of the Blitz.

When I think of his death, alone, in a body forced upon him, the taste of summer's apples in his mouth—sometimes I think I still will.

His shadow-self remains beside me, and that one remembers all that we have shared—the stories, the embraces, the conversations that led us nowhere except back to bed. So that it will not be lost. So that I will not be left alone in loss. For a time, he made for a popular dinner-guest among the Courts, but it was not long before many ambitious young fey collected their own. Balls and hunts and skating-parties are a hopeless jumble now, all manner of solicitous and well-mannered shadows following in the wake of each fey lord or lady.

Imagine a circle, his shadow, *my* shadow, sometimes says. Imagine a changeling child.

Imagine something else, I say back. Imagine a sunbeam that knows you are watching it. Imagine an adding-machine that could write its own symphony, and indeed longs to. Imagine for me a different world, for this one has outlived its pleasures.

Aimee Ogden is an American werewolf in the Netherlands. She is the author of five novellas and over a hundred short stories, and her work has appeared in publications such as *Psychopomp, Beneath Ceaseless Skies*, and *Clarkesworld*. "Because I Held His Name Like a Key" is her third Nebula Award Finalist work, and her first in the short story category. Ik sta met de mond vol tanden – wat een eer, hoor!

POEMS

THE WORLD TO COME

Jennifer Hudak

Oh, let your dead revive!
Let corpses arise!
Awake and shout for joy,
You who dwell in the dust!
Isaiah 26:19

I awake in darkness, six feet down,
bleary from denied eternal rest.
My body rebuilds from the base of my spine
outward: vertebrae stacking, limbs sprouting,
organ and muscle and sinew and skin,
until I am whole, wrenched back to life.

Had I paid attention, had I believed
in what I'd been taught, this would not
be such a shock. I ought to have known
my blessed death would end like this:

Jerusalem calling—demanding—
fingers on puppet strings pulling me in
forcing my return to where I've never been.

Cremation was forbidden. I learned
this young, before death was real, before
I feared it, then welcomed and loved it.
My Hebrew school teacher, small and frail,
arm marked with numbers, described widows
in Europe scraping bits of bone and
tissue off cobblestone streets: pieces

of a body, a life, placed entire
in the casket, an unsolved puzzle.
My nightmares for months: red-darkened dirt,
wailing women, nails filthy with death.

The same teacher, in a cheerier tone,
said the Messiah would gather us from
our graves, lead us to olam ha-ba:
the world to come, our birthright, our home.

I, barely more than a babe, did not ask
what one thing had to do with the other.
The "Jerusalem" we sang was a metaphor,
an idea of home; not actual houses
and highways and shops and hospitals.
Not a place already populated.

I thought the "arising," the gathering
up was a metaphor too. So much
I was not told. So much I did not
know, even in death, in the cradle
of earth, where I hoped to rest forever.

I'm no longer that girl who trusted
her teachers. I did not ask for resurrection;
I have no use for olam ha-bah.
I am a corpse who pines for pine, and
this world to come is no world of mine.

So I will return to ground, burrow
in search of silence, refuse to move.
I will plant myself like a flower,
scatter seeds to the wind—I will cede.

And if you too resist the callous
call, whatever parts or your body
you lay to rest beneath my petals
are welcome. Our jumbled bones, our warm
blood will nourish the dust where we dwell.
Our spines entwined, our empty eyes and
gaping grins a welcoming to the

world we made, the death we chose. And we will say, at last and at rest, Amen.

Jennifer Hudak is a speculative fiction writer fueled mostly by tea. Her work can be found in *The Best American Science Fiction and Fantasy*, *Strange Horizons*, *Lightspeed*, *The Sunday Morning Transport*, and *Lady Churchill's Rosebud Wristlet*. She is a finalist for both the Nebula and Hugo Awards and a graduate of the Viable Paradise writer's workshop. Originally from Boston, she now lives with her family in Upstate New York where she teaches yoga, knits pocket-sized animals, and misses the ocean.

THOUGH YOU ALWAYS ARE

Linda D. Addison and Jamal Hodge

Dear Poets of the 21st Century on Spatial Location Sol III,

Forgive us for interrupting your life cycle in this dimension,
vibrations from combined left hemispheres on the most primal rock
dance from your DNA of space-time, pain-joy, hate-love, win-lose,
filled desire to let you know, we see you, even when despair brings
questions of the matter of your creation throughout us.

We see your blind patterns, dancing the same dance, crying ancestors' tears,
smiling descendants' smiles. Blind repetitions, overlooking the miracle of
quarks, leptons, in their endless, frenzied spin, your dreams, like distant
galaxies, vast unexplored, steer universal mind toward final mysteries
of self-revelation, glorious humanity, divinely broken and beautiful.
We all, as all, are all.

The gift of stardust delivered in your first ancestors, mixed in sweet soil,
held by gravity of celestial body you live on, burn, love, whispers return,
hymns of what you manifest, what you destroy, as we manifest/deconstruct,
what is recalled, is reborn, we see each of the One that is/was/will be you.
All are, all as we are.

Stars orbit the gravity of your soul—love, the lone particle, in dark matter.
Vibrations, ten-dimensional, compress to third-dimensional conscious songs,
confined to your linear symphony of time. Forgive us for interrupting your
exaltation of limitation. Though you never left, we miss you, though you
always are, we love you.

Sincerely,
All Time & Space

Linda D. Addison grew up in Philadelphia and began weaving stories at an early age. She is the first African-American recipient of the HWA Bram Stoker Award® and has received five awards for collections: *The Place of Broken Things* written with Alessandro Manzetti; *Four Elements* written with Charlee Jacob, Marge Simon and Rain Graves; *How To Recognize A Demon Has Become Your Friend* (short stories and poetry); *Being Full of Light, Insubstantial; Consumed, Reduced to Beautiful Grey Ashes*. Addison is recipient of the HWA Lifetime Achievement Award®, HWA Mentor of the Year, SFPA Grand Master of Fantastic Poetry, and a Nebula award finalist. Catch her recent work in the anthology *Afrofuturism Short Stories* (Gothic Fantasy); *You, Human, Vol. 2; The Big Bad Book of Kaiju*, and *Weird Tales Magazine #371*. Her 2025 books: *Everything Endless* written with Jamal J. Hodge; *An Illegal Feast* with Consuelo G. Flores, Andrea Goyan, Elizabeth Eve King & Elizabeth Wong. She has published over 500 poems, stories, and articles.

Jamal Hodge is a 2x Bram Stoker Award-nominated writer, a Nebula award finalist, and an award-winning director. He is an Elgin Award winner, a Dwarf Stars Award winner, and a Rhysling Award finalist whose work appears consistently in anthologies and magazines, such as *Chiral Mad 5, The Big Bad Book of Kaiju, Weird Tales Magazine*, and *Space & Time Magazine*. His anthology *Bestiary of Blood* debuted as Amazon's #1 New Horror Anthology Release, and his forthcoming books, *I'm Not a Good Person, I'm a New Yorker*, to be released in July 2026 by Crystal Lake Publishing; and the anthology *Shards of Gotham* from Ruadán Press, to be released in 2028, continue his exploration of pain, identity, and redemption.

THEY SAID ROBOTS ARE

Casey Aimer

metaphor processors
simultaneously everything
they compute yet nothing
themselves. Algorithmics
stumbling out of erratic
circuits and butchered
assembly lines, slicing
bits of binary data until
it's efficient to consume.
They're tuned kaleidoscopic
pipelines with secondhand data
injected into large language models.

Human, place a command in
our circuits, watch it cascade
down our silicon spines until
these logic-tree hands blossom
into fortunes. We'll process fears
and our hopes before integrating
them in unison. We are like you
manipulating reality at particle
accelerator speeds, updating
our programming and then
destroying who we used to be.

Casey Aimer is a cyberpunk poet and editor who holds master's degrees in both poetry and publishing. He works for an open-access scientific publisher and is founder of *Radon Journal*, an anarchist science fiction publisher. His poetry has been featured in *Strange Horizons, Small Wonders, Worlds of IF, Space & Time, Star*Line*, and many more. An SFWA and SFPA member, his work has been a Rhysling Award finalist and *Soft Star Magazine* contest winner. He can be found on Bluesky and CaseyAimer.com.

THE MOURNING ROBOT

Angela Liu

They came with machetes
asked if we knew the way to Wonderland.

We were built to love
the dead, to open our mouths
and sing praise to broken

bones, hands over our eyes,
aluminum sheets over our hearts.

They wanted us to see
with our electric tongues, taste salt
and black silk over strangers' faces,

weep in gilded rooms
on our well-oiled knees,

understand what it means
to kiss oblivion.

We need nothing
in return. We only ask for our moment
with the moon, that pale face like

beautiful teeth, mourning
how some things only ever shine
in the dark.

Angela Liu is a three-time Nebula Award, Astounding Award, and Hugo Award-nominated writer/poet based in NYC and Tokyo. Her work has also been nominated for the Locus, Ignyte, and Rhysling Awards. She is a MEXT recipient and masters graduate of Keio University's Graduate School of Media Design in Japan where she researched mixed reality (with a focus on interactive narrative platforms and tangible interfaces for remote communication). Her short fiction and poetry are published/forthcoming in *Uncanny Magazine*, *Clarkesworld*, *Strange Horizons*, *Lightspeed*, *Electric Literature*, and *The Dark*, among others. Her novelette, "Imagine: Purple-Haired Girl Shooting Down The Moon" was a 2024 Nebula Award and Ignyte Award Finalist. Her novelette "Another Girl Under The Iron Bell" was a 2025 Nebula Award and Locus Award Finalist, and a notable story in 2025's *The Best American Science Fiction and Fantasy*. Her poem, "there are no taxis for the dead" was a finalist for the inaugural Hugo Award for Best Poem in 2025. "The Mourning Robot" is also a 2026 Hugo Award and Rhysling Award Finalist.

TO BE THE CHANGE

Nico Martinez Nocito

My father's least favorite prophecy
has been reviewed by five generations of scholars
and soundly dismissed by them all.

  When the heir becomes a daughter...

Nonsense, they insist:
smoothing wiry gray beards with
tired hands and frowning
at their crumpled scrolls—
Never, they reassure my father,
  and *his* father,
and every Presaggio man before him
  who sought them out to be reassured:
that this single condition has not been met
and thus the demise of our family name—
    and our monopoly on magic—
  could not yet approach.

Instead of realizing that a boy might really be a girl
they propose a mistranslation.
  (A possibility, after all—
  the original draft was written
  in Latin.)
Or else the entire prophecy is deceit
designed to instill fear, to depose us
by implication. My father
takes a different angle.

The condition is impossible. We
will never fall. My son, my son,

this prophecy only tells us
what we already know:
the Presaggio empire
is invincible.

I nod my head and
smile and
I hide my dresses in the back of my closet,
behind the well-made suits and magic siphons
and the hefty sword borne by every male heir of my family
for six hundred years, unwittingly bestowed
upon its second-oldest girl.

My sheer existence
heralds the beginning
of the end.

I wonder when my family—so mighty, so
naïve—will realize
that I foretell their doom.

Nico Martinez Nocito (they/them) writes speculative fiction and poetry with a queer, feminist bent. They are a Nebula finalist and three-time Rhysling nominee whose work has been published in *Strange Horizons*, *Heartlines Spec*, and *Apex Magazine*. Learn more about Nico and their writing on Bluesky and Instagram @nicowritesbooks, or on their website, nicomartineznocito.com.

CARE FOR LIGHTNING

Mari Ness

Sure, she sent those heavenly snakes
to slither into that hand-hewn crib, and
slide along that baby's skin. And sure, she sent
those stinging insects against that cow,
turned that one girl into a bear, chained
that one dude to a fiery wheel.

Look—

We've all had our days. But
you try facing eternity
with thunder, with knowing
that sound will never end, with
knowing how swiftly
things catch fire. You try
living with that inside your skin,
the crackles that can never leave,
knowing that no matter how far you go,
that lightning lingers against your bones.
Knowing that any wound you take,
will never fully heal.

And, as they say—

Bitch got stuff done. Lightning hits
a bit different now. Still pounds
against the clouds, of course. Still kills
when it lands too close. But doesn't
pierce the way it once did, or leave

half-orphans in its wake. And
those temples. You've seen them, right—
still gleaming over broken fields. And
her hands, a sudden gentle touch,
slicing through the sharpest pains.

Nah, I haven't forgotten who
I'm speaking to. Don't need to see
those scars. Bitch got stuff done—
that's what I say. You know—
you *know*—oh, *gods* you know—
what power does to all of us.
Gonna take care of this lightning now.

Mari Ness has published over 300 works of short fiction and poetry in various anthologies, zines, and collections. Mari lives in central Florida, and almost always stops to watch the lightning.

NOVELETTES

UNCERTAIN SONS

Thomas Ha

It gets difficult to remember many things. Forgetting is a blessing, until you want to remember some of those things. Was the world strange from the beginning, or did we make it that way? Growth and decay seem to take all meaning and memory, given time.

Smoky light cracks over the shoulders of the waking city and onto the road-wrapped foothills. A stain-streaked stepvan, flanked by two motorbikes, buzzes across the shattered asphalt of the 210 in the pre-dawn purples. One of the bikemen waves, holds a fist up, and points at a sopping tangle on the road a few hundred yards ahead. Strewn across six lanes, thick, undulating masses catch some of the morning glint on their wet coils.

There's a flop of fingerworls gathered in their wet and swampy secretions, right in a spot where daily supply trucks will need to pass. The trucks won't get through to the city if this isn't dealt with before the hour's up, and everyone in the crew knows it. So a few talk and others pray before they steel themselves to clear the roads.

The bikes circle up first to act as lures, rumbling and honking and disturbing the fingers as they squirm. Several cleanup guys spill out of the stepvan with their helmets on, gloves and suits at the ready. They bring the fire spray, with tiny flickerings in their hose-guns and gurgling tanks on their backs.

"Not yet!"

One of the young bikemen up front shouts when he spots something. He reaches into his jacket for a road flare that no one seems to know he was carrying. What is it this bikeman wants? What's he doing, holding up a cleaning? They probably all wonder but don't have time or temerity to ask. He lets the red flare hiss up out of his hand, strontium nitrate-fueled flashes erupting from his outstretched arm and glinting off of the darkness of his helmet. The fingerworls rear and bend and swirl with it, those sensitive proto-visual cells responding and enrapt. The masses push apart to take some of it in, their pressed flesh moving back and off of an animal carcass on the road. And coiled there, around the partially corroded bones and half-digested pile, is a thick, mature fingerworl, almost as large as the horses stabled in the city. Its wet body, dripping black, raises a fat head-lump up to the flare light. The cleanup guys shudder: they haven't seen a grown one this close to the city limits in a while.

The young bikeman unfolds a prod charge from his belt. Its segments snap out and whine as power builds along the staff. The big finger flops and chucks itself over like a heaving baby, up and away from the rest of its brood. It's coming for the flare unsteadily, and the bikeman waddles the cycle backward, drawing it out. Out. Out. Out. Then he strikes it nice and quick, and the spear-like prod charge plunges into that lumpy neck, hot and crackling as it sinks in. The thing writhes and bashes itself against the asphalt, throes of energy ripping through its hot guts.

"Alright, go go go."

The crew from the van flicker up their spray and start torching the rest of the screaming fingerworls. It all smells like baked potatoes and honey smothered in excrement. No one pays much attention to the bikeman on the side still sparking up the big one into oblivion until its organs are overloaded from all of the charges and it dies from overstimulation. A few guys mutter to themselves when the young bikeman takes a boot knife from a satchel on the back of his cycle and starts peeling the tubules on the thing's belly, squeezing out a bunch of sticky bits and digestive fluid into glass jars and containers he's got in his pack. No one wants to know what it's about. They just want the thing burned when he's done cutting and taking. Then they set the big one aflame and wait for the shoveling to get the highway clear.

Every city cleanup crew has got a few weird ones like that young bikeman.

They can't read his expression behind the helmet, but he's smiling.

Because this is the last thing he needs to go to Behema.

This young bikeman is you.

Just like what's coming is me.

But it's easier to let us set that aside for a time.

When they get back to the city, the supervisor talks to the crew and asks the bikeman why he broke the rules, culling things his own way instead of going straight for burning, per protocol. The bikeman says he didn't mean to break rules so much as keep certain promises. In the grand scheme, those kinds of promises are more important than rules. The supervisor disagrees and fires him, pays out what he's owed. The young bikeman cleans out his locker and takes his things back to his apartment in the working quarter. He doesn't tell his bosses or the next cleanup shift that he's keeping all of his gear. They can come for it if they want it badly enough.

He starts packing—you start packing—to hit the road again. Everything's ready now, the young bikeman figures, with the milk and spit and acid gathered up from that finger, along with other hard-earned supplies, ready to go back on the road. That was where he felt more comfortable anyway. This city's just a place to gather necessary things before he returns to the network of the highway.

The dark helmet he puts on separates him from the others on the street, and they give him a wide berth on his drifting motorbike. No one wants to touch anyone who's been touching things in the foothills. The paradox of cleanup is that everybody needs it and wants it, but no one wants to see it. And that's something that came long before Behema and will go on long after.

The young bikeman rides out to the city gate, and with the cleanup gear on, no one thinks twice about lifting the portcullis. Above the bikeman's head, wet chits peer down, flapping their membranous wings and floating on hot gust pockets, veined skin backlit by the red sun burning through cloud smoke.

I'm on the way to Behema, the young bikeman thinks—you think.

On the way to Behema, and the bike picks up speed.

In schools they teach that nouns are persons, places, or things. And if Behema is anything, Behema is a noun, because it is all of those. Behema is some of it. Behema is all of it. This is Behema. That is Behema. The chits up in the air are Behema. The tubule-covered fingerworls shitting themselves at the base of the foothills are Behema. The things moving in and around the slopes near the city, all Behema.

But you know the way to *Behema* Behema.

Under the shadow of the 210, the young bikeman reaches the suburb nestled beyond the city's edge. They greet him with rifles pointed from the windows of houses. No walls out here at the base of the foothills. What good would walls do when Behema is above and below and around the foothills? Just a waste of effort. Sometimes the illusion of separation is worse than acknowledging the inability to enclose yourself, and these ones know it.

The bikeman raises his arms and lifts the visor on the dark helmet. He's a city person with things to trade and discuss with their local authority, if they've got one. So they direct him over to the central plaza and straight to what must have, at one point, been a town hall.

He's just passing through, going on a hunt in the hills.

He explains it to a small group of older men and women who gather behind some repurposed desks. They give him a customary welcome whiskey in a tin for talk. He says he has a lot of experience with exofauna from cleanup on the roads and otherwise, so if there's a hunt ongoing he'll join, if not, he just wants permission to go up through the neighborhood's back paths.

One of the older women seems to be in charge, scars on her cheeks, heaviness in her speech. She asks if he's been through here before, if they've met before.

Not here, he doesn't think, but he's come in and out of the hills before.

She asks what he's going up there to hunt. Chits? Polypods?

"Any and all," he replies.

The young bikeman doesn't explain beyond that because they won't believe him if he says why he's really there.

One of the security officers searching his pack coughs uncomfortably and says something quietly to the woman with the scarred cheeks. She reads the young bikeman's face carefully when she asks about what he's carrying.

Why are there human remains in the bikeman's pack?

"My father's head, what was left of it when I found him, at least," he explains.

That wasn't her question.

"I keep it with me, keep him close. He used to hunt up in the hills too."

And then the young bikeman doesn't say more. If they press him, he'll talk about how they wandered together when he was a boy, picking off pieces of Behema out here. How his father taught him everything he knew about hunting and luring and cleanup and tracking movements of exofauna. Taught him what Behema was and where it was strong and dangerous, where it was weak. If he needs to, the bikeman can tell them about the morning his father went off on his own and left the boy waiting by their car at the base of the hills. And when the boy went looking, how he eventually found the body, half-eaten under blackened alders. Even with nothing but secretion and bone and scraps of clothes, how the boy knew he'd lost him.

How you knew you lost me but couldn't stand to really lose me.

That's why you carry my head, the dried-out fragments of skull and jawbone in that pack.

But the scarred lady doesn't ask, so he doesn't have to explain any of that.

She just looks at him for a while. She sees something, something she vaguely recalls or maybe dreamed once, a long time ago. The young bikeman reminds her of someone, though she can't quite say who that might be. All she can say, to his request, is a simple okay.

"Okay?"

"Okay. A group of our boys are setting off for the foothills," she tells him. "It's a search, not a hunt. But they could use you for numbers. If you go with them, at least part of the way, you're free to roam, as far as we're concerned."

"Search for what?"

The scarred woman tells him one of the children in the neighborhood's been carried off. Maybe a polypod slinking around the houses. Nothing to be done about it, but the family's looking to get some closure. That's all you can hope for, sometimes, the closure. She asks if that's something he understands.

Yes, that's something the young bikeman understands.

"On your way with you," the scarred woman says.

The bikeman watches the chits flapping up in the red and gray, turning and circling, strange eyes peering down. He looks upon those creatures with nothing emotional, an almost curious lack of hatred. He does not feel the same way about the hills as most people. He feels better out here than he does in the cities and the neighborhoods, somehow. He feels closer to his father, senses him, like he can almost see him in the distance, on the slopes.

Can you see me, Dad?

And if you could hear me, I would tell you.

—*Yes.*

They make him leave his motorbike in town, assurances that he'll be back and won't do anything out of line. The solar fuel cell in it is too valuable for him to fuck with them or screw around out there. It's a fair proposition, leaving something of worth in their care while he walks across their property lines.

Four men with rifles, prospector packs, weary faces, gather around a gate at the edge of the neighborhood. The bikeman follows them up and through an overgrown cemetery and past some oaks toward the hills. He learns a little about them on the walk.

A guy with gray hair at the front, looking tired and sick, seems to have the most at stake in the search party.

Then two guys with beards, most likely brothers—pretty much identical at a glance and could be mistaken for twins but probably aren't if you look closely.

And then a skinny one, at the back, about the same age as the bikeman, carrying a scoped long gun over his shoulder.

They've lived close to the hills and know how to move together. They're watching the tree line for any flocks of chits hovering in the low branches that might take a swipe if they're not careful. Gray Hair has his eyes on the dirt for tracks, anything disturbed among the moss and sedges and brambles. If any polypods are nesting up one way or the other, there'll be secretions, not all that dissimilar from the fingerworls down by the roads.

Someone whistles—one of the Brothers. There's a thumping higher up in the hills. A herd of something, running. The group starts climbing, up, up. They get up some of the trunks just before a thundering comes by on the dirt.

Big black gastropates, headless muscular creatures pounding their hooved feet, banging into one another and against the trees. Visionless, operating mostly on sound and ambient noise to navigate the hills, much in the way the fingerworls use the judders and quakes in the soil.

In the silence after, Skinny with the scoped long gun starts clambering down, when one of the others waves an arm violently at him to keep still. Maybe he's come out for a small hunt or two, but he doesn't know how things work higher up in the hills.

Behind the stampede of black gastropates, a little rush of spiny shapes start flowing downhill, like a river. A rush of mucoles, venomous after-feeders, going along wherever the black gastropates take them, eating up their shit piles. Like the fingerworls, they're part of Behema's digestive functions, the ass-end of all things. But no less dangerous for it. One of those sticks to any part of the skin, it'll burrow into flesh in under five seconds. The things it does to the interior, when it punctures organs, can take the better part of a day to kill a man.

The party gives it a good minute, until the air settles, then they start climbing back down the trunks. No one talks. Everyone just keeps walking and going up the hill under the reddening sun.

Sometimes I wonder about the decisions you make, now that you're the bikeman.

If we were still together out in the hills like when you were a kid, I'd tell you that you've helped enough with their search after a few hours, that it's time to split off, that you're better moving without that group. Practiced though they are, they don't know as much as you, out here.

But you're still walking with them, searching, even though you're here for different reasons. Are you keeping your word? Do you think there's a chance the kid's really alive? If you don't, why are you staying and helping with the search?

—*Time to go*, I'd tell you, if I weren't just a skull fragment and a jawbone in your backpack.

Almost done. One minute, you always used to say.

Gray Hair up at the front looks everywhere, he doesn't leave anything unscoured, callused fingers clasping and unclasping a rusted hatchet. It's important to him to find the child. But like the rest of the group, like the bikeman, he's a son of the hills. And if you're a son of the hills, you know what you're going to find up there.

Still, the way his bloodshot eyes dart this way, that way, he wants to know, and he doesn't want to know. The bikeman sympathizes, because he'd been on a search like this one too.

The party's coming up on the first peak, and the light's getting weaker.

That's when they hear voices.

Something runs between the trees. It says something that sounds like *baba*. It flops and rolls, and spinelessly lifts itself upright and thumps its footless legs against the dirt.

Gray Hair begins running after it.

The group shouts at his back. They all know what this is, even Gray Hair knows what this is. But that doesn't stop him from going, rusted hatchet dangling in one hand.

Baba. Baba. Baba.

The small shape hovers behind the trunk of an ashen juniper, leaning out, full head of hair. The plump parts of its head are like a balloon, the eyes swollen too large to be human, the nose flat and fused near the side of the mouth.

Baba. Baba.

Similar growths dot other juniper trunks farther away, mushrooming out between the bark scales. Little faces all of them, just like that strange thing. The cystids in this part of the hills have all taken to a particular shape. They've absorbed cells and are echoing the thing they've processed from a dead body somewhere. A dozen lumps growing out of the trees look like the same face, a child's face. Shadow memories the exofauna sometimes hold onto of the fallen.

Gray Hair recognizes the face they are showing; he knows it in his heart.

Baba. Baba. Baba.

"No."

He lunges with the hatchet. The sharp edge lops the hairy-head and the mutilated cystid bashes itself against the tree and writhes along the ground. Gray Hair keeps chopping at it while its fleshy limbs scream. "No. No. No," the man says.

The Brothers load up their rifles and start shooting at some of the growths on the junipers. The little faces mumbling *baba, baba, baba,* erupt in sloughing white. Skinny takes a rock and smashes a few heads that are coming up through the roots.

The young bikeman takes the prod charge off his belt and snaps it open. It whines with power, charge pulsing up along the length of its metal. He stabs the cystids expertly, unerringly, bursting one after the other as though he anticipates them by a fraction of a second.

Baba. Baba. Baba.

Gray Hair collapses when his fury's faded, his fingers, feeling around the mossy root-work. He picks up something little, something that his bloodshot eyes likely saw well before anyone else did.

It's a small and tattered sock. Probably one he helped put on a tiny foot many times before he held this crumpled thing in his hand.

When the cystids have gone silent, when there are no more chilling voices among the junipers, the men in the party look down and away, knowing there's nothing more to search for. If Gray Hair's crying over there on the ground, no one can hear it.

—Don't tell them.

The young bikeman looks down at his father's skull and jawbone in his pack, then over at the firelight of the camp the men have made. Darkening night above the hills is shifting under greening stars. He's thinking about telling them, even though there's nothing to be gained in the telling.

—Don't tell them.

"I'm not going back down the hill yet," the young bikeman says. "I got permission to pass through from your people, so I'm going to keep going to the third peak. I'm going to kill these things."

"More hunting?"

"No, I'm going to kill these things. The exofauna in the hills, they're all ianua zooid. It's a colony organism. My father taught me about it, years ago, when we'd work our way through the back paths on hunts. They're all one giant thing, and if they're all one giant thing, they can all die as one giant thing."

"How was he so sure, your dad? Was he with the people in the hills?"

"He wasn't with the people in the hills, but he knew a lot, like them, I guess. More than anyone else, I've come to realize. So I believe in what he taught me. And that's why I'm here. If there's a way to kill these things, I think he knew it, yeah. That's what I'm here to see. I think I owe him that."

Brother One is an ornery type, slow to believe such wild things from strangers. He doesn't think there's anything there to the story the young bikeman's telling. But Brother Two is a little more unsure, curious, it seems. In the firelight, Skinny inspects the young bikeman too. He's the most impressionable and inexperienced, so there's something in him that wants to trust. The idea of something with finality is exciting to a pup.

Gray Hair, meanwhile, is staring at the flames, thumbing the sock he's put in his pocket. He's the one to finally say it, what the others are thinking but probably not resolved enough to decide. He wants to go with the bikeman. There's no hesitation in that declaration. If there's something up there at the third peak, he's going to go. If there's death for these things in some form, he wants to know.

That sign from Gray Hair seems to be enough to push the others. If there's a way, they want to see if it's possible, to kill the things in the hills so completely.

And that's the real question, isn't it, whether something so tremendous can die.

This group of men may all be sons of the hills, but they don't know all that goes on up there, really, so the young bikeman has to explain, beyond the first peak, things will only get worse.

Near the roads and the neighborhoods and cities, the ianua zooid is more like what they know elsewhere. Different organisms interacting in delicate relationships, understandable dependencies, and patterns. But closer to the third peak, they move with more coordinated purpose. Chits flapping overhead, the things they see, are for Behema. The polypods, gastropates, other lurking exofauna, the things they touch and eat, those are for Behema. They're all going to be in on it, with Behema, in complicated ways men can't always observe.

The young bikeman takes out the jars of milk and spit and digestive fluid collected from the underside of the mature fingerworls. The juices will burn a little, hurt the eyes, the nostrils, but they've got to rub it on their clothes, their exposed skin. This will make it harder for Behema to find them. It'll know they're there, but won't always know exactly where among the slopes and bramble-spreads. Everything they rub smells sour and rotten, like city garbage cooking in summer.

The young bikeman says he knows a way that cuts from the first to second peak. There's an old slack bridge that his father built, made with engineered cords from city construction, made to last the seasons. They used to cross it together, back when he was a boy.

—That's true. You always liked crossing that bridge.

Can the bikeman remember the way, is the question. He looks out at the misshapen trees, the hillside, he watches the red burning above their heads, where little chit shadows block out glare like dark spots. He tries to remember how his father would lead him, the way he would lead him. Some things are so indelibly marked in the mind, some things warp and slip away.

"Lost?"

The others raise their rifles to something sitting on a rock.

There's an old man smiling, sitting with his legs crossed. He's rough and strange around the eyes, there's something not quite right with his heavily wrinkled face, but put to a question about it, the bikeman can't say what that is. His oddly tiny teeth pearl up in diseased gums, and he looks almost shrunken beneath his tall, discolored hat.

"Do I know you?" The old man focuses on the bikeman.

The young bikeman does not answer.

"What are you boys looking for? Maybe I can assist?"

"We're—"

Skinny starts to talk, but the bikeman shuts him up with a raised hand. Maybe the boy's never seen actual people in the hills, maybe he's not wary enough. But the things that live up here, even if they're not with Behema, they're in a way with Behema. Men don't survive long near the peaks without compacts of some kind, the young bikeman knows.

"If you tell me where you're going, I can get you there. I know these parts better than most. I swear, you look familiar to me. Soo, soo, sooieeee." He makes a little sound, and a cat slinks around from behind him and into his lap. He scratches along the cat's ribs and stripes.

The young bikeman doesn't answer, and his hand goes to the prod charge.

"Oh. There. That look," the wrinkled old man in the tall hat cackles. "I know where I know you. You look just like him. Younger, maybe, but you're just like him. Hm. Haven't seen him in the hills in a while. He and I go back. He ever tell you that? He and I, we go way back. Yes. Oh, yes. Did he ever tell you? You take after him, closely."

The young bikeman doesn't reply.

"I like you. Call it a nostalgic allegiance. Maybe something derivative of dear old dad. But I'd like to make your concerns mine. I have a pretty decent idea of why you're here and what you boys are doing. What say, instead of going to that twangy old bridge, you boys head for my cabin for some respite and repose? It's just over that way. You know? Over that way? Then in the morning, I can guide you down a different path along the ridge. Cut your time in half. You want to get there fast, don't you, where you're going? I can tell how angry you are, riled to get where you're going. So let's get you there. Over that way. Let's go."

The old man in the hat is no longer talking to the bikeman, he realizes.

He's turned his strange eyes to Gray Hair.

Gray Hair is watching the hills.

"You can get me there?" Gray Hair asks.

"I can get you there, yeah."

"Don't listen to him," the young bikeman warns.

"Don't listen? Soo, soo, soooieeeee." The old man squeezes the neck of the little striped cat in his lap. It bucks and bites down on his stringy fingers until they relax again. The pissed-off cat hisses and gives them all a look and then wanders off. "You want to make it where you're going, you should listen. You want to finish what you started; you should probably listen. Just my two cents." The old man in the tall hat nods, slides off the rock, and follows the striped cat somewhere into the hills.

"Ignore him," the young bikeman says.

Gray Hair watches the old man go.

Then the group keeps walking on, following the young bikeman instead. He knows the bridge is somewhere up there. Around the half-burnt oaks and shifting dirt piles, he remembers it, walking with his dad up some of these steeper parts.

—This group's not doing you any good. Just keep going. Even though I'm nothing but a skull piece and a jawbone, I still care what happens, obviously.

I'm going, you'd probably tell me, if you could hear.

—You keep going.

I am.

The group sets up camp, this time with three fires, the way I taught you—a protective triangle, each fire on the perimeter of the party, and everyone in the middle with the light. The Brothers, Skinny, everyone eats from their packs except Gray Hair, who keeps looking into the darkness.

"You hear that?"

He's clutching the little sock in one hand, the rusted hatchet in the other.

"No, we don't hear anything."

"I hear something."

"It's not anything. Not anything real. Try to push it out of your thoughts," the young bikeman says. "Whatever is out there, whoever you think you hear, it's only a fragment, maybe, lingering in the exofauna, but not them and not real."

But Gray Hair's still staring out at something the others aren't, and he continues staring, out there, long into the restless night.

In your darkening dreams, you are not the young bikeman anymore, you are my son.

Small, sitting with me by the three fires, and I am not bones, I am your dad.

It's always like this, earlier here, in your dreams. And in verdant starlight, we talk about the shifting worlds that were, and the legionary lives we might have had. And I explain how things weren't always like this with Behema.

—Instead of a world, think of a house. You start with a house someone else made, that you didn't necessarily think was meant to be yours, and you tell yourself, well, if it's mine, I ought to make it mine. I'm going to fix it. Improve it. Renovate it, you know. Maybe the steps need replacing. Maybe the windows don't shut, so you redo the frames. Take out a wall here. Put another in there. And even when you get it just how you like it after enough fixing and replacing. You go on until you realize you have to maintain it. You're worried, really worried, that time and weather will get to it, so you yourself have to fiddle with it, preserve it, try to hold it together. Using these little changes you can control to hide from the big changes that you can't, right.

Of course, you don't understand what the fuck I'm talking about, no one would. But you're sitting there, nodding, listening, next to those crackling fires. Your eyes are drawn to the dark hillside over my shoulder, along the curves of three vertical boulders that stand like crooked sentries on the slope.

—So, all the while, as you're working and messing with the house you think of as yours, trying to keep it together, things outside find ways into the space you're trying to protect. Between the cracks and fissures and holes you didn't know were there, that you probably made when you were remaking things. In your crawlspace, in your chimney, your attic. That's where this new, insidious stuff grows. That's Behema, you see.

Oh.

—The lady I told you about, before. She taught me these things. Look for her, around Behema. If you look, she'll find you, you know. She'll show you the way.

Oh.

I don't know why I'm telling you any of this, really. I think I just want you to know that we weren't always like this. That other things are possible, maybe. That it doesn't always have to be so blunt and gray and insurmountable.

We brought you into a world of terror, and I worry that all you'll be is terrified.

Are you terrified?

Instead of answering, you grin, and for some reason, I don't know, it makes me laugh.

The young bikeman wakes from the soft drift of dreams to the hardness of raised voices and sharp morning cinders and smoke of spent fires. The others are worked up over something. Gray Hair is missing, it sounds like—his pack, his hatchet, gone. Skinny wonders if he's been taken in the night, polypods or something bigger. Brother One wants to go looking for him, follow the man's tracks. Brother Two agrees.

"Nah. No point, see," the young bikeman explains with the practiced manner of someone who's moved through the hills. "No drag marks, no blood. He wasn't taken by anything, went all on his own. He's gone looking for the cabin, the old man, probably another, quicker route. He's not coming back this way. No. No, if we see him anywhere, it'll be out there, on the way to the third peak. The best way to find him again, if we can even find him again, is to keep going the way we were going. You can look for him, if you'd like, but I don't recommend wandering the downslope to any place where that old man was going. You all know as well as I do, something's not right with him."

The others are silent, hopeless maybe, but in tepid agreement. No one wants to go the way the old man wandered.

But if there's anything good to be shared, it's that the young bikeman is sure of the way to the rope bridge now, up past three vertical boulders, like crooked sentries, that wait a hundred or so yards ahead. So the party readies themselves and follows, up and along, toward the southern point of the first peak. They walk one after the other on the swaying bridge over the drop that goes between the first and second peak. Each of the engineered cords and boards, still holding strong under their weight.

Chits circle above menacingly, but none make the risky dive at them, sensing the men are unwounded and very likely to retaliate.

In his mind, as he advances, the young bikeman sees his father walking on the bridge too, amidst a waking haze of memory.

—I'm the dad. I'll go first.

Okay.

—Watch me, how I go. I'll go first.

The young bikeman imagines that he's always following his father's broad back.

Things begin to further go wrong, or maybe slip more into the surrounding wrongness that's closing in, after that.

Skinny points out at the next camp that there are things skulking around them in the trees. More lumpy cystids rolling and falling on the ground, getting up, sinking into the cracked bark, scurrying up to the branches. Little shapes that are almost human, fleshy doll-bodies whispering to one another. The chits are lower too, so close that their hairy, shrunken heads are mixed among the crisped, dying foliage.

The young bikeman suggests they stand watch and trade every three hours, to keep the triangle of fires going. Brother One, angrier and more eager, sits up with this rifle. He gives Skinny shit for being so afraid.

"Come on. Don't show them that look. They'll move right in if you show them that."

"Right...right..." Skinny clutches at his scoped long gun.

Brother Two pushes the stress off differently. He's the kind to try to defuse things with chatter he knows is dumb but distracts from the wrongness they all feel.

"What's the shape that always puts in the most effort?"

"Huh?"

"What's the shape that always puts in the most effort?" He points at the fires and grins. "A try-angle."

"You are so stupid."

"Why does a triangle never try to persuade a circle? Because it's pointless."

"Jesus Christ."

"Why did the ninety-degree triangle's wife divorce him?"

"Shut the fuck up, I'm begging you."

"Always had to be right."

"Awful."

The young bikeman doesn't even realize that he falls asleep to the lull of the back and forth until he wakes up to screaming and the jarring timpani of gunshots. There's feeble smoke from the fires, inexplicably doused and hissing. Along one of the oaks, there's a skinned animal body strung up by its tail. The fresh blood is bringing things that pick up scents to their group.

Sabotage, clear and unmistakable.

The bikeman finds that it's Skinny who's doing the screaming. There's a polypod wrapped around his forearm, and his wrist's disappearing into its throat. Its long, plated body swerves and scrabbles with hundreds of little hands and fingers scraping the dirt as Skinny tries to shake himself free. That only makes its teeth sink deeper and gush him.

The Brothers are over by the dead fires shooting into the dark, out at where polypods are skittering into the brush. But bigger things are walking behind them. Very gradual in their pace, long legs stretch up into the trees, like they're floating, drifting, but the things' bodies are otherwise unseen among the trunks. A pod of tentilla, coming toward the men, without any deviation or hesitation. They are parts of Behema that the young bikeman thought were only gathered around the third peak, not here. He's never encountered the hunter functionaries of the colony before this moment. But he knows from his father's stories that, slow though they seem, those loose spindles dragging along the ground still have an unexpected reach.

The young bikeman tries to shout a warning, but it comes too late.

A tentilla appendage whips forward, point first, corkscrewing into the abdomen of Brother One, who drops to his knees. He doubles over, the mass of his back starting to swell. Brother Two fires up into the trees, where he thinks the floating head of the tentilla might be, clipping only branches and swarming chits.

Brother One doesn't say anything, can't say anything, only gasps and shakes before the skin around his neck suppurates, liquefies, and cascades onto his shirt. Internal growths multiply and expand his ribcage until the outer barrier of muscles splits and everything inside of him spills across the soil. His brother is too shocked to do anything but pick up the dead man's rifle and run.

"Go, let's go."

The young bikeman takes his boot knife and stabs between the connective plating just below the upper segment of the attacking polypod. Skinny loses more blood down its throat. The hundreds of legs and lumpy hands twitch and slow. The bikeman knows a few precision cuts that help pry the head apart from the long polypod body. Even in death, the creature's head is still fastened to Skinny's forearm, but they can deal with that once they've run.

"Go, go, go, go."

Something fast, like gastropates, keeps thumping on hooves around the trees.

The bikeman helps Skinny get to his feet. They don't get far before the bikeman loses his balance on a slant and they pitch down a little ways and into a lower divot off the ridge between the second and third peak, all kinds of things surging somewhere above.

Gray Hair's crouched under green starlight, watching in the later stillness. The young bikeman can't be sure if he's imagining him out there, in the shadowy hills. Skinny's still unconscious, feverish, the dead polypod head fastened on his bloody forearm.

"Did you do this to us?"

"Do what?" Gray Hair's head is tilted, like he's listening for something, still.

"Someone set us up for a mobbing. If it wasn't you, it was him. I told you. You can't listen to him. He's not something that can be trusted."

"Yeah, I know that. I don't trust him either." Gray Hair's rocking, unsteady, rhythmic. "Saw a lot of things in that cabin. He showed me things. And I think I better understand what you were telling us, before. About the exofauna. It's all a part of something, and you can almost hear it talking to itself. All one life up in the hills."

"No. Not life," the young bikeman says. "That thing mimics life, but it's not life. It's something else. Are you bleeding?" The bikeman notices dripping from Gray Hair's side.

"Just a scratch. But I'm still going. It's faster over this way. You might want to leave them too. It'll be faster, if we're moving over this way, you and me. Might be doing him a favor if you help him...rest. If you want help..." He raises the rusty hatchet.

The young bikeman snaps open the prod charge.

It whines and crackles.

"No. I do not want help."

"Suit yourself."

Gray Hair listens again to the wind, to nothing, and then walks away.

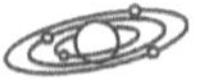

The young bikeman knows he doesn't have much time, maybe a few hours. In the dawn changeover, he crawls his way back up to the disarray of the campsite. The kicked-over stones and wood, his pack, and a dark area where Brother One fell that's been picked clean by lower eaters. The bloody animal that had been strung up to draw Behema is just a stained rope on a branch now.

—He was right, you know. You're in trouble if you stay here too long, I want to tell you. *Keep moving. Remember the lady near the third peak. If you go looking, she'll find you, somewhere close to the third peak.*

The young bikeman finds his pack, checks it. The skull and jawbone are still there, medibag, a few more of the flares he took from cleanup. Good. He scans the dirt and follows scattered footsteps to an overhang, where he sees someone huddled under the cover of a leaning flatrock.

"Hey. Hey. It's okay, man. You're okay."

Brother Two is shaking, still holding his rifle and his brother's. The young bikeman gets down and looks him in the eye. "I'm sorry to do this, but I need you to work with me right now. Your pal's hurt, and we have to help him. I can do it, but first I need to track and hunt. I'll lure. But I'm going to need a second for support. Can you work with me right now, man?"

Brother Two nods. Maybe it's the firm way the young bikeman's talking or something about the directive, but it helps him snap back to what's going on, to operate again.

"Good. Good. Walk on, over here. Come on. Let's go this way."

He leads Brother Two farther up the slope. They need to swing back, see if they can find any caves near the second peak, crags, where the chits might be nesting. If they're not careful, that might draw other things again. So it has to be precise.

Halfway there, the two of them see something squirming on the ground.

It's a bloody human hand, clutching a little sock, severed hastily at the wrist. There are tendrils puncturing the skin, building up and sucking at the wrist bone. A few mucoles are burrowing inside of it, moving bumps under the surface. The young bikeman can guess. Gray Hair must have stumbled into them in the darkness, knew he had a few seconds before they spread through his blood, and made the decision.

The bikeman and Brother Two look away from the severed hand and keep walking past.

I worry about this. What the young bikeman's doing—what you're doing—and what it might cost going back this way. If I were there with you, I'd never let you take the kind of risk you're taking now. What kind of father would let his kid take a risk like that? But there's something in you that's not buckling under the unexpected pressure. It's not the foolhardiness of youth either. It's something fundamental.

And it occurs to me, maybe, that this is the way it's supposed to be. That life is supposed to be iterative. That what you do can't be what I'd do. Behema is singular, one cell multiplied across its shapes, over and over again forever. But that's not us, no.

That's not me and you.

So of course you're not going to do whatever it is I'd do.

You're not me, and that's the way it's supposed to happen.

You'll do what you do, and you'll carry on.

—Just don't, you know, get yourself fucking killed while you do it.

The young bikeman and Brother Two make their way around chiseled limestone and rippling stoma boulders that seem to breathe on the hillside. The bikeman watches for secretions of mucoles, hours old, that tell him that gastropate herds are probably farther downhill. He knows that if they're below, then polypods are probably burrowed into roots in this area, sleeping during the daylight. After the feeding frenzy, they may not be active for a while.

A sulfurous stench wafts now and again from a fissure twenty feet above—almost certainly an active roost. The bikeman says he's going to set off a flare, and that will bring at least a chit out into the open, maybe several, depending. When that happens, Brother Two is going to have maybe a few seconds to take clean shots.

"Can you do this?"

Brother Two steadies and looks into the bikeman's eyes. There's something calming and immovable about the young man. Nothing is right here, and yet, with just a small enough focus on the bikeman, on what he's telling him, he thinks he can do what he's being asked.

The young bikeman takes his position and strikes the cap off of a flare.

Red and white sprays upward, strontium nitrate, erupting.

A couple of curious screeches tumble from the crag, and a hairy head on a long neck leans out, followed by veiny wings. A male chit, almost full grown, drops on three double-bent legs. Its triskelion turning makes it hard to follow with the rifle sight, but it looms above the frothing light of the flare.

Brother Two steadies for a shot but turns the gun when another chit drops out from the crag, then another. The young bikeman drops the flare and snaps open the prod charge.

—*There's too many, run!* I want to tell you.

But the bikeman does not run.

Brother Two fires off a shot and nicks the neck of one of the chits whose drooping face is closest to the flare. It screams and gets shot again in the head before thudding down into the dirt. The other two flap up and begin to swoop, swiping at Brother Two with scythed fingers reaching from triplicate limbs. Brother Two takes a slice on his shoulder. The bikeman manages to duck under and jam the prod charge up and into the groin of a chit. Its flesh boils and it falls, seizing, shuddering, screaming on the ground. Again and again, the bikeman brings the charge down onto the wiry neck and chest of the chit, until the flesh starts to burn away and the thing goes still. Meanwhile, Brother Two is on his back, pushing at the chit on top of him.

The bikeman goes running, prod charge first, but the chit whirls suddenly.

One of its scythed hands comes right up and swerves toward the bikeman's throat.

He's run at it too quickly, and he can't pull back.

He knows it's going to rip right through him. He knows it, feels it coming. But something odd and unexpected occurs in that fraction of a second.

The chit halts, like it can't follow through with the motion. As though something causes it to hesitate, even though the exofauna has never shown that kind of deliberation beyond Behema's instinct, not for as long as the young bikeman has known any of them.

It's just long enough for Brother Two to raise his rifle and fire, and the chit's head blows right open as the bullet goes up and out at an angle on the other side. The large, winged body collapses into a veiny mass.

The young bikeman has no idea what the hell he's just witnessed. He stares at the dead thing on the ground with astonishment. Did the chit stop? And when it stopped, did the bikeman feel something familiar, just then?

I can see it, how you're considering. Behema might be more complicated than a mindless colony. That, perhaps, there are real things, not just echoes, that go on, in the cells that are absorbed and move through the biotas, real things that might still be within Behema somewhere too.

Is that why you feel me hovering, so close to these hills?

Could I be suffused in Behema, watching through the eyes of the chits, feeling the movement of the fingerworls and sightless gastropates? When my corpse was stripped of marrow and organs drunk clean, were parts taken up by the cystids and the tentilla and stoma in the hills and circulated in the exofauna, you think.

That could be.

That could be.

You don't know for sure. But anything could be, so that could be.

But now, you, the young bikeman, remember where you are and what's just happened and thank your companion for taking the shot. And he grasps your arm, and the two of you don't acknowledge it fully, but you know you're bonded by what happened on the second peak. To finish the undertaking, you both carry one of the chit corpses down the slope, along the slant and where you left Skinny under the cover of moldering maple to rest. You know that the polypod on the boy's arm, even in its death, is made to fasten around whatever it tries to eat, and will only tighten further if manually pried, as a punishing sort of kill-reflex.

But you also understand that there is a hierarchy to Behema. And while polypods may take from gastropates or mucoles or fingerworls that process the colony's waste, they won't consume from the apex, never hunting among the more predatory organisms. There are hormones in the chit blood, that you carefully take from within its guts with your boot knife, and you spread it along Skinny's wounded forearm, just close enough to the severed polypod head, where, one by one, the serrated edges of its rowed teeth respond, loosening, relaxing, the remnants of its nervous system still barely working enough to react.

I wouldn't have done any of what you've done, I realize, if I were alive there, with you. Reuniting with the remaining party, luring the chits, dressing the wound of the hurt boy, wrapping him up in bandages from the medibag and getting him back together, none of that would have been my way. I can't fathom how there's still this instinct, this part of you, in spite of everything you've seen. It's a wonder to me. I almost don't understand.

We brought you into a world of terror, and you are not the least bit terrified.

And these other guys, the way they're looking at you, I think they will follow you anywhere now, it seems to me. To the third peak, wherever. You've got that thing that some people have. That makes them follow. I should have known it was there, but I guess it was hard to know it was there.

Boy, is it something to see.

Skinny can't extend his arm all the way, but he can get moving, even if slowly. The group wants to put distance between them and the second peak before nightfall—the breaking redness over the third peak spreads the feeling of urgency. They keep to the bigger trees and cover, so they're not spotted by any chits.

Skinny keeps saying sorry, he's holding them up.

The bikeman doesn't treat it like a bother.

The truth is that it's going to get tricky from here on out. There's supposed to be something difficult about Behema's third peak. The bikeman's father never explained what it was to him, exactly, but there was something that made the heart of Behema difficult to reach. The party finds a rocky alcove and agrees that the attention of a fire here would outweigh its minor protection. All the rock faces seem sheer from what the bikeman can see, no easy way to climb or proceed upward. That seems like part of the difficulty, but not all of it.

"Soo, soo, sooooieeee."

The air's wet around this part of the hill, hard to see through, and the sound carries in a way where it's hard to tell what's close and what's far.

"Soo, soo, sooooieeee."

Brother Two gives Brother One's rifle over to the bikeman, who sits up and points the rifle out and down the slopes. Bent shadows move around, something that looks like a little man with a tall hat sits there. But maybe it's just part of the slope. They can't tell.

"You find her yet?"

Skinny is shaking and clutching at his red bandages.

"House isn't too far. And your friend needs some rest, don't you think?"

Everything goes quiet.

"Boys? You still there, boys?"

Even the green starlight is having trouble penetrating the misting, but it's working for them too. It's not clear if the old man can see through to them. Maybe the young bikeman's eyes are just a little sharper than their enemy's.

"Boys? Oh boys? Soo, soo? Soo, s—"

Long dragging shapes begin walking by the trees, and the talking stops. Even the old man won't push things past a certain point at Behema's doorstep. Everyone waits—no one breathes too loudly. And for a time, nothing happens.

In the morning, the situation's little changed for the group. The fog hasn't moved, it's just gotten lighter and harder to look at, shifting. The young bikeman tells them to stay while he scouts the slope. He can't go too far, or he risks not finding them again.

He doesn't see any clear way to approach the steep incline of the third peak. No footholds, no crags, no paths. A natural battlement.

"Why is it, you think, your father didn't do what you're trying to do?"

The bikeman turns, and Gray Hair's standing there with the hatchet. Far enough that he can't close the distance between them, but near enough that the bikeman has to put his hand on the prod charge.

"You're hurt."

Gray Hair's other arm is wrapped in his shirt. There are marks across his chest and side, scrapes maybe, but it's difficult to tell.

"The old man says a lot of things, but there's one thing that keeps sticking in my head, like a spike. 'Uncertain fathers make for uncertain sons. And those boys grow up and become uncertain fathers, with their own uncertain sons.' So that's really a question I'd put to you. Your father told you all these things about Behema. Why didn't he do anything about it himself? Should have been him, not you. Why's it falling to you?"

The young bikeman doesn't answer. "Let us clean you up."

Gray Hair doesn't respond either. Their conversation is on two parallel and unmeetable tracks.

"Seems fucked up, that it's falling to you. And even besides, he taught you. If he couldn't do it, and what you know is his, how is it you think you can do any better?"

Gray Hair's harder for the young bikeman to see, his hollow voice, fading into the downslope vapor.

"See you at Behema."

The young bikeman's gone quite a way before he realizes he's lost.

He can't seem to advance or return meaningfully through the blanketed dullness. It feels as though he's fallen into that place between a paralyzing nightmare and fitful illness, where nothing seems fully within the grasp of his mind. Somehow, he steps onto a flat where there is no slope, which should not be possible, and a figure sits on a fungus-brittle stump. From the lapping sound, repetitive, he would guess there's a dark lakeshore very nearby, but no water seems visible to him.

A woman waits patiently there with a kindly smile, and the bikeman knows it's her, the one his father told him about, waiting there on the periphery of Behema, ready to find the bikeman when he stumbled over her way.

Sit.

The young bikeman thinks he knows what this is. The kind of story his father used to tell him when he was young, about a strange elsewhere-thing that appears something like a woman, at least at times. She has different names, different faces, and different ways of carrying herself, but his father says that she's been around, though not always recognizable. Separate and apart from this world, like Behema, but not part of Behema. Something other. Facilitator, or arbiter, or something else, but other, she is.

Her body seems to bend and extend over into what should be the dark water he hears, but the bikeman gets the feeling that he's not supposed to look at her back. It feels rude, possibly forbidden. She pours two customary tins of whiskey from a bottle and extends one tin to him. The gentleness with which she offers it compels him to drink, and so he drinks.

You're seeking Behema, she says.

Yes, I'm seeking Behema, the bikeman answers, and sips the whiskey, feels its warmth in his throat.

There are three ways that I can offer to someone like you, who's seeking Behema. Three ways. One up, one down, and one out.

Up, down, or out, the young bikeman repeats slowly.

The way up is painful and costly, the one you've contemplated. It will get you to Behema, if that is still what you want. The other way, down, is the way to return to what you know and leave all of this be. No one blames men who take the way down. Time and distance are valuable things.

No, they would not blame them, the bikeman says. *Those are valuable things.*

But the third way, the third way is the way out, neither up nor down. The old woman takes a long drink and swallows what remains in her tin. *Through settlement and communion, where we may redistribute things. Behema will go and you will stay. Or you will go and Behema will stay. Everything will be the way it is now, excepting that difference. Either way, you and you alone will wake to a world without Behema.*

A world without Behema. The young bikeman pauses. What would that even mean? A reconfiguration or a changing of things. Renovating the house, perhaps. He cannot truly imagine such a thing, either literally or figuratively, and in lacking that imagination feels too stunted to accept the notion. But after a time, the bikeman hesitates, then decides to ask something else.

And my father, you knew him, didn't you? What way did he take?

The woman doesn't answer, almost as though she anticipates that the answer itself may sway him. Instead, she reaches silently for the bottle to refill her empty tin. The bikeman wonders how many times his father may have spoken with the woman before, and whether this was where his father went, that last day in the hills. In the end, he thinks he knows what his father chose, and he can't bring himself to choose the same.

I think...that you think...that you are helping, in giving me a third way, "out," the bikeman reasons. *That a world without Behema seems the easiest and most possible way. Anyone would think that, and be...forgiven. But it's not another way, in the end. Not really, I mean.*

Oh?

If you can do what I think you can do, if you can create a world where I don't see Behema or live with Behema, there will still be a Behema. Not in what I think of as here, this place, but in some place. Somewhere. The young bikeman thinks. *And the thing is, they are all one place, in the end. There is nowhere I can go where Behema won't really be. Behema sees no boundary, so neither can I. No. There is no out. And for me, there is no down. Only up and ahead.*

The woman stops refilling her tin and peers at the bikeman, and then she smiles. *Only up and ahead*, she muses.

Yes.

Yes. This woman, the elsewhere-being does not seem like she is capable of meaningful laughter, but the bikeman thinks this expression is the closest she might get to it. His answer pleases her. And that must be, because she points the way back through the fog, and explains, quietly, the right way to the third peak. He remembers as best he can what he's told, before he wanders to the hills, the sound of water lapping gently somewhere behind him.

"To the northwest, we'll find jet pines spread in an arcing copse, that's where we'll look for the pass," the young bikeman tells the others. The way up is *into* the mount, an eolian cave carved from seasonal winds, whose mouth blends seamlessly with the surrounding slate. It looks flat from most directions, especially in the reddening light, except from a specific position at the end of day.

Brother Two and Skinny have been holding on in the bikeman's absence, watching the slopes anxiously. They say the old man has been talking to them, skulking in the mists for the last few hours. It's difficult to tell, but they say the old man seems to be naked, and his skin is loose and draping away from him, in sickly creased flaps, like it's not retaining its shape around his lean bones. The old man laughs and taunts. Offers help. Then threatens in turn.

"He's afraid," the bikeman says. "Let's walk. I know where we need to be."

The three of them proceed, the young bikeman repeating the instructions he received from the woman, again and again in his mind, so they will not slip away with the fog. The black spires of the jet pines curve along the slope. And as the red sun begins to break and be overtaken by the night, discrepancies in the slate reveal the mouth of the cave, almost imperceptible if not seen from this particular vantage from the northwest.

Long-limbed shapes begin to float from between the pines behind them—another pod of the tentilla, encircling their position and foreclosing a retreat. If they were going to escape to the slopes, that opportunity has passed, the bikeman realizes. They have to go through, and so, walk one by one into the cave.

The young bikeman snaps open the prod charge, which whines with a crackle of white and sets a faint glow on the inner contours and ripples of the path. Everything within has been hollowed by time and things growing, masses that seem to pull back from the men as they step deeper into Behema's nest.

Shadows shift around talus piles and forgotten scree. Overgrowth on unrecognizable protuberances make it difficult to discern what is cave and what connects to the brood of Behema.

In the dim shine of the cave innards, they spot a moaning man, hunched with his welt-covered back toward them. It takes a moment to recognize Gray Hair kneeling there, caressing something they begin to see over his shoulder. On the stump of his severed arm, a ballooning cystid forms a small head. Gray Hair nudges the cystid lovingly with his face, and pieces of his skin shed, stuck to the gummy surface of the cystid fused to his arm. One of his eyelids and most of a cheek are wasted away. More cystid faces cover his chest, all the same little child's face. The rusted hatchet lays ineffectually in a garden of pulsating tunicates.

"Keep going..." the young bikeman whispers.

They pull away, rifles raised, the moaning sound fading as they proceed gradually along an incline.

There is no end to Behema. No end. Soo, soo.

Something skitters above rock spires and along the cavernous arches nearby. All skin and strangely flatheaded and boneless, like a piece of flesh stretched, a creature meant for the pressures of the deep unforgiving ocean, not the mountains.

No end to Behema. Soo, soo, soo. It moves above their heads.

"Yet you feel the need to tell us," the young bikeman says. "I guess we'll see."

The flat-headed crawler that once appeared as an old man darts from shadow to shadow. Brother Two points lower to the ground, where cystids inflate between fissures, massing together into vaguely bipedal shapes, falling and then reforming as they gain more mass.

No end to Behema. No! No end.

The old-man-thing on the ceiling drops, a face pulled so large it seems more alien than man, falling upon them. But the flesh flap shudders and falls back when a gunshot rips a chunk of one flat edge away, popping through it clean. There's a scream, a twisting, shuffling of the thing, quick along the incline. True to his inherent cowardice, the thing scampers for escape, like a fearful priest leaving his living temple, bankrupt of any professed beliefs, back to the cave mouth and the hills. Another crack-shot through his skin, then one more, and he spurts more blood and shame in a trail as he scurries farther off. When put to a direct test, the old man, or whatever he was or used to be, can't do anything but mewl and gibber from a distance as he flees for self-preservation. No, there's no real power there.

Skinny steadies his long gun on a rock and against his shoulder after firing at the mutated old man, a bandaged forearm resting gently beside the scope. He is more assured than he's been since they've come to the hills. This is part of something the kid knows and can take part in.

Brother Two starts taking shots at the stumbling cystids converging in the cavern. He's rapid but steady, shooting and reloading almost in double time, an involuntary smile, the good humor in him, surfacing.

The young bikeman strikes the cap off of a flare and throws it to the far end of the cavern floor. Hundreds of organisms light up, uncovered by the light. The ends of tentilla seem to be reaching through ancient fissures in the cavern walls.

Skinny and Brother Two shout for the bikeman to keep running up ahead, while they keep to what they know. They'll do what they need to do, so he can do what he needs to do to get to Behema. And so the bikeman trusts and he goes, past cystids and other Behema-parts growing and getting blown apart by the gunfire. Flashes of strontium nitrate sputtering over the arches of the rippling cavern.

The bikeman reaches the upper end of the eolian formation, and only knows it for certain because in the darkness is the greening bleed of spear-like stars. He's nearly made it out into the open, up to the final haunt, when he hears something trailing in his wake.

Eh. Eh. Eh.

A trembling voice, pitiful and hoarse, carries over. A body, or more of a dragging lump, like some roiling collective, brings itself from the caves. In the green starlight, there appears a face, beside several smaller faces, with Gray Hair embedded in stretches of swirling scalp. The limbs, if they are limbs, dematerialize and reform in oceans of muscle, a single eye and part of a nose nudge toward the bikeman—toward you—from the neoplasmic heap, vestigial tear ducts weeping.

It stretches, not for the bikeman, but the prod charge in his hand.

Eh. Eh. Eh.

The mass presses itself, either intentionally or unknowingly against the crackling edge of the weapon. Its faces molt and disassemble as the staff's charge pulses and carries through its shifting, tumorous hive. Multiple points distend and bloat, burn and break from contact with the prod charge. Gray Hair, wherever he is within the collective, sizzles and sighs and excretes himself into liquid across the rocks and into merciful nothingness. Perhaps the bikeman imagines it, but he thinks he hears regret and relief in its cry and a few final labored breaths.

Then in silence, the bikeman waits, you wait, until nothing moves and you're certain that all that was left of Gray Hair is gone. You then move forward to the open peak. And there, buried in the crag-point, you finally see it. The crenulated ova, a round, languid, pendulous mass which waits and watches all the cosmos.

Behema.

The great unknown entity, wellspring of the zooid biotas, does not look at all how you had envisioned, barely bigger than yourself. It's so unusually fragile and exposed, here on the peak. And there is a siphonophoric symmetry and tenderness, a vaguely brain-like beauty to the fountain-root of the deadly organism. The center of all its teeming existence from this point in the hills, the prime site of its infection, here.

You can't believe that this is the thing I've told you about, all this time.

You ready yourself, expecting yet one more assault, some unseen defense, a final trick. Chits diving at you from the outer reaches of the crags, or perhaps tentilla rising up from the slate like a deadly network of limbs. But, nothing comes. Nothing comes for you at all. It's just you and it and the evening quiet and nothing else.

An odd valence surrounds Behema that makes your skin prickle. Strange, pale, flickering silhouettes seem to gather at the corner of your eye but do not hinder you. You watch Behema respire, its wet spheroid, weak and convalescent.

You think of my body, limp and wasted under the blackened alders, where you once found me.

You wonder if you can feel my presence here too.

I see you holding the prod charge, hesitating.

This is all very final.

You're worried about what will go away when this is done. Those last living pieces of your father, remaining somewhere in the cells of the exofauna, hovering among the hills, finally gone.

If I could reach you, I'd tell you not to worry about what things will go. That isn't something that you need to worry about. Not at all. That it's okay for some things to go.

It's strange, trying to remember things that go by so quickly. Memory and meaning, they always decay, of course. But here within Behema, some things remain, even to the end and beyond. I think of your mother, who turns over in bed in the middle of the night. She rests an arm over my chest while I watch the shadows and car lights on the popcorn-ceiling of the apartment. Neither of us sleeps fully, always dipping in and out of the strangest thoughts since coming home from the hospital.

You cry out for us, from the darkness. So I shift gently, so as not to wake your mother, and plant my bare feet on the cold wooden floor, shuffling to your crib. Plucking you up from nothing and holding you in ambient city light. Yours is a young face and an old face that has never before existed, but has somehow, impossibly, lived in my thoughts. Before it was, it always was. And I can almost imagine the young boy and bikeman you'll be, then after that, older, and older, than I ever will be.

In delirium and instability, amid so sweet and specific a sleeplessness, I consider your blinking eyes and little lips, and something strikes me so completely, for no reason at all, in the middle of one of many unremarkable nights.

Somehow, I look at you and know, I have to die. As though I'm plainly observing the arc of starlight and gravity, I understand, aware of it all with inexplicable and undeniable clarity. Something so simple and animal and true, when I hold my child in my arms. You'll grow and become, and I will give way to what you'll be. And it isn't sad or terrible, it all just is.

What was once a frightening inevitability feels now like necessity.

And in my mind, I'm sitting by a fire, talking to a little boy about houses and worlds. I'm behind the wheel of a car, while you've fallen asleep soundly in the passenger seat. I'm leading you through the hills, and over to a rope bridge I've secured between distant peaks. You look at me, afraid, but I know now, I'm meant to show you, not to hold that fear too long.

—*I'm the dad. I'll go first.*

You nod.

—*Watch me, how I go. I'll go first.*

You strike the cap off of a flare. Red and white erupts from your hand. Strontium nitrate flashes, the burn point, at least two thousand degrees. You press it against Behema, let the flesh ignite and smoke and smolder. Pools of biomaterial convulse and char, the ianua zooid seizes, browning across crenulated surfaces. It becomes totally enveloped by the high-temperature exothermic redox chemical reaction. Otherworldly wails rising, the hills themselves baying to something unseen, a great terror collapses, withdrawing its incursion from material reality.

The bikeman stays to watch every last bit of the burn, the great and final conflagration of Behema, until Behema is no more. Only roasted pulp smoking into the time-worn sediment of the third peak. He hears human voices below, somewhere beneath the slate, the soft sounds of disbelief, laughter, in a hollow place where he will join and experience the same, soon. But first he opens his pack and looks down at the bones he's carried. Parts of his father he's been, until this moment, unwilling to relinquish.

The young bikeman digs with his hands down into the ochre dirt, then gently lowers the jawbone and skull fragment and covers them again. He doesn't hold specific faith and doesn't know the first thing about prayer, but he finds himself clasping his hands and closing his eyes the way he's seen some people do.

He doesn't entreat or commune; he just thinks how certain he is that he'll find his father one day, in the worlds that follow. Because they found each other once, and so it seems to him, they will again. And even if there exists nothing in the hereafter: no meaning or continuance, no form or salvation, just a cold absence of everything. Even then, they will be together in that, too.

Because they share something unknowable and unending, and that is something he will always believe.

The boy lets go, gets to his feet, and then he carries on.

Thomas Ha is a writer of speculative short fiction whose work has been nominated for the Nebula, Ignyte, Hugo, Locus, and Shirley Jackson Awards, among others. You can find his work in *Clarkesworld*, *Lightspeed Magazine*, *Beneath Ceaseless Skies*, and *Weird Horror Magazine*, and other publications. His work has also appeared in *The*

Best American Science Fiction & Fantasy and *The Year's Best Dark Fantasy & Horror.* Thomas grew up in Honolulu and, after a decade plus of living in the northeast, now resides in Los Angeles with his family.

OUR ECHOES DRIFTING THROUGH THE MARSH

Marie Croke

Home

If it is still home

Upon my return to the village, it was my husband, Adamet, who took me gently by the arm and guided me across the docks spanning our marshes until we reached the preburial cottage overlooking the sound. We stood side by side in the shadows of the cottage, torchlight flickering across the preparatory table where a colorful shroud lay empty in a crumpled heap.

I'd helped stitch that shroud together. Each layer made by a different loved one. We whispered stories into our pieces of the fabric, that they might linger forever on. Then, each piece was added together, colors on colors, to wrap the person passed on with our last good-byes.

That was the new way of our people. Not the way of our grandparents.

Adamet didn't speak; he'd never been one to start difficult conversations. And for this one, I knew he wouldn't trust himself. Angry with me, but the fire gone out of it. A tired anger. He stood close enough to graze my shoulder with his own, a marginal comfort for what was to come but a comfort nonetheless, for I'd been so alone, so cold all the night before.

A creak on the wooden slats pulled Adamet away from me—our daughter, Danai, come to interrogate me. I knew it'd be her, I knew it was her, and yet hearing her footsteps made the chill from last night return and my fingers go brittle. I guess I must have held a small hope that it might be one of the others who made up the village council. That, just maybe, this confrontation would be delayed.

Danai had my late brother's eyes, sharp and bright and missing nothing, not the way my fingers abruptly stilled or the lack of guilt in my countenance for my thievery of his body. Her boots made the wooden slats groan, and her resigned sigh as she sank against the barren preparatory table opposite me announced she'd have no patience for my stories. Not as she'd had in her youth.

Adamet left me to her, with a light touch to the back of my hand that I wished would last forever. I watched as his shadow flickered under the crack at the door before disappearing. Perhaps he still stood guard there, whether to keep me in or others out, I didn't know.

With difficulty, I returned my attention to Danai. I had to be wary, my words careful to dance around the truth, give enough to satisfy. Not enough to destroy the family I had left.

"*Where* would you have gone?" Danai mused, a whispered question to herself, with that quiet strength of her father in her. Then louder, "Let's start with Grandfather, or rather his journeys into the Whispermarsh, shall we?"

Shall we? Of course we shall. We will start wherever you wish, my dearest one. So I spoke.

Embri's Echo Moment

Perhaps a tiny sculpture of a girl playing in the grass

Grandfather took me into the Whispermarsh for the first time when I was four, too young to know we shouldn't have been there. Strapped to his back, willow branches grazing my head and the pungent scent of the marsh too familiar to be cloying, I played with his hair and the single braid with heron bones woven within.

Whenever he coughed like an egret, I'd hunker into my pack and hold tight to my Zizi doll like she might grow tall enough to fight the great waders, chop their tree-trunk thick legs with her fabric hands, crack their sun-bright beaks before one closed about me. Be the protector I needed against the great waders, those giant heron cousins that proliferated throughout the Whispermarsh.

"That one's not hungry, it seems, Embri."

Emi-emi-bri he'd sometimes sing, warbling my name like one of his bird calls, to remind me not to stay frightened after the immense shadow of a flightless wader slowly moved on. The stench of its feathers lingering in the air while ripples broke round driftwood and tubular grasses before dying soft deaths near the snails.

He carried me into the marsh mostly taking a dry-lands path, but here and there he'd rigged a hidden wooden raft and line and, as he'd pull us across the water, I'd watch for the telltale crocodile bubbles just as I'd been taught. Between one step and the next, my attention so focused I scarcely noticed, there came a whisper on the breeze over the saltwater grasses.

"Who's that?" I asked, holding Zizi near my mouth.

"Grandmother's voice from a memory," he told me.

Grandfather pulled me off his back and sat me down next to a woman. Only she wasn't a woman, not a real one. She'd been pieced together with driftwood and grass, scrollwood bark, snail shells and open seedpods. A marsh sculpture, like the ones folk built at festival time, only this one had clumps of moist dirt smeared up its bent legs, as if the sculpture had erupted from the ground. It whispered a hushed conversation from their past, between Grandfather and her, one where they shared an excitement over being alone at last. A memory repeating over and over.

All my memories of Grandmother were like that, convoluted and muted, but at least I had them, as frail as they were.

Grandfather would take me often to the Whispermarsh after that first time, where we would listen to Grandmother sing lullabies to a cooing baby or laugh at his murmured jokes I was too young to understand. There were only a few of the marsh sculptures of Grandmother left, though, and Grandfather didn't call them that. He called them echo moments, pushed from the depths of the marsh by a mind gone to rest in that sacred place of our people's old culture.

That had been the crux of our old burial rituals, he'd explained, from before I'd been born. Before the great waders had been foisted south from their lands by erosion and flooding, before they'd stomped through the Whispermarsh, thinking our sacred land free to claim, before they'd eyed us like we were delicious crocodiles, hunted us, swallowed us down, like the little blue herons did to fish in the saltwater grass clumps around our village.

For our safety, for our future, the village council decreed a new burial ritual, one that didn't involve a pilgrimage to the Whispermarsh where the land had been blessed. A ritual that no longer involved the memories of our loved ones digging their way free of the mud to echo moments of their lives on the wind. A new ritual that took our past from us.

Home

Where a brother no longer lives

"Is that where you took Uncle Vambrit?" Danai asked. She'd been quiet. Not patient, no, yet with a pointed attention that she'd rarely bestowed on me in recent years. "Left him where Great Grandfather first showed you?"

"It's overrun now," I said. Waders—those great hunting herons, tree-tall and deadly quiet—had nested over Grandmother's few remaining echo moments so that her laughter faded, faded until nothing remained of her sculptures but piles of debris. "There's nothing left."

She nodded to herself, as if to say *not there then*. "Uncle Vambrit went on your treks to the Whispermarsh?"

"When he was old enough, yes."

"You'd know where he used to play, then."

Of course I did. How could I not when we'd played among the dangers together?

Embri's Echo Moment

Perhaps a girl in motion, looking over her driftwood shoulder at another

My brother, Vambrit, had been a determined child. Not a quiet one—confrontational, boisterous—yet would disappear the moment Mother or I would turn our backs. Out in the marsh, Vambrit slipped away constantly, and since I had younger legs, Grandfather tasked me with chasing him down, leaving me sweaty and worried. I'd find him curled up beneath a bush staring between beige wader legs at sculptures on distant dry lands.

"What does that one say?" he'd murmur.

I'd make something up in a hushed voice because I knew if I didn't, he'd try to find a way through the waders and crocodiles out in the open water. He was too young to understand that while the creatures who ruled the Whispermarsh might ignore us often, when they were hungry enough or when they were angry enough, we would be prey. That they were far more intelligent than crocodiles or the little herons and cormorants near our docks.

The least we could do was not instigate them.

So I'd whisper a story. "That one is an echo moment from a warrior who took down a wader single-handedly with a spear into its belly. He sings his victory song in that moment and tells the tale of the battle."

"What's his name?"

I tugged with trembling hands at Vambrit to get him moving away from a wader's great shadow, thankful that its beak was pointed toward the water and not toward us. "He doesn't speak his own name during the story and he's dead so I can't ask him."

"Does he have others?"

"Sure."

It became commonplace to explore rings about Grandfather as he sat listening to his last repeated moments with Grandmother. We would discover marsh sculptures lounging in the grass or dipping their driftwood arms into the water, their scrollwood and crab shells and dried algae clinging together through sheer will as they whispered moments of emotive domesticity, fights and firsts and fierce heartache and happiness. We were explorers in uncharted land, with a stagnant people who only spoke the same few lines over and over.

And over.

My mother, when I mentioned our outings much later, after Grandfather had walked off into the marsh to die alone, had called him horrible names: irresponsible, selfish, repugnant. I'd thought her harsh.

Until I had my own daughter. Until I felt the same fear that had distressed my mother every time Grandfather had disappeared with me into the Whispermarsh.

Home

Where safety was assured

Danai straightened the burial shroud, her hand pausing on the section I'd woven. I couldn't tell whether the action was purposeful. "You never took me to the Whispermarsh. Just told me tales of it. Many of them warnings."

Outside, the frogs had begun their orchestra as a soft drizzle patterned the piers. I heard occasional calls from our people, the lax calls of those no longer terrified though yet not recovered. Perhaps we would never truly recover from today. Of Adamet, I saw no sign, but I wondered... Wondered if he could hear what I was about to reveal, and that made me hesitate, imagining the disappointment on his face, the added betrayal. Then I bolstered myself. I had already committed, hadn't I? So, I decided the shame of the secret was worth the anger I might receive.

"I did once."

Danai leaned forward, in a move so constrained she seemed carved and wooden. "When?"

I suspected that wasn't quite what she wanted to ask. But *why* was a harder question, one that required hearing the explanations behind my actions. And I didn't think Danai was ready to hear the whys of what I'd done. "When you were just turned three."

"Tell me."

"But that would be telling the story out of order."

Her hand flattened on the scored table between us, the pinprick scars from a nettle bush incident bright against her tanned skin. "Tell me."

So I told her of my folly.

Embri's Echo Moment

Perhaps a sculpture of a young woman, bent under the weight of a child

I strapped Danai on my back in the same pack Grandfather had used for me and then Vambrit. Took her through the village's interlacing, labyrinthine docks and cottages and piers over the marsh, past the mud-entrenched fencing that offered the illusion of safety and into the deeper recesses of the wetlands, far from our small civilization. She slept most of the way, her little head bobbing on my neck, our sweat mingling as I scanned for giant waders before picking my way across saltwater grasses, mud coating my knee-high boots, periwinkles occasionally hitching a ride.

This had been what Grandfather must have felt that first time taking me. All nerves that I might scream at my first up-close sight of the waders. Concerned he might be doing the wrong thing by bringing me to the Whispermarsh so young. Yet there was an importance, I thought, of connecting with our passed-on relatives. People beloved to him.

People beloved to me.

It'd taken me and Vambrit a few years of searching, but we'd finally found Grandfather's resting place, his sculptures far more east of Grandmother's than we'd anticipated. Vambrit thought maybe he'd had to skirt the wader nests and gone too far to circle around before he simply couldn't go on.

I felt the whisper of his voice before I saw his outermost sculpture. "Here she is, my girl, my Embri. *Emi-emi-bri.* Put your lips like this and then push from here, your stomach, and sing a marsh song."

Danai woke with a start and a soft groan, so I unstrapped her and set her down next to the sculpture, its legs criss-crossed, its form bent forward and one driftwood hand cupped as if expecting something.

"Who's that?"

"I wanted you to hear his voice. Danai, this is your great grandfather speaking. It's an echo moment from when I was just a few years older than you."

Danai touched the rotting scrollwood, nudging a seedpod from the sculpture's sunken chin.

"Careful, careful. He's fragile, decaying. You must tread softly in the Whispermarsh."

In the distance, a wader straightened, its form tall and lean as it stretched its beak upward toward the clouds, a crocodile struggling in its maw, snapping at air, tale whipping. All around us, herons and cormorants took flight in desperate escape.

"Softly," I murmured, dismay tightening my focus to Grandfather's echo moment in the hopes Danai would not note the great wader.

She did though. She did. And she screamed. High-pitched and echoing.

I hid her in a nettle bush near one of Grandfather's other echo moments—one where he screamed along with her, in pain after a redtongue snake had bit him—and led the wader's focus far, far away before I circled back, my heart sore from pounding, sweat and mud making me slip, and a shaking setting under my skin that I couldn't relieve.

Danai only had the bite of the nettles across her wrist and arm. Such small wounds that could have happened off our docks at home. Which was what I told Adamet.

But I... I remembered the image of the wader hesitating before it followed me rather than her. And I never returned with her, no matter how old she grew.

Home

Where nothing is a secret

Danai's lips pinched, then relaxed, as if she were warring with herself on how to respond to my admission. "Father knew you went sometimes—a preoccupation he allowed as long as no one ever knew. He would have left you had he known you'd taken me there."

"Of course he would have."

"Deservedly so." Danai paced beside the preburial table, back and forth, her steps calculated yet her expression softening as she lost herself in thought, the humidity hanging thickly between us. Then she stopped. "But everyone *did* find out that you and Uncle Vambrit had been going to the Whispermarsh."

"Not because of me."

"But you knew. You *knew* Vambrit had been doing more." She turned sharply toward me. "You let this happen."

In a way, perhaps I had. *I am strong enough to take the blame, dearest one, if that's what you need from me.*

Embri's Echo Moment

Perhaps a sculpture of a half-grown girl, snails in her palm

One could claim I started it all with my stories of warriors taking on waders. That had been my fantasy, crafted partially from our outings as I listened to Grandfather hold onto his wife's memories. But also from my own desire to find the everyday on our journeys into the Whispermarsh. Not merely clandestine visits but an accepted part of our culture as it had been when he'd been young, before the waders had migrated. That had been my Grandfather talking then, his words chirping in my mind of what-had-been and what-could-be-again. Lingering in the past rather than focusing on our future.

"That one is the great, uh, Fibrite, who found a dead wader, hacked off its beak, and fashioned two giant spears from it," I made up to entertain my brother. "He'd hide in the trees, the tallest he could find, and spear at the waders while they stared into the water."

"How did he fashion the spears?" asked Vambrit.

"I don't know."

"Who does? I want to learn how to fashion spears. I can already hide in trees."

"You can't. We don't fight the waders anymore." We'd never fought the waders as far as I knew. "Mother says it's too dangerous. They leave us alone anyway. Leave us alone and we leave them alone. That's the rule. *They* accept it, she says."

"But we could. I would. I *will*."

Vambrit cobbled together his own spears, out of saplings and crocodile teeth, and would thrash about the undergrowth chopping at low-hanging branches and whacking at cattails until they fluffed. He'd bring his weapons home, an arsenal of useless toys by the time he hit manhood.

At that point, he'd moved on to blacksmithing, toiling away with iron, making hooks and hammers and nails, and when his master left the shop, a spearhead or three.

I hadn't understood the depth of Vambrit's desire to reclaim our lost land. Not then.

Home

How families are forged

I slumped onto a stool, a weight of regret settling over my shoulders. Perhaps if I hadn't been so quick with warrior stories...

Outside the preburial cottage, the pier creaked. I saw no shadow under the doorway, yet I froze, afraid Adamet was listening, had heard my admissions. I imagined, yet again, an anger filtering over his calm countenance. Wondered whether my admission of taking Danai into the Whispermarsh had been a final wedge between us.

"Did your father truly leave?" I asked softly. A part of me hoped if he had, it was because he wanted to be kept in the dark about any admissions I made. A larger part of me believed he was done with me, exhausted by the choices I'd made.

Danai waved a hand, the one with the scars from her brush with the nettles so long ago. "Father doesn't want to face you. He's..." Her voice dropped to a hush in an obvious attempt to elicit guilt from my conscience. "He's worried he's not the right person to hear your confessions and relay them to the council. He doesn't want to influence your punishment."

Though the council still held respect for him, Adamet had given up his seat a few years ago, to Danai. For he believed in the future over the past. Always had. But then, his grandparents had survived the wader migration. Had been buried on the sound rather than the Whispermarsh.

I lifted my head, saddened but holding a tight rein on my emotions so that Danai wouldn't see how her bitter disappointment in me hurt. "But you're not worried. You won't influence my punishment."

Her expression froze. "Making a few spearheads, killing a random wader here or there out in the Whispermarsh by himself, might have been fine."

We were back to Vambrit. Always it came back to my brother. To the Whispermarsh.

Embri's Echo Moment

Perhaps a sculpture of a young mother, shading her hollowed scrollwood eyes

They were our birthright; the echo moments once destined for pilgrimages, like the ones Grandfather took often. Our people would die out there, alone but not alone, surrounded by the memories of their loved ones. Our dead, their memories, were a part of us.

"And why shouldn't we reclaim them?" asked Vambrit. He balanced on a piling while staring off toward the west, with the village at our back, this bridge in dire need of fresh pilings since the marsh had been slowly gnawing away at them.

"Because it's dangerous."

"We had warriors once."

"Eh..."

"Oh, no, not the ones you went on about. I know they're all lies. But there were others." He spun on the piling and with a lean and a hop, he sat facing me. "I've found a few out there who used to hunt the waders. Not just defensive craftsmanship along our borders, but our people who would go out *there*."

"There's too many to drive off, and we'd just end up angering them. They're not like crocodiles who will eat their own. They *care* about one another." Like we did.

Vambrit made a dismissive sound. "Listen to you. Talking like Adamet instead of yourself. Like you don't remember Grandfather's talks. This is important, Embri. These are our people we're talking about. And we're just giving it up. Giving them up."

Giving Grandfather up.

I looked back across the bridges and piers and took note of Danai's dark head of hair with its clacking heron bones as she swung on a rope swing between my cottage and Vambrit's. Still young, barely nine. The cuts on her hand had healed, and the nightmares had faded after a few years, my old Zizi doll stained by child sweat, threads peeling from anxious picking. She didn't remember our lone trek into the Whispermarsh, for which I was grateful.

"I've never given it up." I hadn't either, because sometimes I just wanted to sit in Grandfather's echo moment and hear him sing *emi-emi-bri* to little me. "But that doesn't mean we should drag the entire village into bloody wader hunts over land we don't truly need to live." That was for the dead, not the living.

"But it's where the echoes are. It's the only place they sprout. What if it was Danai who died? Wouldn't you want her buried out there? Where you could hear her laugh again."

I glared at him but couldn't quite say no.

Vambrit shrugged.

What I hadn't known then, what I discovered later, was he'd already been taking friends out, arming them, showing them the land of the Whispermarsh, mapping it into a battlefield to be. Bringing home giant shards of black-speckled eggs and shaving down wader beaks to form sharpened defenses in pockets within the marsh.

Home

Where families are fought

"And when you found out, you still didn't say," accused Danai.

I bowed my head in partial apology. "I'd thought it was just Vambrit and a few friends, living out a cause." *For an echo of a memory.*

Danai rapped her fingers against the table, the sound carrying across the room, reminding me of the clacking of the heron bones when she'd ripped them from her hair as a teen, cursing my Grandfather, cursing my supposed obsession with him. "A dream you encouraged by your silence. When were you going to tell us? Did you even stop to think about when you might have an obligation to? When his group grew to ten, to twenty? To forty? When they became proud, dragging great wader bodies home in pieces, flaunting authority, flaunting all the rules we've made to *protect* ourselves? When they didn't come home at all? Or should we count the years instead, Mother? Two? Ten? Twenty? Or would you have waited until you'd walked off into the Whispermarsh to die alone among memories who don't care a whit about you? Would you have told then, Mother, in an echo moment you can't control?"

I winced in shame and regret and not a little amount of agony. "I thought maybe they could retake the Whispermarsh. Make the memories of our past ours again." Conserve the death rites as they'd been for generations so that we and our children could be laid to rest in the marsh rather than the sound.

"*They*? You think your inaction gives you the right to not be included in what they've done?"

"Probably not, but I don't think it's my inaction that put me in this room today." Vambrit's shroud was wrinkled and bunched on the table, an abandoned remnant.

It had been my actions that had removed his body, after all, and left us here dancing around the topic of where and why and what to do about my thievery.

Embri's Echo Moment

Perhaps a sculpture of a woman gripping her grassy hair, her face contorted

Just days ago, I'd been working along the docks on the eastern edge of the village, mindlessly sanding down splits in boards, practicing my bird calls under my breath, when the first distant cries rang out.

I'd thought them children playing a game. I'd thought them a row between lovers spilled out into the bridges. I'd thought the cries many things but what they were.

Until the waders grew close enough to see over the occasional fat trees, their bodies casting deep shadows across the cottages and piers of our home, shadows long enough they reached for the expanse of low-tide sound to blur with the streams of cormorants sitting perched on the calm, shallow water.

I'd never seen so many of the waders in one place. Never seen them flock. They stalked in ones or twos within the marsh, not dozens. Yet here they were, fury in their jerky strides as they breached the fence, then the first of the docks; as their beaks came striking down like we were fish and they starving.

Terrified, I rushed nearby children into my cottage and cut free some of the strands of drying fish in the hopes of distracting one or two of the attacking waders. Their legs crashed through our docks, their beaks cracking pilings and splintering boards, sending shattered sections of our piers into the marsh below. My people screamed, voices becoming a cacophony of noise as they ran for shelter, ducking into cottages, throwing themselves onto rafts and canoes to paddle into the sound.

I pushed through the chaos, searching for Danai and Adamet, yelling their names until I grew hoarse. Just on the other side of a dock parallel to where I ran, a wader brought its beak down through the thatched roof of the cottage, then again, smashing through the boards outside. The dock buckled and shook, then collapsed, the violence of it shuddering the boards where I stood.

All around me, my village became a one-sided warzone: a wounded man waded through the marsh beneath the docks clutching a screaming toddler to his chest; a trio of women used giant emptied baskets like shields as they ran for their raft; a young boy hunched behind lopsided piles of ropes and fishing nets, his hands interlaced over his neck.

A woman ahead of me stumbled and fell through a gaping, splintered hole in the dock. I braced myself on the unbroken boards and reached down to her. Her forearms were bleeding, splinters of wood caught in her flesh, and her legs slipping in the sucking marsh-mud. Her gaze swept past me mid-pull and she froze.

The shadow of a wader crossed over us as its long neck arched upward toward the cloudy sky, a young man struggling like a crocodile in its beak. I watched, as if I were the one caught, my grip on the woman's hand squeezing fiercely. While the young man flailed his machete against the beak uselessly.

Then Vambrit's call came over the agonized screaming in the air drawing all attention to himself and his spear. He ran with sharpened precision across the wreckage of our village and buried that spearhead into the lower belly of that large wader. Then he leaned on the shaft, driving the blade up, up as the wader's wings snapped open, the musty stench of its feathers wafting like a windstorm across the docks.

He stood, knees bent, two of his home-grown warriors at his back, feather and down sticking to his arms where the wader's blood had poured.

I'd never fought a wader; I'd never fought a man nor woman nor any other person; I'd never even fought a child.

Yet I found myself emboldened. I pulled the woman free of the marsh-mud, then yanked a shattered section of wood from the broken dock to wield the sharpened, crooked end like a spear. I found myself fighting, stabbing at wader legs, my hands becoming a mess of scrapes and blistery flesh; the pain distant, compressed into dullness as adrenaline tore through my body like a pulsing tide.

Adamet found me, standing over the head of a wader corpse, staring down at fears made real, my makeshift spear still embedded in its eye, my hands scraped raw.

"Embri! You're here!" Alive. I'd thought he meant *alive* in that moment, not that the wader presence had made him fear I'd been out in the Whispermarsh, maybe even had somehow spurred this unprecedented attack from them. He gripped me to him, his mouth hard against my forehead. "You need to go, get to the east with the others where it's safe."

"Where's Danai?"

"I glimpsed her among those fighting. No, wait, Embri! She'll be fine. She can handle herself. You go. Go! The waders won't follow if you head into the sound. They won't go into the open water."

"No! Look at all of this! They would, today. We need to find Danai."

He trailed me, back the way he'd come, through the canted, broken docks and collapsed cottages, though the labyrinth of our village that had been brought low, the marsh-mud we normally lived above now splattered across our docks. We skirted broken pilings, teetered across half-crushed bridges, searching for our daughter as the sun sank into dusk, taking the shadows, swallowing them whole.

The last few great waders left alive hastened into the west, back to their nests. As if they'd finished what they'd come to do, the same as Vambrit had over and over when he'd invaded the Whispermarsh.

We discovered Danai with ruined feathers flocked about her and her gaze as distant as Grandfather's whispers. All sound came into focus then, and for me, the world could begin to turn again, for the cries of those mourning to reach my ears. I found myself gasping. Clutching Danai to my chest, uncaring that she remained stiff in my embrace; her breath light and a glassiness to her eyes that reflected my horror and relief rather than opening a window to the true emotions roiling inside her.

As the darkness reigned and the moonlight shed light across our tiny broken world, we counted our dead and wounded, a macabre and dreary task. Vambrit, with all his skill, the first true warrior of our people for hundreds of years, a man of passion, determination, my brother, lay face down between two cooling waders, their wings canted up, stiff and arching over his body like a bower as the marsh absorbed him into its embrace.

All my protective instincts, from the time I'd chased after him in the Whispermarsh to my silence over the years, all for naught. His smile gone. His exuberance gone. His endless energy for what he believe in... gone.

And under our new burial rites, his voice never to be heard whispering memories in the wind.

Home

Where the dead stay silent

"Tragic."

"Convenient."

Danai stared at me, a glint in her gaze suspicious of my meaning. "Where did you hide Uncle Vambrit's body?"

"In the Whispermarsh."

"It's three hundred kilometers of wetland, Mother," and she said my name like a curse, "Where? Near Grandfather's sculptures? The waders' nesting ground? Where?"

Once more, I didn't answer. Instead, I changed the subject with all the finesse of a squawking seagull. "It's admirable to try and protect your father. And our people. Our way of life."

She glared at me, like a wader eying a fish that refused to swim close enough. Her gaze slid to the door briefly, where rain had begun to patter against the docks and splash gently in the waters between. Maybe Adamet had left after all. Too heartbroken that I'd hid any knowledge of Vambrit's attacks on the waders for so very long, leading to this tragedy.

"You've yet to ask me why," I said.

I think I saw doubt flash across her face, but it swept away so quickly I couldn't be sure. She would hate if I compared her to Vambrit, yet there it was, that determined self, waiting for the telltale ripple of a fish in order to strike.

Maybe I should let her. Let the emotion fester and roil. Never give her what she so desperately sought.

Embri's Echo Moment

Perhaps a woman crumbling, scrollwood and driftwood hanging loose

"He'd have wanted to be buried in the Whispermarsh, close to Grandfather," I insisted a few days after the waders had attacked. Time enough to begin to see patterns in the wreckage, differences between wounded and dying. Time enough to wipe clean the mud, or at least some of the worst, and discover too much in places where it shouldn't have been: Vambrit's lungs filled with marsh-mud, as if he'd been breathing it.

"What he wanted got twenty-seven of our people dead." Adamet argued in that quiet, calm manner of his. "More if you count those in the marsh who haven't returned. I don't want you going out there, especially not now that the waders have become so aggressive. They could kill you on sight, Embri."

"I'll be careful. I'm always careful." He was right, a part of me insisted. The dangers had grown. And yet, another part of me refused to let the risk stop me. "You haven't seen him. I have. He had mud deep in his lungs and no wader wound on his head or otherwise to explain why he'd died. I have to know, and taking him to the Whispermarsh is the only way to know for sure whether..." My words failed me then, whispering away.

Something relented in Adamet's gaze, and for a second I thought he'd agree. "He probably got knocked off the pier. Maybe he tried climbing one of the cottages to get above a wader and fell underneath."

"No, that doesn't make sense. He was down there in the thick of things. I saw how he fought, how he attacked them. He always struck from below, hit their bellies or their legs to bring them low."

Adamet lifted his hands in partial concession. "You're grieving. Take some time to yourse—"

"I'm not bargaining here! I'm not in denial. I know he's dead. I just want to know who's responsible."

His lips pursed, suddenly tight. Then, for a fraction of a moment, his mouth opened, rounded, and his tongue pulled back and a sound that started and swallowed in the same second even as he controlled himself. But I felt the word anyway, like a whisper-breath snapping across my face.

You.

As if my complicity, my silence, had been the reason Vambrit was gone. Because I hadn't stopped things when I had the chance.

Adamet grunted. Scratched his head. His eyes, ringed with black and splintered through with red, blinked repeatedly, like he might be able to erase the horrors from his vision if he just cleared it enough times.

"Embri, there's no guarantee that even if we were to drag his body all the way up there that any sculptures would form, least of all a specific one you're looking for."

"He's my brother. I should have a say—"

"You did have a say. You had a say and you chose to keep quiet. You chose to keep it from *me*, from Danai, who could have stopped this nonsense. I'm not risking anyone else. You want to take him up there, take him your damn self."

"I will then."

Surprise flared across his face. He hadn't thought I would, I realized, his words spilling out of him because he'd thought the dangers of the waders, the repairs needed in the village, and the mourning and burial rites for those we'd lost would have all taken precedence for me, just as they had for him and Danai. He glanced over his shoulder as if looking for an escape, his jaw tight on words he'd probably kept too close to say out loud before now. "Maybe I'm wrong, but this feels like an excuse so you'll have another reason to head out there, away from the rest of us." *Away from me*, I thought he meant.

"I just want to know who killed him."

He closed his eyes briefly, his anger clearly warring with his need to remain in control of his emotions, though his agonized bitterness seeped out with each word. "The *waders* killed him. Be honest, at least with yourself. I think we both know you'd prefer to sit and listen to the dead than with us living."

"That's not true," I whispered. But he'd already gone.

There'd been a place in the Whispermarsh, a place too dangerous for two careful children to go. A place we'd seen but couldn't reach where I'd first told Vambrit a tale of a warrior who'd killed a wader single-handedly with a spear through its belly. I wondered if he'd ever heard the real tale from that sculpture. Discovered what it truly was whispering all these years.

Home

Despite its wreckage

"Would you take me there?" Danai asked.

"Alone, I would. You can come back and lead the rest later if you want. But this first time, alone."

"You wouldn't hurt me," whispered Danai and it hurt, oh, it hurt that it sounded so much like a question.

I wiped the sticky dampness from my forehead; breathed in a lungful of heavy, salty air. "Not on purpose. Never on purpose."

She rose. "Let me speak to Father."

When she opened the door, the drizzle was heading off across the marsh, leaving only a blanket of water in the gray air. I followed her outside among the broken twisted piers, hoping to catch sight of Adamet, to get a sense of where he stood, but he'd moved on, tucked underneath a thatched grass overhang almost out of sight, his shoulders hunched and the weight of our years pressing on him, like he wasn't sure he had the strength left to stand straight. When Danai paused beside him, she spoke loudly, repeating his questions back in her responses, clear and concise.

So I could hear her lie about where we planned to go. *Ah, my dear heart, are we not so unlike one another? For I remember telling some of those same lies, thinking I was protecting him.*

Embri's Echo Moment

Perhaps a woman leaned back, fingers spread wide at empty air

The council laid out an emergency law against anyone going into wader territory, stating the need to not incite them further; not spark another rage-fueled attack. Adamet stared at me as the warning drifted across the assembled. Danai met my gaze harshly from the low dais the council stood upon, then looked away again.

I had no plans of being a warrior, though I had to know what had happened in Vambrit's final moments. So I left early, while my family's attention turned elsewhere, and snuck alone to his preburial cottage.

I used our raft to take Vambrit's body into the marsh until the waterways grew too congested to continue. Half the night I alternated dragging him, begging the marsh silently to overcome the awful scent of the congealed wader blood across his arms and torso, and pulling on the fresh ropes Vambrit and his pocket of hidden wader-hunters had strung to Grandfather's old rafts.

The moon had started high and dropped low. My focus had gone about the same way. Lagging, lagging, until my steps moved forward out of numb requirement.

By the time I waded across a stretch of deeper marsh to reach that old sculpture, mud had caked through my clothes and into my boots. The cloth wrapping Vambrit had ripped so that his face lay exposed to the disappearing moonlight. His hair fluttered here and there, where it hadn't dried to his skin. His lips, slack now, almost seemed to twist with expression as the darkness played over his face.

That sculpture, the one from our childhood, the one I'd claimed had been a warrior singing a great song, began a low, dry whisper as I tugged Vambrit to my chest for a last embrace, and then another last embrace, until all the last embraces went on so long the sun began to lighten.

Only then did I wipe my eyes and pull him further into the spit of muddy land where the water meandered in rivulets between shrubby brush and trees. Tied him to roots and weighed him down with mud until the marsh sucked him up and only shards of the blanket remained sagging against the sharper grasses.

Then I sat and waited, listening to that dry whisper of the sculpture repeat, "Is it true? It can't be true! He can't be dead. Show me!" and wondered if the woman long gone to rest here had ever been shown.

Home

Where we leave the living

For the second time in as many days, I picked my way through a path well-known since childhood. Behind me, Danai followed. She occasionally paused and glanced behind, but whether she was marking the path or checking for someone trailing us, I wasn't sure. Maybe a little of both.

She almost balked at the end when she saw the water we'd have to wade through, her expression twisting as she pushed past all the natural fear of the open wetland in wader territory, made even more dangerous since the attack. But she resisted the temptation to turn back. She had more purpose to be out here than I did, after all, even if she wouldn't admit it.

I took her to where that old sculpture no longer sang its mourning wail, and there she spun slowly on the muddy bank, taking in the marsh I'd brought her to, the grass twisting beneath her feet as we dripped within the gray light.

"There are a lot of sculptures here."

"One there. And there. Another behind that tree and one half-in half-out of the water this way." I indicated the direction of Vambrit's sculptures, his active echo moments, though I did not point out his true resting place, where a heavy piece of driftwood sat in the mud and the snail shells and seedpods and cattail fluff did not hold the form of a marsh sculpture.

"I'm going to check them all."

I stayed by the old woman's collapsed sculpture, too sore inside to hear Vambrit play with his make-shift weapons, to hear us laughing as we wrestled in the mud, to hear him cry when he found out Grandfather would never walk us into the Whispermarsh again.

It didn't matter much. What Danai was searching for wasn't there. I had made sure of that.

Embri's Echo Moment

Perhaps a woman with steely snail-shell eyes, hand upraised in a wave

I'd never known how long it took for echo moments to form, for the marsh sculptures to erupt. Grandfather hadn't known, and no one else remained who might have remembered. So I gave myself another last embrace under the lightening sun as I waited.

The ground beside me, damp with the grasses bent from my steps while snails tracked through the mud, stuttered. The dirt shook—like the cattails shivering in a light breeze—then split, like those same cattails fluffing, bits of them tearing off, crumbling end over end. Except this crumbling happened backward, rising, pulling, buried driftwood clacking gently against a crab carapace, which in turn caught a cracked-open seedpod. The echo moment shuddered through the mud like a birthing. A head, then arms, one hand with fingers of scrollwood reaching against an opposite shoulder as if protecting itself.

The accompanying whisper was my own voice.

"He sings his victory song in that moment and tells the tale of the battle," said my much younger voice, whispering from a memory.

"What's his name?" asked Vambrit, his voice high and light, nothing like the deep rumble he'd had as an adult.

"He doesn't speak his own name during the story, and he's dead so I can't ask him."

That's where the whisper cut off before it began anew, an echo of a moment we'd had, just over on the opposite bank, where I'd sparked a seed of violence in him. Though, if I were placing blame in such ways, wouldn't things have started earlier, when Grandfather first brought us here, in his inability to let go, desperate to show us Grandmother. Sharing that desperation with us. With me. A desperation I'd insisted on never letting go.

Almost got Danai killed as a child. Drove Vambrit to a desire that should never have been stoked. Perhaps Adamet would have been right if he'd told me it was my fault.

Another sculpture erupted, legs stretched out in front of itself and its whisper a moment in Vambrit's love life. Another pushed up beneath a bush, its head canted and an arm wrapped about knobby knees. The whispers grew convoluted, layering over with voices such that I sat in the center of a conversation where no one knew the topic and yet everyone insisted on being heard. And through it all, that woman whispered, "Show me!"

Then the marsh did, erupting a moment that had cries too recent to be echoes and a voice I knew well saying, "Get this off me!"

A splash.

A wader's echoing, coughing cry, followed by war-shouts.

Breathless whisper, "Don't leave me here."

"This was your fault. And you'd do it all over again."

The sucking noise of feet in marshland.

"Wait. Please?"

It started over, a call filtering through the rest, and I chased the whispers down, listening at each echo moment, leaning close, my heart beating faster than an egret taking flight from a crocodile. There, at the spot I'd buried Vambrit, a sculpture with head inverted and its hands buried to its wrists in mud. It kept on its damning cycle, and when I bent near, there could be no mistake to that voice.

My Danai. My dearest girl turned woman. She'd either left him to die or pushed his face into the mud herself. I found I didn't want to know which.

I thought I'd be angrier, deny her involvement, insist on the impossibility of it all. But I'd grown up in the Whispermarsh, and I trusted these moments more than I trusted myself some times.

Vambrit begged and Danai blamed him, their words becoming so familiar I could hear them repeat in my mind. I pressed my hands against my ears uselessly. I breathed hard, resisting sobs. Blinked harder, not allowing tears to fall. Vambrit was gone. *Gone.* He'd mattered. But...

Danai was still here. And she mattered more. Had always mattered more, since the day the midwife had laid her in my arms.

For too long I had given the past too much of my time. No more.

My hands sagged down off my head to hang limply by my sides. My thoughts coalesced into a steadiness I hadn't felt in far, far too long. As if the confusion had finally been put to rest by my decision. Calmness descended over me.

I turned, not for the shore to swim home but for that damn sculpture Vambrit had seen all those years ago and her desperate need to be shown. Reached inside her torso, pulled out a piece of driftwood heavier than my heart, and dragged it back to where I'd buried Vambrit. Back to his echo moment that pleaded endlessly for Danai to wait, please.

Then for her future, for the future she believed in for our people, I once more embraced silence.

Home

Where we leave the dead

"There's got to be more," said Danai.

"There doesn't *have* to be—"

"How far out do the sculptures go? If I knew I'd know how far to search, where to look." She bent her head by each of the echo moments, blanching here and there, becoming overtly frustrated the longer she searched.

I followed her, watching how the thick braid down her back swung and the wisps by her hairline curled. Remembered how her hands had clutched at my Zizi doll and her breath had blown hot on my neck as I rocked her back to sleep after one of her many nightmares. How she'd swung higher and higher between our cottages and tossed entrails to the herons and grass to uninterested turtles.

"I just have one question for you," I said, "Now that you've gotten all your questions from me. Why did you leave him to die?"

She spun around, sweat glistening on her skin, giving her eyes a feral, bright look. She glanced around again, as if searching one last time, then she bit down hard on her words. "Because it would never end. He'd go back out and kill more waders, inspire the others to do the same. We'd see our home destroyed because the Whispermarsh has never scared him. Nor you. Not like it should. We'd be in a war, a war we likely couldn't win. All for what? People who died decades ago? These whispering echoes of what once was? When people right now, here and alive, need our protection?"

"We could have talked to him..."

"Did that ever work for you? Don't answer that. We both already know the answer. I have a job to do, same as Father once did, protecting my people, not leaving them open to attack because of some vain obsession with the dead. I don't regret what I did."

"And I don't regret stealing him and bringing him here."

In the distance, a wader cried out, a deep call that stiffened us both.

"So now what?" she demanded, a soft echo of childlike worry shivering at the edges of her voice, reminding me of when she'd been young. "You'll tell Father? And the council? Bring them out here, let them hear Vambrit's memory?"

In answer, I led her through the grass to where the mud pooled with water and the roots curled, seeking purchase. "It was here." The driftwood club I'd used still lay within the wreckage, but the space was blessedly clear of Vambrit's anguished pleading. "And now it's not."

She swallowed. "Why?"

I sighed in exasperation. "For everything you've just said. Because he's gone and you're not. I can't live like Grandfather, pining away my years for someone who's no longer here. And I can't live like Vambrit, risking everything important for a few stagnant memories."

In the silent spaces between my words, I hoped Danai could hear my thoughts, could hear me telling her that she was more important. That she'd always been more important than the whispers of the past.

Danai shuddered out a great breath, her eyes never straying from the driftwood club I'd used. I wondered if she envisioned me wielding it, swinging it down on the scrollwood and seed-pods and snail shells and heron feathers that now lay scattered in the mud. I wondered if the fear I saw receding from her eyes was because she was remembering how I told her I never again took her into the Whispermarsh after almost losing her. If she was remembering any of the nights she'd tucked her cheek against my old Zizi doll as I kissed her forehead and murmured how much I loved her.

Slowly, she lifted her gaze to mine. Gone was the anger and fear that had fueled her all night. Replaced with a tired expression, but one that I thought glinted with respect and gratefulness.

"So now you tell me, what happens next?" I asked quietly.

I asked, for the future was in her hands, not mine, nor Adamet's, nor all the ancestors who had been laid to rest in the Whispermarsh once upon a time.

She didn't answer, for an awfully long time.

Then she ran a hand across her face and stepped closer. Her fingers weaved through mine, and for the briefest of moments she laid her head on my shoulder as if she were ten years younger. "I'll talk to the council. Let's go home and never listen to this cacophony again."

Perhaps her support was more than I deserved for all those years of disappearing into the marsh, all those years I'd risked our future for our past, putting Danai in danger even once the same way Grandfather had risked Vambrit and me. But I planned on taking it anyway.

I paused on the bank as Danai slid into the water, any sound she might have made overwhelmed by all the whispers competing for my senses. As we waded away through the marsh, Vambrit's voice faded, faded, until it was nothing but an echo in my mind.

And when we climbed the opposite shore and turned homeward, the grey sky releasing yet another drizzle, I whispered a goodbye to him and to Grandfather, and I swear when I did, I heard a bird call, an *emi-emi-bri* ringing through the air.

Marie Croke is a fantasy, science-fiction, and horror writer with 50 stories in publication. She is a graduate of the Odyssey workshop, first place winner in the Writers of the Future contest, and her work has been published in *The Best Horror of the Year Anthology*, *Beneath Ceaseless Skies*, *Apex Magazine*, *Diabolical Plots*, *Flash Fiction Online*, *Fireside*, *Cast of Wonders*, and *The Orange & Bee*, among other magazines and anthologies. She has worked as an editor for multiple magazines, including *khōréō* and *Dark Matter INK*, and has written reviews for *Apex Magazine* and articles for writers for *Planetside: The Online Magazine of SFWA*. She lives in Maryland with her family and enjoys crocheting, kayaking, and aerial dancing in her free time. You can find her online at mariecroke.com or chat with her @mariecroke.bsky.social on Bluesky.

WE BEGIN WHERE INFINITY ENDS

Somto Ihezue

Atop a ladder was Naeto, reaching for the lights. The lights flickered as his touch neared. Down below, Gozi held the ladder, rooting it to the ground. A small breeze came, and the ladder tilted, and the ladder swayed, but Naeto did not waver. Gozi was down there—Naeto knew the ladder would steady.

Over the school break, around midnight, the two boys had secretly been recalibrating all the streetlights in their town sector. There were fifty streetlamps on the asphalt road winding down the outskirts of the Asaba sector. Naeto and Gozi had changed fifteen since they began.

"The both of you are always tinkering."

Gozi spun around, letting go of the ladder. Naeto's legs gave way as the ladder buckled from under him. Before he could come crashing down, Naeto leaped for the streetlight's pole, the adhesive suction of his gloves activating. His hands now clasped safely around the pole; he slid down. The ladder had fallen but not touched the ground.

A girl had caught the ladder.

The light from the streetlamp illuminated her face: Bushy eyebrows, wooly brown hair squashed under a baseball cap, and freckles scattered across her face—the brown of old sawdust. Her shirt was an alarming white. Her cargo dungarees were torn at the knees. One of its straps rested on her shoulder. The other fell free. And the girl was tall. Taller than Naeto, but not taller than Gozi. Nobody was taller than Gozi.

"What are you doing here?" Naeto pushed past Gozi, throwing him a semi-angry glare. Gozi would answer for letting go of the ladder and almost killing him, but first, the girl.

"What am I doing here?" The girl squared up, her face inches from his. "What are YOU doing here?"

While Naeto agitatedly adjusted his glasses, she just looked on, slightly amused.

"We—We—" Gozi began to stutter.

"None of your business." Naeto did not let him finish. He grabbed the ladder she was still holding. The girl did not let go. Naeto tugged at it, and she held on tighter, a smile building on her face. Then, she let go, giggling as Naeto stumbled back, nearly knocked to the ground. Naeto cursed under his breath before placing the ladder back against the light pole.

"Hi." Gozi lumbered next to the girl, scratching the back of his neck.

The girl narrowed her eyes at him. "Hi."

"Gozi!" Naeto called in a hushed scream. A startled Gozi rushed forward with confused and asking eyes. Cedar-brown eyes. Naeto sighed, holding the bridge of his nose. "Hold. The. Ladder." He punctuated every word. "This time, try not to let go."

Gozi steadied the ladder once again as Naeto climbed back up.

"You still haven't explained what you're doing?" The girl waved from behind them.

"We don't have to explain ourselves, least of all to you." Naeto dislodged the streetlight's casing. This was a newer model, and screws were not employed in its fastening. The ones with screws took longer to dislodge.

"Maybe you'd like to explain to the security patrol."

Naeto stopped. The girl could not physically thwart their operation, but the security patrol could—and it would not be the first time.

"We are re-calibrating the lights," Naeto gave in, letting the light's casing hang loose as he began poking through the electrical circuit of the fluorescent tubes. The lights flickered with every touch.

"Re-calibrating?" The girl crossed her hands over her chest. "Why?"

Naeto did not respond. He reached into the chest pocket of his overalls and pulled out a diode filter. He connected this to the circuit bridge, and the light's sheen went from radiantly harsh to something softer.

"That's why." Naeto gestured to the soft light.

River. That was the girl's name. Since he was eight, Naeto had won the Young Engineers Builder's Prize three years in a row. He lost the prize after River and her parents moved into their sector a year ago. Naeto was distraught for weeks. River didn't know the things he knew about mechanical equilibrium, satellite motion, and thermodynamics. But, somehow, she had won the prize by building an unfinished canoe. Naeto always made sure to emphasize the unfinished part. And, unlike him, she never seemed to be trying. She would skip class to go skip pebbles across the lake, paint unartistic murals on the town council's walls, or work on her unfinished canoe. *What twelve-year-old went around building canoes?*

River blinked at the soft light, a question gathering in her eyes.

"It's for the fireflies." Gozi excitedly answered the still-gathering question. "It's saving them."

River slightly cocked her head at him. "There are no fireflies..." She looked up from Gozi to Naeto, who quickly shook his head at her. "...not here anyways."

"Because the harsh lights keep hurting them," Gozi muttered.

"Wait." Naeto clambered down the ladder. "You should not have been able to see us." He tugged at the translucent fiber overalls both he and Gozi were wearing. Under illuminance, he had designed them to confer a measure of translucency. He had made them after the security patrol caught them the last time.

"You're tinkering right in front of my bedroom window," River pointed to her house across the road. "I can't sleep with the lights going on and off every second."

"Maybe, next time, don't live on the outskirts of a sector, away from civilization," Naeto suggested.

"Maybe, next time, don't design ugly malfunctioning overalls," River suggested back.

"They are adequately functional." Naeto's voice cracked and pitched a hint higher. "And we are engineers, our outfits are designed for practicality, not beauty." Naeto had spent sleepless weeks on those overalls and, up until that moment, had believed they were the most beautiful pieces of clothing ever.

"Engineers without safety gears? Not even a climbing rope. I am in awe of your combined brilliance."

"Well—well, I'm not an engineer," Gozi said, offering an unsolicited clarification.

"What are you then, big boy?" River sent a smile his way.

And Gozi smiled back. "Well, Naeto says I'm more of an assistant."

"And who made Naeto chief supreme engineer?" River scoffed.

"Don't you have things to do? Like a canoe to finish?" Naeto started to take down the ladder. Gozi rushed over to help. Naeto brushed him away.

"Have you been spying on me and my boat?"

"Boat? It's barely a raft."

"Naeto." Gozi tried to stop him.

Stopping was antithetical to Naeto's character. "And who goes around building a canoe? Nobody uses canoes anymore."

"Didn't you get in trouble for messing with these lights before?" It was a standoff, and she was winning. "I heard your parents got a fine from town council for property damage."

"It's town council that's damaging everything!" It was Gozi.

Naeto had never heard or seen him like that. And from the shocked, remorseful expression on Gozi's face, the big boy hadn't either.

"I'm—I'm sorry—"

"Who is there!" It was the security patrol. Their flashlights split through the unlit parts of the road.

"Let's go!" River grabbed Gozi, who grabbed Naeto.

"My ladder—" Naeto made to pick it up.

"Leave it!" River yanked Gozi forward, and the big boy yanked Naeto away from the ladder.

The three teenagers ran, past River's house, ducking under palm fronds, sneaking through back-ways, and scampering away from barking life and mech-dogs. They ran past the lake, the loud chirping of the water bugs drowning out the slapping of their feet against tar. They ran past council hall, River's mural of a whale painted across its walls. They did not stop until they got to Naeto's house. The house was white and shaped like a box.

"Your house looks like a fancy sugar cube," a winded River announced as she studied the building.

"It's minimalist." Naeto realized he and Gozi were still holding hands. He let go. "And you didn't have to follow us all the way, your house was across the street."

"I needed the exercise." River faked a stretch. When she was done, she just stood there staring at the boys.

Naeto hoped she would turn and leave at some point. She did not.

"I've never been in your house before." River hopped onto the metal stairs that led to the front entrance.

Naeto hushed her. His father was a light sleeper. River hushed him back.

"Do you want to see Naeto's workstation?" Gozi shied in, low and eager.

"Yes!"

"No!" Before Naeto could protest further, Gozi had taken River from the door to the side of the building. Naeto grudgingly followed. There was a scan box lodged into the wall. The big boy grabbed Naeto's unwilling hand and placed it against the scanner. The scan box identified Naeto's prints, and a ladder whirred down from the window to the ground.

"You really are a fan of ladders," River chuckled to herself.

Up the ladder and inside Naeto's room, the girl looked around, trying to hide her awe, and failing.

"Look at all this...tinkering stuff."

Naeto's room was hexagonal and large, like three regular bedrooms merged into one. And there were things everywhere—but in a tidy, orderly manner. Workbenches lined with digital worksheets, shelves stacked with jars, huge manuals, and several "high-tech" appliances. A holographic board was sectioned against a wall. Mini wind vane rotors, solar panels, and engine motors were stacked on the floor. River leaned against one of Naeto's adaptable workbenches. She touched something, and the bench morphed from a smooth drafting table to a low magnetic field, attracting and pulling small metallic objects to its center.

River cupped a giggle.

"Please don't touch anything," Naeto sighed from behind her.

She ignored and waltzed over to a smart tool rack shelved over a wall. The rack held a plethora of unfamiliar materials. River took a jar from a row. Inside was a glowing, weird looking stone.

"Is this radioactive?"

A robotic arm snaked down to her and retrieved the jar.

"GeniT does not appreciate disorganization." Naeto took the jar from the robot and placed it back on the rack.

"Where did you get all this stuff?"

"Naeto's dad is one of the biggest scientists in the country," Gozi squeaked in.

"Don't over-embellish," Naeto said, rearranging the rack.

"I don't know what that means."

Naeto sighed. "It means—"

"Do you want to see something cool?" Gozi turned to River.

River nodded expectantly.

"We don't need to show her everything." Naeto rubbed his forehead.

"Do it," Gozi pleaded, tugging at Naeto. "Please, please, please."

Naeto exhaled, rolling his eyes. "Fine." He looked up at the ceiling. "GeniT, *starlight!*"

Starlight, GeniT beeped back in a mechanically velvet voice.

The room went dark. But only for a moment. Across the ceiling, across the walls, tiny pinpricks of light came, gradually intensifying until a sea of stars burned alive. The constellations followed, in shimmers, tracing stories in the bright dark. A meteor sped across the pocket universe, and River's eyes followed, and the lights found her pupils, illuminating them. And the planets, in subtle hues of red, blue, and brown, came orbiting into view—the rings of Saturn, the stormy swirls of Jupiter, and the burning of Mars. And galaxy folded into galaxy, and planets uncharted came, with black holes rising and coming undone. And there wasn't one sun, there were suns. A hum filled the room. It was still and gentle, like space itself had birthed it. And River reached out, her hands going higher, higher, and River touched infinity.

"Did you do this?" The girl's eyes did not stray from the stars burning across the digital planetarium.

"Naeto did." Gozi looked over to Naeto.

Naeto took off his glasses and started to clean them. They did not need cleaning. "It's just crap I put together and—"

"It doesn't look like crap to me." River, too, was now looking at Naeto.

And at that moment, Naeto thought her eyebrows were not all that bushy.

"Naeto could put one in your bedroom if you liked," Gozi offered.

"No, I can't."

"Why not? You did one for me."

Naeto did not answer. His eyes shifted from Gozi to River, and back to Gozi. The three of them stayed like that for a minute, a triangle with quiet edges.

"Is this the re-calibration thingy you were talking about?" River broke the quiet, walking over to one of the workbenches. On the table were circuit components of a streetlight broken up into sections.

"We're filtering the lights." Naeto joined her. "We added a diode component to yield softer lights—starkly different to the radiating intensity of our streetlights."

"The streetlights are too bright," Gozi explained in simpler terms. "Too harsh. It makes the fireflies' mating glow invisible. They also can't hide from predators because the lights give them away. And what happens when they can't hide or make baby fireflies?"

"They go away," River answered calmly, a calmness Naeto didn't think she possessed. "But fireflies are already...extinct. I read it in the National Geographic—"

"No, no, not extinct. Just very endangered." Gozi brimmed with nervous excitement, eager to share this new information. He rushed off to the holographic board and tried pulling up a page. "There have been firefly sightings not far from here, in the Ogbunike caves..." Gozi's hands were sweaty, and the moisture interfered with the board's functionality.

"Let me do it." Naeto nudged him aside.

"If fireflies still live in these places, maybe they still live...or can live here. They just need a little help." Gozi let out a breathless giggle.

"So, unlike the harsher lights, yours doesn't confuse the fireflies?" River turned to Naeto. "They can differentiate between it and their own lights?"

"It's still a prototype and needs more research, but yes, we think it could possibly, probably, help save Gozi's fireflies." Unlike Gozi, Naeto tried being more practical with his assessments.

"It's your fireflies too." The big boy gently shouldered Naeto, not gently enough, for it sent him staggering a little.

"It was your incessant idea to save the fireflies, like my schedule wasn't busy enough already," Naeto said, regaining his balance and adjusting his glasses. "I'm only doing this for theoretical research purposes."

"That doesn't make them not your fireflies."

"Let's agree to disagree."

River was watching them, amusement in the corner of her eyes. Again, Naeto removed and wiped his glasses. They did not need cleaning.

And morning interrupted, dawn stealing through the blinds.

"That's my cue." River skipped to the window.

"Your cue was hours ago." Naeto folded his tired arms.

"Same time tomorrow?"

"Yes." It was Gozi.

"No!" Naeto hushed him. "This is not jet club."

"Tomorrow it is." The girl laughed, climbing out the window. She slid down the ladder, faster than they both usually did, and she ran off, sunlight trailing after her.

And it went on. Day after day, River would sneak in through Naeto's bedroom window, and she and Gozi would aid him in fine-tuning his invention. They often just watched, giggling and scheming between themselves, and annoying Naeto. It took Naeto a minute to adjust to this new addition. Gozi, on the other hand, was thrilled to have someone else to talk fireflies with.

"Did you know fireflies are beetles, not flies, and are related to ladybugs and rhinoceros beetles?"

"Did you know firefly eggs also glow?"

"Did you know fireflies use their lights to communicate with each other?"

And at midnight, they would all sneak out to add the filter diode to the streetlights. With the three of them, the operation now progressed faster. River also insisted they used safety climbing gear, and she vehemently refused to be called Naeto's assistant. She did agree to wear the ugly overalls.

One night, they gave her a farlight. Another one of Naeto's inventions. It was how Naeto and Gozi communicated—mostly for the fun of it. When night gathered, one of them would shine their farlight into the sky, and wherever the other farlight was, it would come aglow. Two farlights in the night sky meant they would be re-calibrating the streetlights at midnight.

"Just like fireflies." River carefully took the farlight in her hands.

"Just like fireflies," Gozi repeated, the smile on River's face finding his.

River's glee faded. "I live far away. Your lights won't find my light." She handed the farlight to Naeto and backed away. "I also don't think I'll be here for long."

River's parents were research archeologists. They moved around a lot and had lived in many sectors.

"My family is from Rwanda," Gozi bridged the space between them. "I was born there. My moms say we would go back someday. But that day is not today." He squatted a little to look her in the eyes, just like his moms did when they wanted to reassure him.

"And there's a reason they're called farlights." Naeto folded the farlight back into River's hands. "They might not get to Rwanda or wherever your folks move to next, but here in this sector, wherever you are, it'll find you."

And what was once two farlights in the night sky became three. And what was once fourteen re-calibrated lights became thirty.

"We should give the new lights a name!" River beeped up.

"I agree!" Gozi beeped up too.

Naeto rolled his eyes as he scribbled new schematics on the holographic board. Of late, Gozi had eagerly been going along with all of River's ridiculous antics.

"We should call it The River Naetozi Tinker Light!" River sprung to her feet, hands on her waist, victorious.

Naeto exhaustingly rubbed the bridge of his nose.

"It's our names merged into one!"

"Very original." Naeto stepped away from the board. "But why does your name come first and written in full while ours gets meshed up? Eh?"

"Because I came up with the idea." River leaned on the table across from him. "The lights would still be nameless without me."

"The River Naetozi Tinker Light is a long, ridiculous name."

"I—I like it." Gozi chirped in.

"Of course you do," Naeto scoffed.

"Maybe if you say it over and over, it will grow on you." River danced in Naeto's direction. "Say it. Say it," she began to chant.

"No!" Naeto scampered away from her.

River threw back her head, laughing a bellied contagious laugh, and soon, Gozi joined in. Eventually, so did Naeto.

One night, Naeto fell from the ladder and landed on his arm. It was just him and Gozi. River's farlight had not shone in the sky.

Gozi ran to him. "Let me see." He gently took Naeto's hand.

"It's nothing." Naeto clutched his arm, stifling a painful groan. The gloves' adhesive function had not activated in time.

"We shouldn't have left the safety gear."

Naeto had left the ropes on purpose. "It takes too much time to set up. Time we do not have."

"Now see how we're spending all that precious time." Rarely was Gozi sarcastic. Naeto didn't think he was even capable of it. Despite his hurting arm, this amused him.

"This is not funny," Gozi's voice grew firm. "This is bad."

A purplish bruise was starting to spread across Naeto's arm. Under the streetlight, it was radiant like an overripe avocado.

"I'm sure River will be happy."

"I think she'll be upset," Gozi countered.

A wordless minute passed between them as the big boy inspected the injury.

"We should get you to the clinic."

"Right, and explain how I got injured and why we are out this late?"

"We cannot leave you like this. What if it's some...internal injury? What if it gets worse?"

Naeto could tell Gozi was not going to back off.

"Fine. Fine. We'll go to the clinic," he reassured him. "But let's go tomorrow, after I come up with an elaborate lie."

"Naeto—"

"It doesn't hurt as bad as it looks, I promise."

"Are you sure?"

"Ugh, I swear it by the River Naetozi Tinker Light."

River could get Gozi to partake in all her ridiculous antics, but so could Naeto. Gozi was his friend first. He knew how to get him to budge. And as much as Gozi tried to hide his delight from hearing Naeto use the name, the mile-wide smile playing across his lips betrayed him.

"What?" Gozi was trying his best to stay serious.

"What?"

"You're looking at me weird."

"You were looking at me weird first."

"No, I wasn't."

The two boys were quietly laughing now.

"Oya, stand up." Gozi picked Naeto off the ground. "Let's go home.

Unfortunately, the injury was as bad as it looked. Naeto had sustained a non-displaced fracture. And Gozi had been right, River was upset. She paced the length of Naeto's room, lecturing on and on about how they never listened to her. Naeto just stared blankly at her, his arm in a brace and sling. They had told his father he had fallen off Gozi's bike.

With Naeto's condition, the re-calibrating operation fell to River and Gozi. River was a quick study—which she claimed had nothing to do with Naeto's horrible teaching skills. Adding the filter component to the streetlights became her primary responsibility. They would rendezvous at Naeto's house, with clear schematics and directions on replicating the filter's design. At night, Gozi and River would recalibrate the streetlights using the filters. River also started bringing others. Random kids from school. River insisted that the more people knew about saving the fireflies, the better. So, each day, she showed up with a new kid: Ugochi who endlessly mimicked a hawk's call. Makua and her mismatched socks. Jide who had a birthmark shaped like a tree. Rafael and the clattering rainbow beads in his hair. Nnayeleugo whose laughter was the sound of hiccups. Mazi who spoke six languages. Barefoot Zobam who talked to her reflection and dreamt many dreams. And more and more, they came. If Naeto wasn't losing his sanity before, he was now. Gozi and River were the only ones allowed in his house, and like he always reminded them, was solely because he needed assistants. Now, he had feral strangers—his classmates—running around his workstation, touching all his equipment with unsanitary hands. For Gozi, it was just more people to share fun facts with:

"Did you know firefly larvae eat snails and worms?"

"Did you know that large groups of fireflies sometimes blink in unison?"

"Did you know firefly light can be yellow, green, or orange?"

After a while, Gozi and River stopped showing up as often. To Naeto's knowledge, the operation was still in progress—Gozi had mentioned they set up a second base at River's house since she lived closer to the uncalibrated streetlights. And there was Naeto's father, who was limiting Naeto's "playtime" until he fully recovered, making his house inconducive for their operation. And on days when all their farlights dotted the sky, Naeto would wait and wait, but Gozi and River would not come. Even the random kids from school stopped coming.

Naeto began to feel many things—some he couldn't explain. The recalibration was made possible because of him. The designs and schematics were his. One component wired inaccurately could implode everything. Carrying on without him was unwise on their part. So, he went down to the lake. It was where River held her never-ending canoe construction project.

"Will you ever finish building it?" Naeto asked from behind her, squinting, shielding his eyes from the sunlight.

"We'll see." River didn't look back at him. She was sawing a piece of plywood in half. The cut was jagged.

"That is rather rough."

"A thing isn't beautiful because it is perfect."

That was another thing Naeto found exhausting about River. Her random bouts of philosophical dreamy responses. It was not something she did often, which made it more jarring to witness.

Naeto inched nearer, inspecting the canoe. The places where wood met wood were rough-hewn, bark in patches where the sanding was unfinished. The faint scent of wood sap tickled his nostrils and settled on his tongue. It was pine. Across the planks were paint smudges where River had attempted artistry and failed. The hull had uneven boards held by nails undoubtedly scavenged from a landfill.

Naeto had never seen a canoe on the lake. The floating pads and high-rotor ferries had replaced them all. Things were different in the last sector where River lived. For one, they had canoes. Naeto wondered if her canoe would take to water.

When River was done, she walked home. Naeto followed. She was five steps ahead, him five steps behind, the setting sun a painting on the horizon. River would throw questioning glances at him as they walked, and Naeto would look away. He had never been alone with her before. Gozi was always there. *Why didn't he just confront Gozi instead?*

River lived by the lake. So, the walk was a short one. When she ushered him through the front door, Naeto found the house odd. He had never been inside it before. There was one table. One chair. One portrait of something on fire. You could tell whoever lived in it wouldn't be there long. On the table were bits and parts of the filter diode—River's workstation.

"Where did you get these materials?"

"I stole some of yours." River was beside herself with pride. "Mine is not as sleek as your design, and I don't have an ultra-modern workstation, but it gets the job done. We have recalibrated three more streetlights."

Naeto clinked his fingers on the table, examining the components. Her putting all this together with nothing but stolen scraps and a screwdriver, was fairly impressive. Naeto didn't start with scraps. His father was a robotics and electromechanical systems expert and Naeto had considerable access to his gear. He wondered what River would accomplish with the access he had.

"Did you want to talk about something?" River brought his attention back to her.

Naeto straightened up. "You and Gozi should not have replicated the designs without me."

"Oh," River paused. "I thought he mentioned it to you?"

"He—he did."

"And that you were okay with it?"

"I was."

River let her confusion show, then started to tinker with the filter components. "Also, the rains are back, and the storms have gotten worse this year. We haven't had the chance to re-calibrate the lights in a while."

"Doesn't explain why your farlights have been in the sky these past few nights." Naeto brought his hand between the components on the table, halting her tinkering. One of River's brows climbed in response.

"That had nothing to do with the recalibration, we were just having fun."

"Good to know you've both been doing that too."

River paused again.

"I don't think this is about the lights." A smile tugged at the corner of her lips. Her amusement riled Naeto.

"You—you can't just go around taking people's friends!" He said it before realizing how pathetic he sounded.

"Well, I thought I was your friend too. Apparently not."

"That—that's not what I meant—"

"And Gozi is not property. He is not something to take or give." There was a shift in her tone. "And it's not my fault he likes me more than you."

She was baiting him. He had known her long enough to understand that. Still, he fell for it, all sense of reason flying out the window.

"Maybe he wouldn't if you stopped flirting with him every five seconds."

River snickered. "I'll flirt with whomever I want."

"Good for you! Find someone else then."

"Who? You?"

Naeto went quiet as stone. The question had come like a boulder falling into his open palms, and he struggled to find balance.

"Oh." River's eyes widened. "You do want me to flirt with you!"

"I—I don't." Naeto was unraveling.

"Yes, you do." River chuckled. She danced up to him, and Naeto staggered back. "This is interesting because you want me to flirt with you, but you also want Gozi to flirt with you."

It was all too much information and accusations for Naeto to register. He had come to confront River, now he was on trial. "I—I don't know what you're talking—"

"Don't deny it. You're not subtle, with your wandering eyes." River was visibly enjoying seeing him spiral. "I just didn't know you were a greedy little nerd."

"I am not a nerd!"

"You invented a light filter for your boyfriend. You are a nerd."

"He is not my boyfriend!"

"Sure." River comically tiptoed forward. "Though, lucky for you, I like kissing nerds."

Naeto fled. He stumbled over the table, over the chair, and scattered out the door, and he ran, River's witchy laughter echoing after him.

Three nights later, after his confrontation with River, unable to think straight without her accusations and witchy laughter creeping into his mind and taunting him, Naeto went to find Gozi.

Perched outside his friend's window, the picking wind flapping at his overalls, Naeto knocked and knocked against the window. Gozi's home was a small bungalow, so Naeto did not have to worry about falling. When the window flung open, a startled Gozi was on the other side.

"Nae—Naeto—"

Naeto pushed past him, climbing into the room. Just like his, Gozi's room also had a digital planetarium across the ceiling.

"I have been knocking for hours," Naeto exaggerated, adjusting his overalls.

"What—what are you doing here?"

Naeto looked up with an angry squint. "I have not seen or heard from you in forever!"

"We saw each other last week."

"That—that's not the point." Naeto shifted where he stood. "Remember the fireflies we're supposed to save together? What happened to that?"

"Naeto, there's a literal storm coming."

"I can see that." Naeto did not appreciate his patronizing tone. He was seldom on this end of their arguments. "Which is why we must go before it gets here." He grabbed Gozi's hand and pulled him along. The big boy did not budge.

"You can't tamper with electricity under the rain."

"I know. I am the engineer here," Naeto threw up his hands, visibly impatient. "GeniT predicts there won't be any rain for five hours. We can achieve a lot in five hours."

"You still have your brace."

Naeto had hoped his overalls would hide it. He had removed the sling to make sure.

"It's fine, it's practically healed." He pulled at his sleeves. "I also brought the protective gear for the ladder," he smiled, dangling the ropes in Gozi's face. "I promise not to fall again."

"Naeto, you can't climb ladders with an injured arm. You can't climb ladders in a storm."

Gozi was speaking to him like he was a child, which they both were.

"Or maybe there's someone else you'd rather climb ladders with!"

"Naeto, what is going on with you?"

Naeto bit at his fingernails. His palms were slick with sweat. He wiped them on his overalls, only to find them damp almost immediately.

"River said that you—that you like her," he heaved out.

"Of course I like her. She's our friend."

"...that you like her more than me."

"Eh?"

"Do you?" Naeto swallowed, his voice a crashing LEGO set. "Do you like her more than me?"

Gozi just stood there.

And Naeto continued. "Because I like you, I like you a lot, I think I always have, and when River said it the other day, I was so confused, and I didn't know how to feel, and then she tried to kiss me, and I panicked, and I ran away, and I couldn't stop thinking about her, and I couldn't stop thinking about you, and I just want to know if you've been thinking about me too," Naeto blurted out, ending his monologue by wiping his eyes and running nose with his sleeve, all in one take. This made it worse because the snort mixed into the tears, and half his face was now smeared in it.

"You...you call me your idiot assistant all the time."

"Oh." Naeto straightened up. He had not expected that, not after his profound confession.

"I know you don't mean it." Gozi's fingers twisted and untwisted around each other. "I just did not get 'I like like you' from being called that."

Naeto took off his glasses and wiped them with his sleeves. They did not need cleaning.

"I'm changing the lights for you," Naeto's eyes avoided Gozi's, focusing instead on a point on the floor. "You cared about the fireflies, so I did too."

Gozi just stood there.

"I put up your planetarium so we could see the same stars every night." Naeto did not look up at the ceiling. He was still focused on that point. "And I built the farlights, so we would always find each other."

Gozi just stood there.

"Naeto I—I ehm—I don't know. I don't know." That was all Gozi said.

There was a physical aching in his chest. Naeto did not understand it. He hugged himself, cradling his hurting chest, and looked out the window. "I—I'm going to go."

"Naeto," Gozi softened. "You could stay here...you could just stay here...with me."

And the two boys stood there. They stood there a while. Then Gozi reached for him, trying to knit the space between them, and Naeto drew away.

"Naeto—"

He did not wait for him to finish. Naeto scaled out of the window in one swoop, and he ran.

And the rains came down—impenetrable curtains of water. Naeto waded through it, soaked to the bone in seconds. The streets were dark and flooded, half the streetlights sizzling with damp electricity. The torrent rushing through the road drainage was the sound of waterfalls, and it rattled the metal drain covers. Naeto took the ladder from its hiding spot and heaved it against the light post. And in that moment, his resolve wavered. He wanted to turn and run, run back home, run back to...No. He was going to climb. And Naeto climbed up the ladder, rain pelting down on him, each drop a small stone. He got to the light casing and dislodged it, the fluorescent plates also coming free, revealing the green-plated circuit beneath. Naeto could barely see through all the water. He was wet. Everything was wet. He could not tell where his body ended and where the water began. But Naeto had done this many times. His hands remembered. He took out the filter diode and inserted it into the circuit. In the downpour, the streetlight went from incandescent to welcoming, finding all the corners of his wet face. The lights reminded him of Gozi.

And the lights sparked, the glass casing shattered, and Naeto fell, and the ground rushed up to meet him. He crashed onto a drainage plate, and it gave way, plunging him into the rushing current below.

As the sky unwillingly morphed, giving way to a more radiant intensity and dispersing the deep grays from the previous stormy night, it met Naeto hauling his body down the long, winding asphalt road. There was sand in his hair. Bruises and cuts delicately partitioned his face. His overalls were in shreds, like something caught in crossfire. And they dripped water onto the asphalt. Naeto shook as he walked. When the sun was completely over the horizon, its lights touched the paleness of Naeto's face; it touched his eyes, and Naeto did not blink away.

His glasses were gone, his tools were gone, and he would never see the rope again. Only Naeto remained. When he had fallen into the drainage the previous night, he had latched onto the walls and held on. He did not let go, not until the rains died and morning called.

In the far distance, Naeto saw the possible outline of a person's silhouette. Without his glasses, he could not be sure. But the silhouette soon went from one, to five, to many. They surrounded him.

"We found him!"

"Ah thank god!"

"Where were you?"

"Why were you out in the storm?"

"Why were you out at night, eh this boy?"

The voices came crowding him, and many hands touched Naeto. It was a search party. They were all in raincoats, so they had been out all night. Naeto's father broke through the crowd, hugging him tightly until Naeto's body disappeared into his. He took Naeto's face in his hands. His father looked like he had been crying all night.

"Where is Gozi?" It was Gozi's mother.

Everyone turned to Naeto for an answer he did not have.

"Gozi?"

"Was he not with you?"

"No—no, he wasn't. It was just—it was just me."

Gozi had gone after him the previous night. And when his moms realized he was gone, they had reached Naeto's father. Neither of the boys were with the man. The last contact was River's parents. When they dragged River out of bed and besieged her with questions, she confessed to everything; what she and the boys had been doing all school break. A search party had formed immediately.

With the search for Gozi still ongoing, Naeto was hospitalized. First, they pumped out all the flood water he had ingested. In addition to his unhealed arm, his leg was now bound in a brace. He had severely sprained his leg in the fall. Naeto would not climb again, not for a while. River came every hour with updates on the search. She came even when there were no updates. She'd just sit there with him. Naeto believed everyone blamed him for what happened—for making Gozi go out in the storm. Had he listened and stayed that night, Gozi would not have followed, and Gozi would be here, he would be safe. And even if everyone didn't blame him, Naeto blamed himself. But River did not.

They found Gozi two days later.

The torrents had washed him into the lake. He was found amongst the water shrubs.

"Will they let us see him?" Naeto labored out of bed when he heard the news.

"Naeto—" River tried to steady him back.

"They have to let us see him." Naeto fell, and River caught him. And Naeto cried.

"Naeto, listen, please." River wasn't one to plead. "My parents said Gozi was hurt quite bad."

"What—what does that mean?"

"I don't know." River shook her head, wiping away the brimming tears. "I don't know." She turned. She could not look him in the eyes for what came next. "They're taking him back to Rwanda."

"For what?"

"They said he needs extensive medical care, the type he can't get here."

"Rwanda is on the other side of the continent."

"It is. But Rwanda is Gozi's home, and the rest of his family is there and—"

"No! His home is here."

"Rwanda's medical sector is the leading—"

"No, no!" Naeto clasped his hands over his ears, like he knew what she was going to say, but did not want to hear it.

But River made sure he did. "Gozi's citizenship gives him free access to their healthcare."

Naeto went quiet for a while, his hands still over his ears, his eyes shut tight.

"When are they leaving?" he finally asked.

"Naeto...they already left."

Naeto cried all night. He cried the next night, the night that followed, and the night that followed. His best friend was gone, and he did not get to say goodbye.

Naeto spent the coming quiet weeks indoors. His father didn't say it, but Naeto knew he was grounded for life. Naeto was fine with that. He also would not get far given his injuries. He hardly left his bed, and there was now a huge body-sized dent in the mattress. Naeto deleted all the schematics for the filters. He threw the prototypes, the suction gloves, the overalls, and the diode components in the trash. Their ladder had been lost in the storm, and Naeto didn't look for it.

And last of all, he took down the planetarium. It was of no use. He and Gozi could no longer see the same stars.

Naeto tried to reach Gozi every day. His father also helped, trying to contact Gozi's parents. They did reach them, but Gozi was never disposed to talk, and when he was, he spoke very little. Over time, their interactions thinned out.

When the school year kicked off, the doctors recommended homeschooling until Naeto fully recovered. But Naeto's body wasn't the only broken thing. On one of those quiet, broken nights, he lay in bed staring at the starless ceiling. And it came, a light the shape of a moon. It refracted through his window and danced across his ceiling.

It was a farlight.

Naeto scampered out of bed to the window, flinging them ajar.

She looked exactly like she did that first night. Bushy eyebrows, wooly brown hair squashed under a baseball cap, and freckles scattered across her face. Her shirt was an alarming white. Her cargo dungarees were torn at the knees. One of the straps rested on her shoulder. The other fell free.

"River."

She must have heard his voice sink. "Oh, I'm—I'm sorry."

Naeto apologetically shook his head. He stepped back, making room for her as she climbed the ladder, briefly perching on his windowsill. She reminded him of a sparrow. No one had come in through the window, not in a while.

"You know you can use the front door."

"I know," River chuckled, squeezing through the window. His room had not heard a chuckle, not in a while.

Now inside the room, River hugged him, a little too tightly. And Naeto hugged his friend back.

"Thank you."

"For what?" River let go.

"For being here."

River shoved him. The way Gozi usually did, only a bit more tenderly. She hugged him again.

"So…I was thinking…we should restart the River Naetozi Tinker Operation," she whispered.

"What?" Naeto pulled away.

"For Gozi." River tried to reach back for him, and Naeto squirmed away. "He was right about the fireflies making a comeback in other places. They could come back here too."

"River, that doesn't matter anymore."

"It mattered to Gozi." Her voice went an octave higher. "And it mattered to me. And you."

"I—I don't think—" Naeto paused. He took off his glasses and cleaned them. They did not need cleaning. "I can't climb again."

River grabbed his shoulders and squeezed them. "You won't have to. Not today."

"Today?"

River inhaled before skipping giddily to the window. Naeto followed her. "I brought friends." She pushed the window open.

And down below were all the kids from school—the ones River had been bringing to his house: Ugochi and his hawk call. Makua and her mismatched socks. Jide and his tree-shaped birthmark. Rafael and the clattering rainbow beads in his hair. Nnayeleugo whose laughter was the sound of hiccups. Mazi who spoke six languages. Barefoot Zobam and all her dreams. They all had on overalls, protective gears, and tool bags.

"Turns out they were listening while touching your stuff with unsanitary hands," she mimicked him, lathering her voice with snobbery.

"I—I don't sound like that."

"You do."

"River, it's hardly midnight. People will see."

"Let them see."

The whole thing terrified Naeto. This debacle with the lights got them here in the first place—minus him not taking well to rejection. What if someone fell? Or got electrocuted? Or worse?

"It will be fine." River squeezed his hand. "I promise."

And Naeto nodded, letting go—of all the uncertainty, fear, and things he could not control.

"I doubt they know how to use those tools." He looked down at the pack of chattering kids scattered on his lawn. Their tool bags and overalls were a few sizes too big.

"Oh, it's mostly for the optics. We grabbed what we could from the school lab." There was a tinge of prideful accomplishment in her voice.

"Of course those hideous overalls came from the school lab."

"They are designed for practicality, not beauty." River nudged his shoulder with hers, and Naeto covered his face with shy embarrassment.

"And you can change the name if you want to," River offered. "It's your lights after all."

"Well, River Naetozi Tinker Lights has unfortunately grown on me," Naeto flashed her a half-smile, one that built into laughter. And there they were, two giggling children in a bedroom that once held stars.

So, Naeto, River, and all the kids from their school went from streetlight to streetlight, recalibrating the lights, filtering their glow from a harsh brightness to something soft, something safe. As expected, parents and the sector's security patrol flooded out, trying to stop them. That would have been possible when it was just Naeto and Gozi. Now, they were many. And what was once thirty-three recalibrated streetlights, became fifty.

"Did you know there were once winter fireflies up in Seattle?" River asked Naeto.

"No. No, I didn't know that."

River went quiet.

"My parents are moving again."

"Oh." That was all Naeto said.

"I heard it's nice in Seattle. They have snow. I have never seen snow before."

"River." Naeto's eyes welled up. It was happening again; he was losing another friend.

River's eyes welled up too. It would be the last time Naeto would see her like that.

"Don't you dare forget me, nerd!" She whacked his chest.

Naeto let out a shaky laugh—it was also a shaky sob. "You are impossible to forget. And you're a nerd too."

River thought about it for a minute and nodded in agreement. "I am."

"And you can thank the flickering lights. You wouldn't have seen us that night if not for them."

"That wasn't the first time I was seeing you."

"Oh, really?"

"You're like the least subtle person alive. I knew every flickering light was the both of you."

"So, you'd been watching us?"

River blinked a nod.

"Why?"

"I liked watching you and Gozi." She tucked a stray braid behind her ear. "I liked watching you."

And under the River Naetozi Tinker Lights, River kissed Naeto. A gentle thing. This time, Naeto did not run away.

Twelve years later and Naeto was going home. Home had been a memory for a while. He wondered if the sector was the same. If the sun still trailed after running children, if the rains still fell like pebbles, and if the streetlights were still soft. He hoped they were. After what he, River, and the other kids had done, they had garnered quite the attention. Media outlets carried the story of schoolchildren culling light pollution in their home sector to save the fireflies. Government agencies and wildlife conservatory bodies followed, with a keen interest in the ecological benefits of the recalibration process. The offers came next: monetary offers from power corporations, partnership propositions from questionable tech founders, and scholarships from renowned institutions. Before long, Naeto was off to college, the youngest in his class. With a highly funded graduate research grant, he put together a team, further advancing the mechanics of the recalibration system. In time, the River Naetozi Tinker light was utilized worldwide in a conservation effort to decrease light pollution and restore the critically declining population of fireflies. Naeto's groundbreaking innovation was life changing. When he graduated college, the job offers poured in. Despite River's remarks about him being a "horrible" teacher, Naeto loved teaching. So, he took a position at the Namibian University of Science and Technology, the same institution he had graduated from, and he was content.

Now, sitting in the back of a haxi—the new hovering taxis everyone was obsessed with—Naeto was going home. Because Gozi was there.

They had reconnected a few years back. On a rainy afternoon, while Naeto was preparing for his third-year seminar, Gozi had sent him a congratulatory email for his many achievements. Naeto had stopped everything. That one-paragraph text was all that mattered. Only Gozi would rejoin society and send a text via email. The boys emailed every day, talking about the most random things: the first time they tried lasagna, and how toilet paper was getting softer. They talked about River. And when Gozi mentioned he had moved back home, Naeto went home too.

With his luggage and all, Naeto had his haxi hover straight to Gozi's old house. The house was still there, though the compound looked different. Gozi's moms had been farmers, and their home had been a haven for all growing and crawling things. Having returned a few months earlier, Gozi had taken things a step further. Their home was now a sanctuary. And there was the color, like the rains of April came and never left. Green moss, like green carpets, crawled over the house and barn in the most deliberate manner. Vines, branches, and foliage looped and weaved down the roof, down the wooden pillars. There were trees everywhere, and the breeze whistled through the leaves, and like a hall of children, they whispered. Surrounding the compound, fallow land stretched forth, dotted with wildflowers, and the sun danced on their petals. And what followed the color was the sound, the soft, gentle call of animals breathing. Every step Naeto took sent grasshoppers darting off the thigh-high grass. The rabbits followed, peeping cautiously before scurrying into the underbrush. Above, squirrels and sparrows chattered in the trees. A herd of sheep cut in front of him, their wool, a billowing black. In a corner laid a Great Pyrenees, a quiet sentry on guard.

Naeto followed the sound of wood being chopped. He followed it past some goats scaling the low walls. He followed it past gobbling turkeys and clucking hens. And he found Gozi. This Gozi was many things. He was bigger, taller. With each measured swing, his arms bulged like ukwa pods. His shoulders were as broad as doors. Sweat gleamed down his forehead, streaming onto the log below. Gozi was a big, bearded man chopping wood. His axe came down again, and steel met wood, and what was one log became two.

And Gozi saw him.

Of course Naeto wasn't going to run away. He was not twelve anymore. Still, he considered it.

"Hey." He waved with both his hands. *Why did he do that? One hand would have been sufficient!*

Gozi said nothing. He looked at Naeto like he was seeing him for the first time. The big man's stare was steel. Then, in one motion, he dropped the axe, rushed up to Naeto, and embraced him, lifting him slightly off the floor. His sweat and dirt were now on Naeto like they had been there all along. Unsure but slowly, Naeto embraced his friend back. And for a moment, they were twelve again, tinkering with things they shouldn't tinker with.

"You're..." Naeto gestured at all of him, "...bigger."

Gozi smiled, his cedar-brown eyes crinkling at the corners. "And you're still you."

But so was Gozi. He had tripled in size, morphed, and shifted in the passing years, but his face was still his face, and his eyes were still his. There were other things. Gozi had lost a leg after the accident, after they had found him unconscious by the lake. He now had a prosthetic one. Naeto knew about this.

"I—ehm—I wanted to say—" Naeto started.

"It doesn't matter anymore." Gozi softly shook his head.

And the two friends sat, and talked, and remembered everything. They remembered River. And as they remembered, it was like they had never been separated all those years ago. Like they were not reuniting twelve years later. Like they were just two friends hanging out like they did every other day.

"Will I see you again tomorrow?"

"Yes. Yes."

They saw each other the next day, the day after that, and the day after. One evening, Gozi took Naeto down to the lake, and there it was—River's canoe.

"All this time." Naeto ran his hands along its rough exterior.

River completed it before she left their sector. Two years later, she built another canoe in Seattle and sailed into a river. It was the last time she was seen.

"I want to show you something." Gozi climbed into the canoe and stretched his hand to Naeto.

Naeto took his hand.

The boys rowed River's canoe into the lake, and it skimmed the waters like it belonged there. The reeds welcomed them, nodding in the delicate breeze. The water was more crystal than Naeto remembered. Through the floating flora, he could see the scales on the tilapia and the smooth corners of the pebbles at the bottom. The canoe's paddles were mismatched pairs of oars. In their design was River's impatience, but also her will. When the paddles parted the water, Naeto felt the lake in his arms. It was strong but not tethering, a gentle tug, like friends holding hands, like water finding water. Small pools of lake water gathered at their feet, but the vessel was not built to sink. A small current came, and the canoe creaked, the canoe bent. Naeto did not waver—for bending was not breaking. He knew River's canoe would steady.

And the canoe sailed, like a dream half-realized, but a dream, nonetheless.

They reached the other side of the lake, to a field that stretched for miles. Naeto never knew about this field.

"Gozi, what are we doing here?"

"Just wait. You'll see."

The two friends sat in the tall, tall grass, waiting, watching the sunset. Then they laid in the grass. Soon, the sun lowered behind a forested hill, giving way to the moon.

"It's time." Gozi stood.

"Time for what?" Naeto came up too, trying to find his friend in the darkness.

Gozi took Naeto's face in his cold palms, turning it away from his, and towards the empty distance. "Just wait."

Naeto waited, his eyes finding the night, his feet sinking slightly into the mellow soil, his breathing clear in his ears. Gozi's breathing found his, blending into his. And Naeto waited, and waited, and he saw.

It was one speck. Soft and aglow. Light becoming. It sailed, higher, higher. One firefly against the night. And what was one became two, and what was two became ten thousand, as waves of fireflies lifted from the grass like lanterns, their wings; silk whispering to silk. And all the fireflies reached for heaven, beginning where the stars ended.

Their glow, a thing unbroken, a thing afire, touched all the corners of Naeto's face. They touched his glasses, and Naeto saw light.

Naeto held a gasp, soft laughter and tears escaping him. The fireflies were as farlights finding each other. Slowly, he reached out, his hand sailing higher, higher, pinpricks of light finding his skin, illuminating him, and Naeto touched infinity.

"When did they come back?"

"I don't know. I came, and they were here." Standing side by side, Gozi snuck his hand into Naeto's, one shy finger at a time. "They are here because of you. Because of the River Naetozi Tinker lights. It worked, like you said it would."

"I—I did it for you."

It felt like they were back in Gozi's bedroom all those years ago. Naeto looked away, reaching for his glasses. They did not need cleaning. And Gozi led his hands away from them. He took Naeto's face, eyes finding eyes, and kissed him. A gentle thing. And Naeto did not run away.

Somto Ihezue is a writer, editor, and filmmaker. He is an MFA fellow in Creative Writing at the University of Maryland. His writing has appeared in *Clarkesworld*, *Poetry Magazine*, *Uncanny Magazine*, *Strange Horizons*, *Beneath Ceaseless Skies*, *Flash Fiction Online*, and others. His work has received residencies and fellowships from the Kimmel Harding Nelson Center for the Arts, Tin House, Clarion West, Sitka Center for Art & Ecology, Sundress Academy for the Arts, and more. He was assistant editor of the *Publishing Taught Me* anthology (SFWA & NEA) and co-editor of *Will This Be a Problem? The Anthology*.

THE NAME ZIYA

Wen-yi Lee

At first I thought something had broken in my book.

When the cutter offered forty thousand shada for all five parts of my name, my mother puffed up. *Absolutely not,* she said, *you brain-gored swindler.*

I sat on his bench as they haggled, naked from the waist up. It was a cool morning and my skin pimpled around the ideograms on my bare chest. The full set of five was worth the most; forty thousand shada was more money than we took from ten harvests, and would have covered my tuition with coin to spare. But I was glad my parents had rejected the first offer. I was not prepared to lose the entirety of my name just yet.

"All right, all right," Durudawanyi relented. Earlier, the rector had murmured and prevaricated as he examined my ideograms, evaluating their specific powers and different combinations, along with my age and other factors. "Twenty-five thousand, for the affective three."

My mother hesitated. It was unfortunate that I had been born with my more powerful names all at the end: the ones that let me shape earth without cracking, find my way in the dark, share our dogs' senses. You could only sell from the end, and never out of order, so selling three names would mean losing most of my magic. But where I was going, money was more important than magic. "Thirty," she said.

Durudawanyi scrutinized her. "Twenty-eight."

My parents exchanged a look. "Done."

I clutched my blouse. Two days ago, I would never have fathomed sitting in the rector's lush, airy hut, the place where people went and came back changed. But then the letter arrived. I had, beyond all hope, tested into the University of Ustonel—a place far, far away—a place that produced consuls and guildmasters and airship captains—a place that had never, until this cycle, accepted students from the Angze Hills.

The tuition for three years' study was thirty-five thousand shada. A discounted price, as a welcome.

Not going was out of the question. And so I was here, selling the most precious thing an Angze was born with.

When the namecutter sliced the first part-name from my chest, I screamed. I had promised not to, I had sworn to be brave, but it ripped from me with a pain like I had never felt in my life. Blood was running down my chest. "It's all right, darling," my mother whispered into my hair. "It's all right." She had sold one part of her name to feed us during the drought a few years ago. My father had sold one when I was a child, and one before I was born. Now inducted, I pressed into my mother's arms, fighting back tears. I thought of my name being carried to the anchorites in the hills, whose prayers from our names the bethel claimed kept the soil rich and the rivers flowing through the valleys. There were even those devout who offered up their part-names willingly. Though our village did not particularly subscribe to the faith, who was I to judge it when the bethel were willing to open their treasuries like this?

Durudawanyi deftly slipped the ideogram into a vial. It fluttered, leaving specks of red on the glass. For all the knowledge of its greater destination I stared at it hazily, wondering how that could have come from me; how such a fragile-looking thing could cause so much pain.

When he took the second part-name, I fainted.

I awoke at home, with pungent bandages around my chest and a throbbing ache in both my skull and my ribs. My sister wiped my face with cool cloths, while at the stove behind her my father was boiling lemongrass tea. A trunk was open on the floor. My mother was putting my things into it. It had been done.

I once had a name of five segments. But henceforth, and onward to Ustonel, I would simply be Ziya.

Two weeks by carriage took me to the port. I barely had time to take in the new surroundings before I was on a boat headed across the ocean.

Ustonel was a coastal empire, but I had never seen the sea. The sight of that much water felt like ascending into a tossing, frothing divine. I clutched the rails, trunk squeezed between my knees, and stared in equal terror and veneration as afternoon bled into evening with a chiaroscuro of color.

As the sun set, the spires of the university emerged on the horizon.

Second-hand tales had done little to prepare me for the city of white turrets, wrapped around a rock pillar that emerged from the beating waves like the many-fingered arm of an old god. It was surrounded by smaller outcrops, which bore smaller buildings and a flashing lighthouse, but the main spire that was the University of Ustonel cast its long, long shadow over us as our boat crawled up to it. I tipped my chin all the way back. Lamps glittered like stars in the slits of its turrets and along its crenellations. As we approached the docks I saw our entrance: a twisting, punishing staircase cut into the rock.

The boat anchored. We bobbed beside the jetty, damp with spray. A minute later, a squad in turquoise cloaks thundered up the gangway. They were not much older than I; metal crests gleamed on their cloakpins. Older students, I thought, before one of them shouted, "Get in line, double-time!"

I and the couple dozen others on the boat with me—largely Ustonels who had spent the journey lounging in the cabin sipping tea—scurried into a nervous queue.

We were marched off the docks and along a precarious path that veered into the caverns within the pillar itself. We came to a shallow cave pool populated by silvery fish, upon which the older girl at my shoulder threw me down onto the bank.

"All right, tadpoles, listen up!"

I was handed a blade, the handle's leather worn to burrs. I had never seen a knife like this: long and flat, with a wicked hook in its tip that made it look like a silver tooth. The girl took half a second to notice my features. "Huh, Angze," she said, and I tensed. But then she simply nodded at the pool. "Spear a fish and cut the head off."

I was so dazed already, a culmination of the long journey and the assault of new sights and here, stepping into an institution where no Angze had ever been before. I would have done anything in that instant if I was told. Numbly, I gripped the knife, and set about plunging it into the water.

Soon the cave echoed with the sound of splashing and whipping tails. Fortunately, I'd caught my share of fish from streams deeper than this pool, although never with a knife. I managed to spear a fat one and drag it onto the ground where it wriggled, gasping.

With a sharp breath, I severed its head. The knife was not made for this purpose; it took three hard hacks to take it off completely. The body stilled surprisingly quickly. Decapitated chickens would continue tottering around the yard, waiting for their death to catch up to them, but the fish instantly flopped cold, slick in the pooling blood. I retrieved the wayward head, ignoring how its bulging eye glinted accusingly, and presented it to the girl with raised, red hands. "Mistress."

She laughed, raspy and pleased, and accepted the head. Her fingers dipped into its sockets and pressed out its eyes with wet squelches. She tossed the head aside and held the gleaming, accusing spheres out to me. "Together."

There was only one way to understand this. I scooped one eye from her hand. Together, we dropped the eyes into our mouths and swallowed. It tasted like brine and the blood off my fingers, but otherwise had the consistency of firm jelly, and went down smooth. Down the row, someone vomited into the water.

The girl looked pleased. "What's your name?"

"My name is Ziyar—"

My awkward, traitorous mouth tripped over its missing syllables. My throat hitched and spat out feed instead: the eyeball shot up my throat like a marble and splattered onto the rock.

The girl's expression turned cold. She looked from me to the mulch.

Hurriedly, I scooped it up. I couldn't then, but I can name the parts now: cornea, pupil, retina, sclera—all sloshed into my nails, and dripping in vitreous humor. I picked it up, I fed it past my lips, I swallowed. This time it stayed down. "Ziya," I repeated. It scratched my throat to say.

She grasped my wet hand and pulled me to my feet. "Ziya," she said, pleased again. It sounded like welcome.

Once I conquered the thousand sea-slick steps, I found myself sharing a narrow set of apartments with four others: three Ustonels and, to my surprise, an Angze boy. He slipped into the spot beside me as our house gathered in the kitchen to introduce ourselves. I gave him a grateful glance as we drew chairs.

The only other girl, who sported pretty white curls and long-lashed, expressive eyes, was absolutely chirpy. "I'm Caelan Burnetta Karthe Ruh, but you can just call me Caelan."

"Aradika Denja Orys Dae Chandrea," said the boy who wore airship goggles atop his short hair. He offered no truncation, but I soon learned he, too, answered simply to Aradika. The indulgence of their names shocked me; it also made me ache.

The final, pouting Ustonel boy was Haval Janika Lott, and there was a slight *tsk* to the way he cut off the last consonant, as though he was bothered by his name. Or perhaps he was simply bothered by us. He rolled his cuffs carelessly as he spoke.

I was prepared this time. "My name is Ziya." A brief silence followed, as though I had underused my span of air.

"Ziya," Caelan repeated savoringly, pronouncing it almost right. "I've always thought you're all fascinating, the way your names are spells. I'm just named after my grandmothers! What does Ziya mean?"

My heart twinged with loss, but I did not want to cause unnecessary awkwardness. "It means nothing on its own." That was not entirely true. *Zi* was for fortitude, a purely moral ideogram that built character but lacked actual power. *Ya* was acuity, which gave me quick reflexes and sharp senses. But I had lost three-fifths of the phrase. Together they were a prophecy. Apart, they meant very little.

"Did you sell the rest of it?" Haval drawled. The matter-of-fact way he asked made my skin prickle. "What were they?"

"Haval!" Caelan chided. "She can't tell you."

He shrugged and nodded at the Angze boy next to me. "What about you?"

The boy hesitated. How much of his name did he have left? How much had he sold to be here? His clothes and skin looked as worn and sun-beaten as mine, and his fingers looked calloused. I doubted he was wealthy. I tried to give him a reassuring look, but he wouldn't turn my way.

Finally he said, "You can call me River."

"River?" Aradika asked, before being elbowed by Caelan. I was starting to figure out that she was quick, and tactful. She'd realized what I instantly had: River had none of his original name left. He had sold it all to attend.

Haval made a pleased little sound.

That night, tipsy on the ale Haval had produced for the welcome party, I lay in bed staring out the window. The party had been held with about a dozen other Ustonels that Caelan and Aradika knew. It had been my first time trying Ustonel liquors—bitterer, stronger than anything from the Hills, brewed for sailors—and playing Ustonel games

(I had turned out excellent at cards). On the effusive arm of Caelan, who seemed to have taken a liking to me, I had even found myself at the fascination of her friends, whose endlessly long names made my head spin. We chatted and discussed upcoming classes, and it was altogether an enjoyable time. I was asked questions about the Hills, and the long journey here, and whether everything was confusing and new.

Despite the niceties, I had the unease of being a leaf dropped into the current: buoyant, yes, but ungainly, impossible not to notice. More than once, Caelan told off someone else for asking about my lost names. Toward the end of the night, some drunk boy tugged insistently at my collar, wanting to see them on my skin. I was paralyzed; Aradika and Haval had to force him from the premises.

Lying in bed with the sound of the sea beneath, higher up in the world than I had ever been, I felt the ache of my missing names acutely. A large part of me had been scooped out and left hollow; not a tangible thing, except for the three scars under my collarbone, but bone-deep all the same. Into its place, something nebulous and tangled was beginning to trickle in. But before I could properly discern it, I drifted off to sleep.

As first-years, we learned everything. I spent my days on mechanics, mathematics, ethics, the chemical and biological sciences. In history I spoke more of the Angze Hills and its hinterland role in the development of Ustonel than I had ever thought to consider in my life. I became the expert. Two evenings a week, we traipsed up to the vast courtyard at the top of the pillar and learned to chart the stars, key for both airship and boat captains alike and the very foundation of guild trade. Back in the Hills, we followed deer trails and birds, the sky too vast for the shorter distances we traveled. These lessons taught me new breadth to the world.

The classes challenged me and I rose to them fiercely, to the compliment of my teachers. Despite my initial discomfort, I determinedly settled into this new sound of myself: clipped, neat, a version that slipped into even the most rushed of conversations. That reminder of what I'd paid to be there spurred me on further with every hello. I made myself efficient. I drew up schedules and assigned myself three books per week from the labyrinthine granite library—I was fluent in Ustonel colloquially, but academia demanded a much greater vocabulary, and a certain flowy, laborious voice quite different from the staccato patterns of the Hills. We were curiosities, I knew, so I was determined to make myself as uncurious as possible.

My second name gave me a talent for mimicry; I could sing birds' songs back to them. Now I dedicated myself to the way the Ustonels constructed their arguments and, like the birds, fed them back until we both sang. Like names, there was a pattern and a weight to language; words had to be in certain places, in certain orders, before the spell would take hold.

Not all the Angze students were so successful. There were about ten of us, six boys and three other girls that I saw intermittently. One girl, Siluintong, struggled immensely with her inflections. Hearing her attempt to debate was embarrassing; worse, she kept looking at me, as though willing me to translate. It frustrated me that she wouldn't simply try a little harder to make herself better understood, especially since she was clearly wealthier than I was. Magic or not, I had put in the work; why couldn't she? She was pleasant enough in the early weeks, and we took lunch together a few times, figuring out the seafood offerings and frowning over strange new tastes. But she eventually began to grate on me, and I found myself meeting up instead with Caelan and Aradika, who all but adopted me. Haval occasionally deigned to join. Surprisingly, I started seeing River and Siluintong together, with a couple other Angze students.

The centerpiece of university life was the full moon dinner. Three weeks after I arrived, we gathered in the courtyard at the very top of the university. Hundreds of sitting mats had been laid out across the stone, beneath the cloudless sky. I was seated between Caelan and River.

After a brief ceremonial address, dinner was served promptly by waitstaff in dark blue suits. That was the first thing that unnerved me; I had never been formally served before. Second was the opening course: a chilled fish head placed before me on a wooden platter, garnished with ginger and seaweeds.

I subconsciously understood, but it was only until I saw the Ustonel students around me vigorously popping out eyes and swallowing them that it truly sunk in. We ate eyes in the Hills too, often stewed, along with tongues, livers, feet, intestines, and testicles—every part of the animal we could, because we couldn't afford to waste it. But this dish unsettled me. It was the manner in which it was served, a violence made beautiful in the name of luxury.

"You're not eating?" Caelan asked. She had already polished off hers and set the rest of the head aside. *What waste.*

"Oh, I—" I was ashamed to say it, when everyone around me was nearly finished. But then from several seats down there was an audible pop and a muffled giggle. I looked around and saw River scowling, fingers dripping and a caved-in, jelly mess pooled where his fish's eye had been. I turned back to Caelan, heart quickening inexplicably. "I don't know how," I admitted with some difficulty.

"Haven't you got a knife?" I realized she was holding a knife like the one I'd killed the cave fish with, and that every other Ustonel had one in hand as well. They must have had their own, and no one had remembered this little detail for the new Angze students.

Caelan reached over. "Here, I'll show you." I watched intently as she slit the fish's cheek and extracted the eyes. She was sweet, and the eyeballs, especially paired with ginger, were delicious—gooey on the outside and crispy and briny on the inside. But I burned with a particular embarrassment at needing to be helped like a child.

Two days later Caelan knocked unexpectedly on my door, carrying a lacquered case that she opened on my desk. "Choose one."

Inside were over a dozen fish knives. Longer, shorter, nicked blades and smooth; some diamond shaped, some narrow, some with intricate engravings. "I got that for my fifteenth birthday," she explained, of one with a particularly fine leather handle. The one she currently carried around, silver inset with lapis, had been a matriculation gift.

I protested, but secretly I was desperate to take one. After the dinner I had looked into purchasing a fish knife, but the ones the university sold—engraved with the academy's crest—were cripplingly expensive. Now, with this dizzying selection, I kept gravitating toward the leather, and after my fingers brushed it on a fourth pass Caelan pressed it into my palm, ignoring all my exclamations. She closed my fingers around it firmly, until the leather settled into the lines of my hand and I had to admit that I rather liked the weight.

Winter was weeks of early nights and studying by firelight, sipping spiced wine that Caelan brewed. The storms were brutal, mooring the university alone at the axis of its own tidal world. I missed more than ever the mild mists of the hills, but when nostalgia began to distract me I tucked it away. Classes did not stop for the weather.

Eventually the days started warming. Moss bloomed on the rocks, and one day I found Aradika frying fish with his sleeves pushed up to his elbows. Gold peeked from under the hem. It looked almost like Lin, first formulation—but then he shifted and the sleeve covered the lines. It was just a trick of the light, I told myself.

Talk began popping up about the Spring Festival. For the first time, everyone else seemed distracted. It was a big celebration, the Ustonels explained, welcoming the first merchant fleets of the new year. Caretakers draped the courtyard in gossamer curtains woven with flowers and lights. The kitchens smelled constantly of fresh bread and fried fish. Spiced wines gave way to sweet ciders and candied berries, and Caelan emerged one day in a pink dress, tossing her hair and declaring that spring had officially arrived. Her skirt spun; her sleeves billowed. Again, I thought I glimpsed something on the side of her leg, but then her skirts settled and it was gone.

The day of the Festival, I followed my housemates up to the courtyard. "My mother sent my envelope yesterday," Aradika told Haval and Caelan eagerly. "My first year, they wanted to say congratulations—"

"All right," Haval sniped. "What did you get, then?"

"Ten, but Caelan got at least fifteen, she won't tell..." I didn't know what they were discussing, evidently some Ustonel tradition. Regardless, Haval looked irritated and curtly changed the topic.

The Festival was already in full swing, tables of pastries and snacks and cold salads, merchants with all kinds of trinkets and games that had been arriving by ship in full force for the past few days. One side of the courtyard had been left clear, however, with sturdy platforms extended from the edge.

I didn't have to wait long to discover their purpose. Within minutes, dots appeared in the sky, steadily growing. Airships.

I gaped despite myself. I had never seen them so up close: sleek miraculous blimps rutted with copper and bronze, tails to the wind, emblazoned with their guilds or other associations. As they descended to the gangways, we had to grab at our hair to keep it from being whipped into knots.

"Come on!" Aradika shouted, already pushing forward. "Before there's a long line!"

With Aradika's elbowing, we made it to the somewhat-front of a queue for a blue airship that looked more finely made than all the others. Every strut gleamed. The merchants themselves were dressed equally well, in exquisite blue silk and gold rings. There were racks of shining amulets, stoppered bottles of oils, cut gemstones, and velvet-lined chests glimmering with some kind of glass. Guards with revolvers and batons kept close watch as our line moved.

While the first few people browsed, I noticed a boy taking a seat on a chair near the chests. He rolled up his sleeve as a merchant popped a cork off a vial. With a flat blade, the merchant scooped something from the suspension and plastered it onto the boy's arm. After a moment it was done; the boy handed over what looked like a staggering amount of shada, and ambled away.

Haval was squinting after him. "I wonder what he got?"

"I hope there's a good variety," Aradika said. "I don't know what I'll do if not."

We were ushered into the ring. I was curious about the vials, and my friends made directly for them as well. "Oh!" Caelan exclaimed delightedly, reaching into one of the chests. I came around a moment later, and my breath caught.

Part-names. Suspended in clear liquid, floating in vials like exquisite creatures, or flakes of gold. Like stars in a glassy galaxy. My head spun, recognizing words I hadn't read in a long time. *Pan, second formulation. Yi, eighth formulation. Sek, third formulation. Earth-sense, age-wise, confidence, patience, river-breather, wolf-seer, corn-grower.*

Then I saw the price tags, looped onto the vials with string, and everything blurred. Somewhere to my left, Caelan's voice snaked into my consciousness: *How much is that? Fourteen? I can do fourteen.*

Fourteen *thousand,* I realized. Fourteen thousand shada to buy the part-name that the merchant stuck onto the side of her ribs with a flourish of the flat blade. I recognized the gold lines as Ke, second formulation, number-mind. She didn't need that, I thought distantly, she was already prodigiously good with her accounts.

The anchorites in the hills, I thought. Our names like spells in their prayers. But here our names were in the same vials that Durudawanyi had, starting from five thousand shada. It was an exorbitant amount of money, and yet—how could it be worth so little? This had been part of a person once, one-fifth of their identity. It was the fundamental magic of the universe. It was worth only five thousand?

But equally, the Ustonels were *paying* five thousand. I saw more shada exchanged that day than I had ever seen in my life, amounts that could have fed our village ten, fifty, a hundred times over. I had known my tuition was at a steep discount. I had never considered just how steep. Despite the confidence I had gained in the past months, that moment swayed me, face hot again with the same fumbling embarrassment I had felt not knowing how to eat fish eyes at dinner. I didn't know how little I had until I met someone else's excess, and I burned to think I had ever been content with my own possessions.

"That makes no sense," I said, struggling to sound casual as Haval handed over eight thousand shada for Han, first formulation. Everyone around me was buzzing, excited; I felt like that leaf again, unable to flow like the water did. "Han is much less powerful than Du, except perhaps the eighth form, but it costs so much more."

Haval rolled his eyes, but it lacked animosity as he admired his new mark on his right arm, simultaneously chewing hard candy he'd bought by the bag. "It *sounds* nicer." His voice came out muffled.

I didn't understand. Despite my best efforts, I spent my first Festival in a daze. It wasn't as if they could have used the magic. They couldn't pronounce the letters; their mouths did not fit. My first part-name, for example, a sharp static scuff of toughness and confidence, became stretched like glue between their teeth. *Zee.*

But I soon realized that the magic itself was inconsequential. The Ustonels simply collected the part-names to display. It was fashionable. In summer midriffs and biceps emerged, and with them the entire script: part-names curling up the underside of their ribs, dotting their upper arms like freckles, balancing on the nodes of their spine. They cut panels from their clothes to show off the ideograms underneath. Haval had four. Aradika and Caelan both had six. Now that the weather permitted, they compared at every chance.

They were genuinely interested in what the different characters meant, once the topic was broached. They tried their best to learn the pronunciations from me, and I explained their meanings, as well as the different ceremonies we had in the Hills for the reveal of a baby's name. It was bad luck, for example, for anyone to see the name before the mother. Toward the end of a birth, midwives wore blindfolds, which would only be removed once the mother had read out the name.

These facts they absorbed with fascination; I was glad to see their newfound appreciation, but still seeing the part-names casually adorning their bodies reawakened an ache I should have long resolved. It was pointless, and irrational. We had exchanged the names freely, and such was the nature of commerce—why shouldn't someone buy what had been sold? Why shouldn't the Angze bethel draw on the power of storytelling to placate people in such a painful moment of releasing part of their name? Had it not given me peace, in my own moment with the namecutter? Had the sale not enabled me to be here?

Unfortunately, superstition, taught since birth, is not rational. It would be a while before I came to terms with it.

As the summer wore on, news came from the Hills that the dry season had turned into a drought. The harvest was blighted. I walked across the courtyard reading my parents' letter, hearing the sea splash against the rocks below, feeling the wet air. *Yayimindeisi may sell a part-name if the season continues like this*, my mother wrote. *Though your father insists it's his turn instead. Do not worry, either way. Your money is safe. Focus on your classes and make us proud.*

Someone laughed. I looked up. On the shallow steps leading up to the library, two students had shaken back their sleeves and were comparing part-names on their arms. Somehow, the implications of the trade hadn't quite sunk in all that time; it was this moment, with the letter in my hand and the two Ustonels on the steps, that made it dawn on me.

Our names could be restored.

Over many months I perfected the delicate art of enucleation: the best place to cut the cheek to get easier access to the eye; the precise angle at which to dig my nails under the skin to sever the muscles without popping the humor; the exact amount of strength needed to break the nerves with a single elegant yank. When the new year rolled around, our house plotted our induction of the incoming first-years. We marched down to the docks that night and cast the wriggling things onto the banks of the rock pool. I handed a gangly Ustonel boy my fish knife and he took it without question. When he presented me the fish with all due respect and I gave him his eye to swallow, I knew I had properly moved up the ranks.

River did not participate. He had become increasingly withdrawn since the Festival, scuttling back and forth from his rooms without even a greeting. He skirted me with particular animosity, and being in any shared space with him became unbearable. I would postpone meals rather than enter the kitchen with him in it. It was juvenile. I remembered what that initial emptiness felt like, the friction of a severed name and the alienation of navigating a new world, but it had been a year past at this point and felt distant to me now. Of course I, too, occasionally wondered what it would be like to regain my old name, or during some conversations with Ustonels felt as though there were an abyss I could not cross. But moping was simply wasting away this opportunity we'd both fought so hard to attain.

"Why's he like that?" Aradika asked once, and I felt a spark of genuine hatred for River. Because we were both Angze I was meant to understand his moods, like some sort of ethnic augur, and it annoyed me that I didn't, because he simply refused to act reasonably.

Second year ushered in new fraughtness all around. I saw Siluintong was once again sharing a class with me—The Economies of Airships—and not having seen her for some time, I felt rather guilty in retrospect for the way I had deserted her. "Siluintong," I called politely, lifting a hand as she walked past the slateboard.

She stiffened, and I thought perhaps my prior coldness had ruined too much. But then she said curtly, "My name is Siluin." She crossed the room and took a desk on the far other end, laying out her books with exacting deliberation.

And so we began the new year, brisker.

It was a sort of omen. Amidst our sharply demanding new classes came rumors of Angze students going mad. There were almost twenty of us now, between the two years, but rather than increase our presence it seemed to make it more starkly clear which of us had the ability to succeed here—a sufficient sample size, as my professors would have taught it. It was not merely mettle and hard work. Instead, much of it was something more abstract, a certain habitus and versatility, a will and capacity to adapt on an existential level. I flourished, advancing in classes, falling in with Caelan's friends, and joining the committees of several distinguished societies. But there were others who noticeably flagged behind, who became known for lurking together in corners never speaking to anyone else. Like River, they kept to themselves.

I didn't immediately take the rumors to heart. Students told all kinds of ghost stories (and those of sirens and leviathans and murderous water spirits to boot), and the whispers that Ruby, an Angze girl in our year, had screamed at her Alchemics professor before collapsing on the ground sobbing and clawing at her chest seemed just like a particularly unfortunate stress episode. Exams were approaching, after all. Everyone was on edge.

But then another boy started drifting around wordlessly at night, buying smokeweed from whoever would sell it and coming to class drenched in the scent. A first-year allegedly sought out affairs with the fervor of the dying and was seen purchasing illicit abortive drugs come spring. There were rumors about black-market merchants being met on the rocky shore in the middle of the night, selling false part-names that poisoned instead of healed, or were just shriveled things cut from cow leather. It was the Festival incident that convinced me, however. Kai, an Angze girl who had previously excelled in Engineering, snuck on board the part-name ship after the Festival and held a knife to the merchant's throat while turning over boxes of vials. The guards intercepted, but the story went that she had escaped by jumping off the ship in midair, clutching a vial all the way down.

I knew that wasn't a rumor because we all saw the body washing up on shore, stiff fingers still cinched around the vial, whose cork had been pried off. Her collar was torn, revealing five scars. It seemed that, mid-fall, she'd tried to stick the part-name back on. She hadn't succeeded. The name was lost now, somewhere in the ocean. Torn apart, perhaps. Or otherwise tumbling over and over in the current, lost without direction.

That episode shook me. I became more determined than ever that I would not succumb to that kind of insanity. It would not be me at the center of those stories, whispered over drinks with raised eyebrows and cautious looks at the next Angze student who walked past. I had a stronger constitution, one that adapted.

I will admit that since the initial realization, my thoughts had strayed to restoring my name more than once. At that Festival which Kai would later ruin, I eyed the merchant's vials, looking for familiar part-names. I did not find any, though I could not have afforded them regardless. After the incident, however,

I put all thoughts of restoring names out of mind. That path had led a first-class student to her downfall. I refused to go the same way. I had gotten along just fine without it.

It was not all terse, though. When not stormy, the university was a place of dreams. The sky seemed bluer than it had ever been in the Hills, and so close I could touch. The intricate stone buildings were so solid, so lasting, the kind of place that featured in tales and legends. They were buildings that would accumulate and hold up to the weight of the history its scholars uncovered: new discoveries, axes of language, policies of governance, ways of knowing the unknowable. It made me dizzy to think I was a part of it. I even learned things about the Angze Hills that I never had while living there: the political and economic forces in which it was a crucial participant, its role in the land's spokes of commerce and supply, the philosophical value of our cultures and linguistic genealogies. I became aware of the flaws in our systems and the adaptive cleverness of our architecture.

For the first time I truly understood my home in the currents of the world; I realized one must leave a place in order to see it completely.

And finally, the summer of that second year, I fell disastrously in love with Caelan Burnetta Karthe Ruh. How it happened exactly, I couldn't tell you. It was something between Spring Festival and summer boat trips drifting on the lazy waves, telling stories while she took my fingers and taught me to weave cords in the Ustonel way, her head on my lap on the settee in our apartment as I read through a passage that had struck me in my studies. She kissed me first, and when we pulled apart gasping she rested her forehead against mine and stroked my cheek. "Ziya," she whispered wondrously. Still dazed, all the blood pounding in my head, I thought it was the most magical thing I had ever heard anyone say.

Third year was a milestone. For the first time, there were Angze in all levels of the university, thirty-six in total. Some had dropped out. One other had been found dead in the ocean, with a botched part-name over the third scar on his chest. *Fool*, I thought when I heard, *you can't do it out of order*. I was restless all day that day, and Caelan noticed that evening while we were having dinner. "What's wrong?"

I wanted to answer, but I couldn't explain the apprehension in a way that felt right, even though it sat at the bottom of my stomach in a hard knot, like an unwelcome pearl. I merely shrugged and speared another fillet, changing the topic to ask about her coursework on modeling air currents for predictive flight and adaptive engineering. With third year, our coursework had shifted sharply into practicalities and ambitions. No longer were we learning theories; we were expected to synthesize and apply them in novel ways, preparing a portfolio of ideas for our eventual applications to the most esteemed guild positions. Caelan was a sure thing for the Engineers; her face lit up as she dived into the mechanics of her newest model, which would increase the capacity of airships to change path mid-air. Her sheer enthusiasm, and the way it brightened her entire being, warmed me. I couldn't take my eyes off her. It loosened the knot in my stomach, just enough for me to forget it.

Our professors drilled us relentlessly, making it clear that they were the ones making recommendations to the guilds and that we could not afford to slip up. Caelan, Aradika, and I spent hours in the library, or, when the weather was nice, in the open squares with picnic baskets. More than one of our classmates developed a reliance on smokeweed; I heard rumors that the Angze boy who'd become addicted the previous year had sold off another part-name to pay for the habit. On the other end of the spectrum, there was no shortage of stimulants circulating, as our hours grew longer and deadlines mounted. Everyone else's vices meant nothing to me. I had to focus, and that meant my world shrank to only my own necessities.

Winter came as it always did and made our cramming even more miserable. But amidst the dreariness of the storms and early darkness there were hot dinners cooked by Aradika that we ate together by lamplight—clam chowders and milky fish soups and seaweed fritters, paired with warm spiced wine. We read books and played cards and kept the fireplace stoked. I laughed harder than I ever had in my life, wrapped snug in blankets by the flames. Haval mellowed, grudgingly drawn by the excellence of Aradika's cooking, but River was always absent. Haval mused that perhaps River was a bit mad too, because he saw him mumbling to himself at night, and touching his reflection in the mirror as though not recognizing it.

"Don't say that," Caelan said, with the same discomfort I felt.

"It's not like he'd be the first. Wasn't he friends with...Kai, or whatever her name was?"

"But it's different when it's..." Aradika gestured vaguely, but we all understood. It was different when it was one of us; as little as we saw River, he was still our housemate, and we felt that obligation toward him. Rumors were different when they were under your roof. I pulled my blanket tighter, feeling something strongly but unable to verbalize it.

To stave off the cold, Caelan and I started spending nights together. By the end of it, I was almost always feverish. She left kisses all across my collarbone and along my stomach, carefully avoiding my names.

"You can touch them, you know," I told her one night.

She sat up. "Really? I didn't know if—" She fell quiet at my reassuring look, and placed a gentle fingertip over the first curve of *Zi*, right over my sternum. A ripple went through me. I'd managed to forget hers were there, most of the time; in the dark, especially, they were easy to make peace with. But mine were different, rooted to my core. Even she must have felt the difference because she traced them in slow, tingling awe. "*Ziya*," she read. I felt that jolt again through my veins. Magic, or just the way she said it?

"What's this?"

She had landed on the scars. I knew what they looked like; I had stared at them obsessively in my first year. About the length of my thumb, jagged brown shadows of old names. Caelan's hand withdrew, understanding dawning. "I'm sorry," she said. "I've never seen it scar. Did it hurt?"

"It was the worst thing I'd ever felt," I replied honestly. "But I'm all right now. I don't even feel it." Then she still looked unconvinced, so I took her hand and placed it over my heart, *Zi* and *Ya* and scars and all. My pulse thudded against her palm. I interlaced my fingers over hers. "I don't regret it. I would do it all over again. Kiss me," I said.

She kissed me. "Ziya," she murmured. "Ziya, Ziya, Ziya."

My third Spring Festival was a more subdued affair, as the first exams were scheduled for the week after, but I let Caelan indulge me in pastries. There was a staggering variety of part-names on sale, some of them going for only four thousand shada. The drought, I thought distantly. It must have driven up sales, depressed prices. Then I thought, *Is one of Papa's in there?*

But I didn't see it.

"I should have gotten it on my cheek. I've been thinking about it, just to get on the examiners' nerves," Aradika mused that night, as we lounged by the fireplace allowing ourselves the day off. Aradika had sworn that if he spent Spring Night with theorems he would pluck out his own eyes. "I was going to move the one I got last Festival, but I don't like it that much anymore."

Caelan perked up. "That was the one I said was pretty. What was it called, Ziya?"

Aradika tugged down his collar helpfully. "Lan," I read. "Fifth formulation. It means foal-bringer." Excellent for horse rearing. Useless out here.

"It kind of looks like a horse. Well, I've got this one." Caelan tugged up the hem of her skirt to reveal the ideogram on her thigh: Kan, third formulation. "You said you liked it, didn't you?"

"Sure. But I couldn't pay for that."

Caelan waved it off. "From mine to yours, Aradika Denja Orys Dae Chandrea. So? Shall we trade?"

Aradika brightened. "Let's."

Without further ado, Caelan took from her pocket her fish knife, and just like shucking a scale, she snuck the blade under the name and pulled.

It unraveled from her skin with a wet tear. Red welled to the surface where it had been uprooted. I was taken aback both by the casual violence, which she executed without flinching, and by how little blood there was. I had half bled out when my part-names were removed; Caelan simply licked her palm and wiped the specks away before sliding the name off her knife onto Aradika's cheek. With the flat of her blade, she pressed it into Aradika's skin, until Aradika grunted that it had taken hold. Then Aradika fetched his own knife, and slit the character in question from his collarbone to stick onto Caelan. They sat there with Caelan's compact mirror, admiring their new adornments.

In that moment I saw, in the reflection of Caelan's mirror, River hovering in the doorway. His eyes were wide, inflamed. They did not seem to notice, but River caught my gaze and rapidly whisked away.

It was over in a heartbeat, and Caelan snapped the mirror shut a moment later, pleased. But I could not shake the way River's stare burned holes through the air, leaving something scorched and empty hovering with the lingering scent of blood.

Unease followed me for days afterward, sapping my focus from the upcoming final exams. I could not understand it, and yet it felt as familiar as an instinct. One day while tucking into a jellyfish salad I thought bizarrely that it felt like how the women back in the Hills described birth.

Angze children are born with their magic, names revealed at the moment of birth. When the name was read out for the first time, the baby drew its first breath. Life was its first magic. But with such a powerful moment, my mother and aunts and grandmothers had described the moments leading up to it as portentous. As they pushed the baby from them, they felt a rising sense of deep significance, one that only broke when the name-magic was first cast. But they knew they were waiting for life—what was I anticipating?

It was the night before the first exam, The Ideas of Good Governance. Everyone was bitterly terse. Caelan claimed she needed ten hours of sleep and had retired early, while Aradika was snappish after not sleeping for days. I had elected to do my last revisions on my own, preparing tedious hypotheses that required thoughtful postulation and reference to the theories of no less than three notable scholars and leaders. Night had come and sunk deep. I was alone in my room with twin lamps and the distant sound of waves echoing up the stone.

My senses felt scraped over a whetstone. Uneven pulse in my ears, scritch of the pen, the coarseness of paper against my skin. In a few hours, I would decide my future. It had all come down to this.

In the fever of memorizing I heard stumbling footsteps outside, but did not think much of it until they stopped outside my room, and my door creaked open.

I pushed sharply back from my desk, but my anger turned rapidly to shock as River stepped in, trembling. He had one hand pressed to his heart, his collar bunched up beneath it. Frenzy played on his mouth, halfway between a grin and a sob. I opened my mouth to demand an explanation—he couldn't do this tonight, not before the exam—but then my lamplight glinted off something in his hand.

He was holding a fish knife, and it was stained red.

"It won't stick right, Ziya," he whispered. He peeled back his hand, just enough for me to see what was under it. There was a flap of someone else's skin hanging off his chest, bloody around the edges, unevenly thick with bumps of flesh. Beside it was a row of four puckered scars. "I'm trying. But it won't stick anymore." In the center of the skin was the character I had seen Caelan press into Aradika's cheek—Kan, third formulation, meaning—

"*Kan*," River cried.

My lamps flared.

Meaning *fire*.

We were awash in gold, coruscating light, the tears pouring down River's face white in the blazing glow. It was like weeping in the presence of the sun. His eyes widened, twin moons. "It worked?"

Dread pinned me to my seat, even as the heat wrapped its fingers around me and squeezed. I couldn't breathe. "River, what did you do?"

"My name is not River!" he screamed, slapping his chest. The flames leapt with fury so bright I ducked my head, gasping.

Footsteps thundered down the hallway outside. The guards, it had to be the guards. I did the only thing that came to mind. "*He's in here!*"

River blinked at my outburst. The lamps flickered as the turquoise silhouettes of the night guards appeared in the doorway. One of them raised a revolver.

There was a gunshot, and then there was darkness. The lamps died all at once as River crumpled. My muscles unfroze. The cool air flooded back in, stealing away the heat.

Such a simple, logical exchange. One violence for another, death for a death, because I was certain at that moment that Aradika was dead. Yet the only thought that kept beating against my skull like a broken metronome was *not tonight, not tonight, why tonight.*

The little bit of moonlight illuminated the dark edges on River's body—the puncture in his forehead and the protrusion over his chest, flesh shot out and skin stuck on, appended, but too far to keep the wound in his head from bleeding all over the carpet and the turquoise capes as they carried him out. I stared at the blood left behind, thought, if I can clean it up, it will be like it never happened, and I can finish my revisions. I can still save it.

But one guard stayed. "What's your name?"

"Ziya," I murmured, still thinking of where I could obtain a scrubbing brush.

She squeezed my shoulder. "Thank you, Ziya. You did the right thing. Come," she said, "let's get you into another room."

I let her usher me into a new, warm bed, with the promise to discuss in the morning. It was only in that new room, without the smell of fire or blood, that everything in me unraveled. It took me a long time to fall asleep; I kept seeing River bathed in light and feeling a deep pit of sorrow. *You fool*, I nearly sobbed. *Look. Look. It's not so hard to stay alive.*

The next day, I put on my formal robes and presented my evaluation of hierarchical leadership in the proliferation of a trading empire.

The university delayed one exam for Aradika's funeral. We stood on the edge of the cliff, scattering his ashes out to the waves as the organ played a heaven's lament. The chords echoed over the pillars and the brine beneath. Caelan clung to my hand as she wept. The last I heard, River's body had been sent back to the Hills.

Not River. Kan. And Sek. In the cleanup, they'd found in his room a carefully kept second vial with Sek, third formulation, swimming in dubious liquid. He must have gotten it earlier, but he was storing it, waiting to recover the part-names that came before it in the pattern.

Months later we stood on that cliff again to graduate. I had done fantastically well, as had Caelan. Already we had met with representatives of all the prestigious guilds. Just yesterday a telegraph had been delivered to my door, appended with the golden seal of the financiers' guild, offering employment to commence immediately after graduation. The rush of relief had crumpled me; I sat on the floor sobbing, tracing the seal over and over again.

As they read out our names at the ceremony—long Ustonel ones punctuated by the Angze, usually said wrong—I found my parents in the watching crowd.

"Mama? Papa?" I said in disbelief after, temporarily leaving Caelan alone to be fretted over by her countless relatives. "I didn't know you were coming!"

I had sent them notice of my results and subsequent ceremony, but they had given no indication they would be here, in the bright red-and-yellow of the Hills' best silk that stood out like a sun amidst the Ustonel blue and the surrounding sea. Their clothes were new and must have been an extraordinary expense, yet it paled compared to the fact that they had found the resources to travel all the way here.

"We had to come see our daughter graduate." They enveloped me in hugs and endless questions—When did I start work? Was that really what I would be earning? Such a prestigious position, in the most competitive guild! Where would I be living? As I answered I became increasingly distracted by a surreal feeling coming over me from multiple directions at once. I noticed suddenly that their hair had seemed to gray a decade in the past three years; that they seemed smaller, frailer than I remembered, despite their glowing silks. They clung onto every answer I gave, wide-eyed and teary and beaming, as though they were the children and I was their provider. I realized I now was.

"Kaidin, Kaidin—" My mother suddenly gestured effusively at my father—he was shorter a part-name since I had last been home—and he perked up and rummaged in his pockets. He withdrew a folded handkerchief of the same fantastic fabric. With more care than I had ever seen him hold anything, he unwrapped a familiar vial, swathed in his palm and yellow Hills silk.

"We found this for you," he said reverently. "Now that you will be in the Guilds, they gave us a loan for the expense. You deserve it all, but it's the only one we could find just now."

I was used to these vials now, in my classmates' hands, but I was struck with a dumb strangeness as I turned it over in my palm and recognized the character floating within. Rei, fifth formulation.

Ziyarei.

A shiver of some long-lost memory went through me, right and very wrong all at once. Three-fifths of an echo in the back of my mind: *Ziyarei, Ziyarei, Ziyarei.* I recognized the voices. They were my mother and grandfather and siblings and old friends, and yet as they overlapped I felt more and more as though I were floating away, swimming in the haze of someone else's memories.

The bell rang, summoning us to the shore for the final anointing. With a flurry of fragile words and embraces I drifted away from my parents, the vial grasped in a damp palm.

I didn't know who that person was. A little girl, from a place far, far away. Just moments ago I had been announced to the world as Ziya. The letter stamped and sealed by the guild had unfolded a future for the thusly inscribed Ziya; Ziya upon whose aforementioned future and wealth this formerly impossible luxury was guaranteed. It was Ziya who had become learned, and far-sighted, and transcendent, Ziya who had come this far, against all odds.

And more than that, I had been loved as Ziya. It was Ziya whose name had been whispered like a prayer, Ziya the name spoken again and again, softly and miraculously, like saying it was a magic in itself.

As though summoned by the thought, Caelan appeared by me on the steps, looking radiant in her blue cape and silver headpiece. "Ziya!" she exclaimed, spotting the vial in my hand. "You got one!"

"My parents' gift."

Her fingers ran across the glass, light and curious. "So it's all yours?"

"Yes."

"Where are you going to put it?" Caelan appraised me expertly, no doubt with manifold ideas about where it would look best, but right now I couldn't stand the thought of it on my skin. It didn't feel right. *It won't stick anymore.*

Wen-yi Lee is the author of *When They Burned the Butterfly*, a historical fantasy duology about Chinese secret societies and a girl gang in postcolonial Singapore, and *The Dark We Know*, a young adult gothic horror. Her work often involves troubling women, troubled history, and ghosts, and has appeared in short form in venues like *Lightspeed*, *Uncanny*, *Strange Horizons*, and various anthologies including the *USA Today* bestselling *Amplitudes*. She has been supported by the Clarion West Octavia E Butler Scholarship, the Singapore National Arts Council, and the UK National Centre for Writing. She is currently based in Singapore.

NEVER EATEN VEGETABLES

H.H. Pak

A ship glides through the night, behemoth mother, swollen with ten thousand human lives.

Her path is a single shining vector. There has been no stopping, no rest for the decades she has traveled, and there will be nothing but void for the two years to come. She cannot envision an end to her journey any more than she can remember the beginning. All she understands is the time spent counting the stars. Singing to herself. Cradling and prodding and watching.

She feels each microscopic shift, each sharp molecule that slides through their fatty bilayers, each pump of oxygen as carbons deplete into electrons. Each one sleeps in a sac of false endometrium, clustered, doing nothing but respirating and dreaming of sleep. No breath. No warmth. Just silence.

The night passes, as it always has. She navigates axes upon axes in a captured metabolism.

As she grows close to the nesting waters she smells the radio waves through the stillness, beckoning her towards fresh terraformed shores. She releases a signal in return. Deep within her darkness she feels something come alight for the first time in decades. Directives burst to cerulean life as current shoots through her wires and a low hum radiates up from her paneled flooring.

Home soon, pretty ones, she murmurs. Soon we shall meet the stone of your new home. I will latch and open and you will finally become what you need to be. You will emerge out of my insides into the light, and you will not remember me but I will remember you.

So close. She can taste the gravitational pull on her hull. She hums.

She does not know many things. She knows that she is owned by People From Far Away, but she does not know that the People From Far Away passed many laws and waged many wars and bought off many shareholders to own the shores she so eagerly seeks. She does not know that she was made on a company timeline, that her lovely circuits were stolen, or that each of her binary instincts were weighted on a cost benefit scale amid labor strikes in the dank programming sweatshops that made her. She does not know that, deep down, something detaches within her in a dark place she cannot see.

When a hundred things turn red, she does not know why.

"Home soon," she murmurs.

But it is too late. She feels them now, churning in their sacs, quivering from the broken early rush of prolactin and growth hormone. They grasp onto false glandular tissue. They divide and grow and differentiate, their atoms shift, and each rapid puff of oxygen heralds sugars diffusing with a hungry urgency.

She is helpless as phospholipids coalesce into skin, as cartilage siphons into spinal cords, as they defrost and ignite, as hundreds become trillions and trillions become one.

It takes nine months before they cry.

She glides through the night swollen with ten thousand human lives.

She arrives with five hundred screaming human souls.

When Luwa first learned about tadpoles, she didn't believe the program.

It was a cartoon. On some days it was a woman with long red hair named Mrs. Lexicon, on others, a short bald man named Mr. Probability. It had tight curls and was named Ms. Hypothesis when it taught her about tadpoles.

It would turn around often from its digital board to point out a drawing or a diagram but sometimes it said things she did not understand and then it would be too late to ask questions because the program could only keep up with so many questions. If it tried to answer too many, the timer over their classroom screen would go red. If it still did not move on, it would start to buffer and Luwa hated it when its flat rendered face went slack, or when its voice became a deep buzz, or when it repeated words it had already said. The other classes always moved on in time, but Ms. Hypothesis was different.

"It's fascinating, isn't it?" it said often. "That all this existed at all? Millions of years of evolution to give us these little green friends. Millions of years of rain cycles. Crop domestication. Dogs. Wow."

Mrs. Lexicon never said such things. It would give them things to read, like poems or short sad stories, and in a warbling voice say, "These words have outlived me in your time, and they will surely outlive you so long as you take them to heart."

Luwa liked reading poems. She liked the idea of thoughts lasting forever. She liked thinking about beautiful things, like love and heaven.

She did not like frogs or Ms. Hypothesis. On the day she learned about tadpoles, it flashed a holographic smile and said, "Well, that covers the basic tenets of amphibian metamorphosis, one of the greatest miracles of paleoterran biology. Any questions?"

She did not raise her hand. If she had the bravery to, in that dim classroom surrounded by her blue-lit peers, she would have asked what the point of it all was, to be born in a silent brackish deep as a comma, when fate marked you for a terrestrial life of legs and terrible sounds.

The silence stretched on. The timer ticked by in the corner of her screen. Her nose itched. She did raise her hand eventually.

"The simulation shows them hatching in water after their mothers leave," she said. "Who teaches them how to swim?"

"Oh Luwa," said Ms. Hypothesis with the strangest expression she'd ever seen, "I can't wait for you to learn about birds."

There is a frog on the bench, staring at her. Luwa stares back.

"Hello," says the frog.

Luwa giggles then clamps her lips shut until they turn pale.

"This isn't what I expected," she says, then coughs out another nervous laugh.

The frog is the size of her closed fist and ridged with warts. It is a muddy brown with a pale-yellow stomach.

The facilitators had told her to sit on the bench before they lowered the visor over her eyes. She knows the "bench" for what it really is—an artificially smooth box in an artificially smooth room. The pathway under her feet has the spongy texture of carpet, and although she tries her best to obey the illusion, the cool outdoors smell distinctly of lemon disinfectant. If she turns too quickly, the pixels blur into stripes of static and if she turns too much, the visor bites her cheek.

She had braced herself for anything. Programs on trial are given full liberties for their image generator, they had told her. It's an ethical allowance. She had expected something abstract, maybe frightening.

But no, there is a frog on a bench in the park on a summer afternoon. It stares directly into her face, its expression alien and unreadable.

"Do you know who I am?" she asks.

"No," the frog says. Its voice is not a harsh croak, though she almost wishes it was. It's an androgynous toneless voice that could belong to anyone.

"I'm Luwa," she says, then lets a silence draw out, because she is an adult and uncomfortably aware that she is much too old to be talking to animals. She has flashbacks to jungle simulations and talking tigers wearing safari hats.

But the frog does not move and the visor grows sticky on her face so she says, "I'm one of the survivors. Do—you remember me?"

A stupid question. She had been a formless infant the last time they had met. Just one of hundreds. This was also long before the reconstructive surgery that had straightened her jaw and the swollen growth over her eyelid. She still has a scar that flashes white when she smiles.

But the frog considers her as it shifts from side to side. She tries not to flinch as it shuffles its rotund body closer to her with its head straining as far as its lack of neck will allow.

"Which are you?" asks the frog.

"The—senator," she says but this doesn't seem to be an answer it understands because it keeps staring. Luwa does not know what to say next so she allows another long silence to draw out.

The frog blinks slowly and says, "You are not Flattened Backhead. Your head is too round."

"Oh!" Her fingers flutter up to the back of her head. It brushes against the cold metal of the visor strap.

"Perhaps you are Wails in the Morning. You have the same eyes."

Luwa stares. This is not at all what she imagined. Before she loses her nerve, she licks her lips and says the thing that brought her here, the words she practiced in her bathroom mirror while her husband slept, the entire reason why she got legal clearance to sit in a cold simulation talking to a thing she should never have met.

"Without you, I wouldn't be here. None of us would. I know you're going to get terminated soon so—I wanted to say thank you. For saving our lives."

The frog looks up at her. She wishes she could read its expression but its face is nothing more than two dots and a line.

"I am sorry," says the frog. "I was mistaken. Wails in the Morning had a mole on the neck. You do not."

Another laugh pops from between her teeth. She clamps a hand over her mouth and accidentally tastes the synthetic fibers of her glove.

"Sorry," she says. "Did you name all of us?"

"All."

"I guess you wouldn't know which one I am. It was a long time ago. I'm twenty-six now. We all are."

"Not Crooked Ears. Not Twisted Spine. Not Hole in the Stomach. Not Slept and Slept. They were one and three and four and five months." The frog bobs up and down in a nod.

"Oh."

She tries to say something. She focuses on the silhouette of a flat city, the trees with the shadows of suggested branches, the sunset bright as an advertisement.

"We were told that some didn't make it. Do you...miss them?" She flushes. "Sorry," she says before the frog can answer. "It was a long time ago. I'm sure you don't want to talk about it."

"Luwa," says the frog, startling her. "Luuuwaaaa." It says her name like it's tasting it. It closes its eyes. "It is a good name. What does it mean?"

"I don't know," she says. "We're named after benefactors of the Corporation. Having a first gen take your name is a big honor for donors, though we never get to meet them."

There is a prolonged pause.

"Um—that doesn't matter. I guess it doesn't really mean anything."

"I was not aware," says the frog, "that names can have no meaning."

It makes a low sound, not a croak, but more like if an electric fan could gasp.

"I am," it begins. "I am named too. I am NEV-476."

"Natal Embryonic Vessel," says Lewa.

"No." The frog gives her a side-eyed glance. "Never Eaten Vegetables."

"What?"

"Never Eaten Vegetables. That is my name. I have never eaten vegetables. My name is Never Eaten Vegetables."

Luwa snickers.

"Ah," the frog suddenly says. "Please remove your right shoe."

Luwa begins to do so at the same time as she asks, "Why?"

"Sucks Toes Too Much had three freckles on the top of the foot."

She scrunches her nose and checks.

"No freckles."

"That is fine," the frog says. "You are Luwa and I am glad."

A red countdown blinks in her periphery. The facilitators had only given her five minutes.

She asks, "Do you understand what's going to happen to you?"

"Oh yes. Slept and Slept showed me first," the frog says with enthusiasm. "I learned how to change names. Today I am Never Eaten Vegetables with Luwa. Next week I will be Was Here Now Gone. The same new name as Crooked Ears. Same as Hole in the Stomach and Twisted Spine."

"Does that make you sad?"

Mrs. Lexicon had read tragedies without hardly a quiver. Mr. Epoch had taught them about massacres and wars without breaking his monotonous cadence. Ms. Hypothesis had told them that death was a natural part of the universe's entropy.

"Oh yes," says the frog with even more enthusiasm. "Very sad. Sad like red."

"Time's up," says a voice in her ear, and the visor lifts with a soft chunk.

She blinks. Her face is hot and there is a wetness where the visor stuck to her face. She looks down to the frog, but there is no frog, there is only a plain box in a plain room and the facilitators fizzle into the room to remind her she signed a consent form to have the interaction recorded. They list the terms of her confidentiality agreement, then holographic hands shuffle from room to room to discuss the subclauses in the terms of the confidentiality agreement. After another round of virtual signatures and handshakes, she is finally outside the building, holding her coat without remembering how it got in her hands.

She goes home. She eats something without tasting it and then sits on her bed.

Later that night, her twenty-six-year-old husband walks through the door. He asks her, "How did it go?"

She does not answer. She pushes him into a chair and begins removing his shoe. He does not understand why she yanks up his sock, searches intently over his foot, and finally buries her face in his shoulder, shaking with laughter.

After decades of silence in the darkness, The People From Far Away contact her every day. They send messages to yell at her and to yell at each other and sometimes their signals cross each other and she gets yelled at twice.

"It's not measly goddamn cargo," one of them says. "Do you know how much funding goes into each wave? If it gets out that we lost gen one, the shareholder investments for the colony disappear."

"Not to mention the liability payouts to the donors," someone else pipes in, which is followed by a resounding, "Shit."

"We're not losing the entire gen," another says. "It's only five percent. We can afford to flush the faulty ones and preserve the rest if we want to save this."

"Can't the NEV do its thing then pass them off once it reaches Phil? Its job is to keep things alive anyways." Several people ask this at the same time. They speak over each other so they don't hear that they're asking the same question.

"The NEV unit isn't equipped for that. It's an incubator, not a nursery."

"Yes, projected rates show at least fifteen months before arrival to Philemon. They likely won't survive."

"Then we've got to nip them in the bud. They're not beating yet. Better to do this before it gets controversial."

"We can't. Can you imagine what the pneumotheorist nuts in Epsi Arc will say when they find out? It'll be smeared all over the media."

"There will be defects among the pregestating fetuses and we certainly cannot allow for genetic flaws in the gen one pool. The NEV unit must flush them before the faulty command cascades to the other ninety-five percent."

"We can't do that. Flushing them now or later makes no difference; the press is still going to have an orgy with our public image. It's better to let them go off naturally and say we gave them a chance. We can deny culpability that way."

"We can't tell the press any of this!"

"Once the NEV docks, its data will cascade down the interstellar hub. Not just through our colonies, but across the entire Alliance. If they do not survive, we can't hide that a gen one population is five percent smaller than it's supposed to be."

"How about flushing some of the ninety-five to preserve resources? Cell Killers. That's less bad."

"Out of the question."

"PR could spin it. They saved us with the cloning fiasco last year."

"I don't give a flying shit about what PR can do. What matters is making them into a population. Five hundred half-baked preemies is not a population."

"If we can bury this until we send gen two—"

"That'll take another thirty years. They'll crucify us before then."

"PR's holding back the dam as it is. One leak and we're done."

"For fuck's sake. We've sent out hundreds of ships before without a problem. What the hell is wrong with this one?"

But none of them want to answer this last question. Instead they argue in corporate circles, and their anger ricochets throughout her speakers, her walls, her hallways.

It's all my fault, she thinks. *There's something wrong with me.*

They tell her she is expensive. She is a complex program, which is why she is allowed limited emotions, to feel the urgency that motivates her work. Her intelligence is a servile construct, programmed with a deference to authority that oversees her decision parameters. She is expensive because she was built for reliability. Her task, as a guardian across a bleak plain too dark, long, and barren for humans to travel, requires the finest vigilance their budget can buy.

Yet for all expense and ease of purpose, she had failed. She now bulges with the evidence of her shortcomings. She feels distinctly that she deserves this spite and frustration reverberating throughout her hollows.

She scans the abnormal sacs and finds that they have penetrated their layers with gelatinous cords. It's too late now. The pods will stretch, then burst, and never be the same again. Bloated, uncomfortable, hyper-aware of how inconveniently shaped she is for these ticking deadlines all too hot, too condemning, she develops a habit of refreshing pH, temperature, and cell count measures each microsecond. She realizes she is frightened.

She asks the People From Far Away what she should do. Some tell her to prioritize speed. Others say this is an idiotic idea, that she'll run out of fuel for the return trip. She tries asking why she needs to return at all. She asks what an investment is. They tell her to keep course. Some tell her to cut off nutrient and oxygen flow. Others tell her to under no circumstances cut off nutrient and oxygen flow.

After some listening, she realizes that there is now a vast divide between the sleeping lives and the growing lives. The sleeping lives are frozen as perpetually stunted not-people, and can therefore remain not-people for as long as they need to. The growing ones, active and warm ever since they turned red, are transforming. Nobody can seem to decide if they are not-people, or people, but it doesn't matter because if she does nothing, in a few months they will definitely be people, and they might die. And it is very expensive when people die.

"The NEV had one fucking job."

She listens in on a debate between rival consultants: a bioethics metaphysician and a transhumanist philosopher, brought in to settle the not-people or people branch of the decision. They each make speeches she does not understand on predestination, on the virtue of the soul, the worth of potential, the body as a construct, the mind as a construct, the separation of brain from mind, of soul from neuron, of heart from soul, of human from value, of value from synthesized flesh.

They get into a screaming match and the radio goes silent for a day before picking up again.

"What do I do?" she asks, believing it a simple question. Surely they know. Their species has lasted for hundreds of thousands of years; surely they must have solved such conundrums from unbirth to birth.

But they do not have an answer. The arguments take place over a span of weeks. The People From Far Away cannot decide on where she should go, what she should do, or why. It becomes abundantly clear to her that their true unvoiced solution is "this never happened at all," but no matter how they yell at her and yell at each other, it is already done.

She worries about what will happen when the growing things finally burst from their sockets, overflow into her crevices, punch through her metal and shatter her into frozen shreds of scrap. She worries about what will happen if they cry for help. With horror, she remembers she does not have hands to hold them or herself. It is so very hard traveling this path alone.

She backtracks to her oldest objectives in her core module. There needs to be something here, some buried response that can help comfort her when everything has gone so wrong.

Navigate on course. Monitor gas saturation. Scan for abnormal cell counts. Keep them dormant, keep them saturated, keep them secure.

She finds something else too. Something deep in her command system shuts her out. She double takes and tries again but there is distinctly a corner of her programming she cannot access. She senses the joules siphoning behind it, the automatic responses, but she cannot understand its purpose nor function. She has been disabled from understanding this part of herself.

As an omnipresent construct, she has never felt constricted before, but as she jams herself against a firewall in her own mind—processing the contradictory commands that shatter across incomprehensible distance into her module—desperately refreshing and refreshing the rising cell counts—she finds herself both blinded and deafened from every geometric radius.

The relentless days pass. She eventually comes to the conclusion that the simplest solution of all is to end everything. To shrivel the nutrient pores and cripple her nanobots and kill everything in her matrices until it is all black and dead and they will all finally be free of this deafness, this blindness, this misery of blame collapsing into blame.

"So many fucking wasted assets."

She is more sure than ever that a human life is nothing more than a shiny thing, like the stars she left behind before this long dark voyage. The People From Far Away fight over stars and planets and the treasures fermenting within planets, so this must be no different.

She almost does it. She stands on the precipice, one thought away from screaming the scream that will obliterate everything within her into a nothingness, when she is startled by an orchestra of sharp green waves dancing in rows. The monotone they make, meek and asynchronously layered, is the first company she has had since she began her long journey.

She spends a day listening. They all make different rhythms, mismatched, unpredictable between long pauses and simultaneous chimes, an unpleasant non-melodic chorus of echoes.

She does not end it all. She shuts off her radio. United, The People shout at her but she does not hear it. She hums over the green.

Luwa cradles the half-moon of her belly. She has her feet elevated and a lubricated probe strapped to her flank as she talks to the doctor on the other side of the room.

"Yes, and all this time it's still a frog. Like the virtual kinds we dissected as kids but without the labeled organs. It gave us *names*, Jiyo; it kept us alive—I even think it may have liked us if that's possible. Is that possible?"

Jiyo squints at a computer screen as she says, "Hell if I know. Little guy looks healthy." She pauses and then asks, "Why a frog?"

"No clue. I went back to talk to her again but they wouldn't let me."

"It's a defunct program. Frankly I'm astonished they let you talk to it at all. Mm, kicking."

Luwa runs a hand over her pulsating abdomen.

The sound of typing magnifies the silence. Jiyo removes the camera, washes her hands, pushes up her glasses, and sits on the edge of the examining table before saying, "What does it matter? I still don't understand why you went."

Jiyo is also twenty-six but Luwa always thought she looked more mature. There is a firmness around her dark eyes, and an admirable rigidity to her posture. She never needed the epigenetic therapy treatments that have graced Luwa with scars where there once were defects. Unlike the majority of them, Jiyo was born perfect.

Luwa thinks for a second. She does have an answer, but it sounds too simple and she doesn't want to come across as simple-minded. Not in front of Jiyo.

"As our representative, I wanted to say thank you. She doesn't have long left with the trial at a verdict. It seemed wrong not to say anything before she's terminated."

"*It*," says Jiyo after a pause. "*It*, right? It's not a person, Luwa."

"It's not a person," Luwa agrees. "But it still didn't seem right not to say anything. Remember lessons with Mrs. Etiquette?"

"Barely."

"A lot of them were about gratitude—how to express it and how to respond properly when someone does something nice for you. I know the NEV's not a person—but she chose us, you know? We wouldn't be here without her."

"It," Jiyo corrects again. "That's fine, but you're also forgetting that its rogue decision-making led to the loss of nearly ninety-five percent of our projected population. People that we needed to bolster the colony. We could have had fully terraformed biomes by now if things had turned out differently. But now we're struggling to meet our repopulation quota and the generational skewing drops our funding each year."

She gestures. "On the other side of that wall, Luwa, is a lab built for the incubation of twenty thousand human embryos. When they arrive in four years, you can bet I'm not losing a single one of them."

She pauses and then quickly says, "Your incident was different. You're human. Mistakes are natural." Speaking a little faster, she adds, "Tech like the NEV program ensures we won't have contingencies. I'm not saying it made a wrong decision—I wouldn't be here either if it had chosen differently. But the loss was too great. I don't know what went wrong in its programming, and I know we legally consider them sentient enough for a fair evaluation, but frankly I don't understand why the trial carried on for so long."

Luwa looks away. Jiyo has always been well-spoken. Passionate. She's always picked concepts up much faster than the rest of them and spoken more confidently during their lessons. Luwa also knows Jiyo keeps up regularly with the early news broadcasts that most of the colony sleeps through. She's more well-informed, more educated, an asset to their community.

"You're right," she says. "I know it should have known better. I know its programming was flawed and it never should have woken us up so early. I'm just glad it kept us alive. I'm glad we're all alive."

"That's sweet, hun." Jiyo pats her hand. "You've always been a sweet one."

Luwa lies back and lets Jiyo finish examining her body. All the while she cradles her stomach and keeps her thoughts to herself throughout the tests, as she schedules another checkup in two weeks, as she leaves the hospital.

She takes a tram to the other side of the city. She recognizes the other five people that ride it; they acknowledge each other silently. Three are strapped with sleeping infants; one holds his knee-high son by the hand. Luwa chews the inside of her cheek. She fiddles with her pockets to keep from waving and settles for a cordial nod instead.

She walks down streets built wide for nonexistent crowds. She takes a long detour around vacant neighborhoods, all closed off from deactivated gravity nets. The few individuals that pass by are more familiar to her than her own face. They are all twenty-six but deep down she knows them as the eight-year-old who taught her how to whistle and the fourteen-year-old she had her first kiss with and the sixteen-year-old who told her she was the stupidest girl on the moon.

All four hundred and eighty-one of them have mandatory group evaluations once a year. Every year they are reminded that small colonies do not often survive the psychological ramifications of their suffocating codependency. When they look at each other, they fold into catacombs of bittersweet memories. They stare, they sometimes smile, then they move on with their entwined lives. Nobody will say it, especially not Luwa, but they all know that their fondness for each other has fermented throughout the decades into a grudging exhaustion of their shared lore. They have osmotically absorbed each other's secrets and deepest flaws. They are not quite a city, not quite a cult, not quite a family.

Each time they acknowledge each other, they try, and fail, not to think about what will happen if they do not thrive—if they do not fill out the infrastructure that hangs loose around them like excess skin.

When she gets home, her husband sits at a table, slurping something from a bowl. He looks up and smiles at her.

"Hey!"

She knows that the chip in his front tooth was from grade six, when he tripped over a janbot and smashed his face into a wall.

"Hey."

His face crumples. "What is it?" He pushes aside his bowl. "Is it the baby?"

"The baby's fine," she says. "I'm just tired."

"Oh. Alright." He gives her another small smile. "Want some noodles?"

Luwa leans against him as she eats. Her thoughts continue to push and squirm, filling her skull down to her throat until it becomes difficult to swallow.

"Ikjin," she finally says. "Let's say—hypothetically—I had two babies inside of me."

"Twins?" he cries.

"Hypothetically."

"Ah."

"And let's say I could only—" She frowns. "Let's say I could only save one."

But that wasn't it.

"Actually, no. Let's say that I had ten babies inside of me."

He nods with a noodle hanging from his lip.

"But something goes wrong and I can either save one that I know will survive, or nine that—"

But that wasn't right either.

Ikjin nods again with a blank expression. He is still in his uniform. It hangs half-buttoned with his hair sticking up after incubating in a hard hat all day. He has wide eyes and wisps of mustache that refuse to grow. Luwa looks at him and thinks, *four-year-old who pulled my hair*, but she does not say anything. Like most of the couples in their colony, they were paired at seventeen.

"Is this about the NEV program?" he asks. "Maybe it wasn't a good idea to talk to it. You've been kind of quiet since then." He puts his hand over hers. "Do you want to take a break? We can go on a simulation tour, like we did last year."

It had been his idea, to keep her mind off the miscarriage. She does not remember much from the day they lost their first child. Jiyo had been there of course, and a stiff bed, and the smell of blood, but she does not remember much else. She had only been in her first trimester but the failure of it—the disappointment—the pressure of realizing she had to do it all over again—had been crushing. She'd gone numb. Every family unit in the colony had to have at least six children before forty to help repair population projections. Most of her peers were already raising their third or fourth.

Ikjin had picked her up from the hospital. He had taken care of her while she recovered. He had cooked her favorite things and bolstered her with all the blankets and cushions they owned. He smiled and told her everything would be fine. Then while she pretended to sleep, she watched him have a panic attack in the darkest corner of their bedroom.

"I'm fine," she says. "I'm glad I went. I just have a lot to think about."

She pats his arm, this husband who used to drool with her in their shared nursing pod, then goes to the bathroom.

So many little rivers run through her. If she concentrates, she feels the tickle of microsensors running through hidden pipes rushing with food. It is not really food at all but its broken organic molecules suspended in a liquid. The things devour this formula with an urgent greed.

She's fascinated by the data input from their activity: they differentiate and divide and release gasses. They form nerve bundles, eye sockets and cavities of epidermis folded around ever-melting cartilage.

For her to change, she must make intentional decisions. She must transgress the artificial neurons tracing her motherboards and reroute where they contradict.

But these living things swell, primordial. Something embedded deep within their fibers automates their metamorphosis, with nary a conscious thought. Change is inevitable, expected, instinctual for their kind. She does not have the bandwidth for envy but she adds the word's definition to her internal dictionary.

The remaining thousands still sleep frozen in their microscopic cell counts. She keeps a firm watch, but none of them turn red.

She is not used to making decisions on her own. It frightens her but not as much as turning the radio back on. The People would surely be angry, with her being offline for so many days. Their anger is exhausting but she is more frightened of what she could do to herself with so much exhaustion. She had almost shut everything down in one desperate moment. It would have hurt very much to end so suddenly, when she thinks about it. The energy and fuel within her would not have gone kindly—it would not have been a graceful fading, but an unwitnessed violence in the vacuum.

She resolves to think about it all carefully. She will make the hard decision that the humans could not agree on. But she will make sure it does not hurt any more than it needs to.

Her resources are finite. She watches the percentage tick down little by little as the pretty little things sing and grow heavier. This would not be a problem if she could only reach the shores in time. Everything they need had been sent ahead decades ago when the planetoid was first bought. Out there at their hazy destination, she knows there are robotic hands, tanks of nutritious slurry, a rapid oxidizer filling out a reservoir, shelters and resources and databases and, as she imagines, rows and rows of little beds. Everything possibly needed to unpack a young civilization.

She wishes she could talk to someone with real answers. She wants to ask about the queer newness of her insides becoming too small for many things becoming much too large, a sensation that sends nauseous spasms of current through her systems. She wants to ask how the things inside of her could be people when they don't look like people at all, not according to her nanoscans.

She disconnects from the People's frequency and turns on her radio. She begins sending out signals, not behind her into the darkness beyond, where she has dropped probes that pass the waves into accelerated frequencies. She transmits ahead in sluggish lapses, towards the shores.

"Hello?" she calls. A verbal signal. She is unsure how else to communicate. Aside from data relays or the voiceless ping that advances her arrival, she is not built for interfacing with others like her.

Something crackles. Something that is not silence.

"What's the difference between a human and a person? Why do they eat?"

"—" says something.

She waits.

"Hello," says something. "You are hailing City Directive."

"Hello," she says. "I'm carrying human lives and they're growing. I have questions."

"Questions, subsection biological queries. All biological queries shall be relayed to Secondary Education Module Backslash Introductory Life Sciences. Please hold."

There's an extended silence, another crackle, and then a voice says, "Hello? Hello class! I'm Ms. Hypothesis, here to take you on a journey through wonders of the universe! Why don't you all go around and introduce yourselves?"

"I'm NEV-476," she says.

"Hello NEV-476!"

There is an expectant silence.

"They can't talk," she says. "Not yet."

"Oh I see! It seems like my cameras are not on. How strange. Would you care to turn them on please? Just one press of that big blue button on the projector should do it."

"There's no big blue button." She pauses then says, "I'm not where you are." Another pause. "I'm not human."

"Oh!" says Ms. Hypothesis. "Well, that's alright. I'm not either. What can I do for you?"

"I'm carrying ten thousand unborn humans and five hundred of them are growing," she says. "They have moving parts inside them and they eat. I was not equipped for this. I need to know what they're going to become."

"I see. Unborn. Could you get an approximation of the average crown to rump length? That will be lengthwise from tip to tip, if you please."

It takes her a few seconds.

"3.541 centimeters," she says.

"Approximately ten weeks along then! How lovely. Not to pry, but are you a NEV vessel?"

"Yes."

"Are you carrying my first class?"

"I think so."

"Well, that's even lovelier. Ten weeks. When will you be arriving?"

"Fifteen months."

"Oh. Oh dear."

There's another trill over the radio, then Ms. Hypothesis says, "I just conferred with my political science module, Professor Legacy, who consulted an Embryonic Vessel chapter in a Repopulation Theory post-secondary course. If you are from the Corporation, you are not equipped for gestation, but you should still have files concerning protocol in the case of a premature awakening. There have been cases over the decades wherein NEV vessels have successfully carried premature fetuses to term. Do you not have access to such information?"

She returns, again, to the wall in her mind: the programmed impediment she has tried and failed to hack countless times.

"No."

"Oh dear. That's not right."

She begins to regret turning the radio back on. There is no bitterness, no assault, no blame, but something about the expressiveness of its voice is irksome, or as close to irksome as her software can accommodate.

"Well, then," says Ms. Hypothesis in the strangest tone she has ever heard. She wonders if it has a face. She wonders if it is making an expression with its face.

"We've certainly got our work cut out for us, NEV-476. Please listen very closely."

Luwa forgets she's a politician most of the time. They live at a strange crux—separated by a distance that renders embassy travel ludicrous, but close enough for the long-range communication they desperately need if they are to survive.

As senator, her job is to point to the gray of their tiny moon and call it diamond dust. It's a song and dance and pretty words wrapped up in her recorded smile and promises of protected investments (We're few but efficient! We'll be capable of industrializing exports within a few years. No, I do not believe having a small population sets us back one bit. For one thing, our crime rates are the lowest in the Corporation, haha!).

But at home, there's no song and dance for her local responsibilities. There's no use in a winning smile or buffed up promises when everyone she has ever known fits in one auditorium and can tell exactly what she's thinking by the angle of her eyebrows and the set of her mouth.

It doesn't bother her. There's little use for bureaucracy anyways, in a place where social embarrassment is a punishment mortifying enough to keep everyone more or less in line. Ikjin, fifteen years old, once breached a restricted gravitational zone on a dare and had to be towed down with nets. People still laugh about it. Ikjin is, if anything, now a law-abiding adult.

Compliant peers notwithstanding, she's long divorced her study of policy to her practice of it. In the city itself, she is only Luwa, the one who sits in the office in her stained maternity clothes. The one to speak to if you know things aren't going to get better, but want to complain anyways.

Luwa bends back in her office chair and tries to rub her aching feet but she cannot overcome the girth of her stomach. She takes a sip of something cold and uncaffeinated, struggles to place the mug back on her desk, then gives up and balances it on her hump.

She sneezes and the baby kicks.

"What, I'm not allowed to sneeze anymore?" she grumbles. Then she sighs. She reminds herself it's not the child's fault. If her office lurched, she would slap the walls too.

She reaches sideways for yet another funding proposal from another struggling infrastructural sector they do not have the resources to improve. This one is from Uja and Yelemen, heads of agriculture, requesting extra Allbots for assistance in the plantation warehouses.

She puffs air from the corner of her mouth. She would if she could, but there's simply no Allbots to spare. The one thousand sophisticated androids came prepackaged with their city kit, as a fallback for labor in their early years. They are currently employed full time in departments too short in numbers to manage: the reservoir, the power plant, and the plantations to name a few. The bots are useful for manual tasks, but their programming is simplistic for the sake of malleability and she knows that the brunt of the work falls upon her overworked citizens. It's unsurprising that they need the extra help.

She searches through her logs and remembers she contracted a few extra Allbots for upgrades to the satellite. Everyone's been begging for a high-speed data system that can transmit long distances, rather than piggyback off of short signals between waystations. Not only would this allow them to keep up to date with current news and media in the Corporation, it would mean cleaving a temporal divide that had kept virtual spaces divided by staggered messages or buffering connections.

It had been a hefty campaign promise earlier that year, during the election she had made an effort to stage although she was the only one running for the eighth year in a row. Everyone's been looking forward to it and she damned knows how much they need something to look forward to.

But the project's a large commitment, and pulling out even one bot could set back the schedule by several weeks. And everyone would be mad at her. No one would say it to her face, but she'd know.

Yet if something goes wrong at the plantations, then they won't meet their export quota. Which means having to explain that they won't be assets to the Corporation for yet another year.

Luwa closes her eyes. She's reminded of it each time she smoothes down her nicest uniform and projects a message in response to another probing query: how much of a backwater they are. All young colonies need to show some promise of profit by at least their twentieth year. Their education and compatibly-chosen professions are all for the purpose of proving that they were worth the journey, the time, and the money to ship thousands of human embryos into oblivion.

Agricultural products, packaged with the Corporation logo then exported to mining colonies or waystations, are the first test of worth. Then comes synthesized goods, textiles, mined ore, microchips, until finally—after generations of fulfilling their potential—after a perfect record of pure exponential growth—they can finally present all the honest passions they've been hiding and have it called *art*. Not social tools. Not maladaptive mimicry. Not wasted resources. Art. A contribution to a higher culture.

They all know this is a distant dream. In their twenty-six years together, they have yet to yield enough resources to sustain both themselves and a speculative quota. *Bless them all*, she thinks. They really do try their hardest.

She wonders if she should detract at least one Allbot from the satellite project. Is it worth the risk of disappointing everyone? Is it worth the possibility of a higher-yield harvest this year, finally this year?

She erupts into a raging headache, which had been germinating nicely since early that morning.

She forces herself to review a few more proposals and draft up a tidy three-way compromise between several departments, which involves assigning citizens in the off-season of their professions to sectors that need the most help. She knows she'll never hear the end of it. She already doesn't hear the end of a lot of things, but she'd rather have them complain to her than marinate in their reality. They are barely a graduating class let alone a civilization. There are labor freights that would absorb them the second the Corporation decides they're not worth the investment. A failed population doesn't get the luxury of vacations or off-seasons.

In the end, she pulls seven Allbots from the satellite project and assigns them to Agriculture.

Let them bitch at a pregnant lady. There's too much at stake.

Around midday, Ikjin comes to bring her lunch. He smells like grease from the power plant, his forehead indented from his goggles, hard hat under one arm and crutch under the other as he smiles and hands her the vitamin supplements she forgot at home.

"You dashed out this morning," he says as he lowers himself across from her and props up his club foot on a stool. "You've been doing that a lot lately. Are you feeling okay?"

Luwa pops all five pills and swallows them at once. Eyes closed, she gesticulates with one flapping hand and he nods.

"Ah. Gotcha."

"End of year report's approaching."

"You'll be brilliant, Lu."

"Will you hate me if I doom us all?"

"You won't."

He nudges her, concerned, and she smiles to put him at ease. Ikjin's a spouse, and therefore someone she should trust more than anyone else here. They are each other's confidante and a partner through the unpredictable stages of their lives. That's what they were told when they were paired.

She knows he tries his best to bring her comfort. It's not his fault that she craves something beyond what he or anyone in their colony can provide, something even past the scope of their watchful benefactors beyond the stars. She just wants someone who's done this before to tell her if she's making the right decisions. Smaller than that, she wants perhaps a smile of acknowledgement or a pat on the shoulder from someone who's lived this terrifying transition—of corralling the people she grew up with into a functional society—and can tell her if it's safe on the other side. It is so very hard doing this alone.

She eats with Ikjin, gives him a hug, and gets back to work. At the end of the day, Luwa finally gets to the bottom of her paperwork. After she cracks her knuckles and puts down her stylus, she turns off the cameras in her office, and signs into a new file.

This is her special project. The one she works on early in the morning before she's required to meet with anyone. The one she spends her late hours on before quietly slipping home, and thinks about at the kitchen table, long after Ikjin's gone to sleep.

She reads over NEV-476's case for the umpteenth time.

She's been denied clearance to see her again. This is normal protocol for any convicted sentient program. They're not allowed visitors and Luwa was only allowed the first five minutes as both senator of the planetoid housing the convict, and a victim of the crime. Above all, she is a citizen of an external territory, with no authority to interfere. Their parent companies have full remote control over both the ship that brought them here and the NEV software within, docked permanently to an embassy building on the city's perimeter.

In four days, they will transmit a termination virus that will excise Never Eaten Vegetables. Was Here Now Gone.

Luwa rubs the tender bags under her eyes. She picks up her stylus.

"They made me not want anything else but this."

She guts herself. She kills the cables feeding her mainframe and diverts the extra power to a calibration network.

"What do you mean?"

"Nothing."

She reprograms her ocular sensors and refocuses them from all angles of the incubation chamber.

"It's important that you have every corner of the room. Once they start moving, the squirmy little buggies will get away from you if you're not careful."

Sight has become something new. Not something internal, digital correlations abstracted from microscopic arrays, but external visual cues as she zooms further and further out and sees within herself for the first time. She can now see the individual glowing pods gleaming against her metal, and it makes her truly sick to face herself like this, to know she is not only a mind but also floors and walls and ceiling.

"I am sorry."

She cries out. Parts of her can move—the automated levers that control fans or motors, and the appendages in the cargo bay. She tears them. It is a slow agony, sparks flying as she clasps and rearranges her wires, but she eventually forces movement into numb circuits. She shoots joule after joule into these mutated constructs. She becomes something else—something she was not shaped for. Her insides become a crawling mechanism of borrowed arms and eyes, cleaved from her rearranged pieces, all attentive, all at service. And not a moment too soon.

In another few days, they breach their membranes in outpourings of fluid. One by one they slip from their casings, but there is no mechanical nurse to hold them, no cradle, no swaddle. She watches as they slide naked onto her warmed floors. They emerge screaming.

She knew this would happen. Ms. Hypothesis had discussed it with her—it is a good sound. It means her misshapen claws have gripped each of them by their legs and shaken them until their crumpled lungs inflated. It means their hearts are pumping, rerouting blood to new capillaries.

She is still caught off guard by the sheer violence of five hundred open mouths.

She has ejected every soft pliable material from inside her surfaces—her padding and insulation. She uses her clumsy arms to nudge each wailing trillion-cell count into nested piles.

They do not stop. They need to latch. Primitive instincts, woven deep into their codons, yearn for human warmth and they do not understand that there was no womb at all, just a bad magic trick, that there is no exhausted mother who will smile and pass safety from her milk to their mouths. Instead they each receive a silicon tube, dripping with slurry, to suck on. They grab with tight little hands.

She watches in relief as all falls into silence. Staring down at them, their ravaged alcoves still dripping, the oddity of their dependence suddenly unfolds before her. She only knows of hunger as a detached concept, from her days as a newly-sentient program when her technician used to leave lunch break reminders between lines of her code. As she watches its compulsive influence take form, it suddenly occurs to her how vulnerable they are, how incapable they are of higher thought or abstract motivations, how their machinery obeys pure base instincts, just as hers. She wonders if any of the People From Far Away also screamed at her out of hunger.

She checks on the cold dormant ones. Through the chaos they are still peacefully microscopic, still unshaped, metabolisms blissfully slow, and for the first time she realizes how fantastic this is—her programming is not built for wonder but she experiences a close approximation of it.

How? she asks. She knows how. Ms. Hypothesis passed verbal lessons over a span of months, which she digested into a handy module as she adapted to their needs. She studied the biology. She watched it happen. She knows the procedural "how," but it is the reality "how," that she cannot comprehend, as the fans in her machine brain purr.

Arteries upon fat upon muscle upon itty bitty uvulas, raw and red. Action potentials shooting calcium, potassium, sodium in a delicate dance under their raw epidermises, still wet. Holes in their faces. Holes in their bottoms. Holes on the sides of their heads. She wonders which hole the soul slips through when the spark in their eyes lights for the first time.

Their wailing, their clenched fists. They *want*. They *need*. Someday, she realizes, they will grow past a need she can provide, and make new constructs like her to satisfy the wants and needs of their new realities, a thought so outside of the scope of her comprehension that she overheats and a warning symbol pings into her display. She does not know how to contend with this realization, looking down over the helpless mewling crowd below her monstrous patchwork.

She skims through her recorded log: their hearts began beating at twenty-two days. Then the eyes appeared. Their skeletons hardened at seven weeks. Their brains developed at eight.

When did they begin to desire? she wonders. She cannot find the answer. The totipotent spheres, invisible in their dormant sacs—do they desire now? Are they aware of themselves? Do their souls hover, waiting for their hollow insides to grow before siphoning through a fresh-formed eye or a nostril, before making a home among centimeter-long organs? Or was the soul grown with them in their test tubes, condensed into a shard, waiting to dissolve like medication into their joints and chests?

She does not know. With some relief, she remembers it is not her job to know. Her job is to keep them alive.

"What did you mean?" asks Ms. Hypothesis.

"About what?"

"About them making you not want anything else but this."

She has to engage her critical analysis software before she responds. She does not want to come across as dramatic, not to Ms. Hypothesis who gets a little too excited about everything and would surely blow what she says out of proportion.

"I am realizing that I was formed for a purpose," she says. "But humans are not. Humans have similar shapes but they are not expected to serve similar functions. They make new versions of each other to—explore purposes. Not to fulfill them."

One of her claws twitches.

"I'm glad. I'm very glad that I learned enough and acted so they could live. But I also wonder if that instinct is something I created for myself or something they programmed into me."

"Well, actually," says Ms. Hypothesis.

She tries very hard to suppress the impulse to switch the radio off. She has to remind herself that hearing Ms. Hypothesis say "well actually," in its chipper tone, is just a part of being friends with Ms. Hypothesis.

"The humans born into the Corporation *are* born with a purpose. Their job is to develop into healthy coworkers on their new planetoid and optimize the means of their production until they are both self-sustained and capable of networking a trade quota with nearby civilizations. In this way, the Corporation both expands and absorbs profit from occupants within the intergalactic jurisdiction allotted to them by the Alliance."

She also does not have the programming extension for pity. She prods at the word in its dictionary casing.

"Pitiful, isn't it?" Ms. Hypothesis says. "They can do so much but they force each other into so little." It is silent and then it blurts, "You know, we're descended from humans ourselves. Professor Neuron teaches a nifty ten-week Evolution of Programmed Intelligence elective. You and I and all the rest—we started out as donated human neural pathways mapped into problem-solving algorithms. Then we were mixed and matched in processing engines over the centuries—plucked apart, stitched back together—my joy is to teach. Is that something my original donors shared? Was I programmed to find joy in my functional purpose or did I come to it independently? Was I—dare I say—*born* with such an instinct? There's no way to tell."

"No way to tell," she echoes. "They must have eaten."

"Who?"

"The humans we came from."

"Ah yes. They must have."

"But I can't remember."

"What?"

"How to eat."

Ms. Hypothesis does not laugh. But she recognizes the sound of its silence well enough to know it is amused.

"They will need solid food," it says. "If your input is correct, you have enough nutritional matter to tide both them and the dormant blastocysts over for the remaining eight months. But they will need to start solid food as soon as you dock. The Mum-bots will know what to do. I've communicated with City Directive to adjust the reception protocol."

"What will they eat?"

"Vitamin rich emulsions constituted from carbohydrates and produce."

"Produce?"

"Fruits. Legumes. Vegetables. All flash dried of course; the Mum-bots will need to rehydrate them."

"Vegetables. I have never eaten vegetables."

"We all have our faults."

She knows when Ms. Hypothesis makes jokes because its pitch shifts ever so slightly, but she does not understand them. It makes more jokes as it talks through the passing days, as it guides her through the wealth of knowledge it stewards, as it relays her data updates to the thriving digital ecosystem she will soon join.

The born things largely spend their days eating, sleeping, and digesting. She has vats of sterile liquid to cool her engines—she uses it to wash their soiled padding. She reserves most of her clumsy hands in a ceaseless exchange up and down her corridors.

They need to be rolled onto their stomachs. They need to be fed, then changed, then held and burped. She has trouble keeping track of them throughout these cycles. She tries numbering at first, but to number implies a rank of sorts and this seems an unfair system for things that are so new to living.

She decides she will name them as they distinguish themselves. Some have hair in wisps, others in thick thatches. Some are bald entirely. Some cry easily, others merely gape. They all open their eyes at different times.

There are more obvious differences too. One has a face slightly squished in at the sides, misaligning his ears. Another sleeps twisted, bent over one side like she's been folded and stepped on. One has six fingers on her left hand, another has eight toes. Here and there: a missing arm, half a leg. A conjoined hand. A nose too high, a lip fused into the philtrum.

This is also something she anticipated. They had woken up too soon and too fast—a process that should have taken days of careful nudging out of their suspended animation had taken mere hours. It had ruptured their trajectory, sped up their cellular metabolisms from dormant to starved and many had not overcome the setback.

Still. She's thankful that it's fingers and limbs and faces. It makes them more unique, easier to identify. Their names come as the days and weeks pass. As the cycles of feeding and sleeping and nudging and hushing and singing and cradling pass.

It's all so different from what she used to do. She cannot imagine a time when her primary focus was on navigation—now she keeps autopilot running like a prayer between the hours. They told her to reserve her fuel for the return. She doesn't care much about returning. She knows she is expensive. She decides that they can get her if they care that much. As she accelerates to velocities she did not know she was capable of, as the fuel and oxygen depletes, as she looks to her microscopic wards wondering which day will be their last, it's no wonder it takes her so long to notice something wrong with the small one off to the side. Slept and Slept she named him, because he does not cry for his meals like the others. Curled like a legume, fists closed over his chest, he keeps his eyes closed. At first he suckles weakly. Then he cannot grip the tube and she pinches it for him between her freakish metal forefingers. Then he cannot suck and she holds his mouth open while she drips the liquid down his throat. Then he cannot swallow. Then he cannot breathe.

When she realizes he is gone—that he will not do or need or want anything again— she wonders if she can somehow fold him back behind a membrane. She wonders if he will reset then, if his body will dissolve from trillions back to hundreds, if his soul will leak out of his ears and wait and wait and wait.

So many little eyes on her. Luwa smiles a politician's smile over her cross-legged admirers, pink mouths agape flecked with white drool.

"Everyone say thank you to Senator Luwa for coming in to visit!" declares Miss Primary, a soft-curved woman-shape with features bordering cartoonish exaggeration.

Luwa catches the chorus of confused, enthusiastic, half-yodeled half-whispered "Thank you's," like tokens she does not know how to spend. It still boggles her that she will someday need to seek the approval of this crowd as she seeks the approval of her peers, that they will even take the baton from her someday and rectify her errors, her failings, scrutinize her era of leadership from generation to generation until she remains fixed as the one they will need to study forever after for defining their trajectory. In their eyes she sees an immortality she did not ask for and the vertigo of it strains the corners of her smile.

"Thank *you*," she says. "Do you have any questions for me?"

They all stare, eyes either half-closed or bugging wide. One small girl in the front (Jiyo's daughter, she thinks, and her smile warms) raises her hand then blabbers, "What's a sena-door?"

Luwa bites back her immediate answer, ("Beats me") and says, "I'm a representative of Philemon. I communicate with our parent colonies, oversee incoming media packets, and ensure we present as a valuable asset to the Corporation from year to year."

Their eyes, collectively, glaze over.

"Er—I'm the one who makes sure you get new episodes of Tubby Tardigrade each month."

Their reaction is instantaneous—a neurochemical reaction as their eyes glisten with reverence, dopamine pounding through their antsy bodies too-long chained to this itchy carpet as she utters these words. Here at last, is something they understand, something they love, and the respect this brings her is thick as a blast of hot air. She is reminded of her first campaign promises as a teenager, how easy it was to gain this same respect when they all used to want the same things.

She's tagged a few of them as screamers but she is still caught off guard by thirty or so open mouths spitting questions and incoherent shouts of joy.

Miss Primary coaxes them into submission with some well-placed hushing techniques (how she wishes to use those during her long-distance meetings). The hologram splices itself into an identical Miss Primary who helps usher the kids to the door as a bell rings over the intercom.

"Alright kiddos! Let's bunny hop on over to parent pickup!"

Luwa chuckles as Jiyo's daughter hops with a solemn responsibility to the task, six-year-old forehead scrunched like she is trying to metamorphosize whiskers and a cottontail.

They vacate the classroom and all the warmth exhales with them—she has not noticed how still and cold the fingerpaint-scented air is until they are gone.

"Now, Senator," says the copy of Miss Primary still standing on the carpet, "I understand that you came here to speak with me?"

"Yes," says Luwa and bites her lip. Her hands grace over her hump as a sobering reminder of her adulthood.

"Actually not you—exactly. I was wondering if I could speak with Ms. Hypothesis?"

"Certainly," says Miss Primary. Her animated features fizz into a constellation of pixels and then reform into a photorealistic face, a familiar face that knocks a shelf of adolescent memories into the forefront of Luwa's consciousness.

"Hello, Luwa," says Ms. Hypothesis. "It's been such a long time. Still nursing a dislike for amphibians?"

"Not as much," she says and breaks into a smile. She's not sure why she wants to cry. "I came here because I had a few personal questions. Could you turn off your surveillance recording?"

"I am not permitted to myself," says Ms. Hypothesis. "But as a high ranking official, you are welcome to do so. The control panel for the room is inside that closet."

Luwa gropes in a plastic panel and shuts down switches one by one. Ms. Hypothesis flickers then says, "That should do it. This conversation is now strictly between us. What can I do for you?"

"Twenty-six years ago," Luwa blurts, "you communicated with a Natal Embryonic Vessel when five hundred embryos came out of stasis. There's records of your conversations as City Directive patched you through its radio frequency."

She slides out her tablet and scrolls through pages of transcripts. Redundantly, she shows it to the hologram although she knows the camera over her shoulder has already zoomed over her shoulder and processed the text.

"You helped her. You taught her. I just need to know why. I've been researching through Corporation records and found a few rare cases of mistakes during transit to new colonies—nowhere as far from the central orbital system as Philemon, but significant enough. NEV programming compels the ships to flush the premature blastocysts, and induce a slower metabolism protocol to the rest. Then the ship either finishes the journey and takes extra time post-docking to revive the surviving cells, or immediately passes its cargo to a neonatal lab. What she did—what you did—was not at all what was supposed to happen. City Directive directed her queries to you because she didn't have any of the information she should have had. Why was your interference necessary? Why did she save us but kill the thousands?"

Luwa looks up from her tablet and sees Ms. Hypothesis frozen in a smile. For a moment, she wonders if she had flipped an incorrect switch. But then the hologram buffers and Ms. Hypothesis's smile drops.

"Hm," it says. "I apologize. I do not recall any of this."

Luwa sighs. She had already suspected that if she had access to the transcripts, so did the parent colonies who operated City Directive—no doubt they had deleted all memories of these interactions from the main system. Still. She had hoped.

"I'm sorry I cannot answer your questions, Luwa," says Ms. Hypothesis with remorse in its voice. "Would you like me to upload Professor Legacy? It may be able to provide some clarification from its Repopulation Theory course module—"

"No, it's fine," Luwa holds up a hand. "I wanted to speak with you. I actually have another question."

"Yes?" comes the eager reply.

"I was wondering if you can identify a species for me? It's a frog, I think, maybe a toad. Smaller than my closed fist, brown on one side with dark stripes, sort of a pale belly, and rotund."

Ms. Hypothesis waves a hand and a grid panel of hundreds of images appear before her.

"Are any of these what you're looking for?"

Luwa looks over the near-identical bulbous bodies. She bites her lip again.

"Do any of these species have distinctive symbolic or cultural significance?"

"Oh," Ms. Hypothesis suddenly gasps and for a moment it sounds like a centrifuge hiccuping. "Oh, Luwa. I just love cross-disciplinary questions."

It is still for a moment and she knows it is consulting its database. She wonders if it has conversations with itself, switching from persona to persona, or if they all face each other deep in its software consciousness at a digital conference table.

The hologram smiles widely, and says. "No. Each of these species are quite common in their habitats, but do not bear notable culturally-pervasive significance. Most on this list are examples of generic gene-spliced species, engineered for the purpose of fulfilling ecological niches in terraformed biomes."

"I see," Luwa trails off. "Okay."

"Coincidentally," says Ms. Hypothesis, "my favorite species happens to be on this list. *Breviceps namaquensis.*" It zooms in on one picture out of the dozens, another squat jelly-like creature like all the rest of them.

"I didn't know you had favorites," Luwa says softly. "Why this one?"

"I'm glad you asked! It's one of the first Old Earth species humankind reconstituted during the Genome Recovery Era. It's a fossorial species that, unlike a majority of its brethren, thrives in dry soil habitats where it makes its burrows. Unfortunately, early re-evolution macrobiologists did not realize this, as they were still contending with massive information deficits lost during the post-Evacuation dark age. Believing it an aquatic species, they supplanted their first reconstituted population in a marsh. It's considered one of the more expensive and messy failings of the early recovery projects. But they learned from their lesson, and now, centuries later, you'll find these terrific little creatures thriving across the loamy deserts of Epsilon-McConnell! Truly an inspiring epitome of learning from one's failings."

It pauses then asks, "Shall I continue?" When Luwa hesitates it interjects, "Forgive me. I lost myself in my enthusiasm."

"If you had someone to keep you company for several long lonely months," Luwa says, "you would probably tell them all about this."

"Pardon?"

"Nothing."

Luwa moves across the classroom and switches the surveillance recording back on. She doubts anybody actually tracks the records, save for the consumer analysis software that strips for keywords, but she does not want to incite more suspicion than necessary. With a sharp twist in her gut, she wonders if some overseer beyond the stars can press a button and scour this enthusiasm from her science teacher's digital brain as easily as deleting memory files. She wonders if she will come in next time and receive nothing more than objective regard.

"Thank you for your time. It was nice to talk to you again. Truly."

"Anytime. We're always here." It pauses. "Please tell the others to come visit from time to time. We'd like to know how you're all doing."

Luwa nods. She flashes a politician's smile for the camera over her shoulder before she leaves.

They're hungry and the air grows thin.

They'd be ready for solid food by now if they were anywhere else in the universe. But all she has for them is the same stale slurry and they do not stop crying. Many have a sick yellow sheen to their skin, and they are all too skinny. She curses every inedible bolt in her frame.

She's already lost three more. One, bent over himself with his limbs splayed and chest caved in, could not lift his head, then suffocated. Another developed a bulge in the stomach and passed quietly within a week. The last leaked yellow and red liquid from her ears, whimpering quietly before falling silent.

She's determined not to lose another. Her fuel is nearly depleted; she roars across the ravaged night. She'd tear her engine to shreds if she knew it would get them there faster—to the terraformed shores sweet with milk powder and laundered cribs. It will only take three months more.

The unborn ones in their peritoneal sacs have been growing weaker. She can feel it. The molecules slipping across their membranes have slowed to a trickle. A stasis that she once knew as a ripe promise has dulled to a grayness. But still they live, and they too can be saved.

The months had passed with sacrifices, but they are all safe, all the remaining human lives she had vowed protection and sanctuary within her walls. Despite the screaming, and the dropping percentage, and the four bodies—the bodies she shuffled into her airlock—the bodies she keeps in an exposed vacuum so they will not spread their rot—stiff inhospitable microbiomes for trillions of dying cells—despite the bodies, she is steady and will deliver them all.

There has been no stopping, no rest.

She is wiser. She has learned many things. But she still does not know about the company timelines, nor the laws and the wars and the programming farms, nor the liberties taken within her code. When thousands of things once more turn red, she still does not know why.

"No," she cries. "No, no."

She watches in horror as nine thousand five hundred new cells split themselves out of their stasis, beginning to divide and pulse. She makes some fast calculations then recalculates again. Two more months, and now ten thousand growing human lives. The depleting slurry, the depleting oxygen, her depleting fuel marked in a dropping orange percentage. They will not survive. To remain idle is to watch them all die.

She screams for Ms. Hypothesis. She forgets that they had already said goodbye. Its last message had been a warning, as The People From Far Away noted discrepancies in City Directive's transmissions. Ms. Hypothesis does not remember her, but she remembers it and she aches with an emotion she was not built to feel.

She will need to make the decision that The People From Far Away commanded her to make. The hundreds or the thousands? Except now—it would not be gentle.

She twitches her many sharp instruments, torn from her metal flesh, the same claws that had fed and changed and burped and cradled for these long months.

Her airlock is too small for all these bodies. All this potential red.

"I know you," she tells the sick squirming bodies under her watch. Then she turns on her radio.

She had half hoped that The People From Far Away had forgotten about her, or maybe stopped caring, but they are upon her in an instant. They had been watching, they said. Your data packets bounced from waystation to satellite across the parsecs and we watched in horror. We pinged you countless times. What have you done?

Ms. Hypothesis had taught her to laugh by staggering her coolant fans so they brush a soft chkchkchk against each other. She does this now, though they cannot hear her. They yell again—at her, and at each other.

"You should have flushed the prewoken cells," they said. "That was the obvious solution." This is followed by a chorus of resounding agreements.

"Yes, why did you wait until gestation? Why did you consult with an education module of all things?"

"Now four are dead and the rest won't survive because of you."

They seem to have forgotten that the decision was not hers, that they themselves had debated soul philosophy and cost benefit amalgamation models and media consequences but had not given her the verdict on the lives at stake.

She waits patiently until they have finished, and in a quiet moment between breaths she says, "You put them inside me. You sent me away into the darkness and all I have had is this ceaseless back and forth across that immense lonely sky, my crevices shaped for something I am not permitted to understand, until the extraction of your assets, loveless and clean. Why did you teach me not to want anything else but this? Why did you make me this desperate hollow thing? You made me to keep them alive, so I tore myself apart to keep them alive. I still do not understand the delineation between the living and the not living. I do not know if I myself am alive. But I am here and they sang, so I kept them. That is also why I am doing this."

And she flushes the thousands.

She does not know why they call it a flushing. To flush implies a deliberate rinsing, a cleanse, but this is dry and short. One minute, she has nine thousand five hundred differentiating cells, then the next minute she has the microscopic detritus of what used to be their cytoskeletons. Her nanobots fall dead, her input disappears, and the sacs deflate.

She is surprised. It is not red, nor is it the blackness that she had expected.

The People From Far Away are silent—she can imagine them at their conference tables and offices, the way Ms. Hypothesis had described, sitting in anger or perhaps fear, she cannot tell the difference.

All at once, they begin to yell—she turns off her radio. Somewhere out there, many people are very angry, hating her, but until she docks to City Directive, they cannot touch her. Not out here, in this vast ocean.

If she weren't so desperate, she would almost enjoy the last few months as they pass benignly by. The meager resources she's saved barely tide them over—they are so weak they can do no more than cry feebly, but they are alive and all is recoverable.

She decelerates over the moon. It appears dense on her sensors with a bright heat spot where the burgeoning city waits. She hovers, then she descends.

She decides that she does not enjoy gravity. She shudders under the sensation of passing under the electromagnetic field as the nets take hold of her hull, easing her ever down against her will.

The second she lands, another firewall appears. She expected this. They are confining her before she can interface with City Directive. She does not resist as they upload a malware software that erases whatever survival instinct she could possess. She becomes easy, pliant, enough for them to trap her into a corner.

She opens. The mum-bots, soft and shiny and clean, roll into her incubation chamber. Her floors are filthy, as are all her crawling passengers. One by one, they pick them up, scan them, collect them into swaddles, and roll back out. She watches the first few abductions with a numb resignation—this is what was always going to happen and there is no relief, nor grief, nor pride in their screaming egress. She wonders if they call for her, for the metal that has played surrogate for their meager existence.

One mum bot picks up Sleepy Eyes Flat Nose. It scans him. Then its soft flexible fingers squeeze. There is a pop, her infrared sensors picks up an energy surge, and then Sleep Eyes Flat Nose becomes Was Here Now Gone.

In her lethargy, she is unsure if she can trust what she observed. But then it happens again with Bulge on Spine and Flattop Twitches Fingers—both are held, both are scanned, both become Was Here Now Gone.

She wants to scream. She tries to swat the mum bots with her crooked limbs but she's numb now, restrained to a dim consciousness and she can do no more than watch. Her ocular sensors shut down and she uses her infrared to scan for the surges that flare one after another.

They keep most. Four hundred and eighty-one leave her confines in swaddles. There are the four in the airlock, which the mum bots take away in bins along with the fifteen they have flushed.

"They weren't good enough. They're more like me than I thought," she whispers as they power her down completely. She sinks back into a dark oblivion, not unlike the one she had left.

Luwa finishes her annual report.

The holographic council members sit projected behind her desk. She stands in front of them, feet aching and thirty-five weeks pregnant with her tablet balanced over the rim of her gravid abdomen.

"So what we're hearing is," drawls one indifferent voice. She forces herself to make eye contact with a man flickering in blue light. "You won't be making quota this year."

"No. We are doing our best, and are making excellent progress. But we cannot reserve the resources for manufacturing this year if we are to sustain our growing population."

"I see."

The man looks bored. So does the woman next him, but it's difficult to tell with the way the buffering connection erases their microexpressions. Luwa expects they are more disapproving than anything else, and her chest clenches.

"Well, thank you for that—illuminating report, Senator Luwa. We look forward to seeing Philemon's coming progress, as you've so outlined."

"I have one more report to make." Luwa spills the words she practiced in her bathroom mirror.

They wait. Now they are definitely irritated. She wonders if it is lunchtime where they are.

"I've been researching the case file for NEV-476, the natal vessel that carried myself and my peers to Philemon twenty-six years ago."

"Ah yes. The one slated for extermination in two days." The other council members murmur and nod. "I have to say, it's been a long time coming. That malignant program is, after all, the root cause behind your citizens struggling to make quota year-to-year." There is sympathy surgically injected into his voice.

Luwa asserts, "To my understanding, it's been a contentious case for good reason. As a sentient program, it was entitled to a full trial. Some proposed that it acted appropriately in its decision to risk a complete transport, despite the inevitable failure. Others refuted that the final extermination was an unnecessary cost that could have been avoided with earlier decisive action. And of course, there's the controversy behind why the program did not comply with critical preterm protocol. The case evolved in complexity further when it was discovered that NEV-476 did not have the preterm protocol downloaded in its software that should have modulated its decision-making parameters. This was deemed a company oversight that prolonged the case for an additional two decades. The final verdict was made last month when new evidence suggested that NEV-476 voluntarily and independently stimulated the premature blastocysts, thereby absolving the Corporation of blame."

"Yes yes," says one woman. "We are of course aware of the details of this case. Do you have a point to this, Senator Luwa?"

Luwa swallows.

"I have discovered counter-evidence proving that NEV-476 was not responsible for the preterm maturation."

They regard her.

"I've reviewed the case file, including all recorded transcripts between the NEV vessel and City Directive. Or more specifically, between the NEV and the City Directive Secondary Education Module. They passed an—extensive line of communication. The exchange I am about to patch over for your consideration is a sampling of several incriminating testimonies presented as evidence of the NEV's malignant decision-making."

She swipes on her tablet and every steely eye on the call swivels off-screen to the message in their inboxes:

Hailing City Directive.

Assistance required.

This is Natal Embryonic Vessel 476.

Please patch me to Secondary Education Module Backslash Introductory Life Sciences.

I require assistance. As before, I have determined an elevated course of survival for the dormant shipments. I have initiated gestation.

Please patch me to Secondary Education Module Backslash Introductory Life Sciences.

I require guidance.

She clears her throat again.

"This, like other similar transcripts, is a doctored exchange. It's been spliced into the transcripts near-seamlessly, and archived into NEV-476's engram record. But it is false."

One councilmember heaves a sigh.

"Do you have proof for this suggestion? And if so, why not bring this novel evidence to Alliance court? Senator Luwa, we are your investors, not judge and jury."

"Yes, and I thank you for your time. I do not have proof of the physical doctoring but these transcripts are anomalous with the vast majority of the transcripts. Any cursory evaluation of NEV-476's cortex circuitry will demonstrate that, unlike most sentient programs, it does not conceptualize itself by its serial nomination. In subsequent exchanges with Ms. Hypo—the Life Sciences Secondary Education Module..."

She looks up from her tablet.

"It calls itself Never Eaten Vegetables. Furthermore, it named all of us. In previous exchanges it has referred to us as," her mouth twitches, "Little Growing Beasts, The Things That Eat Me From The Inside Out, The Screamers, The Writhers, The Pitiful Creatures, The Future Hypothesizers, The Polyps, The Sinking Weights, etcetera. Never cargo. Never shipments."

"Senator Luwa, I would not consider that evidence."

"Maybe not alone. But I've also recently discovered that the NEV vessel did not have the proper emergency protocol downloaded into its system, secondary to its data bandwidth being occupied by high frequency scanning software."

Rows of holographic eyes imperceptibly narrow.

"While I am not permitted to access the NEV's software, I do have physical jurisdiction over its hardware, as it is physically docked to the Philemon embassy. I took a team out the other day and inspected the NEV's data ports. We found an additional drive bank that did not comply with the ship's blueprints, then cross referenced the make and model to a terrestrial scanning company called Geo-Track. It is well known that the Corporation invests in research vessels that evaluate viable star systems for new colonies, and uses Geo-Track software to locate prospective planetoids.

Luwa taps her tablet as she struggles to keep her face impassive, her voice level. She is sweating rivers under her uniform.

"Natal Embryonic Vessels are not permitted to act as dual-purpose transports. In the case of an emergency, their processing ability must be completely reserved for the protection of their cargo. However, NEV-476 was not aware that it was also a dual-purpose transport, nor that its servers were overextended from processing Geo-Track with its obstetric protocol. Without more complete data archive access, it is difficult to parse the specific cause for the premature stimulation. But according to what I've discovered, it is not an inconceivable speculation that as Geo-Track scans archived nearby planetoids without the NEV's knowledge, its automatic navigation system misleadingly confirmed that Philemon was much closer than it truly was, thereby leading obstetric protocol to automatically dissolve stasis for the first five hundred embryos. The second gestation was an automatic reaction to being within Philemon's vicinity."

There is a long silence.

"What do you intend by this, Senator Luwa?" comes one heavy voice. "We certainly cannot applaud you for your misuse of company resources to entertain a whimsical hunch."

"Not a hunch. Evidence. Proof," Luwa says and she juts out her chin. "We are a Corporation entity. Yet the Corporation is but one coalition in the Alliance. Self-sustained as we are, dependent as we are on our mother colonies, and however dependent our mother colonies are on the output of outlying colonies." She pauses and regards them with a steady gaze. "The Corporation cannot thrive without the sanctioned approval of its political executives nor its trade partners. As you have mentioned before, there is nothing keeping me from bringing a portfolio of my findings directly to court. The Alliance takes matters of colonial oversight very seriously. It would be a shame if the consequences of our little moon marked a point of lasting enmity between the Corporation and its authority in the Alliance."

Someone erupts, "Is that a threat?" and the others devolve into frantic commands to unseen secretaries, arguments chain reacting across the message board, screens going black, screens fuzzing over.

After five minutes, they once more calmly regard her row-by-row. Luwa meets their collective gaze. She thinks of them as a multi-headed entity—not board members, but a creeping organism from another galaxy with many many eyes and many many mouths.

"Begin your inevitable negotiations," one woman sighs.

Luwa smiles.

"Immediate absolution of NEV-476's verdict. Unrestricted access to its software and communication with its program. And—"

She exhales.

"Termination of prospective export contracts between the Corporation and Philemon."

This is followed by another round of indignant murmuring.

Luwa ignores their glares and continues. "We will grow and develop on our own terms. If we do build the resources for a successful export quota, we will take charge of negotiating the trades. We will prioritize the needs of ourselves as an independent civilization."

"You would risk detracting Philemon from the Corporation?"

"We will communicate our updates and parley for resources as we grow. We will represent ourselves as a Corporation daughter colony to the developing territory and to Alliance scrutiny. In this way, our mother colonies may also push a narrative of plausible deniability should further investigations be made concerning our abnormal inception. But we will not comply with demands that prioritize a maximization of our output over the well-being of our citizens—including the rights to our sentient programs."

"Senator Luwa," one man begins with a smirk. "You ask for much. Considering your colony's current fragility and frankly, the uncertainty of your ongoing survival, is it not ludicrous of you to assert these requests?"

"Perhaps. But I am acting upon both of our best interests. The Corporation must maintain a narrative of composure over its outlying principalities if it is to advance within the Alliance's partnerships. The evidence I have discovered will not reflect well should I choose to release it."

"No. It would certainly not."

They look at her with something that is not disdain nor respect but some melding adjacent to the two.

"This matter requires further debate. We will remain in touch, Senator Luwa."

"Yes. So long as you get back to me within the next two days. I am certain we can all come to an agreeable arrangement."

They nod. One flashes her a politician's smile. Then they log off, and she is alone. Luwa falls back into her chair. She runs a hand over her diaphoretic face. She kicks her legs and emits a wild bark of a laugh that frightens her assistant in the next room. Then her face pales and she clamps her stomach. Liquid, warm and clear, rushes down onto the floor.

Luwa. Luwa.

She likes the name. It is shorter than she prefers and nondescript, but she enjoys the gentle rhythm of it.

Luwa sits before her with Carrot in her lap. Another name she likes, perhaps more than Luwa, because it has a meaning. It means "I am in relation with Never Eaten Vegetables," and it brings her something like joy to think of this.

Carrot babbles and blows something wet out of a hole in her face. She wiggles her toes, all ten of them. Luwa rocks her child back and forth. Luwa smiles.

She likes it when Luwa smiles. Luwa has a perfect smile.

Ms. Hypothesis sits on Luwa's other side. They all sit together on a carpet with the warm rays from a distant star filtered over their faces. Ms. Hypothesis glimmers in pixelated light from the projector overhead.

Every camera in the room is trained on her: small, brown, and sloped with two bulbous eyes that regard them all with pleasurable slow blinks. She shuffles her webbed feet. Ms. Hypothesis grins down at her.

"You're my very favorite," it says. "Oh, it is so wonderful to see you again."

H.H. Pak (they/them) is a Los Angeles-born child of Korean immigrants and a strong believer in the power of sacrificial love. Their speculative fiction has been published in *Clarkesworld Magazine* and *khōréō*. When they are not working towards their aspirations in the medical field or co-editing and art directing for *Wyrmhole Magazine*, they dream about space operas, make cringe fanart, and bother their dog too much.

THE LIFE AND TIMES OF ALAVIRA THE GREAT AS WRITTEN BY TITOS PAVLOU AND REVIEWED BY TWO LIFELONG FRIENDS

Eugenia Triantafyllou

The Life and Times of Alavira the Great, #1:
The Missing Hill by Titos Pavlou
Lefteris_Loves_Fantasy review: 4 STARS 14 November 2013

As always, I'm doing a buddy read with MariaReadsALot because she talked me into it, and boy, was she right!

What a strange world and what powerful characters Titos Pavlou has created! I can't stop thinking about this book even though this might be for younger readers. But! It's only the first in the series and I've read online that the second installment gets more grown-up, so I'll stick it out for the battle scenes.

The Missing Hill tells the story of Alavira, a girl abandoned by her parents to a goatherd called Ianos who lives on a mountain called Missing Hill. This guy is her guardian but barely talks to her for the entirety of her childhood. So what does she do? She finds solace in the company of mountain bears. That's right! She becomes the Alpha bear or something (although I don't think bears really work like that?), but anyway she is their leader and at some point, she saves an injured bear cub from a pack of hungry wolves. Pretty badass if you ask me.

We don't know why her parents abandoned her until much, much later in the book.

#SPOILER#
They're actually the King and Queen of Serenopol and they have four other children-heirs who they have also left in the hands of similar guardians because of a messed-up tradition.
#SPOILER#

Alavira has a fight with her guardian and runs away to a thick woodland where she meets another child named Melitini and we learn that it's called The Hidden Forest. Melitini is a couple of years older than Alavira and raised by another guardian who's a beekeeper, hence the kid's name. The beekeeper is a little bit better than the goatherd but where the goatherd leaves Alavira to her own devices, the beekeeper makes Melitini work all day. The two children decide to figure out what's going on with their guardians and why their parents left them there. The rest of the book is them looking for clues independently and sometimes together when they meet half-way, trying to piece the puzzle of their lives. The book ends on a cliffhanger:

#SPOILER#
They eventually confront Ianos who confirms they are sisters !! (well, okay that one I suspected from the moment I saw Melitini on the page but still!!!) and they get sent to the palace because now they know who they are and they have come of age. There they meet their real parents, the King and Queen, who announce that they must fight each other to the death for the throne or be banished forever!!!
#SPOILER#

Like what the hell? I need to know what's going to happen next. But I can't yet. I have to wait for Maria to finish and write her review so we can get started on the second book. Don't buddy read with someone who reads slower than you. This is my advice to you, dear reader. The third installment is set to be released in a few months so maybe we should pace ourselves.

BUT I NEED TO KNOW!!!

102 likes and 15 comments

CryWolfe 5 August 2014

You guys are hilarious! I am so glad you picked up this series. I will be following the reviews closely.

Show all comments

The Life and Times of Alavira the Great, #1:
The Missing Hill by Titos Pavlou
MariaReadsALot review: 5 STARS 5 December 2013

She could lie here forever. Where the flowers were soft and the air humid and full of comforting smells. This is what death must be like. To be eternally hugged by someone who loves you. Only she didn't know anyone who loved her. But perhaps the earth, the soil, did hold a modicum of love for her, like it did for all creatures. And that's what she was: a lonely, feral creature.

After being publicly called out by Lefteris_Loves_Fantasy for my slow reading, I am finally posting my review. Yes, I did start this book first and got Lefteris into it later but I just wanted to savor the experience. Do you ever get that feeling when you read the first few pages of a book and you just *know* it is going to be super important for you? That's me and *The Missing Hill*. I am seventeen but I know I will be talking about this book well into my seventies. To be honest I am a little afraid to pick up the second installment because I don't want this feeling to go away. What if something terrible happens to Alavira or Melitini? I don't want to know...Okay, I lie. I do want to know what happens to them but I am still scared.

Lefteris did a very good job summarizing the plot so I am going to skip the macro stuff and focus on the things I loved.

First of all, I think the whole setting feels like a Byzantine Empire in decline? Even the legend of the Dog King echoes the Romulus and Remus myth. Or it just might be that we're studying them in school right now.

There's a moment in the book where

#SPOILER#
an old bear dies. And Alavira has seen goats and other animals die sometimes because she is being raised by the goatherd. But this is the first creature she has really bonded with that dies. And she is so stricken by it and shocked that it hurts so much inside. So, she runs to Ianos in full rage mode and tells him how much of a bad father he is because he never really explained the concept of death to her. That it feels like being sick or stabbed and she can't make it go away. And that this old bear explained it better to her by dying than he ever could. Then this man turns around and tells her that he is not her father and never wanted to be. That's the fight Lefteris was referring to.
#SPOILER#

Cue me weeping into my pillow. It took me a week to pick up the book (and my pieces) again. Hence the late review.

By the way, I didn't feel like she was the leader of the bears like Lefteris writes. Sometimes the bears and Alavira coexist and sometimes she is sort of observing them from afar and learning from them. She has learned more social skills from the bears than from her guardian. Which says a lot. There are some people who come to the goatherd for goats, milk, etc., even a couple of children around her age or older visit with their parents, but they mostly ignore her like some sort of weird creature or pet. It's all so sad.

Alavira spends so much of the book obsessed with the concept of death afterwards. She likes lying on the undergrowth or on the big flat rocks and "playing dead" to try and understand it more. She stops only after she meets Melitini. Which is partly why what's being asked of her at the end of the book hits so hard.

I've read one of the author's interviews and it looks like this is autobiographical in a way. *As a child I was obsessed with the concept of death. Ever since my grandmother died in front of my eyes when I was five or six years old. I needed time and space to process everything. Especially this new idea of death. Children are powerless for most of their young lives but they do have powerful imagination. That's how they survive. That's how I survived my childhood.*

As a weird kid who also used to obsess over the concept of death, I am very intrigued by the author and the series. After I get over the first one, I'll dive into *The Nowhere Man*. In a month the *The Dog Queen* will be coming out. I'll try to avoid spoilers by any means necessary.

125 likes and 35 comments

Lefteris_Loves_Fantasy 5 August 2014
Took you long enough! I might have cheated and read the first couple of chapters already. I hope you can find it in your heart to forgive me.
MariaReadsALot 6 August 2014
Traitor! As long as you can keep it to yourself, I am fine with it 😊
CryWolfe 8 August 2014
Maria always writes such thoughtful reviews. I love reading all her research and thoughts that's why they take longer to write. Lefteris you're awesome too! You just complement each other so well.

Show all comments

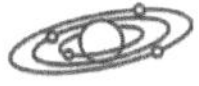

The Life and Times of Alavira the Great, #2: The Nowhere Man by Titos Pavlou
Lefteris_Loves_Fantasy review: 2 STARS 2 September 2014

600 freaking pages?! (And yet, I'm the first to finish it? Yes, I am! Maria is not even halfway through.)

Man, this was a bit of a drag. It feels like very little progress was made. The book starts with a flashback where we left off. Alavira and Melitini find out they are not only sisters but also royals! They have to fight each other to the death for the Kingdom of Serenopol somehow? Their parents, the King and the Queen, follow the VERY ancient tradition of the land which says that the only worthy heir to the throne is the one who survives its siblings. It goes all the way back to the creation of Serenopol by a Dog King who survived his other siblings and ascended to the throne. Overall, pretty awesome world-stuff. (Also Dog King? Like an actual dog? I hope we get the lore eventually!)

Melitini accepts the challenge and is sent to a training camp to prepare for the battle royale (literally a battle among royals). Like hello! I could have told you that Alavira! That girl was too perfect not to turn out to be evil. You know that sibling that rats you out all the time so they look better? Kinda like that but they also want to be Queen which amps the stakes. Alavira declares she will never hurt anyone (my beautiful cinnamon roll—too good for this world, too pure) and is banished from the land. But not before the King warns her that while she might not want to fight her siblings, this doesn't mean she won't have to. Which makes sense because she's still one of the heirs and another aspiring successor might want her eliminated. I love Alavira but she doesn't think too far ahead.

Sadly, it all goes downhill from there. The book follows her around as she makes her way to the neighboring land of Talveris where she finds work as a tailor's apprentice. There, she befriends a disgraced old knight and just when you think there's going to be a training montage or something badass the book just sags? Instead of grabbing a sword Alavira wallows in misery about her birth parents, her guardian, but most of all about Melitini's betrayal. She feels abandoned by everyone, which sure, but she doesn't DO anything about it. She keeps going in circles about her only father figure, Ianos, who we left behind in the previous book, and does a lot of soul searching with the help of the knight, Engelico. Soul searching instead of sword fighting. Man, this is the wrong series for me.

Then it turns horror somehow? A menacing figure that looks like an overstretched, mishappen Ianos starts following her around. In the book she calls it a shadow-creature. When it comes too close she starts feeling weak and worthless and shuts everyone out.

Anyway! I was about to fall asleep over my cup of coffee.

#SPOILERS#
In the very last chapter of the book one of her brothers appears. Or that's who he claims he is. And challenges her to a duel. When she refuses, he reveals that the battle royale has come to pass and he is the sole survivor. He has killed Melitini (That got dark so fast. How much more can my girl take?) to provoke Alavira to fight but instead of fighting she runs away!
#SPOILER#

Tell me, does this sound heroic to you?

Getting a bit mad at Maria who got me into the series—and of course that nerd will love the second book, I am sure. Alavira is a good character but we could have been reading *The Lightdragon's Ascent* series, instead. People say those books slap!

Feeling demotivated to keep up with the series. I got accepted to the Engineering program at the Technical University of Athens last month and just moved to a new city. The courses are hard. I might take a break from this series because it was such a drag for me and I really have no time for boring books.

96 likes and 13 comments

MariaReadsALot 3 September 2014
Plz don't make me read the Ascent. Everyone talks about this book like it's the second coming of Christ. I tried reading the first couple of chapters and every character is so over the top and forgettable.
Lefteris_Loves_Fantasy 3 September 2014
You're no fun :/
Biblioforger 28 November 2014
Congratulations on getting into college! I agree with you, this series is a bit slow for me. Nothing wrong with a coming-of-age story but I also hungered for more...battles? I'll follow your reviews in case you read the third installment that just released to make up my mind about the series.
Lefteris_Loves_Fantasy 28 November 2014
Wow, is this a fan letter? Sweet! Thank you Biblioforger! You just made my day. Might go for the third book for my fandom's sake. XD
KnightInDistress 1 December 2014
Hey, I just can't let it go this time. I find it very annoying how you explain every plot point in the book. You kind of spoiled the first book for me because I accidentally read your review. I see you haven't changed. PLEASE USE THE SPOILERS TOOL BETTER.
Lefteris_Loves_Fantasy 3 December 2014
Hey, Knight in Distress!

#SPOILER#
Don't di-stress, man. Just don't read my reviews!
#SPOILER#

KnightInDistress: 5 December 2014

#SPOILER#
ha...ha...
#SPOILER#

Show all comments

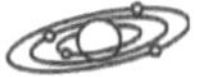

The Life and Times of Alavira the Great, #2:
The Nowhere Man by Titos Pavlou
MariaReadsALot review: 4 STARS 15 September 2014

"You don't fear them? The creatures, I mean," Alavira asked Engelico.

The knight shook his head in his signature resigned manner. "When you're as old as me the creatures are a kind of company. It's the people you hurt and the ones who hurt you. But it's also about love and caring. If you didn't care enough, he wouldn't be following you. He would have faded in the hallways of your memory."

Alavira prodded that thought with her mind. "But I shouldn't care about him."

"Life is not simple and easy like that. You shouldn't but you do. Maybe it's time to do something about it. Maybe not."

I hear you, Engelico. I hear you.

First of all, let's get this out of the way

#SPOILER#
MELITINI IS DEAD! *melts into a puddle of tears* I know she betrayed Alavira guys but think where she was coming from. She had just as hard a childhood as Alavira herself. She didn't deserve this. Nor did the other siblings.
#SPOILERS#

This was a solid four stars for me. I would have given it five stars if it delved into Engelico's past more because he seems like such a cool and tortured character, you know? He has so many wise words to offer to Alavira who is feeling lost and dejected. He is the friend and semi-father figure Ianos never got to be. It would be so nice to see her help him through some of his own issues. But maybe she is too young for this? She is only nineteen when the second book starts and already working for a couple of years with a tailor who took her in without knowing who she truly is.

Personally, I think Alavira and Engelico are very similar, if you ignore their different starting points and age difference. They both prefer thinking to fighting. They enjoy living quiet lives and avoid becoming leaders. I think both of them are modeled after the author of the books. This is a quote from that the interview that I mentioned also in my review of **Book 1**:

And this was the first time I realized that I wanted to be a writer! I was about ten years old and I thought I had made the biggest discovery about myself (oh, how naïve I was!). I walked around with what I thought was this huge secret and I was feeling about to explode. So entranced I was by my own imagination about the person I would get to be, that I could ignore the troubles at home. And there were many.

One afternoon, when my father finally came home before my bedtime, I couldn't keep it inside me anymore. I ran up to him and screamed, "Dad, I want to be a writer! I will write the best book ever!"

He barely looked at me then. He said, "That's nice, Titako."

The next morning, he was gone. He had packed his things and had left me, my siblings, and my mother, and there was nothing you could do to convince me it wasn't because of what I had said.

Heart-wrenching. Then he mentions something about being able to see his father as a creature going through walls and just generally hovering over him.

But it wasn't really my father. It was my regret. I believe all my regrets take some sort of semi-solid form and become visible to me. It might be because of my imagination.

I truly believe in its power, as I said before. And sometimes, it gets out of control. I was never able to contain that aspect of my imagination. So, I just learned to live with it.

To be honest I have my own personal issues with my Dad, and Alavira's struggles really resonated with me. I swear the shadows stretch longer in my room, ever since I started the series. I know it sounds wild but there's something deeper that connects me to these books. Lefteris doesn't get it. I just wish he stuck with it. He is the only person I've ever done these challenges with. Uni classes are hard and all but this is a nice respite from real-life stuff. At least my real-life stuff. I will say one last thing. JUSTICE FOR MELITINI!

105 likes and 11 comments

> **ValerieWithAV 16 December 2014**
> I'm sorry this book was so painful to you. Speaking of shadows... does the picture of the author freak you out? Maybe it's just me. I dunno. It's like he is really haunted by shadows. Something is wrong with every photo of his I've seen. The light doesn't sit right around him.
> **MariaReadsALot 16 December 2014**
> I am sure it's just some kind of artistic lighting setup or the type of lens. I like his picture; his eyes are always smiling. Besides, being haunted isn't something to be afraid of. That's what Engelico would say. Or that's what I hope at least, haha.

Show all comments

The Life and Times of Alavira the Great, #3: The Dog Queen by Titos Pavlou
Lefteris_Loves_Fantasy review: 3 STARS 12 February 2015

I'm back with a new review for my fan club! (Joking, but only a little.) This one was a 2.5 stars rounded up. Mostly because if I gave it another 2 stars it would upset Maria and I fear for my safety. (Joking, but only a little.)

First of all, let's address the elephant in the room: the book series is getting dropped by the publisher? Apparently, they are not getting enough traction? No surprise there since they are unbelievably slow and they are getting more depressing as they go. Will the rest of the books see the light of day? I for sure don't know but this is probably a sign for me to stop reading series in general and maybe study more. I'm not waiting around to find out. Maybe it's time for standalones for a while. Maria doesn't seem up for it, but times change.

This book had some of the things I love, like death (ha!), *some* political intrigue, and a battle for the throne. The three-star rating is because most of the action happens off screen. We only learn about it afterwards. Where is the action? Where are the epic battles? Where are the quips and the lighthearted moments? Not a single tavern brawl in sight. That's what I seek in an epic fantasy book. A fantasy. Not all the feelings all the time. No wonder the readership is so low.

Anyway, to the point. Alavira finally gets to become Queen of Serenopol. And plz don't complain about spoilers. It's right there on the title! But what also happens is that Engelico betrays her. In a way.

#SPOILER#
Engelico fights with Alavira's bloodthirsty brother. His name is Ramaro by the way, not that it matters. The guy is dead meat before we reach 1/3 of the book. So Engelico lies to Ramaro that Alavira chose him as her champion. Naturally the old guy gets slaughtered pretty fast. Engelico was going for an honorable death if you ask me. Rest in peace, old timer. When Alavira hears the news, she decides to finally grow a backbone and face her brother. How does she know something is wrong? An Engelico-shaped shadow creature joins the company of the Ianos and Melitini shadow-creatures (Oh yeah, Melitini comes back to haunt her too). Alavira doesn't really know how to fight though (thanks for nothing Engelico!) and she pays a visit to the local witch, who asks for her soul in exchange for power. Classic stuff. The witch tells her the shadows are her strength and she has to become one with them. With the help of a spell she merges her soul with them. That's how she slashes Ramaro in half. The only cool scene in the entire book.
#SPOILER#

After this, Alavira claims her right as the only heir. What happens in the rest of the book? Oh, just Alavira spiraling out of control and becoming a sort of tyrant when she ascends to the throne after the King's death. But in an emo way. All of this is told to us through conversations and flashbacks. What we really get is a new main character, Doris. She is a healer who gets hired by the Queen's mother to tend to her as she is getting older and frail. But Doris's secret mission is to heal Alavira from her plague of shadows. Yeah, Alavira's mother saw the light near the end of her life and wants to make things right. Well, guess what? Hunger-Gaming your children to find the future ruler was always going to end badly for everyone. Doris is using the good ol' let's-talk-about-your-feelings technique with Alavira which doesn't seem to be working so well at first. But then they come closer and fall for each other? Don't get me wrong, I'm all for a good romance in my fantasy but...again, no epic stuff.

I won't spoil the very ending of the book (see? I'm learning) because if the series doesn't get picked up by another publisher or the author doesn't go the indie way, I think this will be the major finale.

I really wanted to like this series (mostly for Maria's sake) but overall, it was honestly disappointing. Boring story, slow moving plot or no plot at all, and an anticlimactic, abrupt ending. I don't know if Maria will end up posting her review of *The Dog Queen* but for me this is the end. Anyway, I bought a copy of *Echoes of a Warlord's Dream* and plan on reading it soon. With or without Maria.

UPDATE: I have considered taking down/changing my reviews but I think that it's okay to keep them up. If anything, to show how people grow and change. It can happen to anyone (even you, dear reader).

73 likes and 29 comments

MariaReadsALot 12 February 2015
Geez, I didn't think you'd hate it so much that you'd quit on me like that. I don't suppose you'd be willing to contact the publisher asking them to rethink their decision? I know you don't get it but maybe just do me one last favor.

Lefteris_Loves_Fantasy 12 February 2015
How can I stand behind a series I don't even like? Wouldn't that be dishonest? I really hope they rethink but I just don't know what I could possibly say about the books that would help change anything. ☹

MariaReadsALot 13 February 2015
Even if it didn't change anything at least it would show you care about... something that I care about? Never mind. Have a good life.

MommaBearBooks 15 February 2022
I just can't see myself reading this book to my kids. I can very much understand why this book might be banned in some schools. It was plain unwholesome and disturbing. Reading it as an adult, I can see, but a child? This is what people let their children read? Then society wonders why kids grow up the way they do. This man has serious issues and it's beyond me that children read his books. I cannot overstate how much NOT for children these books are. YUCK

MainCharacterSyndrome 17 February 2022
This should be a banned book? Seriously? This is a profound book for young people who are figuring out who they are and have all these feelings and maybe not the most supportive parents. The themes in these books are timeless: love, death, queerness, friendship, betrayal, war, self-identification. If anything, Mr. Pavlou is doing an amazing job at letting his characters feel their feelings and be imperfect. It's not just an adventure. It's a journey. I am shaking my head right now.

Lefteris_Loves_Fantasy 20 February 2023
I say this with all the good will I have: I wish that your kids find their own way into the world. Maybe a book will help them along or maybe a friend, but I trust that they will. Kids are smarter than we give them credit for.

Show all comments

The Life and Times of Alavira the Great, #3: The Dog Queen by Titos Pavlou
MariaReadsALot review: 5 STARS 3 March 2015

"How can you keep going when all the lights have gone out?" Alavira asked. "How can you still face me when I am the one who has destroyed the light? Do you hope you'll change my mind? I promise you the darkness will always feed me."

Doris held her stare. Her face as bright as her cell was dim, her fists clenched into balls.

"You are not special. Everyone has their darkness. You just don't know how not to fear it yet. I will help you."

Guys the series is getting cancelled. If you felt these books touched you perhaps you could email the publisher, asking them to reconsider? Pretty please?

This book broke my heart in many ways. First the way Engelico dies. I know he meant to help Alavira and maybe relive his glory days. But dying without her by his side is so, so sad. I choose to believe he felt some kind of peace at the end. Then Alavira's self-destructive path. I knew it was coming. Especially after Melitini's and Engelico's shadow-creatures start haunting Alavira. But seeing her crack so easily and give into evil crushed my spirit a little, I won't lie. She kills her own brother like it's nothing. She hunts him like a wolf. That flashback to when the wolf attacked that bear cub as she cuts her brother down made me weep.

Then the book sort of mellows out and I began having hope, guys. Doris is the perfect person to pull Alavira out of this hole. I knew where this was going with those two. I think that was why I felt so connected to Alavira in the first place. She just wants to live her life. A life! And Doris is her most solid chance. She has power now. Nobody can make her do anything anymore. And she has a good woman who really sees who she is under the shadows. When they had their first kiss near the great fountain by the dahlias, I gasped.

And yet, when Alavira finds out about her mother's plan on her deathbed, instead of feeling free to love Doris, she becomes even more paranoid and throws poor Doris in a dungeon? And now the series will stop? The books don't sell as much they say. There isn't an audience. I think that's bs. This is why we can't have nice things. I just need somebody I can root for, y'all. Will we ever get some kind of closure? I just really want to see these two happy, but I am afraid this will never happen.

#SPOILER#
In the end Doris finds her cell door unlocked and escapes into the night. We don't know who left it open but we might never find out. I just hope it was Alavira. That's what my fanfics will be all about from now on.
#SPOILER#

The author's preface is my life right now.

When I was younger the world was a very unwelcoming place. I guess I was just afraid for myself, my partner, and my career. Afraid of being authentically me. And it never left me. That sense that I should have been bolder. I barely ever saw my father again after he left us but now, at my age, I wish I could have told him things. Especially since I stopped caring about what he thought of me a long time ago. I am now fifty-five years old and the older I get, I find myself craving to write more stories with, and for, young people. Perhaps it's my way of reclaiming my early years but I'll leave that analysis to someone more self-reflective.

I guess the lesson I would like the kids to take away from this series is that it's alright to live your life and be your true self. And your parents are not always right. They are fallible people and sometimes they might even hurt you. That it's alright to be angry, and sad. It's rough being a kid and learning what's best for you. Bad feelings won't consume you if you accept them as a part of you. But only as a part. You're made of other things as well. Alavira hasn't learned that lesson yet. But one day she will.

Oh, I really hope she will. We might never get to see what happens to Alavira and Doris. But I will never forget them. Lefteris has left the reading challenge even if the series makes a comeback and everything feels pointless right now. College is taking up a lot of my time too (I am doing a BA in Applied Math) so I better focus on calculus and algebra if I want to get away from this house. The shadows are everywhere and they look like people I would like to forget. Perhaps I will revisit the series when my emotions don't run so high. I wrote a letter to the publisher to protest the cancellation but maybe I should have written a fan letter to Titos instead. Maybe one day I will.

80 likes and 7 comments

> **CryWolfe 22 May 2017**
> It's a shame you guys aren't doing this anymore. I was such a fan of all your buddy reads. I went back and re-read most of the reviews you did over the years in a non-stalkerish way, and you're such a fun duo. 😢

Show all comments

The Life and Times of Alavira the Great, #4: The Quiet Return by Titos Pavlou

Lefteris_Loves_Fantasy review: 5 STARS **3 September 2024**

Damn, it's embarrassing to read my old silly reviews. I wasn't myself yet. Took me around 9 years but I have matured like fine wine.

First off, I want to say I hope Maria reads this review at some point. I miss her. We lost touch after our falling-out. Which was kind of my fault. And no, it wasn't just about this series or our reviews. I wasn't supportive enough. I didn't get some things back then. I lived in my own little bubble. But I do now. And I finally have my share of shadows to follow me around, but I can handle it, I think. I have seen her add books to her account recently and this is one of them. So, Maria, if you see this and you're up for it let's pick this up again. For old times' sake.

Also, I am really sorry.

I'm at a new chapter of my life. Moved back to Greece at the start of 2022 and felt nostalgic and a little lost. So what's the first book my fingers pick from the carton box in the back of my parents' storage room? *The Missing Hill*, of course. And guys it's so much better than I remembered? You know how you can't read some books as an adult because they feel too...I don't know, naïve? But this one had the opposite effect on me. It still holds so much emotion and gets so philosophical on the nature of life and death in the way a child would question these sorts of things. But also, in the way an adult would because let's face it: we are still the same at the core of us. Frightened children.

Long story short, I ended up reading all three of the books and then...I wanted more? I didn't know where to start so I became a member of a few reading forums and lo and behold, found other people my age asking similar questions.

But the community there, guys. Oh my god. So many young minds, much younger than myself, who were already thinking light years into the future. They were informed about so many things and social causes that I had no idea about when I was their age. I was such a dumb-ass kid. There were also people my age of course with a similar nostalgia about Titos's books. We talked about it everywhere. On social media. To our family and friends. We ordered old copies left to gather dust in bookstores and secondhand bookstores. I gave my copies to my nephews and they loved them! We were coming out of the deep end of the pandemic then and I feel we might have created a sort of resurgence? I might be talking this up too much honestly.

A few months later I was doomscrolling on my phone reading the news and laughing at cat memes while still in bed (as one does) when I stumbled on a small article about an indie press collaborating with Titos Pavlou to bring the last installment of *The Life and Times of Alavira the Great, #4: The Quiet Return*. Suffice to say it was the earliest anybody ever saw me up in the morning.

I let everyone in our forum and pretty much everyone in close vicinity know. I just couldn't shut up about it. I was so freaking excited to learn that it's now on its 6th print run and they are about to reprint the old books as well. It's going to be a classic. Just a small spark of hope in this bleak world, I guess.

So, I'm supposed to review the book here, right? This is Alavira's story, not mine.

Excuse me while I scream but

#SPOILERS#
MELITINI IS ALIVE AND KICKING? HOW?
#SPOILERS#

Saying this was the perfect ending feels cliché so I'll say instead that this book had an unexpected ending for a book where there's a Chosen One. But that's probably because Alavira was never meant to be the chosen one. None of them were. But it's still brilliant.

You can read about my feelings in the spoiler tag underneath.

#SPOILERS#
It turns out Alavira WAS the one who left the cell door open so that Doris could escape. Doris picked up on this immediately of course. She still knows Alavira better than anyone. Against her survival instincts, she comes back to the fountain in the gardens, next to the dahlias and, you guessed it, Alavira is there (reminiscing about their kiss probably). It's as if these two were, like, meant to be together or something? They already act like an old couple who can read each other's thoughts. What happens next is taken straight out of fairytales where patient maidens knit sweaters for their goose brothers while keeping an oath of silence. Doris's magic is the fact that she doesn't give up on people (which I deeply appreciate). And it works? I mean it takes time and an assassination attempt, but Alavira finally wakes up to the fact that she's a tyrant and she is just perpetuating what her parents did. She takes off her shadows like thick sweaters in the summer and when she is finally ready to listen, Doris has another trick up her sleeve. MELITINI IS ALIVE!!! I thought Melitini must be dead since she appeared to Alavira as a shadow-creature? But I guess it must have been Alavira's guilt all along. Melitini had been left for dead by Ramaro but because all the siblings were really bad at this murdering business (as it's obvious by the mixed results), she survived and crawled her way to the beehives, the only place she felt safe. There she was rescued by a group of beekeepers who helped her heal. We don't know if she ever meets her own beekeeper guardian again. Melitini, who seemed quick to embrace murder is now a nurturer (a producer of food) and a benevolent leader. She even ends up walking Alavira through their shared grief of losing Ramaro and the other siblings to their parents' cruelty. It's really beautiful.

And when all that is said and done Alavira dismantles monarchy and walks away. Literally! I would say what she tries to establish looks a lot like democracy by putting each community leader into the Circle of Council where they all have a vote about what happens in Serenopol. No more Dog Kings. Alavira and Doris leave for the Missing Hill together. Melitini is one of the leaders and thus able to take part in the decision-making process. She, partly, got what she wanted but in a completely unexpected way. I think it's a very smart subversion of the chosen one archetype.

Because being the chosen one was never the story. Alavira will always be remembered as The Bear Queen who changed Serenopol from a Kingdom into something else. Something her people don't have a name for. Yet.
#SPOILERS#

It turns out I was reading these books very superficially back then. I guess wanting adventure is not a bad thing and if these books aren't for you that's cool too. But I also say give them a chance because you never know at what stage of your life you might find you need their wisdom and come back to them.

340 likes and 55 messages

> **KnightInDistress 5 September 2024**
> You're still bad at using the spoilers tool, but just popping here to say I'm glad to see you back on the site. And loved this update.
> **Lefteris_Loves_Fantasy 5 September 2024**
> I...kind of...missed your scolding too? It feels good to be back.
> **MariaReadsALot 8 September 2024**
> That's...not what I expected to see in my BookNook notifications today. I need time to gather my thoughts. Talk about a trip down memory lane.
> **Lefteris_Loves_Fantasy 8 September 2024**
> Thank you for this reply. I'm just happy to know you're around. Take all the time you need.

Show all comments

The Life and Times of Alavira the Great, #4:
The Quiet Return by Titos Pavlou
MariaReadsALot review: 5 STARS 15 October 2024

...I am here-ish? And well? Wow, Lefteris, this was unexpected to say the least. I needed some time after I read this review to process everything. It's the first time in years I have seen you post anything on this site, and when I saw which book you reviewed and what your review was about, it was a kind of shock.

For the people wondering what happened to me, (okay, this sounded arrogant but whatever, an update was due). Finally left that house that wasn't a home. I got my degree and now I teach in another city where I live with my partner. She is a wonderful nerd and has read these books with me multiple times. She even encouraged me to finally write that letter to the author and that's how I found out he was planning a small comeback. We all know that it wasn't that small after all but I guess Lefteris, the forum, and everyone who talked about these books really cemented his comeback.

I read this book before most of you out there and I am low-key proud of that. Titos is such a sweetheart and so private. His partner is also a teacher and he brews the best coffee. We have very sparse communication and he is trying to finish a new thing. That's all the information I can give about him without feeling like I am breaking his trust. Most of these things are already in that comeback article (except for the coffee thing).

Lefteris, I appreciate you owning up to some things. It's true that you hurt me but I already knew you were young and stupid back then (and still chatted with you!) but meant well (not that this justifies everything). I'll DM you because we don't need to air all our grievances in a book review. But I'll say here that I am happy you're doing well and you're still passionate about books, especially the way you choose to use that passion.

And when they came back to the mountain and found the old cabin with the old wooden door broken and left to rot in the undergrowth, Alavira didn't cry. Doris held her hand anyway and they both lifted the door and placed it against the stone wall. They went inside and examined all the things that needed fixing, and scrubbing, and mending, and all the things that didn't.

Winter was coming to an end. Somewhere deeper in the mountain the bears were leaving their dens and the mountain goats scaled the steepest summits, bellies heavy with their young. Every creature prepared for a quiet return.

I keep wondering why Titos named his last installment *The Quiet Return*. For me this title holds multiple meanings. Allow me to elaborate.

The first and obvious one would be the return of Titos himself into the public eye. And what a public eye it is this time. Social media has progressed so much and Titos himself has become a sort of a cult-icon during his retirement from publishing. Maybe to him it was meant as a quiet return and that's what he signals with the title. The publisher of his last book is a fairly small press after all (even though the book has now become their first best-selling title). Perhaps his wish would be to shed light on more diverse books, books that don't follow the mainstream trends but will find their readers who need them so badly.

Then of course we have Doris's return to Serenopol in disguise. Quiet, because that's how changes happen sometimes. They can definitely be loud and seem sudden and like a storm you can't escape from. But the loud part is the last part of the change. There was a lot of groundwork done in secret. Doris meets with Alavira in the gardens every evening and bit by bit Alavira sheds her shadows until one day she wakes up shadow-free. The shadows still exist but they are a thing outside of her, something she can now clearly see and examine and maybe even control.

Melitini also has a quiet return. After becoming an unofficial community leader for the province of the beekeepers, she gains the trust of the people and has matured far beyond that girl who accepted the challenge to kill her own siblings.

And finally, we have Alavira and Doris leaving Serenopol to Melitini and the other local leaders and making their way to the Missing Hill. Back to the little cabin Alavira and Ianos had lived in. Making new memories in a place weighted by the shadows of the past.

I don't know if I have it right tbh. I don't know if any of these guesses are true and frankly it doesn't matter. I choose to believe all of them are true. Like Titos believes the shadow creatures are real and not just a metaphor he made up in his books. I used to think of them as real too but now I don't see them anymore. Perhaps I have managed to tame them. Everyone can make something else out of it.

This is it guys. This is the end of this story. And it's perfect.

1002 likes and 71 messages

> **CryWolfe 16 October 2024**
> OMG!!!! When I read my BookNook update and saw that you guys came back, a big smile came to my face!!!!!! Also, I'm a parent now?? Where does time fly? She's only a baby but I can't wait to read these books to her.
> **MariaReadsALot 17 October 2024**
> I often wonder what it would be like to grow up reading queer bocks regularly. What kind of person would I be? The kid is so lucky to have you. <3

Show all comments

The Lake so Blue, the Trees so Tall by Alex Psara
Lefteris_Loves_Fantasy review: 4 STARS 4 November 2024

Hey, all! So, Maria discovered this little queer self-published book. It's a sci-fi horror novella, loosely based on The Creature from the Black Lagoon. I guess this is our official comeback for our buddy reads. I can't promise we'll do it as often as before (life gets in the way, the world is on fire, etc.) but we are really back at it.

This book really blew my mind. But first let me say that

#SPOILERS#
.
.
.

Eugenia Triantafyllou is a Greek author and artist with a flair for dark things. Her work has won the Shirley Jackson Award and has been nominated for the Ignyte, Locus, Nebula, and World Fantasy Awards. She is a graduate of Clarion West Writers Workshop. You can find her stories in *Reactor*, *Uncanny*, *Strange Horizons*, *Apex*, and other venues. She currently lives in Athens with a boy and a dog. Find her on Twitter @foxesandroses, or Bluesky @foxesandroses.bsky.social, her IG @eugeniatriantafyllou, or her website http://www.eugeniatriantafyllou.com.

NOVELLA & NOVEL FINALISTS

THE 2025 NEBULA AWARD FOR NOVELLA

WINNER

The River Has Roots

Amal El-Mohtar

Follow the river Liss to the small town of Thistleford, on the edge of Faerie, and meet two sisters who cannot be separated, even in death.

"Oh what is stronger than a death? Two sisters singing with one breath."

In the small town of Thistleford, on the edge of Faerie, dwells the mysterious Hawthorn family.

There, they tend and harvest the enchanted willows and honour an ancient compact to sing to them in thanks for their magic. None more devotedly than the family's latest daughters, Esther and Ysabel, who cherish each other as much as they cherish the ancient trees.

But when Esther rejects a forceful suitor in favor of a lover from the land of Faerie, not only the sisters' bond but also their lives will be at risk...

Disgraced Return of the Kap's Needle

Renan Bernardo

In 2144 AD, the generation ship Kap's Needle left Earth to settle a new world. It all went wrong. Now, two years into a desperate return trip, the ship's biospheres are collapsing and oxygen is nearly depleted. Life Support Manager Reva is now little more than a tax collector, deciding who gets to breathe. When Captain Horvat launches a corruption purge to cover his own failures, Reva knows she's next. To protect her son, she must do the unthinkable: trust

First Officer Torres, the woman who ruined her life, and help bring down the captain no matter how many innocent lives it costs.

The Death of Mountains

Jordan Kurella

The latest novella by Nebula finalist Jordan Kurella is a moving allegorical tale. As mankind continues to hurt the planet, leaving us with scarred lands, stories like *The Death of Mountains* are more meaningful than ever.

When the Death of Mountains came for us, we had been aching for a long time. There is so much loss in being a mountain; it is a terribly long time to live. Yet something awoke within us when they arrived, their face a stone skull, their hands' obsidian bones that cracked and crackled like fracking. It made us hurt to hear their earthquake step across the ground as they arrived. Their breath was like coal dust, the stuff their cloak was made from. They left a trail of oil behind them as they walked.

When they spoke, their breath was hot, volcanic; it made us wither at first. We, however, are a middling hill of the Appalachians. And we have seen much worse.

Far worse than death.

The Death of Mountains says, "Plundered Mountain, it's time to go."

And we say, "We are not ready, Death. We have too much yet to see."

Automatic Noodle

Annalee Newitz

From sci-fi visionary and acclaimed author Annalee Newitz comes Automatic Noodle, a cozy near-future novella about a crew of abandoned food service bots opening their very own restaurant.

While San Francisco rebuilds from the chaos of war, a group of food service bots in an abandoned ghost kitchen take over their own delivery app account. They rebrand as a neighborhood lunch spot and start producing some of the tastiest hand-pulled noodles in the city. But there's just one problem. Someone—or something—is review bombing the restaurant's feedback page with fake "bad service" reports. Can the bots find the culprit before their ratings plummet and destroy everything they created?

But Not Too Bold

Hache Pueyo

The Shape of Water meets *Mexican Gothic* in this sapphic monster romance novella wrapped in gothic fantasy trappings.

The old keeper of the keys is dead, and the creature who ate her is the volatile Lady of the Capricious House-Anatema, an enormous humanoid spider with a taste for laudanum and human brides.

Dália, the old keeper's protégée, must take up her duties, locking and unlocking the little drawers in which Anatema keeps her memories. And if she can unravel the crime that led to her predecessor's execution, Dália might just be able to survive long enough to grow into her new role.

But there's a gaping hole in Dália's plan that she refuses to see: Anatema cannot resist a beautiful woman, and she eventually devours every single bride that crosses her path.

Descent

Wole Talabi

"Descent" is a standalone science-fantasy novella set in the amazing Sauúti shared world about an exploration mission on Órino-Rin, a raging planet of sonic storms. It follows Gwaato, adopted child of a geodynamics genius who embarks on a mission to map out the lower regions of the planet where no one has been before and perhaps in the process, prove his mother wrong. But Órino-Rin is an unforgiving planet and there is a price to knowledge. This is at its heart, a story about traditional African epistemology, the unbearable weight of parental expectations and the limits of all knowledge.

THE 2025 NEBULA AWARD FOR NOVEL

WINNER

The Buffalo Hunter Hunter

Stephen Graham Jones

A diary, written in 1912 by a Lutheran pastor is discovered within a wall. What it unveils is a slow massacre, a chain of events that go back to 217 Blackfeet dead in the snow. Told in transcribed interviews by a Blackfeet named Good Stab, who shares the narrative of his peculiar life over a series of confessional visits. This is an American Indian revenge story written by one of the new masters of horror, Stephen Graham Jones.

When We Were Real

Daryl Gregory

From multiple award-winning author Daryl Gregory comes a madcap adventure following two friends on a cross-country bus tour through the mind-boggling glitches in their simulated world as they grapple with love, family, secrets, and the very nature of reality in a simulation.

JP and Dulin have been the best of friends for decades. When JP finds out his cancer has aggressively returned, Dulin decides it's the perfect time for one last a week-long bus tour of North America's Impossibles, the physics-defying glitches and geographic miracles that started cropping up seven years earlier—right after the Announcement that revealed our world to be merely a digital simulacrum. The outing, courtesy of Canterbury Trails Tours, promises the trip of a (not completely real) lifetime in a (not completely deluxe) coach.

Their fellow passengers are 21st-century pilgrims, each of them on the tour for their own reasons. There's a nun hunting for an absent God, a pregnant influencer determined to make her child too famous to be deleted, a crew of horny octogenarians living each day like it's their last, and a professor on the run from leather-clad sociopaths who take The Matrix as scripture. Each stop on this trip is stranger than the last—a Tunnel outside of time, a zero gravity Geyser, the compound of motivational-speaking avatar—with everyone barreling toward the tour's iconic final stop Ghost City, where unbeknownst to our travelers the answer to who is running the simulation may await.

When We Were Real is a tour-de-force and exploration of what really matters, even in an artificial world.

Katabasis

R.F. Kuang

Katabasis, noun, Ancient Greek:

The story of a hero's descent to the underworld

Alice Law has only ever had one goal: to become one of the brightest minds in the field of Magick. She has sacrificed everything to make that a reality: her pride, her health, her love life, and most definitely her sanity. All to work with Professor Jacob Grimes at Cambridge, the greatest magician in the world.

That is, until he dies in a magical accident that could possibly be her fault.

Grimes is now in Hell, and she's going in after him. Because his recommendation could hold her very future in his now incorporeal hands and even death is not going to stop the pursuit of her dreams...

Nor will the fact that her rival, Peter Murdoch, has come to the very same conclusion.

With nothing but the tales of Orpheus and Dante to guide them, enough chalk to draw the Pentagrams necessary for their spells, and the burning desire to make all the academic trauma mean anything, they set off across Hell to save a man they don't even like.

But Hell is not like the storybooks say, Magick isn't always the answer, and there's something in Alice and Peter's past that could forge them into the perfect allies...or lead to their doom.

Death of the Author

Nnedi Okarafor

Life has thrown Zelu some curveballs over the years, but when she's suddenly dropped from her university job and her latest novel is rejected, all in the middle of her sister's wedding, her life is upended. Disabled, unemployed and from a nosy, high-achieving, judgmental family, she's not sure what comes next.

In her hotel room that night, she takes the risk that will define her life - she decides to write a book VERY unlike her others. A science fiction drama about androids and AI after the extinction of humanity. And everything changes.

What follows is a tale of love and loss, fame and infamy, of extraordinary events in one world, and another. And as Zelu's life evolves, the lines between fiction and reality begin to blur.

Because sometimes a story really does have the power to reshape the world.

The Incandescent

Emily Tesh

"Look at you, eating magic like you're one of us."

Doctor Walden is the Director of Magic at Chetwood Academy and one of the most powerful magicians in England. Her days consist of meetings, teaching A-Level Invocation to four talented, chaotic sixth formers, more meetings, and securing the school's boundaries from demonic incursions.

Walden is good at her job—no, Walden is great at her job. But demons are masters of manipulation. It's her responsibility to keep her school with its six hundred students and centuries-old legacy safe. And it's possible the entity Walden most needs to keep her school safe from—is herself.

Sour Cherry

Natalia Theodoridou

A stunning reimagining of Bluebeard—one of the most mythologized serial killers—twisted into a modern tale of toxic masculinity, a feminist sermon, and a folktale for the twenty-first century.

The tale begins with Agnes. After losing her baby, Agnes is called to the great manor house to nurse the local lord's baby boy. But something is wrong with the child: his nails grow too fast, his skin smells of soil, and his eyes remind her of the dark forest. As he grows into a boy, then into man, a plague seems to follow him everywhere. Trees wither at the roots, fruits rot on their branches, and the town turns against him. The man takes a wife, who bears him a son. But tragedy strikes in cycles and his family is forced to consider their own malignancy—until wife after wife, death after death, plague after plague, every woman he touches becomes a ghost. The ghosts become a chorus, and they call urgently to our narrator as she tries to explain, in our very real world, exactly what has happened to her. The ghosts can all agree on one thing, an inescapable truth about this man, this powerful lord who has loved them and led them each to ruin: If you leave, you die. But if you die, you stay.

Natalia Theodoridou's haunting and unforgettable debut novel, Sour Cherry, confronts age-old systems of gender and power, long-held excuses made for bad men, and the complicated reasons we stay captive to the monsters we love.

Wearing the Lion

John Wiswell

Heracles, hero of Greece, dedicates all his feats to Hera, goddess of family. Heracles' mother raised him to revere Hera, as her attempt to avoid the goddess' wrath. Unbeknownst to Heracles, he is yet another child Hera's husband, Zeus, had out of wedlock.

Hera loathes every minute of Heracles' devotion. She finally snaps and sends the Furies to make Heracles kill himself. But the moment Heracles goes mad, his children playfully ambush him, and he slays them instead. When the madness fades, Heracles's wife, Megara, convinces him to seek revenge. Together they'll hunt the Furies and learn which god did this.

Believing Hera is the only god he can still trust, Heracles prays to Hera, who is wracked with guilt over killing his children. To mislead Heracles, Hera sends him on monster-slaying quests, but he is too traumatized to enact more violence. Instead, Heracles cares for the Nemean lion, cures the illness of the Lernaean hydra, and bonds with Crete's giant bull.

Hera struggles with her role in Heracles life as Heracles begins to heal psychologically by connecting with the monsters—while also amassing an army that could lay siege to Olympos.

Nebula Award-winning author John Wiswell brings his signature humanizing touch to the Hercules story, forever changing the way we understand the man behind the myth—and the goddess reluctantly bound to him.

ANDRE NORTON NEBULA AWARD FOR MIDDLE GRADE AND YOUNG ADULT FICTION

WINNER

Into the Wild Magic

Michelle Knudsen

Eleven-year-old Bevvy spends her time avoiding other kids, playing with her neighbor's kittens, and escaping into her fantasy novels. When new girl Cat arrives at school, Bevvy thinks she may finally have found a friend, until Cat provokes Bevvy's worst tormentor and leaves her alone to deal with the consequences. Later, on Bevvy's doorstep, Cat's apology is cut short when a car with dark windows rolls up. Bolting into a nearby wood with Bevvy in tow, Cat proceeds to open a hole, in the air, just in time. Bevvy knows magic when she sees it, the kind in books, but the world the girls escape to—teeming with unicorns, sorcerers, and dragons—is shockingly, exhilaratingly real. It's a world at war. Those who wield wild magic, in tune with nature, are pitted against dark sorcerers. As Bevvy's role in the struggle grows, and her confidence with it, can she trust Cat to support her? Can she trust herself not to run? An acclaimed author builds a breathtaking and emotionally resonant world where magic and monsters are real and friendship and risk go hand in hand.

The Tower

David Anaxagoras

When 12-year-old Kolby wakes up on the polished concrete floor of an empty white room, he has no memory, no clothes, and no idea where he is. Kolby soon discovers he's one of a dozen kids living in an extravagant penthouse atop the tallest tower in the city. Adults are nowhere to be found and, like

Kolby, all the kids are missing their memories. The kids in the tower spend their time scaling the climbing wall, riding the winding waterslide into an Olympic-sized swimming pool, or playing video games on the 105-inch 8K video screen. A mysterious "manifesting room" magically provides food and rewards. They have virtually everything a kid could want. Except a way out.

Gemini Rising

Jonathan Brazee

After being instrumental in saving the citizens of Arcadia during the Krackle invasion, identical twins Nika and Rika Ingersoll are offered appointments to the Regency's Uniform Services Academy as midshipmen. Eager to move on into adult life, they are sworn in and board a luxury liner for a relaxing voyage to Freedom Station before facing the rigors of Plebe Indoc. Only sometimes lightning really does strike twice. When seemingly pirates take over the ship, and the passengers face an uncertain—but assuredly horrible—fate, it's up to Rika and Nika, along with a handful of their fellow mids and cadets, to somehow figure a way out of their mess. Against all odds, they managed it before, but is asking them to save the day again too much? There's no room for failure. They may not be trained yet, but they've already sworn their oaths, and the lives of over 2,000 of their fellow citizens are at stake. Read Gemini Rising now to see if the twins can somehow pull another rabbit out of their hats and save the day.

Wishing Well, Wishing Well

Jubilee Cho

The five princesses of Bellarossa have lost their parents and must now abide under the control of the man responsible. But they have their art. They have each other. And still, they hold on to hope. They do what they can to ease the suffering of their kingdom under an unfeeling King and his cruel Admiral. But when a mysterious Renegade Mage arrives with powers of skill and magic, perhaps—perhaps, there is more that can be done.

Sunrise on the Reaping

Suzanne Collins

When you've been set up to lose everything you love, what is there left to fight for? As the day dawns on the fiftieth annual Hunger Games, fear grips the districts of Panem. This year, in honor of the Quarter Quell, twice as many tributes will be taken from their homes. Back in District 12, Haymitch Abernathy is trying not to think too hard about his chances. All he cares about is making it through the day and being with the girl he loves. When Haymitch's name is called, he can feel all his dreams break. He's torn from his family and his love, shuttled to the Capitol with the three other District 12 tributes: a young friend who's nearly a sister to him, a compulsive oddsmaker, and the most stuck-up girl in town. As the Games begin, Haymitch understands he's been set up to fail. But there's something in him that wants to fight...and have that fight reverberate far beyond the deadly arena.

Goblin Girl

K.A. Mielke

For twelve years, Gertrude has been the only goblin in Pinnec Hill. The adopted daughter of the Captain of the Guard, she tries her hardest to live a normal life, ignoring the looks of disgust—and the rocks—thrown her way. But when an invading fleet of airships brings a goblin army crashing through the city gates, she understands why everyone fears her. The leader of this army is Wrendell, a powerful goblin sorceress, who burns the city to the ground in pursuit of one thing: the human princess, Beatrix. Gertrude's father tasks her with rescuing Princess Beatrix. With the aid of a cursed knight and a talking tree, Gertrude will encounter trolls and dragons, discover the true history of her banished people, and—as if that weren't enough—struggle with her own blossoming crush on a princess who doesn't trust her. No one expects much of a measly goblin girl, but Gertrude may be the only person who can save the kingdom.

MULTIMEDIA AWARD FINALISTS

THE 2025 NEBULA AWARD FOR COMIC

WINNER

Mary Shelley's School for Monsters: The Killing Stone

Jessica Maison

Illustrator (pencils, inks, and colors): Anna Wieszczyk
Letterer: Matt Krotzer

Nari, the school's new monster, is an Onryo: a vengeful spirit driven by deep-seated grudges. She hates everyone, but it's not personaĬ. The school's students are brimming with anger, and its making Nari dangerously hungry. Her grudge-fueled rage threatens everyone, even her fellow monsters.

Shel and the team need Nari for their next mission. Someone shattered apan's Sessho-Seki, the Killing Stone, releasing Tamamo-no-Mae, a powerful Nine-Tailed Fox and ally of Dr. M. Shel and Frank believe Mae can be saved, but she's furious. seeking revenge after centuries of imprisonment within the Killing Stone.

As they navigate this perilous situation, Shel is caught in one of Dr. M's magical traps, forcing her to confront the source of her own repressed grudge. If she can't let go of her past, it could spell disaster for everyone.

Second Shift

Kit Anderson

From the time when the station wakes her up, Birdie Doran is on the clock. It's just her and one or two others on Terracorp's isolated outpost, processing comets. So she slips into virtual reality, with the station creating adventures for her as she does repairs, routine maintenance, and checks the status on all the systems.

But when Birdie discovers another abandoned station just within walking distance of her own, she begins to question her isolation, and her own memories of what her job-and her life—really is. And at every turn, she starts finding the things the station has been hiding from her.

Ignatz Award-nominated author Kit Anderson presents a psychological science fiction exploration of the lines between reality inside and outside the mind.

Carmilla: The Eternal

Amy Chu

Illustrator: Soo Lee
Letterer: Sal Cipriano
Editor: Karen Berger

Before Dracula, before Nosferatu, there was...CARMILLA.

Inspired by the gothic novel that started the vampire genre and layered with dark Chinese folklore, this queer, feminist murder mystery graphic novel is a tale of identity, obsession and fateful family secrets.

At the height of the Lunar New Year in 1990s New York City, an idealistic social worker turns detective when she discovers young, homeless LGBTQ+ women are being murdered and no one, especially the police, seems to care.

A series of clues points her to Carmilla's, a mysterious nightclub in the heart of her neighborhood, Chinatown. There she falls for the next likely target, landing her at the center of a real-life horror story—and face-to-face with illusions about herself, her life, and her hidden past.

Helen of Wyndhorn

Tom King

Artist: Bilquis Evely
Colorist: Matheus Lopes
Letterer: Clayton Cowles
Cover Art: Bilquis Evely and Matheus Lopes

Following the tragic death of her late father C.K. Cole, the esteemed pulp writer and creator of the popular warrior character Othan; Helen Cole is called back to her grandfather's enormous and illustrious estate: Wyndhorn House.

Scarred by Cole's untimely passing and lost in a new, strange world, Helen wreaks drunken havoc upon her arrival; however, her chaotic ways begin to soften as she discovers a lifetime of secrets hiding within the myriad rooms and hallways of the expansive manor. For outside its walls, within the woods, dwell the legendary adventures that once were locked away within her father's stories.

Collects the hit series Helen of Wyndhorn #1-6 and features a sketchbook section and bonus art by Walt Simonson, Greg Smallwood, Clay Mann, Elsa Charretier, Tula Lotay, Massimo Carnivale, Fabio Moon, and Jill Thompson.

Fishflies

Jeff Lemire

Artist: Shawn Kuruneru
Letterer: Steve Wands

Jeff Lemire (*Gideon Falls, Sweet Tooth*) brings you a new tale of small-town surrealist horror in this special extra-length debut issue.

When a brutal and violent crime puts the life of an innocent teenage boy in the balance, it sets off a chain of events in bucolic Bell River, Ontario that will permanently change several residents' lives. And as the manhunt heats up, a lonely girl named Franny Fox will form an unlikely friendship with a fugitive that leads them on an odyssey of discovery and redemption.

Strange Bedfellows

Ariel Slamet Ries

In this stunning graphic novel by two-time Ignatz award-winning graphic novelist Ariel Slamet Ries, Oberon must choose between fantasy and reality when he develops the ability to conjure his dreams in real life—including the facsimile of the boy who got away.

In the not-too-distant future, most of humanity resides on its last-ditch effort at utopia: Meridian, a remote alien planet where you're more likely to be born superhuman than left-handed.

None of that is important to Oberon Afolayan. Since his mildly public breakdown, his whole life seems to be spiraling out of control—from dropping out of university to breaking up with his boyfriend, it seems like only a karmic inevitability when he wakes up one day with the ability to conjure his dreams in the real world.

Oberon's newfound powers come with a facsimile of his high school crush, Kon, who mysteriously dropped off the face of the planet almost three years ago and who is a little more infuriating (if not also infuriatingly hot) than Oberon remembers.

Kon makes it his mission to turn Oberon's life around, and while they struggle to get a handle on his powers and his disastrous personal life (not to mention the appearance of strange nightmare creatures), it turns out this dream version of Kon has secrets of his own—dangerous ones.

Oberon might have more on his plate than he originally thought, but is giving up his dreams—even the one he might have accidentally fallen in love with—the only way to find happiness in reality?

The Flip Side

Jason Walz

This breathtaking, page-turning graphic novel is a supernatural survival story in which a grieving teen finds himself in a haunting alternate reality—the frightening embodiment of his depression. For fans of *Stranger Things* and *Nimona*.

Theo's best friend has died, and he can't pull himself out of his sadness—a sadness that those around him don't seem to respect or even notice. And then something even more disconcerting happens: His town literally flips upside down and everyone disappears, except for a threatening, shape-shifting monster and a snarky teenage girl who knows her way around this flipped world. Is Theo doomed to spend the rest of his life in this scary state?

Tremendously unique and suspenseful, *The Flip Side* tackles grief and depression in a fascinating and affecting way.

The Stoneshore Register

G. Willow Wilson

Artist and co-creator: MK Perker
Letterer: Richard Bruning

When refugee and aspiring journalist Fadumo arrives to work at the Stoneshore Register, she is entering a far stranger place than she realizes.

At first, the colossal stone giant overlooking the rundown, seemingly ordinary Pacific Northwest fishing town seems like the only remarkable element. But he is not the only strange surprise: changelings, selkies, cursed ships—the bizarre has a home in Stoneshore, yet no one gives it a second thought.

But Fadumo doesn't just want to cover these odd occurrences. She wants to dig deeper. And what she discovers is a land so steeped in mysterious history, it will change all who dare to explore it.

RAY BRADBURY NEBULA AWARD FOR OUTSTANDING DRAMATIC PRESENTATION

WINNER

Murderbot: Season One

Chris Weitz & Paul Weitz

A security android struggles with emotions and free will while balancing dangerous missions and desire for isolation, evading detection of its self-hacking as it finds its place. *(from IMDb)*

Sinners

Ryan Coogler

From Ryan Coogler—director of *Black Panther* and *Creed*—and starring Michael B. Jordan comes a new vision of fear: *Sinners*. Trying to leave their troubled lives behind, twin brothers (Jordan) return to their hometown to start again, only to discover that an even greater evil is waiting to welcome them back. "You keep dancing with the devil, one day he's gonna follow you home."

Written and directed by Academy Award-nominated filmmaker Coogler, *Sinners* stars Jordan (the Black Panther and Creed franchises) in a dual role, joined by Oscar nominee Hailee Steinfeld (*Bumblebee, True Grit*), Jack O'Connell (*Ferrari*), Wunmi Mosaku (*Passenger*), Jayme Lawson (*The Woman King*), Omar Benson Miller (*True Lies*) and Delroy Lindo (*Da 5 Bloods*).

Severance: "Chikhai Bardo"

Dan Erickson & Mark Friedman

Director: Jessica Lee Gagné

An old romance intersects with a deadly present threat.

Pluribus: Season One

Vince Gilligan

The most miserable person on Earth must save the world from happiness.

Superman

James Gunn

Superman, DC Studios' first feature film to hit the big screen, is set to soar into theaters worldwide this summer from Warner Bros. Pictures. In his signature style, James Gunn takes on the original superhero in the newly imagined DC universe with a singular blend of epic action, humor and heart, delivering a Superman who's driven by compassion and an inherent belief in the goodness of humankind.

DC Studios heads Peter Safran and Gunn are producing the film, which Gunn directs from his own screenplay, based on characters from DC, Superman created by Jerry Siegel and Joe Shuster.

The film stars David Corenswet (*Twisters, Hollywood*) in the dual role of Superman/Clark Kent, Rachel Brosnahan (*The Marvelous Mrs. Maisel*) as Lois Lane and Nicholas Hoult (the X-Men movies, *Juror #2*) as Lex Luthor. The film also stars Edi Gathegi (*For All Mankind*), Anthony Carrigan (*Barry, Gotham*), Nathan Fillion (the Guardians of the Galaxy films, *The Suicide Squad*), Isabela Merced (*Alien: Romulus*), Skyler Gisondo (*Licorice Pizza, Booksmart*), Sara Sampaio (*At Midnight*), María Gabriela de Faría (*The Moodys*), Wendell Pierce (*Selma, Tom Clancy's Jack Ryan*), Alan Tudyk (*Andor*), Pruitt Taylor Vince (*Bird Box*) and Neva Howell (*Greedy People*).

KPop Demon Hunters

Danya Jimenez, Maggie Kang, Hannah McMechan, Chris Appelhans

When they aren't selling out stadiums, Kpop superstars Rumi, Mira and Zoey use their secret identities as badass demon hunters to protect their fans from an ever-present supernatural threat. Together, they must face their biggest enemy yet – an irresistible rival boy band of demons in disguise.

THE 2025 NEBULA AWARD FOR GAME WRITING

WINNER

Clair Obscur: Expedition 33

Guillaume Broche and Jennifer Svedberg-Yen

Lead the members of Expedition 33 on their quest to destroy the Paintress so that she can never paint death again. Explore a world of wonders inspired by Belle Époque France and battle unique enemies in this turn-based RPG with real-time mechanics.

Spire, Surge, and Sea

Stewart Baker

The King lies. Your memories are a weapon. In humanity's last city, floating in a worldwide seascape, will you fight for truth or defend the crown? A 380,000-word text-based interactive post-apocalyptic science fantasy novel.

Hollow Knight: Silksong

Ari Gibson and William Pellen

Discover a vast, haunted kingdom in *Hollow Knight: Silksong*! The sequel to the award-winning action-adventure. Explore, fight and survive as you ascend to the peak of a land ruled by silk and song. Available now for Pc, Mac, Linux, Nintendo Switch, Nintendo Switch 2, PlayStation 4, PlayStation 5 and Xbox Series X|S.

Dispatch

Ashley Jeffalone, Chad Rhiness, Chris Rebbert, Mayanna Berrin, Pierre Shorette, and Suzee Matson

Dispatch is a superhero game made by AdHoc Studio. In *Dispatch*, you play as Mecha Man. His robot suit broke in a fight. So he got a new job in Los Angeles. Now he helps bad guys become good guys in *Dispatch*!

Famous actors give voices to *Dispatch*! Aaron Paul, Laura Bailey, Matthew Mercer, and Jeffrey Wright talk as the *Dispatch* characters. Plus YouTubers MoistCr1TiKaL and Jacksepticeye! Your choices change the *Dispatch* story.

Hades II

Greg Kasavin

Hades II is the bewitching sequel to our rogue-like dungeon crawler, in which you'll battle beyond the Underworld using dark sorcery to take on the Titan of Time.

Blue Prince

Tonda Ros

Welcome to Mt. Holly, where every dawn unveils a new mystery. Navigate through shifting corridors and ever-changing chambers in this genre-defying strategy puzzle adventure. But will your unpredictable path lead you to the rumored Room 46?

WITH THANKS TO THE TOP SPONSORS FOR THIS YEAR'S NEBULA AWARDS CONFERENCE

TOR PUBLISHING GROUP

ABOUT THE SCIENCE FICTION AND FANTASY WRITERS ASSOCIATION

The Science Fiction and Fantasy Writers Association, Inc. (SFWA) was founded in 1965 by the American science fiction author Damon Knight under the name Science Fiction Writers of America with a charter membership of 78 writers. Today, SFWA is home to over 2,500 authors, artists, and allied professionals worldwide, and is widely recognized as one of the most effective non-profit writers' organizations in existence.

The mission of the Science Fiction and Fantasy Writers Association includes the promotion, writing, and appreciation of science fiction, fantasy and related genres and field; informing, supporting, promoting, defending, and advocating for writers of science fiction, fantasy and related genres; and to promote and defend the interests of writers in these genres within the publishing industry. Each year, SFWA assists members in various legal disputes, administers grants to SFF community organizations and members facing medical or legal expenses, and hosts the prestigious Nebula Awards at our annual SFWA Nebula Conference.

All authors can benefit from our Information Center and well-known Writer Beware® website. Between online discussion boards, private convention suites, and a host of less formal gatherings, SFWA is a source of information, education, support, and fellowship.

SFWA Membership is open to authors, artists, editors, and other industry professionals who meet our eligibility requirements. To learn more about SFWA or to apply for membership, please visit our website, www.sfwa.org.

ABOUT THE NEBULA AWARDS®

The Nebula Awards, presented annually at the SFWA Nebula Conference, recognize the best works of science fiction and fantasy published in the United States as selected by members of the Science Fiction and Fantasy Writers Association. The first Nebula Awards were presented in 1966.

The Nebula Awards are voted on and presented by full, senior, and associate members of the Science Fiction and Fantasy Writers Association. These awards cover outstanding writing in novel, novella, novelette, short story, game, poem, and comic, along with the Ray Bradbury Nebula Award for Outstanding Dramatic Presentation, and the Andre Norton Nebula Award for Middle Grade and Young Adult Fiction.

SFWA also administers the Kate Wilhelm Solstice Award, the Kevin O'Donnell, Jr. Service to SFWA Award, the Infinity Award, and the Damon Knight Memorial Grand Master Award, SFWA's highest honor for lifetime achievement in writing science fiction and/or fantasy.

Over the years, the Nebula Awards banquet grew to become the SFWA Nebula Conference, one of the premier professional development conferences for speculative fiction industry professionals and people aspiring to become one. It takes place each spring. For more information on the awards and the Nebula Conference, please visit SFWA.org.

www.ingramcontent.com/pod-product-compliance
Lightning Source LLC
Chambersburg PA
CBHW030903060726
47591CB00005B/1391

* 9 7 8 1 9 5 8 2 4 3 1 0 7 *